The Ship Inspector

**This book is to be returned on or before
the last date stamped below.**

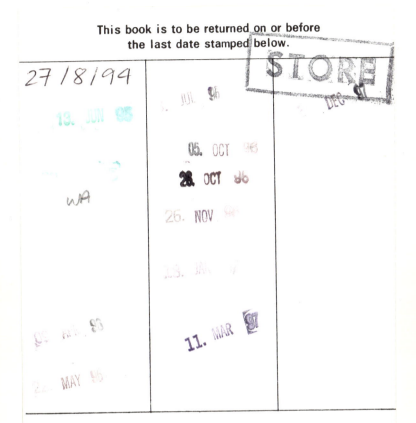

27/8/94

19. JUN 95

WA

JUL 96

05. OCT 96

28. OCT 96

26. NOV

11. MAR 97

STORE

DEC 97

MAY 96

SUTTON LEISURE SERVICES

FERDIA MAC ANNA

The
Ship Inspector

MICHAEL JOSEPH

LONDON

MICHAEL JOSEPH LTD

Published by the Penguin Group
27 Wrights Lane, London w8 5TZ
Viking Penguin Inc., 375 Hudson Street, New York, New York 10014, USA
Penguin Books Australia Ltd, Ringwood, Victoria, Australia
Penguin Books Canada Ltd, 10 Alcorn Avenue, Toronto, Ontario, Canada M4V 3B2
Penguin Books (NZ) Ltd, 182–190 Wairau Road, Auckland 10, New Zealand

Penguin Books Ltd, Registered Offices: Harmondsworth, Middlesex, England

First published in Great Britain 1994

Typeset by Datix International Limited, Bungay, Suffolk
Set in 11/13 pt Monophoto Plantin
Printed in Great Britain by Clays Ltd, St Ives plc

ISBN 0 7181 0021 2 hardback
ISBN 0 7181 3838 4 paperback

The moral right of the author has been asserted

To Kate and Sienna

ONE

Daniel

As THE TRAIN pulls into Redrock station, I am relieved to see that there is nobody on the platform. I don't want to meet anyone who knows me. I don't want to answer any questions about my family.

I step onto the platform and the sea air pokes at my nose and eyes. I can taste the salt on its breath. I have heard old fishermen swear that the air in Redrock is cold and sharp enough to revive a corpse. My friend Paulie Reddin claims to have been present when some fishermen hauled a man out of the sea, cold and lifeless as a sack of turf. After a few moments in the air, the man sprang up suddenly, shouting for someone to give him a sweater for Jaysus' sake.

It is Monday morning, 10 am. I should be at work. Instead, I am in Redrock, my old home town. Being here is not something that I planned. I simply found myself walking to the railway station this morning instead of catching my usual bus to my job at the airport. Taking the train to Redrock seemed as natural and exhilarating as rolling down a grassy hill. I forgot all about work. Instead I spent the journey thinking about my family: Mother, who worked so hard to keep the family together after Dad disappeared; my sister Maeve, a year and a half older than me, who worked so hard to keep Mother together; and my elder brother Rory who, when he was sixteen, was so anxious to be a rock star that he accidentally dyed his hair purple instead of blond because he was too impatient to check the instructions on the packet. We haven't had a family reunion for years.

I

The last one ended with Mother going for Rory with a kitchen knife. Rory never forgave Mother for that. He left for Manchester a month later.

Now that I am finally in Redrock, my anxiety about dodging work has receded. There is nothing like opening up old family wounds to take your mind off things.

I have not been back to this town in ten years. I will not stay long. All I want is a quick look at the old place. After that, I will go home. No big deal.

When I was at university I would sometimes go on the bounce and catch a bus or a train somewhere I had never been, just for the hell of it. Once I went to Dundrum. Another time it was Saggart. The furthest I ever went was Donabate where I spent a morning walking around, exploring, kicking sand on the beach, eyeing Donabate girls. I never knew where I was going until I got there and I never told anyone afterwards. Once I started fulltime work as a ship inspector though, I gave up wandering. There didn't seem to be any point to it anymore.

Then I met Carla.

Carla is my ballerina on a motorbike. I love to see her slight, skinny figure bouncing along on top of her Kawasaki 150, her black helmet way too big for her body, from a distance making her look like a Martian. When she comes home I watch from the window as she takes her helmet off to reveal her delicate head, her bleached blonde hair shaved to a crewcut. I worry about her getting run down. I am always telling her that as soon as I get money, I'll buy her a car but she just smiles, crinkles her slanted green eyes and tells me not to be such a fusspot.

When we moved in together, we agreed that we could see other people if we wanted to, as long as we were always honest with each other about everything and promised never to abuse the integrity of our home. She said she doesn't want to cramp my space. I promised that I would never compromise her freedom to be herself. We both know that there is absolutely nobody else in the world we would rather be with. We never fight. Everyone says we have a great relationship.

For the past year, we have been looking for a house. We are both eager to settle down in a place of our own. The apartment in Fitzwilliam Street is comfortable but it is not home. There is nothing like living in your own space.

Carla has her own business, making stage clothes for rock bands. There are always guys dropping into our apartment to pick up glitzy jackets and shirts. It's not unusual for me to come home to find a rock musician wandering around in his underwear while he waits to be fitted with tight trousers for his stage show.

When I left the apartment this morning, for instance, Carla was sitting around waiting for Donald Logan, the lead singer with The Silent Screams, to call around to collect the special Doc Martens, one orange, the other pink, that she has designed for him. Donald has wavy blond hair that covers his ears like a helmet, a big goofy laugh, and small deep-set eyes. He has an anchor tattooed on his right arm. Carla hates tattoos, but she thinks Donald is 'really nice'. Donald's pink and orange Docs have been lying around the house for weeks. I told Carla the Docs looked brilliant, but deep down I thought they looked as though a hippy had puked on them.

I'll phone Carla later and ask her to call in sick for me. Carla has a cool telephone-style. She could make a person believe that aliens have landed.

As I pass through the station house, I look for the old ticket-seller's office. I remember a tall brown wooden booth. Buying a ticket made you feel like you were on your way to a funfair or a circus, instead of going on a boring train ride. The booth is gone. In its place there is a grille set in the wall and protected by a shiny red plastic cover, in case someone might try to steal it.

Outside, the station steps are stubby and chipped just as I remembered. A small boy sits on the bottom step reading a comic in the breeze, waiting for a bus to take him up Redrock Hill. Overhead, the sky is grey with pudgy dark clouds rambling in from the sea. The cold air feels heavy with the promise of rain.

Across the road is Molloy's newsagents where I used to

3

buy macaroon bars as a kid. It has been transformed from a dark cave lined with shelves loaded with sweet jars and packets of washing powder into a brightly coloured mini-market. I feel a sudden urge to eat a macaroon bar, but I am afraid to go into Molloy's in case I meet someone I know. On the street, walking fast, there is a good chance that people will not recognise me. If they do I will fire off a quick howarya and be on my way before they can latch onto me. In the enclosed space of a small shop, they would crowd around me like wolves, peering eagerly into my eyes the way people do when they haven't seen someone in ages. How's your mother? She's a wonderful woman. What's Rory doing? How's little Maeve? What are you up to yourself these days? If that happens, I am sure that my stutter will come back. I don't want to risk it. It will certainly be an intriguing trick to re-visit my home town after fifteen years without meeting at least one person I know.

Leary's Seafront Hotel and Disco still has its mascot outside – a round black, World War Two sea mine. The mine's spikes are hung with lunch menus, beer slogans and room offers. Old Leary used to tell people that his merchant ship had struck the mine during the war, but the mine failed to go off. He had interpreted this as a sign of good fortune, and brought the mine home to the family hotel as a lucky mascot. Rory always swore that Leary had never bothered to have the explosive removed from inside. Rory knew it was true because he had been told by a fellow who had heard it from Old Leary's cousin who was home from Australia. For years, people kept their distance, and every time a drunk from the disco next door stumbled into the mine, all the local people ducked.

At the harbour, most of the fishing boats are out. Yachts, rowing-boats and speedboats are scattered on the dark blue waters like a child's toys in a bath. The harbour is still dominated by the new yacht club, a huge, yawning, modern construction of tinted glass, concrete and metal. The yacht club started out as an imitation of Sydney Opera House and somehow ended up like a crashed mother ship from a Star Wars movie.

4

Mother had been against the yacht club all along. She dedicated her last big political campaign to stopping the club being built. On a wet Saturday afternoon, she delivered an impassioned speech from the top of a banjaxed fishing boat in the repair yard. I can still see her at the prow of the boat, arms out like a saviour.

'People of Redrock, I want you to rise up now to save the natural beauty of your harbour. Don't let these blue-blazered bureaucrats bulldoze your home.'

The speech was going well until it began to rain. Suddenly, it began to really pelt. Hordes of people scampered for cover, coats and jackets over their heads like celebrities fleeing the press.

'Cowards, come back here,' Mother yelled, but it was too late.

Within minutes, the yard had cleared except for half a dozen umbrellas and two dogs.

'Right, if that's your attitude, then you all deserve a kip like this,' Mother shouted.

She stood like a martyr in the downpour with her head high to show that she wasn't afraid of a little rain. Mrs Donovan hauled her down before she caught pneumonia. Mother caught cold and lost the election anyway. Six months later, the yacht club was completed.

Now the entire harbour area appears worn out, dull, passed over. Even the lighthouse at the end of the east pier, that had once seemed an exotic, solitary place full of mysterious light and shadows, stands lost and forgotten like some ancient watchtower left over from colonial days. The only thing that remains the same is the smell, the heavy, insidious tang of fish guts that the fishermen carry with them to the pubs, to their homes, to Mass on Sundays.

When I was fifteen, going to sea seemed a romantic, dashing life: all day on the ocean with nobody to bother you except the captain; then coming ashore after a big catch like a soldier on leave from the front to swagger around the town with a wad of money and twenty cigarettes poking out of the top pocket of your denims. I envied guys like Hatchet Hardy, the toughest man in Redrock, who left school at fifteen to go to sea. Within weeks, it seemed, he was driving around in a second-hand MG and dressing better than anyone outside of a James Bond movie. At the weekend discos at Leary's seafront hotel, he flung money around like Smarties. That Christmas Eve, at a big party on Redrock beach, Paulie Reddin, Manus Rock and I plus a couple of hundred others watched in horror as Hatchet Hardy, who looked like a barrel with teeth, got off with petite, beautiful, blonde-haired Leonie Powers.

'Now I know there's no God,' Paulie Reddin said.

When my best friend Manus Rock started going to sea at weekends on his father's fishing boat, I begged him to find me a part-time job. He said that there might be a berth going at weekends on his Uncle Jamie's boat if I wanted it. Manus's Uncle Jamie agreed to take me, on one condition: I had to promise not to smoke joints while on watch.

'I'm sick of smelling that stuff in the dark,' he said. 'When I catch one of them at it, I'll shag him overboard.'

Euphoric with the prospect of a new life, I told Mother that I was going to be a fisherman. Her immediate reaction was to grab my arms so that I couldn't escape. She stared into my face, narrowed her eyes and blinked until they grew moist and tears appeared at the corners.

'I can't believe you want to do this to me,' she sobbed. 'You're out to kill yourself. I'm trying to cope on my own and it's very, very hard.'

My enthusiasm for my new life slid away like a herring on a wet deck. I now felt insensitive, selfish, an oaf. How could I have put my own ambitions before the needs of my family? What could I have been thinking of? When Mother asked me to please promise her that I would never ever under any circumstances set foot on the deck of a fishing boat or any boat for that matter, I swore that I wouldn't.

Mother beamed, 'I knew you'd make the right decision in the end. If your dad was here he'd give you a big hug.'

I pass the harbour and arrive at the bottom of Main Street. The snug seafront cottage, where Manus Rock and his family once lived has been transformed into 'Rock's Seafront Bar and Lounge'. A new storey with a thatched roof has been added. All the windows have been turned into oversize portholes. 'Traditional Sessúin Tonight, All Welcome,' says a poster on the door.

On the corner, the old courthouse is boarded up, apparently awaiting demolition. This is where my brother Rory used to hang around with his friends, Malachi Spain and Joey Boland. They would stand on the courthouse steps acting hard and practising their surly stares on passersby. Rory was too cool to be seen talking to me. The only time he ever acknowledged my presence in public was the day I was knocked down in front of him by a Mr Whippy van. Then, when he saw I was all right, he just gave me a thump on the head. Later, he admitted that it was his way of showing that he was glad that I hadn't been hurt.

'That's why I didn't put my full weight behind the punch,' he explained.

When he wasn't beating me up, we got on quite well really.

Just as I pass the courthouse, a green Volkswagen pulls out in front of me. For a moment I think it belongs to Maisie Dorney. I look for some place to duck into but I am exposed on the street corner, about to cross the road. She is sure to spot me and pull over. I remember Maisie Dorney as a dour, stooped, religious maniac with a face like a boiled squirrel. I was friends with James, her youngest, who was a year older than me but liked Jethro Tull and The Beatles and supported Manchester United. Once, when James missed Mass because he was playing football, his mother took him into the front garden and whipped his legs with a belt in front of everyone on the road. Manus Rock said that Maisie Dorney would sacrifice her children if she thought it would bring her closer to God.

I huddle into my coat to make myself small. But as the car passes I realise that the driver is a young woman. The Volkswagen is a recent model, nothing like the chugging old ruin that Maisie drove for years until the day the engine plopped out outside Grogan's hardware shop on Main Street and lay there smoking like the first customer in a pub. The next morning, Maisie was seen driving around in a sparkling new green Volkswagen.

'She probably breeds them in her garage,' Manus said.

I notice that the Dorneys' house has been decorated with a facade of white Roman columns supporting a new balcony. The columns look fragile and temporary, as though a good push might bring down the whole shebang. In the driveway, there is a green Volkswagen with a brightly coloured statue of Jesus hanging in its rear window.

On Main Street, I lose my bearings momentarily. I can find no trace of the small, ugly shops of my childhood, shops that seemed attractive back then only because of the sweets contained within or because they sold single cigarettes to children. They have been replaced by big, modern chainstores, no different than anywhere else. Yet at the same time, I am disturbed by a feeling of familiarity. Despite the changes, it is as if I have been away for a summer instead of leaving for good a decade ago.

Arnold Schwarzenegger and Sigourney Weaver loom out of the window of Mahony's mini-market, where Mother worked for a few years after Dad disappeared. The film stars tower out from the neatly packed rows of brussels sprouts and green cabbages. In the window, squeezed between them, is my own reflection – tight fair hair, narrow face, skinny as a rake in a trenchcoat. I can still see my sister Maeve, thirteen years old, her determined little face, her coolly defiant brown eyes under a black fringe, striding purposefully out of the shop clutching her first brown Aisling copybook in which she said she intended to write Mother's speeches.

I am glad to see that the library is still intact, though much changed. What was once a squat, flat-roofed building with bars on the windows, like a prison for bookworms, is now a gleaming block of shiny glass and white walls. The County Council has apparently succeeded where pudgy Norman Diamond failed. Norman attempted to burn down the library at least half a dozen times. The last time he tried it, he brought Deke, his Alsatian. When the police arrived, they found the dog beside a smouldering pile of thrillers, chewing on a Frederick Forsyth. Deke led them straight to Norman's house. Norman answered the door, face blacked-

8

up like a commando and a can of petrol in his hand. In court, Norman explained that the compulsion to set fire to the library was a result of having been ejected as a child for defacing Noddy books. The experience had traumatised him, he said. The judge didn't buy it. Norman got twelve months.

The concrete playground of the old national school is full of yelling, windmilling, screeching, rampaging kids, all plunging about as though determined to kill themselves. I was a high baby and a low baby and a first-classer here before moving to St Michan's in the city. When I was five, I disgraced myself in alphabet class by having a sudden attack of diarrhoea. When I tried to call for help, everyone thought I was trying to be funny until they noticed the runny brown trails under my desk.

'Sir, Buckley's shit hisself,' Giles O'Hara shouted.

It took them an hour to clean up the area around my desk. They sent me home with a cardboard box around my waist. For years, I had nightmares that Giles O'Hara would come up to me one day to gleefully remind me that I had crapped my trousers in front of the whole school. As I pass by, I expect him to appear at any moment.

Opposite the school is Redrock's oldest row of terraced houses where the inhabitants are so proud of their Redrock roots that they won't even nod to you unless your family has lived in the town since before the dinosaurs. Even families who have lived in Redrock for over a hundred years are regarded as mere 'runners-in'. Because my father was from Sneem in Co Kerry and my mother from Newry in Co Down, we never even made it to 'runners-in' status. Families like ours, who had lived in the town for under a hundred years, were ranked slightly higher than tourists in the Redrock social order. Even when Mother became a TD, we were still considered to be outsiders, playing out our lives on the surface of the place.

Many of the people I grew up with still live in Redrock. Most have bought houses within a mile or sometimes down the road from their old homes. I hear that Norman Diamond actually lives next door to his parents.

I wonder what would have become of my family if we had stayed in Redrock. Would we still be together? Would we ever have graduated from 'runners-in' status?

I come to what appears to be the new community centre, a huge, flat construction not unlike a cattle shed. Then I have a look in the window of The Tall Ships pub. I consider dropping in to to see if the lounge has changed from the days when Paulie Reddin, Manus Rock and I drank there. For a moment, I think about going in to phone Carla from the pay-phone in the back, if it is still there. Then I remember that Donald Logan will probably have arrived by now. I will call later, I decide.

Last night, Carla went to a Silent Screams gig. I lay there in our big double-bed unable to sleep. For hours, I stared at pale shapes drifting across on the ceiling and listened out for the chug-a-lug of her Kawasaki coming down the street. I was still wide awake when she came home at four in the morning. When she came into the room, then slowly undressed for bed, I pretended to be asleep. Carla slipped under the sheets, nestling her cold body into mine and startled me with her freezing hands. I jumped, and she giggled. She smelled of Guinness and cigarette smoke.

'They were brill, you should have come,' she said. 'Donald's a really good singer.'

'Good.'

'Cuddles,' she said. 'I want cuddles.'

We cuddled. Gradually, she got warmer. After a few moments, she dropped off. I lay awake, listening to the thin mumbling of cars in the distant night and to Carla's soft breathing. I eventually fell asleep about half an hour before the alarm clock went off.

When I reach the corner of Church Street, I look up at the tall grey church with its jagged looming spire. There are still a few ugly gargoyles left leering out on the whole town.

Church Street is the smallest and narrowest street in Redrock, and this is where I used to live. It consists of six terraced houses in a row with Butch Cassidy the butcher on the corner. The front door of each house opens directly onto the street. As I pass the butcher's, I am glad to see that Butch is inside, hacking energetically into a side of bacon with a meat cleaver. He is a large, thick-jowled man with a lopsided nose, who used to love playing jokes on people. He was once the most popular butcher in Redrock. Then one day he joked to a bunch of noisy schoolkids that he chopped up bold children at weekends and sold them to the townspeople. He was holding a cleaver in his hand as he spoke. The kids didn't get the joke. For months, no child ventured near the place. A rumour swept the town that Butch had dismembered his parents and sold them as hamburgers. Even the older kids avoided Church Street on their way to school. People went all the way to Grandview to buy their meat. In the end, Butch had to call around to every house in the town to reassure parents that he had no intention of selling their children as housekeepers' cut.

I walk quickly past Mrs Donovan's. She used to be Mother's best friend, and she probably still lives next door to the butcher's. A nosy, abrasive woman with a round, blank face and weak, pale blue eyes, she always seemed to be imploring you to feel sorry for her. Rory called her 'The Foghorn'. He said she had a voice that could strip the tiles from a roof. Mrs Donovan's husband spent every spare moment either at sea or in The Tall Ships pub. Nobody blamed him. Mrs Donovan was bad, but her two fat, ugly kids, Barry and Jane, who we knew as the Things, were obnoxious. Whenever they came to our house, the Things broke our toys, stole our sweets and invaded our room. The girl Thing screamed like an air-raid siren when we tried to get our toys back. Whenever Mother wanted to shut us up, she only had to say that she was going away and leaving us in the charge of Mrs Donovan. Our hatred for Mrs Donovan and the two Things was perhaps one of the few times that Rory, Maeve and I ever felt truly united as a family.

Our house is smaller than I remember, but then I was smaller when I lived here. The splotchy paintwork on the front door and window-sills is the same. I can still make out traces of white left over from the time the handyman

Mother hired to pebbledash our front walls accidentally pebbledashed the front windows as well. When Mother saw it, she chased him down the road with a coal shovel. There were no half measures with Mother. Mother was a very great woman.

It is a shock to find myself suddenly standing outside my old home. I want to knock on the door. Even after fifteen years, I still expect Mother's face to appear at the window. She was always able to sense when one of us was outside. Maeve believed it was because she was waiting for Dad to come home. But I think she just had a sixth sense where family was concerned. She could even tell when Ulysses the cat wanted in. Even on the coldest, darkest night, no matter how late it was, your hand had only to touch the front door for Mother's face to suddenly materialise, like the white face of a ghost darting across a landing to vanish again just as rapidly. Within seconds, the door would creak open and Mother would appear, tall, full, fresh-faced, with hard, brown eyes that went right through you like lasers. Everyone who knew her agreed that she was like a tall Elizabeth Taylor, only better looking. The problem with having a mother who looked like Elizabeth Taylor was that many of my friends fancied her. I remember the horror and mortification I felt when 'Conker' Connelly, who sat next to me in school and whose ambition was to emigrate to India, smoke lots of dope and screw loads of women, called around to the house to ask my mother to go out with him. He was fourteen. He assured my mother that age would not be a factor in their relationship.

'Go home and take a bath,' Mother told him.

When I was a teenager, I often came home from school to find the kitchen full of Mother's friends. Later, when she got involved in politics, the whole house was often taken over by cumann members, local politicians and the occasional celebrity or visiting TD. The weekends were sometimes like political rallies. The walls reverberated to speeches and singing and loud drunken arguments – 'debates' as Mother liked to call them. Rory used to say that Mother wasn't passionate about politics, she was just obsessed with Fianna Fail. Maeve told him that he was just jealous because Mother was so popular.

I can still see the faces of Mother's cumann sitting around our table in the front room for their monthly meeting while Maeve and I served them endless cups of tea. Some of them, like Jenny Donovan, Alberta Biggins and Dessie O'Hanlon, who yearned for Mother with a passion that we thought was truly pathetic, spent more time in our home than we did. Rory used to say that Mother had two families, her real family and Fianna Fail. At the time, though, Maeve and I thought it was great to have so much action in our home.

Friday nights after the pubs closed were sometimes the most exciting, particularly if Mother invited the cumann around for a 'social'. She said there was nothing as beautiful, uplifting or as noble as the sound of good old-fashioned political 'debate'. Occasionally, people from Head Office in town came out. Once, a 'good, old-fashioned political debate' about sending UN troops into Northern Ireland turned physical. Dessie O'Hanlon, the treasurer of Mother's cumann, grabbed John Joe Sullivan, Fianna Fail's regional organiser, by the neck and smacked him into the wall. Within seconds, their respective friends and supporters joined in. The room was full of large, beer-bellied men huddled together in a loose rugby scrum, all slapping punches at one another. To restore order, Mother took off her shoes and waded into the middle. I can remember the looks of shock and disbelief as each of these large men was hauled out of the group in turn by a glamorous, elegant woman who then whacked them across the head with a high heel and sent them out of the room. Dessie O'Hanlon was the last to get hit on the head and thrown out. The next morning, two things happened: John Joe Sullivan put Mother's name forward as Fianna Fail candidate for TD in the next election and Dessie O'Hanlon asked Mother to marry him.

Usually, though, the gatherings were without hassle. Mother had a great talent for making everyone feel warm and loved and exciting. When she looked at a person and smiled, it was like being bathed in warm bubbly water. Men just fell in love with her and women wanted to be her friend.

When Mother was angry about something, she saw only the negative side. Everything was a horror story. She would light on me, eyes ablaze, the minute I came in the door from school or from being out with friends.

'You would not believe the cheek out of Maeve just because I asked her to clean up her room. That girl doesn't need a mother, she needs an exorcist. And did you hear what Rory did? He punched the Henshaw boy from Seashell Drive twice in the stomach. The poor fellow wasn't able to eat his tea. I've had the father in the house all afternoon baying out of him for Rory's blood. And, of course, what do you think but Rory ignored everything I said even though I was only saying it for his own sake to stop him going to prison. I'm run ragged trying to do everything in this house. I'd be better off just leaving and putting you all in care, it would be good enough for you . . .'

If you got home late, she would be waiting up. The moment she saw that you hadn't been mangled by a lorry or beaten up by Hatchet Hardy or converted into a Hare Krishna, the look of worry would change to fierceness. Her anxious questions would become a doorstep interrogation: 'What kept you? Look at your eyes, were you drinking? What do you think you're doing coming home at this hour?'

Once, when Rory was so drunk that he couldn't remember where he had been, she told him to sleep in a boat at the harbour and closed the door on him. 'If your father were here he'd deal with you,' Mother said. 'I can't cope any more. Your father has it easy, wherever he is.'

Rory had to sneak round the back and tap on our bedroom window until I let him in. In the morning, he still couldn't remember where he had been.

It is a good feeling to be standing on our doorstep again. I realise I have lost touch with this place where I spent the most important years of my life.

The familiar sound of the latch being clicked on our door

startles me. Slowly, the door opens and Mother's face appears. As soon as she sees that it is me, she smiles. I am surprised to see her, but in another way, it is as I expected. This is the reason I have come, to touch my home again, to see my mother, to listen to her rich, sometimes scolding voice, to watch those vivid, brown eyes pierce me like swords, to be again my mother's youngest boy, her favourite. I am delighted to be cuddled and warmed by my mother's smile. At any moment, she will ask me where I have been, how I am, if I am feeling all right. I can tell that she is in a good mood. Her eyes shine and her lips are full and smiling.

It is great to be home.

She beckons me to lean my head down to be kissed. I expect to feel her soft breath brush my cheek. I close my eyes. I lean forward and wait to be kissed. For a few seconds, nothing happens.

When I open my eyes, the image of Mother is gone. Instead, a man I have never seen before is standing in front of me. He is a stooped, middle-aged man with blue eyes and a high forehead. He is staring at me as if I am insane. It takes a few seconds before I realise that I am still leaning forward with my cheek turned, waiting to be kissed. I straighten up and attempt to compose myself.

'Yes?' the man says. 'What is it?'

Behind the man, someone is running a vacuum cleaner. There are strange pictures hanging on the walls in our hallway. I glimpse a yellow vase of coloured flowers on a shiny high table just inside the door. The house has suddenly come alive. The man coughs and I realise that I am blocking his path.

'Excuse me.' He tries to move past me.

'Sorry.' I take a step to the side.

Embarrassed and shocked, I walk in the direction of The Tall Ships. Behind me, the door closes. The steady vroom of the vacuum cleaner cuts off neatly. I hear the man's footsteps going in the opposite direction. When I turn, I can see his long figure turning the corner, heading up Redrock Hill. I stare after him. The thought of the house where I had lived being taken over by a complete stranger and his family disturbs me. This man and his family now live in the space where we lived. Someone sleeps in my old room, looks out my old window, stares at posters on my walls. These are obvious thoughts, but they are new and strange to me. I am surprised to feel this way. What did I expect to find? Mother still there? Us still there? A shrine in our honour at the front door? Dad waiting for me?

A speck of rain hits my cheek, followed by another. Overhead, the sky is blotching into an ugly mixture of grey and blue. I cannot decide what to do. The image of Mother smiling at me is still so clear in my mind that I find it hard to accept that it was just an illusion, a daydream. I suddenly feel an urge to go back and knock on the door of my old home, even though I know that Mother and the rest of us are long gone from the place. 'Excuse me, I used to live here', I could hear myself saying as I brushed past whoever answered the door. I wanted to tour the house, to see my old room, feel the bed, check the walls, examine under the stairs for forgotten items of my youth, touch the kitchen table . . .

After a few moments, the feeling passes. Without really thinking about it, I find myself going through the door of The Tall Ships. I enter the lounge just as it begins to pour down outside. Going from the cold into the heat, I shiver briefly. Outside, the rain makes popping sounds on the pavement, like popcorn crackling on a pan.

I signal the barman and he comes over. Tall, acned complexion, sullen, weary-eyed, he is nobody I know.

'Just a coffee, please,' I say, and he goes away.

In a moment, I will call Carla. I'll tell her I'm coming home. I'll ask her to phone work to tell them that I'm sick. Maybe Carla will meet me at the station with the motorbike.

The barman comes back with my coffee. I reach into my pocket for money. I can make out the silhouette of the phone at the back of the pub. I am about to ask for change for a phone call but then I think about Donald Logan, sitting in the apartment, drinking coffee with Carla. They will have discovered the Doc Martens by now. I forget about the phone call.

This morning, when I got up after a sleepless night, the first thing I saw was Donald Logan's Doc Martens, one orange, the other pink, staring at me from the shelf on the far wall as they had every morning for a week. They stared at me while I got dressed. They stared at me after I came out of the bathroom. They even stared at me while I was eating my cheese-on-toast. I turned around to drink my coffee but I could feel their gaze boring into my back. In the end, I couldn't stand it any longer.

As soon as I finished breakfast, I went over to the shelf, took out my Swiss Army penknife and slowly ran the sharpest blade across the toes of both boots.

When I left the apartment, the Docs were smiling. And so was I.

TWO

Mother

MOTHER CREATED the sea. She lifted me above the harbour wall and waved her hand and the glimmering water stretched out before me to the end of the world. Wave tips sparkled like the hundreds and thousands on the icing of my birthday cake. Mother made fishing boats with coal-black hulls and creamy cabins that chugged in from the sea, trailing gulls. She made the bobbing sailboats with their milky sails, the sleek speedboats, the snubnosed rowboats and the elegant yachts, their tall masts tinkling pretty tunes. She even made the squat red fireboat with number 46 on its hull which was always anchored across from the lighthouse at the rocky end of the pier. I felt reassured by its snug shape, the clear bold whiteness of the numbers.

In the summertime, Mother would bring me and my elder brother Rory, and sister Maeve down to the pier to wave at the boats. Whenever a boat came swishing into dock, Mother waved and someone on deck always waved back. Mother knew everyone. At the fish merchants on the pier, the gulls cawed and dipped and dropped their little white bombs everywhere except on Mother. While Mother bought a bag of wet, slithery mackerel for breakfast, we stepped over the pink-flecked fish guts that were scattered on the wet floor. At home, the fish tasted of blue skies and rolling waves and the mysterious light that shimmered on the surface of the water on calm sunny days.

Rory was Dad's boy because he was the eldest. Maeve,

because she was the only girl, belonged to everybody. That left me as Mother's boy. At home, when Rory and Maeve were in school and Dad was away on business, I had Mother all to myself. She took me on long walks, sometimes along the east pier. Other times we went along the cliff walks or up to the top of Redrock Mountain. People always wanted to stop and examine me. Some thought I was the spit of my father, others said I was the image of Mother.

'He's a mixture of both,' said Mother. 'And that's how it should be.'

Mother said that Dad spent a lot of time on the road because that was his work. He was a travelling salesman who sold different types of goods to shopkeepers around the country. Someday, soon, Dad was going to get a job in the city and that would mean that he could come home to us every night. I thought Mother might have created Dad too. After all, I only saw him now and again. It was as if Mother kept him in a big box, someplace secret, and only produced him on special occasions.

One day, while Mother and I were walking on the pier, a sharp wind suddenly swept in from the sea, rocking the sailboats and sending white-capped waves shuddering against the harbour walls. Flails of surf shot up over the wall of the pier as we tried to run home, and crystal droplets stung our cheeks like flung pebbles. Then the hailstones came down. Then vicious cracks of thunder. Mother put me under her coat and held me tight as she ran all the way up dark, wet-cheeked Main Street. The smell of Mother enveloped me – a sweet, warm, pungent aroma that made me want to close my eyes and crawl inside her. Inside, I knew things would be peaceful; there would be warmth and shelter and a moist, easy feeling of calm. Hailstones rattled on the cobbles around us and pinged off the gutters of the houses on either side like ricochets. Dodging the puddles was a game: we had to make it home without splashing in them. Every time we hit a puddle, we giggled. When we got home, Mother was drenched and breathless but I was dry from head to foot.

'God, you're a handful,' Mother said.

'Do it again Mammy,' I said.

I wasn't sure about the mountain which began in our back garden. At night, it loomed above us, silent, immense, scary. Mother explained that the mountain was a friend.

'It's there to protect the town from the big storms and the hurricanes that come sometimes in summer. It brings rain so that the crops can grow and everyone has enough water to drink. Rain is good, almost as good as the milk that helps you to grow strong and healthy.'

I believed what she said, but I preferred the taste of her milk.

Dad was always away. There were times when Mother lost her jaunty manner and turned solemn, preoccupied. Now and then, she gazed at us as if she had suddenly found herself in the house with strangers. I did cartwheels on the lawn in the back garden and she smiled. I made funny faces that made her laugh. I told her jokes that I picked up in comics but she didn't get them. I sang pop songs that I heard on the radio, but Mother only liked traditional and I didn't know any of those.

Sometimes, at night, Mother took us down to the harbour to watch the lighthouse probing the darkness with darting shafts of light. I loved the anticipation as the light danced giddily across the pier towards us. In the beam, the rough stone walls of the pier turned into a pale patchwork quilt, tall masts were bleached white to become an army of skeletal lances marching to battle, a cat x-rayed for an instant on a wall stared at us with eyes that were red and luminous before being plunged back into blackness. The light found us, dazzled our eyes in thrilling whiteness for a brilliant second, then passed along the pier, a showbiz spotlight searching for a star. There was no sound except the jangling of boats against the soft lowing of the water. 'The lighthouse is talking to all the ships at sea,' Mother said. 'It's making sure that they all come home safe and sound.'

When Dad was home, the front room was spacious, a great place to run about. Now you couldn't move without bumping into a chair, a table or a lamp you had never noticed before. At night, the room still resonated with Dad's voice telling cowboy tales.

'I was a sheriff in a previous life,' he boasted once. 'I wore a black stetson and a pair of pearl-handled Colts. Once, the gunslinger Johnny Ringo shot a gambler in a bar in Tucson while I was sheriff. I had to take him in. Johnny stood at one end of the saloon and I stood at the other. 'I'm going to have to ask you for your gun, Johnny,' I said. 'I'm afraid I can't do that, Sheriff,' he said. I looked him in the eye, 'Then it's your move, Johnny,' I said. He was fast but I shot the gun out of his hand. As I was putting the cuffs on him, Johnny looked at me with tears in his eyes. 'Ain't nobody ever taken my gun away from me before.' 'That's OK, Johnny', I said, 'I won't tell anyone.' I can remember it all as clearly as yesterday. Sure, every time I step outside the front door, I expect to find a white horse waiting for me.'

'What's a previous life?' Maeve asked.

'There is no such thing as a previous life,' Mother said. 'There's just this one and that should be enough for anybody. So make the best of it.'

Rory winked at Dad, 'I was a prospector in my previous life.'

'Now see what you've started,' Mother said, but Dad just laughed a big, rolling laugh.

Dad loved to play with us. He rarely shouted at us and he only gave Rory the clatters when Rory really deserved it.

The front room was where we played 'Divebombers', Dad's favourite game. I was the divebomber because I was the smallest. Rory was a tank and Maeve was the ground troops, and I buzzed down from the skies to bomb them. Faster and faster Dad twirled me around the room, making growling aeroplane engine sounds. All the paintings on the walls blurred and streaked into a maze of colours, a vase on the table stretched tall as a lamp post, the television set melted onto its stand and chairs blended into the flowered wallpaper. I loved the way that Rory's and Maeve's laughing faces and Mother's agonised look spun before me in dizzy, whirling confusion. I felt as though I was a kite flapping in the wind inside my own front room, with Dad down below holding onto the string. I always got shot down and crashed into the sofa where I blew up, nose pressed into the cushion as Dad made the sound of the explosion.

Mother frowned, 'John, give it up now, he's too small.'

Dad picked me up and looked at me, 'The lad is just grand.'

Rory always wanted to be a divebomber but Dad said he was too big. 'Besides nobody else is any use at being a tank.'

I was sure that Mother had created the sky with its puffy, rolling clouds that watched over everything in summer and the edgy black shades that crawled across the greyness in wintertime. But when I started school, the teacher said that the clouds were God's eyes. Nobody could see or hear or talk to God but God loved me and everyone else on earth equally.

'It is important to do God's will,' he said. 'God is the Father of all mankind.'

I had a hard time believing that stuff. After all, I saw Mother every day and smelt her smell and touched her face and hands and watched her bake bread and do the shopping and handle the daily chores around the house, making sure that we all had enough to eat and that there was always milk in the fridge. Mother could protect me from hailstones and she could make my nightmares go away. It seemed to me that Mother was the one who was all-powerful and all-knowing and all-loving.

On Sunday morning, we went to Mass in the big grey-faced church opposite. I thought the queer-looking gargoyles on the roof were funny, and I loved to look up at the tall spindly spire that leaned out as though about to topple onto Butch Cassidy the butcher's. Inside, the red-faced priest boomed out about the power of God until his face looked as though it was going to explode. But I didn't pay any heed to him. As far as I was concerned, Mother was the most extraordinary person in the world. I decided that

God, whoever He was, was simply another invention of Mother's.

A couple of weeks before my ninth birthday, Dad disappeared for good. He got up early, ate breakfast and set off in his Triumph Herald. He hated goodbyes. Whenever he was embarking on a long journey, he liked to leave before anyone woke up. This time, nobody even heard the car pull off. A few days before, Dad had asked me to think about what I wanted for my birthday. After much deliberation, I finally settled on a bicycle but I never got the chance to tell Dad. When he didn't come home that night, Rory cried that Dad had promised to build him a treehouse in the back garden. Rory's friend Joey Boland had a treehouse in his back garden and Rory wanted one the same. The fact that we had no trees in our back garden didn't bother him.

'Dad promised,' Rory said. 'When's he coming back?'

'He'll be home soon,' Mother said, and carried on writing a letter to the bishop. She was writing to complain about having to live in the perpetual shade thrown by the big grey church opposite the house. The lack of sunlight kept killing off her plants. The gargoyles stared at our front window reproachfully. When she finished she read the letter to us:

'We are a family condemned to live in darkness. Surely a man of your eminence and compassion can do something to lower the spire of the church or at least take down a few of the gargoyles. My family and I want to enjoy the beauty of God's sunshine.'

We gave her a round of applause. The letter was brilliant, we thought. Surely the bishop would do something about our plight. After all, he was a man of God.

Dad didn't come home next morning or that night or the morning after. There was no phone call or letters or even a card.

'Dad must be very busy,' Mother said. 'You'd think he could pick up the phone.'

'What about my treehouse?' Rory said.

When anyone rang looking for Dad, she told them he was down the country on business. To us, she only said that he would be coming home soon. The weekend went by without a word from Dad.

On Monday morning, there was a letter from the bishop. He wrote that he was delighted to receive Mother's letter but that unfortunately the matter was entirely out of his hands. While he appreciated the gravity of the situation, he regretted that he did not have the authority to alter the church spire or to remove without good cause any of the gargoyles. He promised to pray for a solution.

Mother read out the bishop's letter at breakfast. Then she tore it up.

'He's a Fine Gaeler, I knew it. You'd never find a good Fianna Fail bishop treating his own people like this.'

After breakfast, next morning, just as we were about to help Mother to water her plants, the big orange clock radio that Dad had brought back from America one summer gave a sudden low pliiish, like a balloon deflating, then it cut out. We all gathered around it.

'God, this yoke,' Mother said. 'Your Dad is the only one who knows how to deal with it.'

'I'll fix it,' Rory rose and reached for the radio but Mother shouted, 'No.'

Rory stared at her. We all stared at her. Mother's eyes were wide. She looked terrified.

'Wait for your Dad,' she said.

'Why?' Rory said.

'Because he knows what he's doing and you don't.'

When we came home from school the next day, Mrs Donovan was in the front room with Mother. The two Things had taken over the kitchen and were making our tea. We could smell something burning. Mother had the telephone on her lap. She and Mrs Donovan were organising a petition among the neighbours and townspeople for a campaign to get the gargoyles removed from the church roof. They planned to send the petition directly to the Vatican. So far, all of our neighbours and over fifty people in the town had pledged support. Mother looked at us as if we were somebody else's kids invading her house. Nobody mentioned Dad. In the evening, we sat in front of the television. Mrs Donovan and the two Things hijacked the sofa. Like zombies, we watched 'Lassie', 'Voyage to the Bottom of the Sea', 'Bonanza' and 'The Undersea World of Jacques Cousteau.' When the ads came on, Mrs Donovan sent the girl Thing to the kitchen to make a cup of tea for Mother. I think we were all waiting for the phone to ring or a knock at the door. There was no call and no knock came. I tried to tell Mother a joke I had heard in school but she gazed right through me. I gave up telling the joke but she didn't notice. When I turned around, the boy Thing was glaring at me, waiting for me to continue. When I didn't, he shrugged his fat shoulders.

'I've heard it before, anyway. It's crap.'

Before Mrs Donovan took her Things home, she and Mother had a hushed exchange by the front door. Mother looked distraught, inconsolable. Mrs Donovan patted her head.

'Don't you fret,' Mrs Donovan said. 'All things come to those who wait.'

Maeve beckoned for us to follow her outside. Her expression was horrified, 'Do you think they're moving in with us?' she whispered.

Rory stuck out his chin, 'Well, they're not bloody coming into *my* room anyway.'

Rory and I lived on the top floor, in a long room that stretched from the front to the back of our small house. Rory had the front window. I had the back. Rory hated having to share his room with me. In fact, he had stopped talking to me since the day, nearly three years before, when Mother moved me out of her bedroom into his.

'What about my space?' Rory protested. 'I'm never consulted about anything in this house.'

'You had the room to yourself for long enough,' Mother told him. 'Besides, Daniel is your little brother. You should be glad to share with him.'

'What about me? It's my bloody room. Don't I have any say?'

'You've had your say. If you don't like it you can sleep in the hall.'

'Maybe I will,' Rory said. 'I'm fed up being treated like a fool.'

Rory stormed out. I was left standing by my new bed in my new room with a bag of toys in my arms and a stupid, frozen grin on my face. After that, Rory did his best to ignore my presence. In the mornings, we usually dressed without a word. My attempts at dialogue were greeted by a stony glare. An atomic bomb could have exploded in Dublin and we would still have risen in the morning and dressed in silence. Once, I tried to reason with him but he grabbed me by the ear, led me to the bathroom, plunged my head into the toilet bowl and pulled the chain.

'What's that?' he yelled, as the rushing water soaked my hair and splashed my ears. 'Speak up, I can't hear you.'

'Toilet-training' – as Rory called it – cured my desire to be on speaking terms with my brother while we were in our room. Afterwards, I decided that it was wiser and safer to keep silent.

On Saturday night, Mrs Donovan and the two Things came over to cook our dinner and watch our television. Afterwards, we sat in the front room in silence except for the chattering of the two Things and the occasional remark from Mrs Donovan who liked to answer back to the News. Mother and Mrs Donovan talked about what was going to happen to the bishop when the petition went to Rome.

'He's heading for a fall, that fellow, wait and see,' Mrs Donovan said. 'God won't let him get away with it.'

It seemed as though Dad had been removed from the life of the family as abruptly and completely as a smudge of dirt rubbed from a face. Now he had been replaced by Mrs Donovan and the two Things. Mother was quiet and thoughtful and smoked cigarettes one after another. Sometimes, she had two cigarettes going at the same time. I was sure Dad would miss my birthday and that I would never get my bicycle. I considered asking Mother for it but it never seemed like the right time to approach her and besides Rory was always going on about his treehouse.

That night, after Mrs Donovan and the two Things had gone and Mother had gone to bed, Rory called a meeting in the back garden. We stood under the mountain while we talked things through. Rory was sure Mrs Donovan knew something about Dad.

'I heard her telling one of the Things that he was in America.'

Maeve shook her head, 'Dad would never go back there.'

'Why not? He was there before.'

'He would have told us first,' Maeve said.

'Maybe he's just sick of us,' Rory said.

Maeve was disgusted, 'How could he be sick of us? We're his family.'

In the morning when we woke, Mother was in the front room, slumped on the easy chair with the phone tangled at her feet.

Maeve looked grave, 'I bet she was talking to Dad.'

'It was the cops,' Rory said. 'She was on to Missing Persons.'

At breakfast, the Rice Krispies tasted stale. There was something peculiar about the taste of the tea as well. On the shelf above us, the hulk of the American clock radio lay there with its face all lopsided. A few nights before, Rory had secretly taken it apart in a vain effort to find whatever was wrong. Then he found that he was unable to put it back together again. Now it was waiting for Dad to come home and fix it. Rory was worried. If Mother discovered what he had done, she would tell Dad, when he finally arrived home, and then he might never get the treehouse.

'Is Dad ever coming home?' Maeve asked. 'I miss him.'

Mother turned her bloodshot eyes on Maeve. Her expression softened, 'Of course he's coming home. I miss him too, love.'

'When is he coming home?'

'Soon. Now stop asking stupid questions.'

The phone rarely rang. When it did, it was one of Mother's friends to talk about the bishop, or else it was Joey Boland for Rory. There was no word of Dad.

In the mornings, we continued to eat stale Rice Krispies, drink funny-tasting tea and stare into the patterns on the tablecloth. It was like being condemned to eat the same breakfast for ever. When we left for school, Mother came with us to the bus-stop. Every morning, just before we got onto the bus, she whispered the same terse warning.

'Whatever you do, don't say a word to anyone about anything.'

On the bus to school, Rory scratched his jaw. 'Maybe he's been kidnapped.'

'Kidnapped?' Maeve scoffed. 'Why would anyone kidnap Dad?'

'He could have been a spy for the Americans.'

'I don't believe you.'

'Wait and see,' Rory said. 'Any day now, we'll get a ransom note.'

But no ransom note came. In fact, there were hardly any letters at all, except bills which Mother collected and put in a drawer in the kitchen.

Even though the television was always on and the American radio too, – once Mother had got it back from the repair shop on Main Street – the house seemed empty. Footsteps on the stairs sounded hollow. Upstairs, Mother's bedroom remained dark. Even in the daytime, she never opened the curtains. Across the landing, our bedroom was filled with an expectant hush as if Dad were about to burst in and sprinkle us with water, as he sometimes did in the mornings to cheer us up. Downstairs, the hallway had a tighter, more restricted feeling about it. The kitchen had lost its rosy, comforting glow. Maeve said that there was a weird smell in her bedroom at the front of the house.

'It's not coming from me, and all the sheets are clean.'

Nobody else could smell it.

'I think it's just your imagination, love,' Mother said. 'Don't think about it and it will go away.'

Dad's presence grew larger the longer he was gone. We developed little routines. Every morning, we stepped around Dad's winter coat that was still hanging on the rack in the hallway, as if to touch it would bring bad luck. We avoided Dad's chest of drawers in the front room. We never played Beatles albums or took down any of his paperbacks. We entered Mother's bedroom only rarely and when we did, we never stayed long. Everywhere in the house, we found something to remind us of the new gap in our lives.

'I wish that Dad had taken his coat,' Maeve said. 'He's going to get cold without it.'

For my birthday, I got a gun and holster set from Mother, a belt with a shiny silver buckle on it from Maeve and from Rory a week-old copy of *New Musical Express*.

'There's a big photo of Jethro Tull inside,' Rory said. 'I saved it specially for you.'

Mother produced a small cream flan with nine candles on it and forced everyone to sing 'Happy Birthday' to me. When the song was over, everyone seemed relieved. Afterwards, Mother invited Mrs Donovan and the two Things over to watch television.

The two Things bounced into the room, carrying a plate of sandwiches each. They occupied the sofa Maeve was sitting on, squeezing Maeve out. Maeve sat on the floor in front of the television. 'The Fugitive' was almost over when the boy Thing decided that he didn't want to watch it anymore. He swivelled his fat face to Rory and said, 'Turn.'

Rory just stared back at him.

'Turn it yourself.' Rory said and gave him two fingers.

The boy Thing put down his plate of sandwiches and lunged at Rory. To prevent a fight, Maeve turned the television to another channel. Ken Dodd appeared on-screen, waving a large frilly duster.

'About time,' the boy Thing said and the girl Thing let go a high squawk, like a duck falling down a liftshaft.

Maeve leaned over to whisper to me, 'I think we might have to kill them.'

When Mother's favourite plant died, instead of depressing her, the sight of the dead plant seemed to give her a boost. Mother wrote another letter to the bishop:

'Your Grace, As you well know, I am a lifelong supporter of the Fianna Fail Party. During the recent election, I couldn't help but notice that you were always to be seen at the side of the Fine Gael candidate at all his rallies.

Therefore I have come to the conclusion that your callous dismissal of my reasonable request to lower the church spire could only be due to political bias. I feel it my patriotic duty to point out to you that lowering the church spire or at least removing some of the gargoyles is a question of human compassion, not party politics. I wrote to you in the mistaken impression that I was appealing to a man of God. Instead, I find that am wasting my words on a Fine Gael party functionary. Yours sincerely, Kathleen Buckley.'

Posting the letter put a gleam in Mother's eyes, 'Now, we'll see what he's made of.'

We were glad to see Mother motivated, involved, on top of things. The colour was back in her face, her eyes were moist with mischief. The meek, vague-mannered woman of recent days was gone. For the first time since Dad disappeared, Mother brought Maeve and me down to the pier to wave at boats and to buy fish. Rory refused to come. Mother had no money with her. She offered to write a cheque but Mr Wallace the fishmonger told her to take the mackerel.

'Pay me another day,' he smiled.

At home, we cooked the fish and ate it while it was still steaming, followed by lashings of tea and buttered batch loaf. By the time Mrs Donovan and the two Things arrived, only a few fish bones were left. To me, it was evidence that we had become a family again. Watching television, it was as if Mrs Donovan and the Things were in another room. Mother winked at us and we giggled at each other. It was like being involved in a hilarious conspiracy. In the end, the two Things got bored with our television and went back to their own house. Mrs Donovan followed, muttering something about being made fun of by her own neighbours.

That night, I awoke with my heart pounding. I needed to see Dad again, hear his rumbling laugh, smell his musty smell. I put on Dad's red dressing-gown. I prowled around the house, touching Dad's things – his coat, scarf, his paperbacks, his records. Dad had all The Beatles' albums and singles. He was the only father on the road who bought Beatles records. He pretended that they were for us but he played them himself. On Saturday mornings, he liked to play 'Sergeant Pepper's Lonely Hearts Club Band' really loud and wake everyone up. We would stumble in bleary-eyed from our beds and Dad would try to get us to dance around the front room. Dad liked to have fun in the mornings. I rubbed the sleeve of 'Sergeant Pepper's Lonely Hearts Club Band.' I thought that touching Dad's things might bring us good luck, as if the very feel of something of Dad's could cause him to erupt from the album in a stream of smoke just like the genie from the bottle in 'The Thief of Baghdad'.

In the morning, Mother pushed away her bowl of Rice Krispies and looked at us. We stopped eating too.

She had a grave face. 'Children, I have a only few good plants left. It's up to us to keep them alive, now that the bishop has decided to ignore us. I want you all to be brave and supportive and help me water them first thing in the morning and last thing at night. They need care and attention. We'll have to buy better plant food and at least half a dozen sunlamps. So I'll be selling off some things – a few bits of furniture, the old iron, the bedroom firegrate, a wardrobe, plates and cups and saucers. I want you to give me anything you don't need – toys, comics, books, dolls or any money you have saved. I'll repay you all when Dad gets home.'

We were a bit surprised about the plants. We had no idea they needed such care. Mother's words made us determined to help. We all promised to give whatever we could to Mother to sell.

Mother was delighted, 'I knew you wouldn't let me down.'

On Saturday morning in the front room, we made a big pile of things to sell. Rory gave his collection of Charles Dickens hardbacks, plus the *Life of Thomas Aquinas*, that Aunt Ethna had given him, as well as some records that were scratched. Maeve donated a bunch of her dolls but not Barbie. I gave Mother all my *Beanos* and *Dandys* as well as the Johnny Seven gun I got for Christmas.

'Oh Daniel, are you sure?' Mother said and I nodded.

I didn't really mind about the gun. Besides, one of the siderockets was broken. A Johnny Seven gun was not much use if only six of the guns worked.

'You're my best boy,' and she gave me a kiss on the crown of my head.

Then we put the things in black plastic bags and carried them to Mrs Donovan's car which was whining outside our front door. We filled the car with chairs, bags, boxes of plates and cups and saucers. We helped Mother to tie our old wardrobe to the roof with twine. When we were finished packing, the car looked as though it belonged to a family of refugees.

'I'll be back in a while,' Mother said. 'Tonight, we'll eat big steaks and drink wine.'

After Mother left, we went into the kitchen to watch Rory trying to fix the American clock radio.

'Do you think the money's for Dad?' Maeve asked.

'It could be. The wardrobe is worth lots, I bet.'

'I'm glad we're selling things,' Maeve said. 'It's terrible just sitting around doing nothing. Maybe next time she'll bring us with her.'

'She wouldn't get much for you,' Rory sneered.

'That's not what I meant. Anyway, she'll get a lot more for me than she'd get for you.'

Rory eyed me, 'I wonder how much we'd get for him.'

'I'm n-n-not for sale,' I said.

Rory looked worried, 'I don't have anything more I want to sell.'

I was burning to ask. I opened my mouth and took a deep breath, 'How m-m-much – how m-m-m-uch . . .'

They waited patiently for me to get it out.

'How much m-money will it take to g-g-get Dad back?'

'I don't know,' Rory said. 'A lot. Maybe more than we've got.'

While we waited for Mother to return, Rory had another go at taking apart the American clock radio. This time, he was determined to understand how it worked. He gave up after breaking a spring.

32

'Of course, it could be amnesia,' Rory said.

'What's amnesia?'

'It's where someone loses their memory and wanders around not knowing their name or where they are.'

Maeve became curious, 'How do you get it?'

'Well, you can get it from a bang on the head.'

'Who would give Dad a bang on the head?'

'I didn't say anyone gave him a bang on the head. I was just saying what it could be.'

'And you can't remember anything?'

'Not even your own name.'

'Then how do you cure it?'

Rory looked suddenly stricken, 'Eh, I think you have to give the person a bang on the head.'

'That's stupid,' Maeve said and walked off in a huff.

Nothing Rory could say to her afterwards could convince her that he had not been making fun of the situation.

'Some people should keep their big traps shut until they know what they're talking about,' she announced sternly.

Mother came home from the pawnbroker's just before teatime.

'The pawnbroker took everything, even the broken lawn-mower. Now we have enough to pay the mortgage and feed ourselves for months. I bought steaks in the city, big juicy steaks that are so fresh they're dripping.'

'Yuck,' Maeve said.

'What about the plants?' Rory asked.

'Oh yes, of course, the plants,' Mother said and drifted into the kitchen to cook the steaks. 'Tomorrow, we'll buy sunlamps.'

On Monday, a reply came from the bishop. It was very short and signed by his secretary, a Mr Keefer:

'Dear Mrs Buckley, His Grace has advised me to thank you for writing to him about the matter of the Church roof. His Grace wishes you to know that he is concerned at your distress but he has asked me to point out to you that Catholic bishops are unconnected in any way to national politics. In fact, as most good Catholics can testify, the primary duties of an Irish Catholic bishop are to serve God and Ireland. Please do not hesitate if there is any way in which the bishop can be of any assistance in the future. With Every Good Wish etc.'

Mother got a pen and underlined certain words. 'Service, God, national politics, future.' In the end, she drew lines under every sentence.

'This entire letter proves my point. It is evidence of a depraved and vicious mind. That's a truly shocking thing in a clergyman, let alone a bishop. It's proof that we have a rabid Fine Gaeler on our hands.'

She phoned Mrs Donovan, 'We've heard from Your Man. It's time to go to work.'

At the weekend, they canvassed people in town. When they had three hundred signatures, they put the petition in a large jiffy bag, enclosed a letter and sent the package to the Pope.

'That'll shake him,' Mother said.

We came home from school to find Mrs Donovan and the two Things gone and in their place on the sofa Mother's sister, Ethna, and her bald-headed husband, Brian, who always kept a pipe in his mouth. Ethna came to see us at Christmas and Easter. Dad always went away when she called and came back when she left. Ethna was always giving out to Mother for not taking us to Mass every morning and for not rearing us correctly and for not telling her what Dad did for a living. Ethna gabbled a breathless hello to each of us and spent a little time fussing with Maeve's hair.

'Oh, isn't it just gorgeous, now. You're going to be a real Hollywood star like Maureen O'Hara, isn't she, Brian?'

Brian smiled and his pipe bobbed at us, 'A real little Maureen O'Hara.'

Over tea, Ethna stared at Mother. Mother wouldn't meet Ethna's gaze. 'Tell me, Kathleen, have you told the priest?'

'No, I haven't and I've no intention of doing so,' Mother said and forked another rasher onto Ethna's plate. 'I have enough problems with men of God at the moment, thanks very much.'

'Oh Kathleen,' Ethna looked troubled. 'You know there's

no problem in the world that can't be helped simply by involving a priest. It's what they're there for. I just thought I'd tell you.'

'Fine, you've told me. Now, eat your rasher.'

Ethna was worried that we weren't getting the proper care. She thought Maeve looked a bit peaky.

'I thought I was a Hollywood movie star,' Maeve protested.

'Yes, of course you are, darling,' Ethna gushed. 'It's just that you could use a little more meat on your bones, that's all.'

We couldn't understand why Mother was being so nice to Ethna. The last time Ethna had started criticising our family, Mother slammed a cup of tea into the saucer, 'Why don't you go away and make your own children.' Mother glared across at Brian and said witheringly, 'If you can.'

Maeve said that Mother felt sorry for Ethna, 'You'd have to feel sorry for anyone who was married to Brian. Look at him. His pipe has more life in him than he does.'

Mother and Ethna retired to the kitchen to continue their talk. Brian stayed in the front room to watch television and smoke his pipe. Mother gave us permission to stay up and watch television with Brian if we wanted, but we all decided to go to bed.

'Life's too precious,' Maeve said. 'Why waste it by being in the same room as him.'

Even in bed, we could still hear Ethna's voice, 'Kathleen, the situation cannot go on indefinitely. Think of the children. At least, let me take them off your hands for a while.'

'I'll think about it,' Mother said. 'I'm expecting a call from John any moment.'

Dad's brother, Bernard, arrived with a Kylemore cake in a box.

'I'm sorry to barge in like this,' he said. 'Ethna phoned me, so I thought I'd better drop in to see if there was anything I can do.'

'Well, you can sit yourself down and have a cup of tea,' Mother said.

Bernard was a tall, stooping man with a long, sorrowful face. We saw him only at Christmas. He always arrived with a Kylemore cake in a box. He stayed long enough to drink a cup of tea, eat a slice of his own cake and apologise for not being able to stay any longer.

'I'm sorry I couldn't come earlier,' Bernard said. 'I'm sorry there isn't more I can do.'

We watched him as he built himself up for a big confession, 'I'm sorry I don't know where John is. Otherwise, I could tell you.'

Bernard beamed nervously at us, like an explorer who had suddenly happened upon something unique and wonderful and was waiting for us to confirm it.

Mother nodded, 'That's all right, Bernard. Now let's see what you brought. Oh, a cherry surprise. That's very good of you.'

For the rest of the afternoon, Bernard crossed and re-crossed his legs, scratched his forehead and played with his fingernails. After tea, Bernard said goodbye and left our house as though he had been fired from a cannon. Mother threw the remains of the cake in the bin.

'He always brings a cherry surprise. You'd think he could buy some other type now and again.'

Father Barrel was bald, fat and bad tempered. His real name was Darrell but he looked just like a barrel in a cassock so the nickname stuck. He always seemed to be laughing about something we couldn't understand.

'Naha, naha,' he went.

He liked to put his hands in boys' pockets when he had them up at the blackboard. He often kept boys in after school for private lessons. Sometimes, he invited boys to meet him down in the bicycle sheds at lunchtime. Conker Connolly said that The Barrel was a complete psycho and should be put away.

'If President De Valera knew what was going on he'd close the school down.'

The Barrel made me so nervous that I couldn't speak properly. First, I got sent to the line in geography class for being unable to pronounce Saskatchewan. Then I couldn't answer any of the questions in the geography oral test. I knew the answers, the words just stuck in my mouth. The Barrel said my stutter was put on. He had heard loads of fellows try it before, he said.

'If your problem doesn't improve by Friday, you'll get the bamboo,' he growled.

At the end of the week, everyone who had failed to answer a question, been discovered smoking in the bicycle shed or been caught copying the homework was lined up in single file along the wall while The Barrel went to the book cupboard to fetch the bamboo cane. I was first in line. The Barrel usually gave us three on each hand with the tip of the bamboo. He liked to lash the cane across the tips of your fingers. That meant your fingers always stung for hours. During the short break before the final class, Conker Connolly and I had sneaked down to the urinals. Conker had discovered a new trick that prevented pain and blistering.

'Piss on your hands,' Conker Connolly said.

'What?'

'Piss all over them until they go red, then you won't feel a thing.'

We stood in line with our wet hands by our sides while The Barrel slapped the cane against the desk.

'Naha,' he said. 'I'm telling you, there'll be no more cogging the homework in my class, naha.'

Then The Barrel was lurching across the floor towards us, vast belly wobbling under his cassock, his brow corrugated.

'Naha,' The Barrel said. 'Naha.'

Conker's trick didn't work. Afterwards, our hands stung like hell. The only difference was that now they stank too.

We were all surprised when the the police called to the house. At first, we thought it had something to do with the bishop. But the sergeant said that they were following up a report from a Mrs Ethna Tyrell about a missing person and were making some enquiries.

'Typical,' Mother said. 'Go ahead.'

The sergeant had a few questions. How long had Dad been gone? Where had he last been sighted? Where was he supposed to have been heading for? Why hadn't Mother reported Dad missing before now?

Mother listened patiently, hands on her hips, a lit cigarette dangling in her mouth. You could see that the sergeant was intimidated by her. He kept licking the wrong end of his pencil.

'Excuse me,' she said when the sergeant had finished. 'I'd like you to know that, despite what certain people say, my husband is not missing. He's away on business. I'm expecting a phone call any minute.'

'Is that a fact?' the sergeant said.

'My sister is upset over a family matter. There is really no cause for alarm. John often goes away for long periods, doing business. Ethna has really no right to interfere in my family's affairs.'

'Oh, well if that's the case.' The sergeant apologised for bothering her and put his pencil back in his pocket. 'Maybe you could tell himself to give the station a ring when he comes home, you know, just so's there's no misunderstandings.'

'I'll be delighted,' Mother said.

'My father is away.'

The others could say it quickly and get it over with. But every time I tried it, it was like being kicked in the stomach. In school, The Barrel made me stay behind after class. He asked me how things were at home.

I tried to tell him, 'My father is away.' I jammed on the word father, like a drunk trying to curse. 'My fa-fa-fa,' I said, over and over, 'my fa-fa-fa.'

'It's stupid to keep up this little game of yours, Daniel, naha,' The Barrel said. 'It'll only make things worse for yourself in the long run. You get me, ha?'

'Y-yes,' I said.

'Now, how are things at home?'

'My fa-fa-fa,' I said.

'Oh dear, dear, dear,' The Barrel said. 'Naha, things are looking black for you, Buckley.'

Then he sent me home. I was glad he hadn't tried to put his hand in my pocket.

Next morning, Father Caraher, the head priest who looked like an ape with a crewcut, summoned me to his office on the first floor landing. He gazed at me with something like fondness as though he knew that I had committed a mortal sin and could not escape punishment.

'I hear you're having a bit of trouble with the old verbals.' Caraher gave a big grin, 'Never mind, we'll straighten you out. Now come with me like a good man.'

He led me down to the statue of Jesus in the ground floor corridor, at the entrance to the school yard. He went down on his knees and told me to do the same beside him.

'There's more to this than meets the eye,' he said knowingly. 'The only thing to do is go directly to the Your Man Upstairs. Now. Our Father who art in heaven . . .'

When the bell rang for lunchbreak, we were still on our knees, chanting. Everyone in the school paraded past, looking down at me as if I were a convict on the way to the gallows. I stuttered like an old banger but Caraher didn't seem to mind. He kept his eyes closed as he prayed.

'If you do this for a couple of hours every day, your little problem will go away.'

At the time, I was sure he was playing a cruel trick. When I get big enough, I vowed, I am going to turn Protestant.

Soon Maeve was the only one I could talk to without rat-tat-tatting like an old machine gun and then only if there was nobody else around. Whenever I tried to have a conversation with anyone other than Maeve, I got pains in my stomach and back. I thought I was going to have to give up speaking altogether. I imagined having to carry little signs with me everywhere that said, 'Yes' and 'No' and 'Could you please show me the way to the nearest toilet.'

Mother wasn't worried about me, 'You do *not* have a stutter. You have to have been born with a speech impediment. Your problem will clear up once Dad gets home.'

At home, whenever I tried to say something, Mother would tell Rory to shut up and insist that I be allowed all the time I needed to complete my sentence. 'See, he'll be fine,' Mother said. 'He just needs a little time.'

She thought she was helping, but it only made me worse. It also made Rory angry and sullen.

'You're only doing it to get attention,' he said. 'You don't fool me, little crybaby.'

Deep inside, I thought it was all my fault that Dad had vanished. I figured that I must have done something to displease him last time he was home. Perhaps it was because I was so quiet or because I always got shot down during 'Divebombers'. I learned that I could hide behind my stutter. It meant that people didn't expect much from me. Now that there was something wrong with me, I was either ignored or talked down to. It was like living at the side of people's lives.

'Would Daniel like a biscuit?' Alberta Biggins asked when we were over at her house.

'Ask him yourself,' Mother told her.

'Oh, I thought he . . .'

'He can still hear you,' Mother said. 'He's not a vegetable, you know.'

We knew the letter contained bad news because Mother scrunched it into a ball and put it in the ashtray. Then she set fire to it. We stood in silence as fritters of blackened paper spiralled towards the ceiling. Maeve finally plucked up the courage to ask.

'Is it about Dad?'

'No love, it's not about Dad. It's about our home.'

Mother watched the flames burn out in the ashtray, then she poked the remains with her finger.

'The bank will evict us from our house if the mortgage falls any further into arrears. We owe over two hundred and fifty pounds.'

I remembered a family who had lived under a large white tarpaulin on the green outside the courthouse. We saw them standing around every morning on our way to school or on Saturdays when Dad took us for a drive in the Triumph Herald – a tall man with white hair, a small red-faced wife and seven or eight kids. Dad told us that the family had been evicted because the man lost his job and couldn't pay the mortgage. The family had lived there for months. Then one morning they were gone. Nobody knew where. I asked if we were going to have to live under a big white tarpaulin.

'Over my dead body,' Mother said. 'This is our home. We're not leaving for any bank.'

Next day, Mother got a job as a clerk in Mahony's mini-market, three days a week. At weekends, she cleaned and sold fish in Wallace's fish merchants on the pier. She brought home enough money to pay the mortgage and feed and clothe us. She also brought the smell of fish into every room in the house.

'Pooh,' Maeve said and held her nose.

'I'll teach you to pooh me,' Mother said and chased Maeve with a wet mackerel.

Mother got Maeve on the bed and hung the mackerel over her nose.

'I'll never say it again,' Maeve giggled. 'I swear.'

Mother took the fish away from Maeve's nose, 'I should hope so.'

She held up the mackerel to Rory and me who were standing in the doorway of Maeve's room, 'Have either of you got anything to say?'

Rory and I looked at each other.

'Pooh,' we said and ran for it.

After a few weeks, Mother was too tired to play chasing when she got home. Sometimes she didn't even hear us when we spoke to her. We gave up saying things about the fishy smell.

'Did Dad ring yet?' Maeve asked.

'It's only a matter of time.'

'What's only a matter of time?' Rory asked.

'Before he comes home,' Mother said. 'I'm amazed that you would even ask such a silly question.'

★

Manus Rock found it difficult to believe that my dad was missing. He sat up on the grass bank and studied my face for clues.

'Your dad must be somewhere. It stands to reason.'

'Yeah.'

'After all, everybody's got to be somewhere.'

'T-true.'

'If he's not here, he's somewhere else, right?'

'Eh, well . . .'

'And if your dad is somewhere, then he isn't really missing at all, right?'

I thought about this for a moment.

'W-w-where is he then?'

'How the fuck do I know? But he's not missing.'

Rory beat up Dominic Jones because he said that he had seen our dad staggering out of The Tall Ships, langered out of his mind, the night before last.

'I wouldn't mind, but Dad never drank in The Tall Ships. The guy could at least get his facts right.'

Maeve came home crying when Shivaun Fennessy told her that our dad had run off with a young one. A few months before, Mr Garrison the dentist had run off with his sixteen-year-old temporary secretary from down the road. After that, the whole town was obsessed with the notion of middle-aged men running off with young ones. A few in the town reckoned that our dad had done the same thing. No female of any age for miles around had also gone missing, but that didn't seem to bother the gossipers.

Mother was amused, 'It doesn't matter what other people think. People are always resentful of the brave and the beautiful. You are peacocks, proud, haughty, beautiful, full of light and talent and mystery. Peacocks are not ashamed to show their colours to the world. They shrug off criticism and carry on with whatever they're doing because they know they are in the right. As long as we all stick together, we can do anything. Do you hear me? *Anything*. I want each of you to say it.'

'Anything,' we said.

'Again, please.'

42

'We can do anything.'

Mother's words made us feel good. We drank them in like the freshest, sweetest orange juice. At home, we were confident, secure and warm. Once we were out in the world however, we reacted to every word of criticism as a direct assault on our family. We forgave no one who attacked us. The postman, who delivered our post to the wrong address, became an enemy for life. The shopkeeper, who over-charged Mother, was a criminal who should be locked up. People who came looking for money we owed were treated like burglars trying to rob us.

Maeve wouldn't eat her tea. Mother asked her what was wrong, but Maeve just stared at the table. Mother kept on at her to talk.

'I heard something,' she said eventually.

'Tell us.'

'Never mind.'

Maeve kept peeping at us though, so you could tell that she really wanted to tell us what she had heard.

'What was it? Was it that little Fennessy bitch again? Maeve, if you don't tell me, I won't be able to help.'

Maeve gave her a grave look, 'Shivaun Fennessy said that when a father goes missing, they take the children into care.'

'I knew it. That little Fennessy bitch. None of that family can mind their own business for a minute.'

'I asked Mrs Milton and she said that it was true.'

'I've a good mind to go round there now and eat the head off the lot of them.'

'Mrs Milton said that it's too much responsiblity for a mother to carry.'

'Don't mind that woman, she's only a schoolteacher, not the Pope. She doesn't know what she's talking about.'

Maeve began to cry, 'I don't want to go into care.'

Mother went over to her and gathered her in her arms. Rory got up to leave. Mother pointe at him.

'Don't anyone go anywhere. I've got something to say so sit down please.'

Rory sat down. Maeve stopped crying.

'We are a family and we will stay a family. Don't mind what others say. Just feel sorry for them. They don't belong to this family and they never will. They don't know what goes on in our house. Tell them nothing. Just be proud of yourselves and remember that as long as we stay together everything will be all right. I will never let anyone break us apart or move us out or interfere with our life as a family. Next time that those Fennessys say anything, just throw your head back and laugh. Then they can't hurt you.' Mother threw her head back and laughed, 'Say "ha ha ha", go on, say it.'

'Ha ha ha,' we laughed.

'Our father is away' became a secret mantra in our heads. None of us believed that he was really missing. He was just somewhere else, for reasons of his own which would become clear in time. We knew that if we could remain a family, then one day Dad would walk back into our lives, carrying a suitcase filled with presents.

One day we came home from school to find Alberta Biggins making our dinner. She gave each of us a pat on the head and said in her soft English accent, 'It's lamb chops, dearies, now who wants gravy?'

The next night, Mrs Vincent was standing in front of the stove struggling with a can opener that was stuck in a can of beans. 'Everything's under control. I just need someone to help me with this shaggin' yoke.'

The can of beans twisted out of her grasp and flew through the air. Rory caught it one-handed, like he was taking it down from a shelf. We gave him a round of applause.

'It was nothing,' he said. 'Anyone could have done it.'

Dessie O'Hanlon, the treasurer of the local Fianna Fail cumann, called around after Sunday dinner. We hated Dessie because he always appeared to stare right through us whenever he spoke to us, a trait that confirmed our suspicion that he was only being pleasant to us so that Mother would think he was a great man. Maeve objected to the way he kept playing with the ends of his small, wiry moustache.

'Now, I want you to treat me as an uncle,' he said, touching his small moustache and beaming at us as if we were imbeciles. 'If there's anything I can do, anything, don't hesitate to ask.'

Rory put up his hand, 'Uncle Dessie, I have something you can do for us.'

Dessie was ecstatic, 'Yes, Rory, what is it?'

'How about finding our dad?'

After Dessie had left, Maeve called me out to the back garden.

'Wait till you see what I have.' Maeve fished in her schoolbag, removed a small envelope and held it to her chest.

'Do you remember what Dad looks like?'

'Sure I do.'

'Well, what colour were his eyes?'

I tried to remember Dad's face, his mouth, the colour of his eyes. Every time the face swam into focus, it immediately swam out again. The only things I knew for sure were that his teeth were small, white and perfect and that his eyes were blue.

'Blue,' I said.

'No, they're brown, like mine. Look.'

Maeve took a black and white photograph out of the envelope. The photograph showed our parents in O'Connell Street. They looked so young. Dad was wearing a long greatcoat, and a white scarf. Mother had on a long dress and a coat with a high collar. Dad was smiling at someone off camera. It had been taken before we were born, perhaps while they were still courting. Our parents looked like a typical young couple, out for a night on the town. It was difficult to believe that your own parents had ever done that sort of thing.

'I was looking through Dad's books and it fell out, so I kept it.'

'It's great.'

'See, he has brown eyes,' Maeve said. 'Like me.'

'I always thought he had blue eyes like me.'

'No, brown,' Maeve smiled. 'I'm going to keep this with

me wherever I go. As long as I have this, I'll never forget his face.'

I thought about this for a moment. I looked at the photograph again. How could anyone tell the colour of a person's eyes from a black and white photograph?

'He had blue eyes,' I said.

'No, brown,' Maeve said sternly. 'Like me.'

Joey Boland's mother refused to let him have anything to do with Rory. She said that a family without a father would have a bad influence on a young lad.

Giles O'Hara's mother wouldn't let me into his birthday party even though Giles himself had invited me.

'There isn't enough room for you, Daniel, I'm very sorry,' she said and closed the door in my face.

I got the feeling that she was afraid Giles would catch my stutter.

On the street, Mrs Fennessy from Grace Road Gardens led her entire family across to the other side of the road rather than come face to face with us.

'What's the matter with them?' Mother said. 'Do they think we can make people disappear at will or something?'

As the months passed, and word got out that my father was missing, many of my friends drifted away or suddenly didn't want to know me. I saw Robert Cusack and Damien Donnelly on the street and they just nodded to me and walked on. I could tell they were under instructions. At school, Conker Connolly ignored me for months, as if we had never been to each other's houses or met each other's parents and sisters and brothers or attended each other's birthday parties or made our communions together. I felt I did not have the right to say anything to him having, somehow, mislaid my father.

I could not get used to my home with its tight, cramped rooms, narrow stairs and hallway. Nor did I like to walk out the front door to come face to face with the big grey church. I kept expecting to see Dad's Triumph Herald parked on the pavement. Living in the town meant that I was always aware of the fact that my family was not from around here, neither were we well-connected, nor wealthy, nor influential. Before Dad disappeared, there had been a feeling that one day we would be well provided for, that things were just beginning for us. Afterwards, I felt alien, unwanted, a real 'runner-in'.

'Get up,' Mother said.

'S-s-sick,' I said and pulled the covers up to my throat.

Rory stuck his head back into the bedroom, 'What's the matter with him?'

'He's all right. He'll go to school tomorrow. Won't you, Daniel?'

'S-s-sick,' I repeated.

The next morning, Mother sent Maeve in to get me up.

Maeve smiled, 'You have to go to school.'

'No, I don't.'

'They'll make you.'

'They can try.'

When Mother was at work and Maeve and Rory at school, I got up and roamed around the house. I wore Dad's dressing-gown so that I could hop back into bed if anyone came home early. It was boring being in the house on my own. There was nothing on television except pro-grammes for schools. It was a strange feeling to know that school was going on without me. I could stay at home for ever, I thought, nobody would miss me. I would die of boredom. The next morning, Mother sent for Manus Rock.

Manus sloped into the room. He looked curious.

'Are you really sick?'

'W-w-well, I . . .'

'OK, you're not sick. Why are you in bed?'

'I-I-I . . .'

'Ye don't know. OK, well, you don't want to stay in bed for ever, do you?'

'It's n-n-not as s-s-s . . .'

'Only an eejit would stay in bed when they're not sick, so get up and don't be wasting everyone's time,' Manus moved to grab the bedclothes.

'OK, OK, j-j-just leave me alone.'

I got up and went to school.

47

Manus Rock was a Protestant which meant that he didn't go to my school or to the big church opposite my house. It meant he was somewhat removed from the attitude of some others in the town. He didn't care about being seen with someone whose dad was missing. He was my friend and that was that.

'Some people are born stupid,' he said in his gruff voice. 'Others have to work real hard to get that way.'

One day, Manus's mother and sister came to our house to offer to help out. Mother thanked them but told them we were doing fine now. Occasionally, though, if she was exhausted after work, she sent Maeve and Rory and me down to the Rocks for dinner.

'The Rocks are the best people in Redrock,' Mother said. 'A family that makes its living from the sea is never going to adopt airs. Not like that Fennessey woman from Grace Road Gardens who still looks at me as if I've three heads, the silly goose. She thinks that if I walk up to her and say "boo", she'll vanish on the spot.'

'Spontaneous combustion,' Rory said.

'What?'

'I was reading a book about weird and unexplained events,' Rory explained. 'There have been cases of people suddenly bursting into flame for no reason and burning up.'

'Why?'

'Nobody knows. They think it might have something to do with the atmosphere.'

'Are you saying that Dad burst into flame and burned up?'

'No, I'm just saying things like that can happen.'

'That's the stupidest thing you've come up with yet.'

'Well, I'd like to hear you come up with something better.'

'Wait till I tell Dad when he gets back.'

Sometimes, in bed when I couldn't sleep, I tried to imagine what it was like to belong to a family that was intact. My fantasies always broke down when I tried to picture the face of a father. The memories of Dad coming through our front door or laughing in the front room were still too vivid. I knew that there were a lot of families where one parent had walked out. That meant a lot of pain for everyone. But it seemed to me that, in those families, the kids could at least still see the other parent from time to time. They would know that their father or mother was alive. Even kids in one-parent families, I reckoned, knew that the other parent had deserted them or run off with someone or that they just didn't want to live with the other person anymore. At least they had that knowledge. In my family though, there was just a gap, like a fire-blackened hole in the middle of a family portrait. Occasionally, I wished that they had found Dad's corpse. Then, at least, we would have known, we would have been able to tell people that our dad was dead.

One day, about three months after Dad disappeared, Maeve and I found a large, mysterious-looking box under the stairs. Inside was a black stetson. I tried it on. It came to below my ears and it smelt of sun and dust. I thought I could hear horses' hooves galloping in the distance. When I showed it to Mother, she laughed. As she held the hat, her eyes shone.

'Where did that yoke come from?' Rory asked.

Mother tried the hat on. It came to below her ears. We laughed. She took the hat off and held it.

'He was wearing this the first time I met him. It was in a lift at the airport. I was working as a ground stewardess and he had just come back from America. You didn't see too many fellows who were wearing a black stetson, blue jeans and a buckskin jacket. So I noticed him. He gave me a nice smile and before I knew it, I smiled back. He's like that, he can catch a person off-guard. When he followed me out of the lift and asked me to go for a coffee with him, without knowing why, I said yes. We got married six months later, against the advice of my family. Ethna said she did not think it was a good idea for a young woman in my position to marry an Irish cowboy. Mind you, I was relieved to find that he didn't go around in a stetson all the time.'

As she spoke, Dad appeared before us, a tall, sloping man with a sly grin under his black stetson. To me, he had the face of Marshal Matt Dillon from 'Gunsmoke'. The image of Dad as a straight-talking lawman of the Wild West was more real than anything on television or in any of the family photographs.

'What did Dad do in America?' Maeve asked.

'He worked, he travelled around. Before he met me, he spent five years working in various places, Texas, New Mexico, Wyoming, a year and a half in Tucson, Arizona. He did a bit of everything – ranch hand, short order cook, mailman, oil worker, stuntman.'

'Stuntman?' We were amazed.

'Oh,' Mother said vaguely, 'I think he worked on a couple of films as a stuntman. He said the money was middling but the work was too dangerous so he gave it up.'

Mother couldn't remember the names of the films or anything about them but she thought they might have been Westerns. I went to bed that night thinking about Tucson and Wyoming and Arizona and New Mexico and Texas. Arizona sounded like music. Texas was like the sharp snap of a dry twig in summer. For months, we watched every Western on television and leaned into the screen to scrutinise the credits for Dad's name. Rory swore he saw it at the end of 'Rio Bravo' but none of us spotted it.

'Don't worry,' Mother said, 'John Wayne's in it, they're bound to show it again soon.'

A Dad story before bedtime became a ritual. We became desperate for any new snippet of information. It seemed to me that if we didn't talk about him, he would fade away. Talking about him kept the wish for Dad's return burning in some deep, unknown part of ourselves. As time went on, we grew even more ravenous for stories. Each evening, we would tidy up the house, feed Mother's plants and adjust their sunlamps, then settle down in the kitchen for Mother to tell us about Dad. We didn't even mind when Mother began to tell the same stories over and over. If, however, she began to appear distracted or if it seemed that she was talking about one thing and thinking of something else, we were outraged.

The stories kept Dad alive, but after a while they made Mother feel depressed. Gradually, the stories grew less frequent. Mother found something important that had to be done or else Mrs Donovan, Alberta Biggins or Dessie O'Hanlon called to the house to talk about politics. Dessie O'Hanlon was very keen for Mother to join the local Fianna Fail cumann. We were not allowed to talk about Dad in front of anyone so we bit our lips and watched television instead. Automatically, I scoured the credits at the end of 'The Man From U.N.C.L.E.' and 'Mission Impossible' for Dad's name. I even checked the credits at the end of 'Doctor Who'. I never saw his name listed. Deep down, I never expected to.

On teatime, six months after Dad had disappeared, Mother held up her hands and shook her head, 'No more stories,' Mother said. 'I can't remember anymore and I'm sick of repeating myself.'

'Aw, Mother.'

When she saw that we were sad and disappointed, Mother gave us a big smile, 'I could tell you stories about De Valera and Lemass and Michael Collins. There are some great heroes in Irish history.'

Rory shrugged, 'We get those in school.'

'I think De Valera is incredibly boring.'

'Maeve, that is no way to talk about the founder of our State.'

'Well, he is. I want to hear about Dad.'

I wanted to tell Mother that to us, Dad was more alive, more real, more relevant than any historical figure. I knew the stutter would turn my serious statement into a farce so I didn't even try. Instead, I nodded to show that I agreed with Maeve.

'Life goes on,' Mother told us. 'There is no point dwelling on the past.'

'But Michael Collins is the past,' Rory said.

Mother gave him a look, 'That's different. Michael Collins is our heritage.'

'Dad is our real heritage.'

'Rory, your father is gone,' Mother said.

'You said he was coming back one day.'

'Yes, love, he will. But for the moment, I think we should get on with things, don't you?'

'Get on with what sort of things?' Maeve asked.

'Get on with our lives,' Mother said.

'Yeah, yeah, that's just great, get on with our lives,' Rory stood up, walked to the doorway and held the top of the doorframe. He hung there facing the hallway for a moment, then he went out.

When the new bishop was appointed, Mother and Mrs Donovan were sure it was their doing. Even though they had not received any acknowledgement from the Vatican, they were positive that it was because of the petition. The fact that the previous bishop was in his late seventies and rumoured to be on his deathbed was discounted.

'We overthrew the Fine Gael hack,' Mother boasted.

Mother spent a lot of time on our doorstep, a hand cupped over her eye, as if measuring the church roof with the idea of removing the gargoyles herself.

Within days, Mother wrote to the new bishop to complain that her plants still kept dying due to lack of sunlight:

'It wouldn't hurt anyone just to move a couple of gargoyles. Even if the church spire cannot be lowered or the gargoyles removed, we should at least be entitled to a special grant from the Vatican in order to cope.'

The Bishop wrote back:

'My Dearest Kathleen, God's will is truly a great mystery. I am heartily sorry about the plants. All life on earth is sacred. I promise you that I shall look into the matter and get back to you as soon as I have conducted my investigations. With love and best wishes etc.'

'At last, a man of honour,' Mother declared. 'It goes to show that whenever you want something done right, you have to go right to the top.'

On a sunny afternoon, almost a year after Dad vanished, Mother pulled a big box into the hall. She had brought it home from Mahony's. It was time to put Dad's stuff in the attic.

'We'll keep it safe for him, otherwise, it'll just get wrecked. We can bring it back down when he comes home.'

Reluctantly at first, then with more enthusiasm as we began to enjoy the thrill of tracking down individual items, we gathered up all of Dad's belongings – clothes, ties, shoes and boots, shaving stuff, football shorts and boots, letters, notebooks, snapshots, records. We put them into the large box and when that was full, Rory went down to Mahony's and got more boxes. Mother was going to put the Beatles albums up in the attic as well but Rory protested.

'Dad bought them for us,' he said.

Mother relented, 'They can stay where they are. Just don't keep playing that Sergeant Pepper thing all the time, it drives me mad.'

In the end, we filled four boxes with Dad's things. We all helped to put the boxes into the attic. When everyone else was up in the attic, I hid the black stetson under my bed. I couldn't explain it; it just felt right.

Afterwards, it was as though Dad had disappeared for the second time. Only this time it had been our fault.

'You didn't see many men wearing a black stetson, blue jeans and a slow smile. She thought he was the funniest, most charming man she had ever met,' Maeve said.

We sat on the floor in Maeve's room while Maeve told the story about Dad meeting Mother at the airport. Afterwards, we felt purified, liberated, ecstatic. We felt as though we had somehow reclaimed our father from the box in the attic. Maeve produced an Aisling copybook and a felt-tipped pen.

'Now I'm going to write it down. We'll have it forever.'

The next night, I brought the black stetson. Maeve was overjoyed to see it.

'It's like he's here with us.'

We put the hat on the floor between us and took it in turns to tell stories. I didn't stutter much, just on the big words or words beginning with 'a' or 'p'. We repeated and embellished Mother's stories and when we tired of them, we made up astounding, colourful adventures which portrayed Dad as a hero to rival any big screen cowboy. In mine, Dad rode into town, dressed wearing his black stetson with twin pearl-handled six-shooters strapped to his waist. He was always involved in shoot-outs and fistfights and forever taking on and outdrawing the notorious gunslinger, Johnny Ringo. I gave Dad some of the lines Matt Dillon said on 'Gunsmoke': 'I'm gonna haveta take you in' and, 'Now son, think about what you're doing.'

Maeve's Dad was a wizard who appeared only to children and helped them when they were in trouble. Children loved him and all the animals in the forest were charmed by him, especially the deer who came to the edge of the forest to gaze lovingly at him. I always listened quietly until the story was finished.

'Brilliant,' I said when she asked me what I thought.

I didn't wish to appear impolite, but I preferred my stories. They were more realistic.

Once, Rory appeared in the doorway. Maeve saw him but carried on with the story as though he weren't there. He was gone before Maeve got to the bit about the deer.

At the end of the storytelling session, we carefully hid the red Aisling copybook under Maeve's mattress.

'Now we'll always be able to remember,' she said.

The next morning, we woke up to the sound of loud banging. Mother came running.

'Get up quick, everyone. There's something you just have to see with your own eyes.'

We gathered on the doorstep and watched as workmen on the roof of the church removed a gargoyle. When Mother asked the foreman what was going on, he told her that the church roof required certain 'renovations'.

'Some of the gargoyles on this side of the roof are being removed for good, due to safety considerations,' he explained.

Mother gave the foreman a kiss on the cheek. Then she gathered us to her in a big hug, 'It's a miracle. Now, we'll get a bit of sun on this house at last.'

That afternoon, we saw Mrs Fennessy on the corner of

our street, outside Butch Cassidy's shop. The moment she noticed us coming her way, she pretended to look in the butcher's window. Mother went up to her, stood behind her and tapped her on the shoulder. When Mrs Fennessy turned around, Mother put her face right into hers and said, 'Boo.'

Mrs Fennessy scampered away.

THREE

The Ship Inspector

I AM SITTING on a red plastic chair in the Department of Agriculture office, trying not to drop off. It is 7 am. I have been on nights for the past week and I am wrecked.

Across from me, Frank Nails plonks his briefcase on the table. He opens it and takes out his breakfast, two Mars bars and a can of Coke. Yesterday morning, I watched him eat a large Cadbury's Wholenut and guzzle a can of Fanta. The morning before that, it was a packet of Tayto crisps. Frank has a square jaw and wears a crewcut. When he smiles, he looks like an escaped mental patient. When he is not eating, he likes to talk about hurling. Hurling is a subject about which I know nothing.

I am glad that there is only one more night to go with Frank.

Above our heads, the black and white monitor shows that there are no flights on the ground and none expected until the Boston jumbo at nine. The Arrivals lobby is deserted except for rows of gleaming trolleys standing to attention beside immobile baggage belts. For hours, there have been no engine noises, no announcements, no sudden rushes of wind as the glass doors to the tarmac slide open. Frank Nails is the only human being I have laid eyes on since three this morning when the Torremolinos flight landed, depositing two hundred sun-baked passengers who danced down the stairs in a human chain, waving sombreros and chanting 'E Viva Espana'.

56

In ten minutes, I will inspect the airport incinerator. After that, Frank Nails should give me a lift home.

Carla's flight, EI 167, is due in from London at eleven. I have promised Carla to have breakfast ready for her when she gets home.

'That would be so much more fun than having you wait around at the cold, cold airport for hours,' she said.

I am going to make Carla her favourite: scrambled eggs on toast with raspberry jam and a pot of rosehip tea. As a special welcome home surprise, there is a bottle of Möet et Chandon in the fridge.

Carla has spent the past three nights in London with The Silent Screams. The Screams were doing a series of show-case gigs and Carla's stage costumes were an essential component of their show. Donald Logan insisted that Carla should be there to make sure everything went well. The band paid for her flight and hotel expenses.

'It will be great experience,' she said. 'And besides, it isn't costing me a penny.'

Every night, she phoned to say how much she missed me and to let me know that the reaction to her costumes has been 'immense'.

She said the band was going down a storm, 'You really *have* to see them when you get the chance. Donald is *such* a performer.'

Just before midnight last night, she phoned to say that she loved me madly and missed me terribly, more terribly than she ever thought she could. In the background I could hear squeals of laughter, the clinking of glasses and what sounded like someone playing a trombone.

'Oh, and by the way,' she said, 'The Screams have just signed a record deal for an absolutely huge amount of money. Isn't that utterly *amazing*? Aren't you just *thrilled*?'

I told her that I was thrilled.

After the incident with the Doc Martens, I came home to find a handwritten note taped to the fridge:

'Daniel, you're a very, very bad boy. I'm really quite vexed. Love, Carla.'

There was no sign of Donald Logan's pink and orange Doc Martens.

That night, I bought Carla a bouquet of roses and booked a table for two at The Penguin which was Carla's favourite restaurant. Her frosty manner melted the second she saw the roses.

'I love you, Daniel,' she said. 'You're my man.'

'I love you too,' I said as she kissed me on the mouth.

At The Penguin, she had the swordfish steak. I gave her half my salmon teriyaki. She said it was a sign of real strength in our relationship that we could still go out to dinner and enjoy each other's company even after seven years of living together. She didn't mention the Doc Martens. For dessert, we ordered Death by Chocolate. It was wonderful. After each mouthful she gave herself a little squeeze and went 'mmmmm'. Over espressos, she told me about the tour with The Silent Screams.

Two days afterwards, Carla left for London. I really miss her. In her absence, our apartment is cold and bare and too big. I feel empty, as though a chunk of my insides is missing. I just mope around the place or watch television. I can't read and I don't feel like going to the movies or renting videos. I am so fed up, I don't even wank. Even the *Playboy* with the special section on 'Cheerleaders of Detroit' that I have hidden under the mattress for when Carla is away, doesn't turn me on. I am just numb.

Frank Nails yawns a big yawn and stretches himself. With an athletic flourish, he tosses the empty can of Coke into the bin beside his desk, followed by the chocolate wrappers.

'Now,' he says as he slams his briefcase shut and turns to me, 'that'll keep the wolf from the door.'

It is time to visit the incinerator.

I walk through the empty gleaming lobby, under the 'Nothing to Declare' green customs channel and out through the doors to the main Arrivals hall, deserted except for a few cleaners and a security man. One of my duties as a ship inspector is to visit the airport incinerator two or three times daily and file a report to the head of the department.

I don't feel like walking all the way, so I take the escalator to the Departures hall on the second floor, stroll over to the huge windows overlooking the car parks and the airport buildings and look out. A tiny wisp of white smoke is rising from behind one of the buildings. I go back to the office to type my third incinerator report for that night on the battered Remington:

'To Whom It May Concern, This is to state that I visited the incinerator at 7:21 am today and found it to be working perfectly. A quantity of recently deceased Department of Agriculture officials were in the process of being fricasseed. The refuge operatives were having a rare ould time. Yours sincerely, Daniel Buckley, Ship Inspector.'

For months, I have been filing misleading incinerator reports. I have brought hysterical news of Martians taking over the airport, given advance warning of an impending revolt by baggage handlers and alerted the country to an outbreak of cannibalism amongst customs officials. Nobody has noticed.

Frank Nails is almost ready to go, 'Now, let's do a quick checklist. Mats?'

'All the m-mats in the Arrivals hall have been disinfected.'

'Watering-cans? Plastic bags?'

'Yes,' I say. 'The watering-cans have been f-f-filled with disinfectant. I left the plastic bags beside the l-ledger.'

On all international flights, the stewardess is required to announce that anyone who had been on a farm should contact the Department of Agriculture in the Arrivals hall as soon as they disembark. When passengers come in to say that they have visited a farm, we spray their shoes with disinfectant. If they have shoes in their luggage that have been in contact with animals, we spray those too. Then we put the shoes in a clear plastic bag so that the passenger can place them back in the case without dripping disinfectant over everything. Finally, we enter the passenger's name and address in a big red ledger. If a passenger is rude or abrasive or if he gives me a hard time, I hold him up for ages by spraying every shoe in his baggage, taking my time about putting them in plastic bags. If the passenger is particularly obnoxious, I rip a small tear the plastic bag with my thumb before putting it back in the case so that the disinfectant will leak. On boring nights, when nobody turns themselves in, I sometimes make up names. It fills the ledger and gives me something to do. In the past year, according to the ledger, the department has sprayed the shoes of Benito Mussolini, Sigmund Freud, Mata Hari and Tinkerbell.

On nights, I usually do all the work while Frank sleeps on the couch in the back room. I consider that spraying mats with disinfectant is a lot more interesting than staring at the flight monitor and listening to Frank's snores.

Frank is delighted, 'Good man. Then, with the blessing of God, we have everything done for the next man in.'

On the way out, we pass the relief man. Desperate Dan Doyle is a tiny Kerryman with no neck and a hunched, grumpy face. He seems even more displeased than usual to find himself at work at such an early hour. Frank greets him and Dan says, 'Good morning.' Then he sees me.

'Hello Big Balls,' Dan says and walks past before I can say anything.

Desperate Dan was the first ship inspector I met when I started at the airport as a part-timer. He was the only one in the office when I arrived to report for work. He immediately insisted that I accompany him out into the glare of the Arrivals hall so that he could look me over. After staring at me for what seemed like an age, he took a step backwards and scratched his nose.

'Christ, boy, I think you're the biggest Big Balls we've ever had,' he said finally in his velvety Kerry brogue.

I wasn't sure what to say to this. I was still trying to figure out if he was my immediate boss or just another ship inspector. He poked me in the stomach with his forefinger.

'Show us your hand. Are ye married?'

'No,' I said.

'No. I'm not a bit surprised.' He walked away. 'Sure, who'd marry a Big Balls like you?'

The morning is chilly and grey. We drive into town in

Frank's black Austin Cambridge. Frank smokes a Benson and Hedges' Gold Brand and tells me again about his early life as a hurler. He could have made the county team for the final against Kilkenny but for a dreadful head injury, he says. If I look closely, I can make out the scar. On cold days he often smells smoke and a couple of times he has blacked out altogether but never while driving.

'Touch wood,' he taps himself on the head.

Frank changes gears suddenly and the car lurches to the other side of the road. With a grin, Frank brings it back again. He gives a big pull on his cigarette.

'Good job there was nothing coming, eh?' he beams.

'Yes,' I say. 'G-g-good job.'

In four hours, Carla will be home.

It started the moment I finished my Leaving Cert exams.

First, it was the Army. Every day for a week, Mother followed me around the house telling me what a wonderful life it was in the Army.

'You'll always have your feet on dry land,' she said. 'It's good money as an officer. And you'll be perfectly safe because the Irish Army never gets into fights.'

'I da-da-da-don't want to join the Army.'

'It's a wonderful life in the Army.'

I would have been happy to lie around the house for the rest of the summer. The way I saw it, I had earned a rest after surviving a lifetime of school. Next it was the library.

'Think of all the books,' Mother said.

'I have ba-ba-books. When I want a book I can go to the library and ga-ga-ga-get one.'

'Wouldn't you like to have a job that offered security?'

'I da-da-don't understand the question.'

'Think of your poor Mother then. Who's going to look after me in my old age?'

I thought for a moment. I glanced across at Maeve. We smiled.

'Rory,' we both said.

Mother walked out, 'I do my best. You're just not taking this seriously.'

One morning, I was lying on my bed reading Kurt Vonnegut when Mother came in. She removed the book from my grasp and threw my newly-ironed white shirt and a blue tie at me. I had never seen the tie before.

'Come on,' she said.

'Where to?'

'Never mind. I've got something more important for you than books.'

I held up the tie.

'One of your father's,' she explained. 'I rescued it from the attic.'

'Wha-what's going on?'

'Just hurry please, we've got to get going.'

Mother ignored my questions and led me out of the house to our new Ford Escort. She had bought the car from a car dealer, a Fianna Fail cumann member recommended by Dessie O'Hanlon. Dessie assured her it was a great deal. Mother was very proud of it. She said it was a Fianna Fail car.

'It gets me where I want to go and that's enough for me and should be good enough for anyone.'

Mother drove, leaning forward into the steering wheel, keeping a lighted cigarette in her mouth. She squinted against the smoke as she concentrated on everything in front of her, other cars, the road, the pavements, jaywalking pedestrians, traffic-hopping motorbikers. Whenever she saw someone she knew, she always beeped the horn and waved. She paid particular attention to the sky.

'It's important always to be on your guard. You can never tell what's going to come at you.'

On the way into town she was smiling, as if she knew something wonderful was about to happen. Every time I asked her what was going on, she winked, 'Wait and see.' She parked the car in Kildare Street, then led me to a large building with tinted windows. We kept stopping along the way so that Mother could shake hands or talk to people she knew. Before we went in, Mother straightened my tie.

'Now, go to the desk. Ask for Mr Dorris. Say I sent you.'

'M-Mother?' I said.

She turned an imploring look upon me and told me to get on with it. 'Oh Daniel, do what I say, just this once for me will you, you won't regret it, I promise.'

I did as she asked. The fellow at the desk was a hard-faced, sallow-skinned man with glasses and a sandy fringe that favoured the right side of his forehead. He could have passed for Adolf Hitler's younger brother. In my mind, I called him Herman. Herman asked me my name. I told him and he looked up a chart that was on his desk.

'Oh, yes, Mr Buckley.'

Herman noticed Mother and gave her a weak smile. He told me to hang on a moment. Then he made a phone call.

'The Buckley boy has arrived,' he said. 'Do you want me to send him up?'

Mother made herself comfortable on the couch across from the desk, gradually enveloping herself in smoke from her own cigarette. Herman rapped on the desk until he had my attention.

'Right, the third floor, ask for Mr Dorris.'

He handed me a card with the number 46 on it and pointed to where the lift was. Mother beamed as we waited for the lift. When it arrived, she looked radiantly happy. She waited until the lift doors were closing on me before reaching in to swiftly adjust my collar.

'Don't let me down, sure you won't?' she called as the doors closed.

I don't recall going up in the lift, or walking along the corridor to Mr Dorris's office. I remember a door opening and being shown to a chair in front of a long table where sat six dull-suited men. Each had a name plate in front of him. Dorris sat at the extreme left chewing a pipe that stuck out from his grey whiskers. He gave me a weak smile too.

'Now, Mr Buckley,' he said as he took the pipe from his mouth. 'What makes you think you'd make a good ship inspector?'

I looked around the table. Each man was gazing intently at me. Mr Dorris was doing his best to look encouraging. He had his mouth open waiting for my reply.

'I think . . .' I began.

'Yes?' Mr Dorris said.

'I think I'd make a ga-ga-ga . . . make a ga-ga-ga . . .' I could feel my mouth filling with air as my jaws began to lock, '. . . make a ga-ga-ga . . .'

I couldn't get past the word 'good'. I got even more nervous. The men stared at me with concern. One of them lifted a glass of water and offered it to me. I shook my head. Then I took a deep breath and tried to speak in a rush, which sometimes worked.

'I think I'd be good with pa-pa-people,' I heard myself saying.

The interview board looked relieved. Mr Dorris looked at the others and they nodded.

'Well, I think I can speak for everyone here when I say that it stands to reason that any son of Kathleen Buckley's would be sure to possess an excellent touch with the public.'

'Here, here,' someone said.

'How is your mother?' Mr Dorris asked.

'Fa-fa-fine.'

'Good, good, good,' Mr Dorris made a pyramid of his fingertips. 'Now, Daniel, how would you see your role as ship inspector? There is more to the job than dealing with the public, isn't that right?'

I wanted to tell him that I had absolutely no idea how I saw my role because I had no idea what a ship inspector was. I wanted to say that this interview had been arranged by my mother without my being consulted. But I didn't wish to appear impolite or ungrateful. After all, if I disgraced myself it would reflect on Mother. I didn't want that. It would cost me nothing to play along as best I could. If my stutter got any worse, I wouldn't be able to answer the questions anyway. I decided to tell them that I would try to put a lot of myself into the job.

'I will pa-pa-pa-pa-put a la-la-la . . .'

I felt as though I was suffocating. I let go an unintentional hiccup and kept jamming between 'put' and 'lot'. I made a huge effort to get the words out but it only made things worse. I was aware of some movement at the table but I was too caught up in the battle to take any notice.

'Put a long?' Mr Dorris said helpfully.

'Putter along?' said someone else.

'Pa-pa-pa-pat-ala-la-la . . .' I gave it up.

When I stopped they appeared relieved. I realised that the stutter was now in complete control of me. I would probably not be able to answer a single question with any coherence.

Mr Dorris smiled at me soothingly, 'Excuse us a moment, won't you, Daniel?'

The six men had a brief conference. I heard someone say, 'I wasn't told.' Someone else, Mr Dorris I think, said, 'A speech impediment is a simple fact of life.' After a short time, they agreed on something. Mr Dorris turned to me. He was leaning forward with a look of understanding.

'How would it be with you if we ask questions and you answer with a yes or no or else simply nod your head? Would that be all right, do you think?'

I nodded.

'Good. Then we'll proceed.'

Mr Dorris looked at his fellow board members. They nodded their approval. Mr Dorris gazed at me with seriousness.

'Tell me, Daniel. Do you like planes?'

A week later, I got a letter congratulating me on my appointment as a temporary ship inspector. I was to report to a Mr Magaw, Chief Ship Inspector, at the Department of Agriculture offices at Dublin Airport at 10 am the following Monday. Mother said it was a good job and I should be delighted to have it.

'I had to pull a lot of strings to get you that job,' she said. 'If you do well, you could be made permanent some day.'

That Monday, Maeve kept me company at the bus-stop. 'Are you going to work now?'

'Yes.'

'What does a ship investigator do?'

'I'm not sure exactly, it's my first day, for God's sake. And it's ship inspector.'

'If you're a ship inspector, why do you work at the airport instead of the docks?'

'I don't know.'

'I mean, ships sail on the sea. They don't go anywhere near airports. Planes land at airports.'

'I know that.'

'So why aren't you called a plane inspector?'

'I'll ring you the moment I know, I swear, now let it go, will you?'

'Do you want me to come out there with you? It's a long journey . . .'

'No, thanks. I think you'd better look after things at home, you know, in case anything happens.'

The bus came around the corner.

'Gotta go,' I said.

I got on and gave Maeve a wave. Maeve waved back and shouted something. I gestured to her that I couldn't hear. She ran after the bus and shouted again. I opened the top window.

'Tell them it should be plane inspector,' she yelled.

An hour after I first reported for duty, Chief Magaw appeared. Squat and bowlegged, he spoke in a whisper. His legs were so stiff that he appeared to scuttle forward rather than walk. He said he was delighted to have me on board.

He winked, 'Your mother's a great woman. You're a lucky lad to have her.'

In the office, I was given a white armband which said 'DEPT. OF AGRICULTURE' in thick black letters. Chief Magaw assigned Harry Dunne to show me around and teach me the job. Harry Dunne was tall, slow-talking and distant, with a habit of never looking at whoever he was speaking to. He walked with a slow, awkward, halting gait, as if his feet were being pulled forward by invisible magnets. His fair hair stood up around his scalp like a fortress.

'Now, this is a mat,' Harry Dunne said, indicating a mat at the bottom of the escalator while looking in the opposite direction. 'That's an escalator. You probably knew that already though, didn't you?'

For a week, I simply followed Harry everywhere. He showed me how to disinfect mats and make my way around the tarmac to inspect the baggage holds of planes for animals. He showed me where the incinerator was. I learned the procedure for dealing with passengers who had been on a farm. I found out about the dangers of Colorado beetles and other pests that ship inspectors were always on the look out for. Harry told me that people could bring their pets into the country from England but animals coming in from the Continent had to do six months in the quarantine stables in Malahide before their owners could take them home. Animals from America were sent straight back. Dublin Zoo was the only institution in the country that could bring in animals from anywhere in the world. They always had to notify us in writing first.

'You could say that we're the animal police,' Harry said with a wry smile.

Harry even showed me how to make tea in the official ship inspector teapot. He pointed at a silver toaster in the corner. The toaster was wrapped in a plastic bag.

'That belongs to Chief Magaw. If you want to make toast you have to ask permission.'

'Don't fill the boy's head with shite,' Desperate Dan said. 'The toaster's for everyone. You can use it anytime you want as long as you fill in the form.'

Harry Dunne gestured vaguely in the direction of the toaster, 'So be it.'

At the end of the week, Harry shook my hand and said there was no more he could do for me.

'I think you'll make a fine ship inspector.'

Then he went to Chief Magaw and asked to be re-assigned to normal duties.

The Chief put his hand on my shoulder. 'I'm glad to see you fitting in so well. Now, I want you to keep a particular eye on flights from the Continent. There was a dog found on a jumbo at Cork and an Alsatian nearly got through here last month.'

Later, Desperate Dan came up to me. 'Go out onto the tarmac, Big Balls. Check the baggage hold of the New York jumbo that has just landed. We're expecting a consignment of red-arsed monkeys. If you find them, tell the loaders to put them back in the hold and we'll get them sent straight back.' He looked at me solemnly, 'Don't make a bags of it now.'

On the tarmac, the blasts of wind from the engines were warm but their screech was deafening. I made my way to the jumbo where the handlers were unloading bags onto a baggage cart from a conveyor belt. I had to shout to make myself heard over the engine din.

'H-h-has anyone seen any r-red-arsed monkeys?'

The second the words were out of my mouth, I bit my lip. One of the handlers threw me a look. Having satisfied himself that I was some idiot who had wandered onto the tarmac, he went back to unloading bags.

Back in the office, Desperate Dan grinned when I came in. 'Welcome to the wonderful world of ship inspectors, Big Balls,' he said.

When things were slack and Chief Magaw wasn't around, Desperate Dan, Harry Dunne, Old Brendan Toombs, Dominic Root and I sat on the red plastic-covered seats outside the office waiting for a flight to land. The ship inspectors scrutinised the death notices in the newspapers for the names of former colleagues.

'I only have one wish,' Dominic Root said. 'I hope I'm sitting here the day Granny Magaw's name appears so I can have a good fuckin' laugh.'

Dominic Root was a dumpy, red-faced Dubliner who wore large garish rings on each finger and went drinking on weekends accompanied by his mother. When he laughed he threw back his head and gave an infectious 'ak-ak-ak'. Desperate Dan called him the ship inspector's answer to Liberace. Dan told me that Root had been a ship inspector for nearly fifteen years, but nobody could remember him ever checking a baggage hold or spraying a mat with disinfectant. Dominic had gone onto the tarmac only once, and that was to meet his mother off a flight on her way home from visiting her brother in London. Dominic Root had never been on a plane and he admitted that flying scared him stiff.

'I'd rather eat a farmer's arse through a hedge than go up in one of those things.'

Dominic was worried that I hadn't received sufficient training.

'This poor lad doesn't know what's what out here. I think we should tell him about the dangers of the job, don't you, Dan?'

Dan folded his arms and gave a little shrug.

Dominic put his hand on my shoulder, 'First of all, you have to watch out for customs. They're a bunch of stuck-up wankers. When ye see one coming, just run. Ground stewardesses are snooty-nosed wagons and all pilots think they're God's gift to women. Did I leave anyone out, Dan?'

'Baggage handlers,' Desperate Dan said.

'Fuckin' baggage handlers are poison. Keep away from them. This place would be a whole lot more efficient if all those fellas were kept on fuckin' leads.'

The only person at the airport that Dominic had any time for was the red-haired Statistics girl, Donna. Donna's job was to get passengers to fill in questionnaires about their travel habits and preferences. She was easy-going and witty, with a clear, open face and a large bust. She sometimes joined the ship inspectors on the red plastic-covered seats.

'She's the only one in this kip who can take a joke,' Dominic Root said.

After a while, Harry Dunne stood up, stretched himself and wandered off in the direction of Customs. We watched him disappear around the corner. Dominic Root turned to Desperate Dan, his eyes lit up like a maniac.

'What did I tell you? He's gone to meet Verna.'

For months, Harry Dunne had been disappearing. Sometimes, he came to work in the morning, changed into his uniform and vanished, only to re-surface just before it was time to go home. Dominic was convinced that Harry was sneaking off somewhere to meet Verna, a cleaning woman with an Afro-hairstyle who worked on the Departures floor upstairs.

'She'd hop on anything, that one. Last Christmas Eve, she went through all the chefs in the Skyways Grill upstairs. For dessert, she had the lounge boy.'

Desperate Dan shook his head and folded his arms, 'It's not Verna at all. I've seen him and Mary Dunlop from customs exchanging secret looks.'

Dominic looked horrified, 'Mary Dunlop? She's fuckin' cross-eyed. How could you tell she was looking at him?'

'I tell you, I saw them with my own eyes.'

'Sure, the poor girl only has to say "excuse me, sir" and half the passengers in the place stop dead, thinking she's looking at them. She's always causing ferocious traffic jams in Customs.'

Dan was trying to explain when Dominic looked up and saw Chief Magaw turning the corner at the Nothing to Declare sign.

'Look out. Here comes Granny.'

Everyone stood up. Desperate Dan went off to disinfect a few mats and Old Brendan Toombs walked into the office to check the flight monitor. We watched the chief draw closer. Dominic Root leaned over to me.

'Look at the fuckin' scuttle on her, will you?' he whispered. 'You'd swear she'd just been fucked up the arse by an elephant.'

When Chief Magaw came to within hailing distance, Dominic greeted him with an expression of joy.

'That's a cold one. I hear we're in for a storm tonight.'

'It'll be a bad week, by the looks of it,' Chief Magaw said. 'Please God, we'll get a few fine days next week.'

Dominic took out a packet of twenty Carrolls, 'Will you have a cigarette, Chief?'

'Thanks, I will.' Chief Magaw took a cigarette and Dominic gave him a light.

They sat down on the red plastic-covered seats and puffed their cigarettes. I went around to join Desperate Dan who was mixing the disinfectant. When we came out carrying watering cans, Dominic Root and Chief Magaw were still on the seats, chatting away like old pals.

'Will you look at them,' Desperate Dan snorted. 'They're like an old married couple. The only thing that keeps them alive is their hatred for each other.'

I often stand with the other ship inspectors at the bottom

of the escalator to watch the passengers coming down. The others keep a look out for people who are carrying meat products or trying to smuggle animals into the country but I am sure that one day I will see Dad. It stands to reason that he will have to come through the airport someday. I just hope I am on duty at the time. Sometimes I think that Mother got me the job just so I can keep a watch out for Dad. Sometimes, I fantasise that I am the only one in the office when a man walks in to have his shoes sprayed. I don't recognise the man but I get the feeling that he knows who I am. The man stands on the mat with his back to me and lifts first one shoe, then the other. Perhaps we make chit-chat about farms he has visited. Maybe he wants to know what the weather in Dublin is like over the past while. When I finish spraying his shoes, I sit down at the big red ledger and ask him his name.

'John Buckley,' he says.

My heart jumps, does a little pirouette. I look up and Dad is smiling at me.

'Hello, Daniel,' Dad says.

That is where the fantasy always stops. I simply cannot imagine anything beyond that point. Perhaps I don't want to.

Occasionally, I see a face that reminds me of Dad, but there is always something in the man's eyes, the way he moves or even the way he stands that shows me that he is not Dad.

I read a magazine article once about a man who hadn't seen his father for fifty years. One day, standing on a street corner, a little old man walked up to him and said, 'Hello son.' It was completely unexpected, neither knew that the other had been living in the same city for years. They just bumped into each other on a street corner. Earlier that day, though, each had been thinking of the other. I was sure that their thoughts had actually brought them back together.

I often wonder what I would do if one day a stranger should step out of the milling crowd of passengers, walk up to me in front of all the other ship inspectors and introduce himself as my father. What if he turns out to be fat and bald? What if he has another family?

71

I am not sure that I would recognise Dad now anyway. My memories of his face are dim. I can't remember what height he was or his build or the colour of his eyes, though Maeve is still convinced that his eyes are brown. I don't know how she can be so sure. We could ask Mother for confirmation but for some reason we never bother. Perhaps we want to hang onto our own visions of Dad, rather than the true image. If Dad ever does come through the airport when I happen to be on duty, I tell myself that I will still know him, no matter how much he has changed. I will sense his presence first, the recognition will come afterwards.

Many years ago, I had a vivid and terrifying dream. In the dream, I am meeting Dad at the airport. Dad is wearing the black stetson and holds his suitcases like a pair of six-guns. He looks like Marshal Matt Dillon. He comes up to me, squinting, and says, 'Daniel, is that you?' I open my mouth to greet him, to welcome him back, to tell him that the family has been waiting for him for years and that everything at home is fine. That is when my stutter kicks in and I start choking on air. The only sounds that come out of me are weird choking rasps. Dad measures me for a while, decides that this unfortunate couldn't possibly be his son and walks past, looking all about him for another Daniel, one who isn't a freak.

I never talk to any of the ship inspectors about Dad. As far as they know, my father vanished, presumed dead, sometime in the sixties. I rarely socialise. I go to the Christmas parties, play in the occasional soccer game against the Customs guys and once in a while go upstairs to The Sky High Lounge for a pint or two with Desperate Dan after work. But I never talk about myself or the family and I never allow myself to get too close to anyone. All the other ship inspectors really know about me is that my Mother used to be a TD, and that I sometimes develop a bit of a stutter when I get rattled.

I have left nothing to chance.

The eggs are on the counter. The small pot has been filled with water and placed on the cooker ring. Bread has been sliced and the crumbs cleared from under the toaster.

72

A new jar of raspberry jam is waiting on the table, with its seal still intact. Two bags of rosehip tea are in a saucer next to Carla's favourite cup. One is for the tea, the other as standby in case I mess things up first time around.

I am too excited to prepare anything for myself. When Carla arrives, I will just have a cup of coffee. It will be fulfilling enough to watch Carla eat. Her enjoyment of scrambled eggs on raspberry toast is contagious.

Seven years is a long time to be with someone. It is like being married. We have never really discussed marriage. We both value our individuality too highly. Carla says that the best way to prove that you really love a person is to refuse to tie them down. That is what an adult relationship is all about. The whole notion of people as possessions is completely absurd. Nobody should be encouraged to believe that they own another person.

There is a knock on the door. When I open it, Mrs Macken stands there in her brown overcoat and slippers.

'Oh, Daniel, I heard you come in earlier but I didn't like to disturb you in case you were having a snooze.'

'That's OK.'

'It's just that I heard a noise in the lock-up last night and didn't like to go down on my own. I thought you might want to check the bike?'

Carla's bike. I have forgotten all about it. I grab my jacket. On the way down the stairs, Mrs Macken gives me her weekly soliloquy on city life.

'It's good to have a man in the house. I always rest easier when I hear you come in. This used to be a great city. You could leave your key in the door. I think people had respect for each other then. Now when I watch the news I do have the fear of God in me for days.'

Mrs Macken unlocks the door to the back yard. Carla's Kawasaki looks fine. The lock is untouched. The tyres are hard. I touch the smooth, cool metal of the petrol tank and I brush the back of my hand across the leather saddle.

'I don't know how Carla does it. All that running around. And you to look after as well. She's a great girl.'

'I'm perfectly capable of looking after myself,' I tell her.

73

Mrs Macken laughs, 'None of ye are. I was married fifty years, I know what I'm talking about.'

On the way back up the stairs, Mrs Macken pauses for breath a couple of times. She tells me to go ahead only because she knows that I won't leave her there. She gives a performance that includes most of her usual repertoire of wheezes, racking coughs and deep sighs, with occasional brave smiles from what she believes is a martyr's face.

I worry that Carla's plane could land early. I don't want Carla to breeze in home to find nothing ready. I am impatient for the moment when I can leave Mrs Macken at her door. Finally, we are outside the chattering woman's apartment.

'You're a nice man, God bless you,' she says.

I race up the stairs. The phone is ringing. It is Carla. She is really sorry that she will not be home this morning. She's staying in London for another night. The Silent Screams have lined up a special gig this evening to celebrate their recent record deal. She can't possibly miss it. She will be home tomorrow instead. She'll take me out to dinner to make up to me.

'You don't mind, do you, Groover? It really is a very special occasion. Otherwise I wouldn't dream of staying away from you for another moment. You do understand, don't you?'

'I understand pa-pa-perfectly.'

'Thanks, you're a pet.'

'Go and enjoy yourself,' I hear myself say. 'Don't worry about me, I'll be fa-fine. See you tomorrow.'

'Daniel, I love you. You're still my man.'

She makes the sound of a kiss and hangs up.

I tidy away the breakfast things. I put the eggs back in the box and place the box in the fridge. The butter, now soft, goes in the fridge too. I toss the bread in the breadbox and dump the teabags in the bin.

It occurs to me that today is a good day for visiting Mother. I have nothing else to do. Of course, I will have to phone first, to check on how she is feeling. The last time I visited her, she rose to her feet and clapped her hands together the moment I came in the door.

'Oh look, it's the handsome man again. He's come to see

74

me.' She clapped her hands in time as she performed a joyous dance. 'Oh, the handsome man, the handsome man, the handsome man . . .'

It was a difficult visit, but at least she seemed to have given up her obsession with the British invasion of Ireland. A month ago, after a perfectly normal dinner that she and Maeve had cooked, Mother had appeared to be her old self. Then, over the fruit cocktails, she had leaned over to me, 'It's still going on. The Brits are kidnapping Irish people and replacing them with their own. Just like they did hundreds of years ago.'

Later, the conspiracy turned into a full-scale European plot. The Germans and the Dutch had invaded Kerry and west Cork. She had proof. She was going to bring it up in the Dail during the next session.

'Soon, the Irish race will be just a memory. We'll all be bloody Europeans.'

Maeve says that Mother is just working things through. She is slowly coming to terms with her disappointment at not being a TD. anymore. She's making good progress, Maeve says. She hasn't mentioned Dad in weeks.

When I think of going home to visit Mother, I see her in our old house in Redrock, not in the new house in Clontarf. To me, the place in Clontarf is nothing more than a temporary shelter for Mother. When Dad returns, we will buy back our old house in Redrock and become a family again.

I decide that it is not a good idea to visit Mother today after all. Maybe at the weekend, after Carla gets back and things have settled down.

I go over to the stereo and put on Tom Petty and the Heartbreakers. I turn the volume up loud. I dance over to the fridge and take out the Möet et Chandon. I fiddle with the cork until it blows. Fzzzzt. The foam shoots all over the carpet and splatters onto the back of the settee. I drink straight from the bottle. I larrup it down. The champagne tastes cold and fizzy and sweet on my tongue. It freezes my throat as it goes down. By the time it reaches my stomach, I feel fresh and alive. It gives me the shivers.

I turn the volume up higher.

FOUR

The Politician

WE KNEW THAT something was up the moment we saw the six jam tarts arranged on a plate in the centre of the table. Another clue was the Teatime Express box that stood on the kitchen counter, its flap open so that we could peek at the coffee cake inside. There were neatly folded serviettes at each of our places for tea. Mother stood with her back to the gas cooker, fiddling with the brass cooking rings as if she was afraid that we were going to take a bite out of her instead of the nice things she had bought. She folded her arms and told us to sit down.

'Children, your mother has become a soldier of destiny.'

Nobody was surprised. In the three years since Dad disappeared, Mother had spent almost all of her free time going to Fianna Fail meetings. The only surprise was that it had taken her so long to join. She had been laying the ground work, she said, it didn't do to rush things in politics.

'I am now a member of the one true party, the party of the past, present and future. I hope you're all proud of me.'

Even though we were too young to know what it meant, we could sense that Mother's decision to go into politics was important for her and for the family. Our attitude was that if it made Mother happy, then it made us happy, too. We wanted to make her feel good so we hugged her and we were dying to get stuck into the jam tarts.

'Congratulations,' we cheered.

'Sit down, Mother,' Maeve said. 'I'll make the tea.'

'Would you? Oh, that would be grand.'

Mother sat down. Maeve filled the kettle. Everyone sneaked a glance at Rory as he took a crumpled cigarette out of his top pocket, even though he wasn't allowed to smoke at home. He flicked his straggly fair hair out of his eyes and stuck the cigarette in his mouth. It bobbed up and down as he spoke.

'You've joined Fianna Fail, is that all? With all the fuss, I thought you were going to tell us that you were marrying Dessie O'Hanlon.'

Mother had been trying to smile to give her eldest the benefit of the doubt, but now Rory's cocky attitude made her face get hard.

'Excuse me. That man is a good friend to this family. You've no right to make fun of him.'

'He couldn't be much of a friend if he made you join the sleeveens.'

'Rory, that's not fair.'

'The truth is always difficult.'

'There is nothing wrong with supporting your country. I'm looking forward to seeing what kind of a contribution you are going to make to Ireland's future.'

Rory smiled, 'I'm going to be a prospector. I'm going to discover gold on Redrock mountain.'

Mother waited until Rory had lit the cigarette. Then she walked over to him, took the cigarette out of his mouth and put it out in the sink, 'Well, I hope you find some soon. God knows I could use a little extra cash around here.'

Rory got up and slowly shuffled out. In the doorway, he paused to yawn and perform a languid stretch. He threw us a sideways glance to demonstrate that he was leaving of his own accord.

Mother folded her arms, 'What about your tea?'

'I'm not hungry. When you get to be Taoiseach, give me a shout,' he said as he ducked under the doorframe and went out.

Mother sighed and sat down at the table, 'I don't know what that fellow's problem is at all.'

77

We ate our tea. We put aside a jam tart and a slice of coffee cake for Rory.

Everyone in the family was normal except Rory.

When he was fourteen, Rory was just under six foot tall. In the year after Dad disappeared, he shot up to six feet two. Indoors, he banged his head off the tops of door-frames and walked into chandeliers and low-hanging bulbs. Outdoors, he was nearly tall enough to see into Mrs Donovan's top floor windows. Rory liked being tall.

'It's my way of protesting against society,' he said.

Maeve took me aside to talk about Rory. She was convinced that he was one of the world's tallest people.

'He must be the tallest person for his age in Redrock, maybe in Ireland. I think we should enter him for the *Guinness Book of Records*.'

I was five eight, Maeve was five five and Mother herself was an inch taller than Maeve.

'I don't know where we got him from at all,' Mother said. 'There must have been a basketball player on his father's side of the family.'

Maeve sat up late one night and wrote Rory's biography for the *Guinness Book of Records*. In the morning, Rory found it and tore it up.

'What do you mean, "in his spare time he doubles as a goalpost"?'

At sixteen, Rory stuck at six foot five and a half. He told everyone that it was only temporary, that he was bound to start growing again soon.

Mother was relieved, 'Lucky for you that you stopped growing. Otherwise, you'd have been painting ceilings for the rest of your life.'

I think Rory was relieved too, but it didn't stop him being sullen and cynical at home. Even when he played Cream and Beatles records on Dad's old hi-fi, he listened with a constipated face. He kept his albums in plastic sleeves and arranged them meticulously in alphabetical order on the rack beside the hi-fi. He had appointed himself official caretaker of Dad's Beatles collection. In the even-

78

ings, he tended them like flowers. The ritual was the same every night: he deftly removed the record from its cover, wiped the surface with a damp cloth until you could see your reflection in the glistening black vinyl, then gently restored it to its sleeve, like bedding down a pet. We kept waiting for him to kiss the records goodnight. At times, it seemed as though our brother cared more for records than people. If anyone played his collection when he was out, he went spare. Maeve was the chief culprit. She was always leaving records lying around out of their sleeves.

'It's only a record,' she said when Rory accused her of destroying his 'Sergeant Pepper'. 'Keep your shirt on.'

One Saturday night, Rory came home drunk after the pubs closed and put on 'Sergeant Pepper's Lonely Hearts' Club Band' at top volume. Mother came out in her dressing gown and ripped the record off the turntable. Rory reacted as though he had been slashed with a knife. I watched from the doorway as he stood, face twisted, fists clenched, glaring down at Mother. Next to him, Mother looked like a child. For a moment, I thought he was going to punch her.

'As long as you live in this house, you'll have respect for the others who live here or else you're out,' Mother shouted.

'One more year of school, then I'm gone,' Rory said calmly and went to bed.

In the morning, Rory left early for school. Mother was worried that she might have failed him in some way.

'I've done everything for him, haven't I?'

'Yes, Mother, everything.'

'I've been a good mother to him, haven't I?'

'Yes', we said, 'you've been a good mother.'

'Then why is he behaving like this? Is he on drugs?'

Maeve produced a notebook from the pocket of her anorak and consulted it. She studied it while we watched her. Mother looked at me and raised an eyebrow but I shrugged. I didn't know what Maeve was up to either.

Maeve closed the notebook, 'I think that the main difference between Rory and the rest of us is that we like to wake up in the mornings and he prefers to lie in until the afternoon.'

'Pardon?' Mother said.

'We are always looking forward to whatever the new day has to offer. Rory just wants the light to fade from the sky as quickly as possible so that it can be night and he can go out with his friends. I think Rory has lost his joy somewhere, he's at a stage where he just doesn't seem to think that anything is all that exciting anymore. He'll be grand though as soon as he finds his feet.'

Mother looked at her daughter in astonishment, 'What age are you?'

'I'll be fourteen in a month.'

'Maybe I should let you take over, you seem to know what you're doing.'

Mother's politics kept her very busy. We saw her at weekends and holy days and at night before bedtime. At first, when Mother was working late, Mrs Donovan and the Things came in to cook our tea and look after us, but after a week of eating miniscule portions of fish fingers and beans and fighting a losing battle with the Things for control of the television, we rebelled.

'We're old enough to take care of ourselves,' Maeve argued.

'Have it your own way,' Mother said. 'But who's going to cook your dinner?'

'Mother, for heaven's sake. I can cook a dinner now and again. Besides, I'm always first home from school.'

We always knew that Maeve was cooking dinner when we saw black plumes of smoke floating over the house. It was not unusual to come home to find the kitchen filled with smoke or Maeve whacking a blackened frying pan off the back wall of the house, trying to get hamburgers off. Rory swore that it was more nutritious to eat a slate off the roof than one of Maeve's hamburgers. Even I found it difficult to sit down to soggy chops, peas as solid as bullets and mashed potato that ran all over the plate like milk. Mother got so tired of the moaning and arguing that she offered us a choice: Maeve's cooking or Mrs Donovan and the Things.

'That's like a choice between a firing squad and a guillotine,' Rory said.

In the end, we went with Maeve. She was overjoyed, 'I'm getting better all the time, really I am. I'm going to try spaghetti bolognese next.'

Sundays were 'quality time' for the family and Mother rarely allowed anything to interfere. Once she took us to Butlin's for the day. Rory wouldn't have anything to do with any of the rides. He refused to get into the paddle boat and he said the miniature golf was for midgets. He even turned down the candyfloss that Mother bought.

'I'm too mature for this stuff,' he said.

Maeve and I went on all the rides and nearly broke our legs on the skating rink.

When Mother took us to the zoo, we had time to see the monkeys and a couple of polar bears before we had to leave. Mother had suddenly remembered an important meeting that she just could not afford to miss. On the way out, we waved to the giraffe.

'We've lost both our parents,' Rory declared. 'One to forces unknown and the other to Fianna Fail.'

'What's a scumbag?'

'Where'd you hear that filth?' Mother demanded.

Maeve told her she'd seen it written on the wall of the bus. She had been sitting right across from it all the way home and she couldn't help reading it. The full sentence was 'Giles O'Hara is a scumbag.'

'Well you've no business reading the walls of buses, you should always bring a good book with you.'

Mother went on a big campaign to clean up the buses. It was her first proper political issue. She contacted all the newspapers as well as the radio and television. Nobody rang her back, but Mother didn't let it bother her. She and her cumann made a special excursion on the Redrock bus from town. Mrs Donovan jotted down a list of the rude words they found and Mother asked all the passengers if they had seen anyone acting suspiciously with a marker. Nobody had seen a thing.

As soon as the bus pulled up at the bus terminus in Church Street, Mother handed the list of words to the bus conductor.

'Thanks, I'll read it later,' the driver said.

Mother informed him gravely that if action wasn't taken immediately to stop the spread of evil graffiti, they'd take the matter to the head of CIE. The cumann gave her a round of applause and she led them off the bus into our house for tea and biscuits. The campaign made Mother feel better but it didn't stop people writing rude things on the bus walls. After the campaign, Maeve bought another tiny notebook. This one was to list interesting words she came across, she explained.

'You mean bad words,' I said.

Maeve gave a quick smile, 'Don't tell, sure you won't? They might come in handy some day.'

Mother called me 'the family glue'. It meant that I was good at holding it together when things went wrong. Even though I had a stutter, everyone admitted that I had a knack for calming down a situation. When Mother and Rory were having a row, I often took the sting out of the argument by making a joke or a funny face or performing some silly stunt. Once, when Mother and Rory were shouting at each other over something, I ran between them and poured a glass of water over my head. Even Rory thought that was funny.

When my brother and I were getting on well, we often went out to the back garden to play 'Mountainball'. It was a game that Rory had invented. You kicked a football as high as you could up the mountain at the foot of our garden. The other player had to wait for it to come down, then try to kick it back up again. Using your hands was out. You had to kick it first time. If you missed or if the ball went past you or if it rolled down into one of the neighbours' back gardens, the other player got a point. Rory always won. We rarely talked. I was quiet because of my stutter, but Rory only seemed to be able to find the right words if he was being smart to someone or when he was fighting with Mother. Our close periods never lasted long. The football sessions traditionally ended when Rory abruptly 'tackled' me, dumped me on the grass and strode off.

I became good at drawing. I sketched excellent likenesses of everyone in the family as well as most of the neighbours. I spent hours carving lifelike animals out of wood with a penknife. Once Mrs Donovan took fright on seeing a mouse I had made and shot out of the house screaming.

'Next time, make it a snake,' Maeve said, 'that should keep the old wagon out for a month.'

I was the most placid kid in Redrock. I never got angry or difficult. I prided myself on being easy to get along with. Whenever anyone said anything mean or nasty to me, I just shrugged and said they probably didn't mean it. I seemed to have no temper. I was no threat to anyone. And I had a stutter which meant that I couldn't chat up anyone's girl-friend. Even Hatchet Hardy, to whom casual violence was a way of life, only hit me once.

'It's just for appearance's sake,' he explained. 'In case anyone would think I'm too soft to hit a bloke with a stutter. Do you get me?'

I nodded and he hit me a clatter on the head.

After that, he always gave me a big smile when we met.

'The only reason everyone gets on so well with you is because you're a lickarse,' Rory said.

'Don't mind him, Daniel,' Mother said. 'He's just jealous because you happen to have a great gift with people. You'll always be a much loved person.'

Rory lit a cigarette, blew the smoke into my face.

'You'll always be a lickarse.'

The night that Mother was made Cathaoirleach of the local cumann, Maeve baked a sponge cake which looked wonder-ful but which tasted like sandpaper. Afterwards, Maeve admitted that she might have used a sheet of sandpaper for a base.

'I thought it was edible cardboard,' she explained.

Mother took Maeve aside to explain that there was no such thing as edible cardboard. We all quietly decided to skip any cakes Maeve might bake in the future.

Maeve had big brown eyes like Mother. She also had Mother's ability to stare with such unnerving directness that whoever was on the receiving end often forgot what they were talking about. Mother called it 'the Buckley look'. Despite the gift of 'the Buckley look', boys liked Maeve. Sometimes a boy called around to ask her out. Occasionally she went, but Maeve was more interested in reading difficult poems or finding out about politics. She always read Mother's speeches and queried any new words.

'What does reverie mean?'

'It means "to dream",' Mother said.

'What's an idealist?'

'To be an idealist means to really believe in something. For instance, Padraig Pearse was an idealist. He believed in an united Ireland, a nation free of the yoke of British imperialism. He gave his life for his beliefs. I also believe in a united Ireland. I'm an idealist, too. Remember that, Maeve, your own mother is an idealist.'

'What does impet . . . what does impet . . .?'

'Show me it.'

'There, impet-something.'

'Impetuous,' Mother said. 'It means to be hasty or rash or do something without thinking. Your brother Rory will tell you all about that.'

Maeve often went along with Mother to cumann meetings. Sometimes, the cumann let her take notes. Dessie O'Hanlon began to refer jokingly to Maeve as Mother's official 'handler'. She helped Mother to organise fundraising dinners and special events and they were great successes. At the end of her first term as Cathaoirleach of the cumann, Mother had brought in more money in a single year than her predecessors had managed in five. John Joe Sullivan, the regional organiser from Fianna Fail HQ, appointed Mother district organiser. Mahony's mini-market promoted her to store manager and doubled her salary.

'The money still doesn't amount to much,' Mother said, 'but at least I can give up selling fish on the pier at weekends.'

Mother quit the fishmonger's next day but it was months before the smell of fish left our house.

Conker Connolly wanted to kill The Barrel.

The Barrel had taken him down to the bicycle sheds after school the day before and tried to put his hands in his pockets. Conker had had to stuff his own hands into his pockets to stop The Barrel feeling him up.

'He tried to queer me,' Conker said. 'I think we should at least tell the newspapers.'

The Barrel had felt up most of the boys in the class. For some reason, he had never tried anything with me.

'That's because your mother is in Fianna Fail. I think he's a bit afraid of you. He never asks you hard questions anymore.'

At lunchtime, there was a class meeting in the toilets. Barry Newman, the class captain, was against telling the newspapers because they would just sensationalise things.

'Something like this could ruin our job prospects.'

Conker's proposal to assassinate The Barrel was eventually voted down.

'Nobody has the right to take human life,' Barry Newman said.

'Nobody has a right to put their hands in my pockets and feel my balls,' Conker said. 'Especially not a fat smelly old queer priest.'

Conker tried to get me to help him with his plan to get revenge on The Barrel.

'We don't have to kill him. Let's just put him out of action for a while.'

He wanted me to hold his legs while he leaned out of the top floor window to drop a basketball on The Barrel's head. I told him that I couldn't possibly get involved.

'My mother's in Fa-Fa-Fianna Fail,' I explained. 'I have her career to consider.'

Fianna Fail. The words sounded so reassuring. They gave off an aura of powerful magic. When Mother said them, they formed the first bars of a soft, irresistible music. Mother seemed taller, livelier, more forceful, definitely more important. Her eyes had a lustre about them. She was charismatic, radiant. People wanted to sit beside her at meetings, they ran to her when they saw her in the street. Fianna Fail had helped her to take control of her life again.

Nobody ever mentioned my dad now, or if they did, it was done quickly, by way of explanation and not in the hushed, accusatory tones of before. The fact that her husband was missing gave Mother a tragic, heroic quality.

'She's like Penelope in the Greek myth,' Dessie O'Hanlon said. 'Only instead of weaving while her man is away, your mother is dedicating herself to helping the Irish nation.'

Mother was no longer a deserted wife, a sad case or, as someone in the town said, 'a widow waiting to happen'. Now she was Kathleen Buckley, Fianna Fail councillor and party activist, supermarket sales manager, mother of three. Mrs Fennessy even said 'hello' to us on the street. Mother got a great kick out of ignoring her. I was keen to make sure that Mother knew that Maeve and myself were behind everything she did. We sat up with her at night. We helped her to write speeches and plan campaigns. We knew that if we wanted to see our mother, we had to come into her new world. Fianna Fail had become a part of our family, like an invisible uncle whose presence you could feel all around you. It seemed to me that Mother's relationship with the party was making the family strong again. Even Rory was beginning to accept that there was life after Dad's disappearance. As long as Mother stayed in Fianna Fail, we had a future. We were a family.

I didn't pine anymore when I saw a mother and father with their children on the street or in a friend's house. I no longer got sad for what had been. I stopped thinking about the day when Dad would come home and learned to live in the present.

Sometimes, when Rory and Maeve weren't around, Mother snuck up behind me to give me a hug. Her hair fell over my face. She smelt of smoke and stale rooms and musty perfume.

'How's my best boy? I am very proud of you.'

I loved it when her hair fell over my face. I wanted to stay close to Mother. I wished that I could stay twelve for ever.

Mr Calhoun had Frank Sinatra in the back garden again.

'Strangers in the Night' blared out all over Church Street. Even the customers in The Tall Ships could hear it.

It was Sunday afternoon. Mother was outraged that anyone should interfere with our family's 'quality time'. She thought about calling the police. Then she decided that she wouldn't give Calhoun the satisfaction. She would handle the matter herself. Even though Calhoun only lived two doors up from us, Mother phoned him to ask politely if the music could be turned down. Calhoun told her the record player was set as low as it could go. He said that he would see what he could do.

By the time Sinatra had crooned his way through a live version of 'Lady is a Tramp', complete with tumultuous applause, Mother had decided that she had heard enough.

'That man has no right to ruin our Sunday,' she said.

The Calhouns lived next door to the Lallys, in the last house on our street. Maeve and I followed Mother down the street to the Calhouns' front door. Sinatra had just started 'That's Life' when Mr Calhoun opened the door. We stood by Mother's side as she politely asked Mr Calhoun to please turn down the music. 'It's my day off and I want to spend time with my family.'

Calhoun was a small man with a pockmarked face. He belonged to the Labour Party and liked to go around saying that Fianna Fail were a bunch of strokers and crooks. Mary Calhoun appeared beside him, thin and birdlike with a hoarse voice. Maeve and I were fascinated by the thick jungle of black hairs that was sticking through Calhoun's string vest.

Maeve whispered, 'I dare you to pull one off.'

Calhoun scratched his nose, 'It's my day off too, you know. I've a perfect right to listen to music in my own back yard.'

Mary Calhoun leaned forward, 'That's right. He works hard and needs his Sinatra to relax.'

'That's all very well but what about the rest of us?' Mother argued. 'We work hard, too.'

Calhoun considered for a moment, 'Well, I've no objection if you want to play music in your back garden.'

'Now,' Mary Calhoun said 'you can't get fairer than that, can you?'

'The last thing some of us need on a Sunday afternoon is a racket like that at full volume.'

Calhoun scratched his vest and looked stern, 'Racket? What are you saying about Frank?'

'I'm not saying anything about Frank. I just don't think it's right that you should be playing him so loudly.'

'Frank Sinatra is the greatest singer in the world.'

'That's not the point.'

'Are you saying there's someone better?' Calhoun bristled. 'Listen to that voice. Now there's a real artist for you. No one in their right mind could possibly deny that.'

'I just want you to turn it down.'

Calhoun considered for a moment,' OK, I'll do better than that, I'll turn it off.'

'You will? That's great.'

'As soon as I'm finished listening to it,' Calhoun smirked and closed the door.

We heard Mary Calhoun's cackle from behind the door.

'Right,' Mother shouted, 'Just remember I asked you nicely.'

We went back to the house. Mother's mouth was tight as a zip. She marched us straight into the back garden to get out the hose. We attached the hose to the back garden tap and brought it to the fence. Mother pinched the nozzle between her fingers to make it spray further. Then she pointed it in the direction of the Calhouns and turned it on full blast. After a couple of minor adjustments, the jet of water shot across the Lallys' garden to fall neatly over the fence into the Calhouns' back yard. Immediately there was a shout, followed by a lot of tumbling and crashing noises. There was a sudden screech as Frank Sinatra had his throat cut, then silence. We heard the banging on our front door even before Mother turned off the hose.

'Sometimes,' Mother said 'you have to take matters into your own hands.'

Everyone spilled out of The Tall Ships to watch the row.

Mr Calhoun was soaking. So was Frank Sinatra.

'You're a typical Fianna Fail fascist,' Mr Calhoun shouted, waving the LP around. 'You're always imposing your will on the innocent.'

'I'm terribly sorry about the accident,' Mother said meekly. 'With all the noise from your record player I just found it impossible to concentrate on what I was doing.'

Neighbours, passers-by and townspeople joined the circle of spectators. Passengers getting off the buses stopped to watch as well. Soon, Church Street was packed. Mother maintained a dignified stance while Mr Calhoun ranted.

'You're a crank, a sleeveen and a third-columnist.'

'That's what you are,' Mary Calhoun said.

In the end, people began to boo and Mary Calhoun was forced to haul her husband home.

'You haven't heard the last of this,' Mr Calhoun shouted.

'I don't mind,' Mother allowed herself a small smile. 'As long as I've heard the last of Frank Sinatra for a while.'

The crowd gave her a round of applause for that. Mother took a bow. Mother closed the front door behind her and took a deep breath with her eyes closed.

'I think I've made my point,' she said.

After Mother was elected to the county council, her picture appeared in the Irish press. The caption said she was 'an energetic, can-do politician in the traditional mould, one to watch'. We were surprised to read in the brief biography that Mother's late father had been a prize-winning amateur boxer and an influential Fianna Fail councillor and activist. Mother's parents had died when we were very young, but none of us could remember Mother ever talking about her father or mentioning his achievements. It was reassuring to know that Fianna Fail ran in the family. Soon afterwards, people began to call around to the house to ask for favours. Most asked for straightforward things – they wanted a telephone installed or the council to repair their drains or whatever. Some wanted Mother to get their sons into the Gardai or the Army or to get their youngster a job – any job – to get them out of the house. Mother always told them she would see what could be done.

She got Joe Shaughnessy a job in the corporation; she got Miles Connors into the Army Dispatch Corps; she convinced The Tall Ships to give Joe Spain another chance as a barman – Joe was fired for staying on after the bar closed with a young woman called Noeleen Hennessy; in the morning, Joe and Noeleen were found asleep in each other's arms on the floor, empty bottles of Jack Daniels all around them. Joe had been wearing Noeleen's skirt. Mother even got the two Things part-time work cleaning the lighthouse and picking up debris on the pier.

'This is for Herself,' Butch Cassidy said, slipping me an extra chop with a big grin.

'Tell your mother I was asking for her,' the postman roared whenever he passed Rory or Maeve or myself on the street.

At school, Father Caraher started being nice to me.

'I never had you figured for a son of Kathleen Buckley – more's the pity you're not a bit like her.'

Conker Connolly decided to convince his mother to go into politics.

'It's the only way to make sure that you get treated right,' he said. 'The only problem is that my Ould One always votes Fine Gael. I was kinda hoping maybe that you could drop round and have a word with her.'

Conker put his plans to bump off The Barrel on hold.

'There is no point getting into trouble for a rotten old pervert like that,' he said, 'unless you're sure you can get away with it.'

There was a chance of a house on Redrock Hill. On Mother's new salary as manager of the mini-market, we could afford to move. But Mother refused to move from Church Street.

'This is a snug, safe house. It's a good place to bring up a family. Maybe it doesn't have the space and style of the houses on the Hill, but it's solid and the roof doesn't leak. Besides, this is a Fianna Fail house now. It would be high treason to leave just when life is beginning again.'

Mother got Maeve to recite a Yeats poem for the cumann. Maeve delivered the lines in a grave monotone, as if she had just seen our cat Ulysses being flattened by a steam-roller. The cumann gave her a thunderous ovation. Mrs Vincent sneaked a pound note into her hand. Rory went up to Maeve.

'Lickarse,' Rory whispered. 'I can see through your act.'

Later, Rory waited in the kitchen until Maeve came through to get drinks for the cumann. When she had her back to him, he slipped a piece of soggy bread down the back of her neck.

'Now. That shook you,' Rory said.

Maeve behaved as though nothing had happened and carried the drinks she had prepared back to the cumann meeting.

'You have to make allowances for Rory,' she said, 'he's a bit immature.'

My stutter was an embarrassment. Whenever Mother called upon me to say anything in front of the cumann, I often gagged convulsively, especially at the beginning of a word. In front of strangers or at school, I jammed on certain words, 'book', 'bus', 'happy', or anything beginning with 'a' or 'p'. It was like being slowly suffocated. I always felt that I was fighting desperately for air.

Mother decided that I needed help, 'What's going to happen to you in a few years when you leave school? Life is not a dress rehearsal, Daniel. Your first job interview could be the crucial one. This is a bad reflection on me as a mother.'

'My cousin was the laughing stock of Ballaly,' Dessie O'Hanlon said. 'Then I sent him to Mr Wolkenski. He was cured in a month.'

Mother was intrigued, 'Do you think he could do the same for Daniel?'

'In Poland, Wolkenski was a household name,' Dessie O'Hanlon said. 'He has been known to cure a stutter simply by touching the person's head.'

Rory thought the whole idea was hilarious, 'Daniel's going for stutter lessons. Now I've heard everything.'

Mr Wolkenski's office was on the top floor of an old

Georgian building in Mountjoy Square. There was no lift. The room was bare as a dungeon except for a couple of wooden chairs and a table. The walls were pockmarked and peeling. Lumps of plaster were piled in the corner. I spent the first ten minutes of the lesson listening to Mr Wolkenski slowly clumping up the stairs. I wasn't surprised when Mr Wolkenski turned out to be old, skinny and wrinkled. His eyes were like two dark caves. Occasionally, I caught a glimpse of something moist peeping out. He didn't smile or say 'hello'.

'Breet in deep, pleez,' Mr Wolkenski said.

I took a deep breath.

'Now, holt breeth.'

Then he walked out of the room. I wasn't sure what to do. I held my breath until I thought I was going to explode and then let it go in a big rush. Mr Wolkenski came back in.

'Gut, ver gut, now ve try again, yes.'

For half an hour, Mr Wolkenski made me breathe in, then hold it until it burst out of me. He didn't attempt to explain what he was doing. Nor did he show any interest in listening to my stutter. He kept saying 'ver gut' and making me do it again. I thought he was under orders to punish me for something. It was difficult to see how he had gathered such a great reputation. Could it be that people swore that they were cured just to get away from these stupid exercises?

'Well what was it like?' Mother asked the moment she got home from her meeting.

'A ba-ba-bit weird. I don't feel any different. The stutter is still the sa-sa-sa . . .' I said.

'Still the same?' Mother said. 'Ah well. These things take time. You have to be patient. If he hasn't cured you by the end of next month, I'll send you somewhere else.'

The cumann members all adored Charlie Haughey, except for Mrs Cassells from Redrock Boulevard who said that Des O'Malley should be the next leader of the party.

'O'Malley's only a pup,' Mother said. 'He doesn't have the maturity, the vision, or the style of a Haughey.'

'There's more to politics than style,' Mrs Cassells said knowingly, and flinched as Mother handed her a cup of tea that was overflowing onto the saucer.

'O'Malley doesn't have the gumption of a goat,' Mother said.

Mrs Cassells gave Mother a smug, superior look, 'We'll see about that.'

Mother said that Mrs Cassells was a Fine Gael spy. Mrs Cassells was not to be trusted, she said. Before the next meeting, Maeve, who had the job of serving the cooked chicken and bread rolls, was taken aside by Mother.

'Give you-know-who the you-know-what end of the chicken,' Mother told her. 'It's what we give to spies.'

Maeve served the rear end of the chicken to Mrs Cassells.

Soon, Mother had brought the other cumann members round to her view. Mrs Cassells was ignored at meetings and any proposal she put forward was dismissed out of hand or ruled out of order for some technical breach of the rules. 'This isn't democratic,' Mrs Cassells said. 'I feel like I'm being railroaded by my own people.'

'Democracy is about action, not stupid blather,' Mother said. 'People who want to discuss railroads should take up train-spotting.'

Mrs Cassells left the cumann. A few weeks later, she joined Fine Gael.

'I told you she was a traitor all along,' Mother boasted.

The others nodded their heads.

'You've an amazing insight into human nature,' Mrs Donovan said.

Mother sighed, 'It's a gift from God.'

Whenever Mother travelled down the country to attend a party function, she always took Maeve and myself with her. Rory always refused to go. 'Why should I go down the country? I see enough sleeveens in this house as it is.'

We got used to hanging around in smokey rooms, being pawed at by the party faithful who always told us what a great woman Mother was and how lucky we were to have her. We learned to recognise instantly the smell of whiskey

93

on people's breath. We always nodded and gave big grins when John Joe Sullivan told us that Mother would be Taoiseach one day.

Rory was going to kill himself.

My brother was poised in a supermarket trolley at the top of the Hundred and One Steps, waiting to be pushed.

Maeve grabbed my arm, 'I can't believe he's going to go through with this.'

Earlier, we had come across the supermarket trolley lying in the street. It was bright and shiny and the tiny metal rollers were working. We were having fun pushing each other around in it when Rory and Joey Boland and a bunch of older guys came up behind us.

'Let's take it up the Hundred and One Steps,' Rory suggested.

The Hundred and One Steps was a steep, narrow, stone pathway halfway up a little-used bothareen. For years, local teenagers had used it as an obstacle course. Kids had been carted off to hospital with broken legs and arms and occasionally a fractured skull. Some had tried to slide down on planks of wood. Others had attempted to cycle down. One kid had tried to roll down in a barrel and broken everything except the barrel. Nobody, to the best of our knowledge, had ever attempted the descent in a supermarket trolley.

'I'm going to be the first,' Rory announced.

He checked the position of the trolley, re-examined the tiny black rollers, walked up and down the one hundred and one steps until he was satisfied that there were no unforeseen obstacles. Finally, he positioned the trolley at the top of the steps, and got a bunch of us to hold it steady while he climbed in.

'I know a foolproof way to do this,' he smiled. 'You just have to lean back at all times. Coming down on this thing is as straightforward as cycling down Redrock Hill without brakes with your feet on the handlebars.'

We all gathered at the top for the historic attempt.

Manus Rock leaned over to me, 'Your brother's mental.'

94

'I know,' I said.

At the bottom, a crowd had gathered, yelling, laughing and shouting encouragement. Paulie Reddin had turned up and was standing at the side, taking bets.

'All right, let her go,' Rory said quietly.

Joey Boland and Malachi Spain let go of the trolley and stepped back. The trolley bumped down the steps making a noise like thousands of gates being clanged. People at the bottom cheered and roared.

'Go on, do it, Rory,' someone shouted.

Halfway down, the trolley suddenly flipped over completely and pitched Rory out. A girl screamed. Rory tumbled down the steps, arms and legs flapping like a circus clown. Finally he plunged into heavy gorse at one side of the steps. The trolley landed on his head.

'Rory,' Maeve shouted. 'Oh God, Rory.'

When we got to where he was lying, we were sure he was dead. He lay without moving or appearing to breathe. There was blood all over his face. Someone ran for an ambulance. I was worried for my brother, yet strangely exhilarated by the activity and the crowd. I bent down to check if he was breathing. Rory came to and squinted at me. He seemed confused, hurt, vulnerable. My heart leapt when I saw that he recognised me.

'Dad?'

'It's me, Daniel.'

Rory blinked 'What the fuck are you looking at?'

I was glad that he was alive. Rory tried to rise but couldn't because of the pain in his arm and back.

'Hang on,' Joey Boland said 'there's an ambulance on the way.'

A little while later, we heard the nee-naw sound coming up the bothareen. Later, everyone agreed that the two stretcher bearers carefully picking their way down as Rory moaned on the stretcher was the most impressive descent of the Hundred and One Steps ever made. Whenever the stretcher bearers stumbled and nearly dropped Rory, the crowd gave a big ooooh. It was far more thrilling than Rory's crash.

'Think he's broken anything?' I asked Maeve.

'I hope so, the eejit.'

'You don't mean that.'

Maeve reflected, 'No, I don't mean it. Well – maybe a toe.'

In the excitement, none of us thought to ask which hospital the ambulance was headed for. We spent an hour making frantic and frequently grovelling phone calls on a temperamental pay-phone before I was able to phone Mother to tell her which hospital Rory was in.

'*Hospital?*' she screamed. 'What do you mean hospital?'

It took a while before she calmed down enough for me to explain what had happened.

'I'll murder him,' she said.

Rory had a fractured arm. He went around with his arm in a sling for a month. The doctors told Mother that Rory was lucky not to have broken his skull or his back. He could be a vegetable now, they said. At home, everyone was deferential to Rory. He never had to lift a finger. All his meals were served to him and Mother was always asking him if there was anything more she could do for him. Around the area, he got a nickname, 'Evel Kneivel'. We had not seen Rory so happy since before Dad disappeared. In the end, even Mother believed that the accident had actually done Rory good.

'Any time you're thinking of going down a flight of steps in a trolley, just go right ahead,' she told him.

Mr Wolkenski leaned over me like an ancient vampire.

'Press-hips, yeh, ver gut,' he said. 'Do, do.'

After a while, I gathered that what Mr Wolkenski wanted me to do was to get onto the floor to do twenty press-ups. I gave up at twelve. Mr Wolkenski made me try again. And again. When I finally managed twenty he clapped his hands.

'Ee-nuff. Gut.'

As soon as I was back on my feet, he handed me a telephone directory. He wanted me to walk around the room reading aloud pages of surnames that he had marked.

He wouldn't let me read the addresses, phone numbers or first names. Just the surnames.

'Murphy, Murphy, Murphy . . .' I went.

He never gave me a page with interesting or unusual names. It was maddening. I couldn't grasp the logic behind it at all.

'Smith, Smith, Smith . . .'

Mr Wolkenski clapped me on the shoulder.

'Gut,' he said.

I noticed that when it came to reading simple surnames from a telephone directory, I stuttered only occasionally. The more I thought about Wolkenski's techniques, the more confused I got. The strange thing was that my speech began to improve. For some reason, I was no longer as self-conscious about my stutter. After a dozen lessons, I found that I could occasionally hold a conversation, even with a total stranger. Even though Mr Wolkenski's methods didn't make any sense at all, I began to look forward to 'stutter lessons'.

This time, it was jam doughnuts.

We sat down at breakfast, staring at the big bowl of fat doughnuts on the table. Next to the doughnuts was a packet of cinnamon rings and a jug of orange juice. Steam was still rising from the doughnuts. Mother must have run out to The Kerry Creamery at the bottom of Main Street before we got up to buy them fresh from the baking tray.

'God, this is serious,' Maeve whispered. 'Maybe she's going to marry Dessie after all.'

When Mother came in, we pretended not to notice the goodies. For a while, we all ignored the doughnuts and the cinnamon rings. Even Mother joined in the charade. In the end, Rory spoiled it.

'Don't tell me, you've joined Fine Gael.'

Mother smiled, 'Just eat your breakfast, please. And I hope you'll all join me in a glass of wine.'

Mother produced a bottle of white wine from the sink where it had been standing under a running tap. We were stunned. Maeve threw me a look to say, 'told you so'.

Mother got Rory to uncork it and pour everyone a glass. I was surprised at how cold and bitter the wine tasted. It was 8 am.

'This is very civilised,' Rory said.

'Come on, Mother, will you,' Maeve said. 'You're just teasing us.'

Mother gave a shy smile, 'If you must know. Last night, your mother was chosen by Fianna Fail to contest the next election to the Dail. I hope you're all very proud of me.'

Rory spilled his wine on Ulysses. No one said anything for a few moments. Outside, birds sang. Maeve knocked back the remainder of her wine in one gulp.

'Well, what do you think of that?' Mother smiled.

Maeve recovered first, 'That's great news.'

'Yeah,' I said, 'g-great news.'

We looked at Rory.

'Don't say a word,' Maeve hissed.

Rory shrugged, 'Congratulations.'

Mother put on her serious face, 'I can't stand idly by and watch the country go down the Swannee. The political arena is the only logical and reasonable course left open to any decent Irish patriot. Besides, last night, the cumann nominated me to contest the seat left vacant by the death of Dinny Blackstone who has represented the area in the Dail for twenty years. Who am I to argue?'

'Sure he's been dead for at least ten years,' Rory said. 'It's a wonder that anyone finally noticed.'

'Rory,' Maeve exclaimed. 'Don't ruin things.'

Mother lost her proud, cheerful face, 'Always in with the smart remark, aren't you? You couldn't say congratulations, Mother or well done, Mother or I hope everything works out well for you, Mother. Oh no. Maeve, Daniel, take a good hard look at your brother, that's what happens to you when you spend all your time listening to long-haired trash.'

Everyone kept quiet after that. The wine made me feel funny. I kept drinking it though; I really liked the taste and it was giving me a whole new feeling towards mornings. We ate the rest of the doughnuts in guilty silence, hoping that

Rory would keep his mouth shut at least until breakfast was over. When the doughnuts were gone, we filed out to the hallway to collect our coats and bags. It took us ages to find our stuff. Maeve knocked over the coat-rack in the hall, trying to pull her her schoolbag out. Rory hit his head off the hanging bulb. We looked at each other and giggled. In fact, we stood there until Mother came out to see what was going on. Before we left the house, she thanked us for our support.

'I will need your help over the coming weeks. Daniel, you and Maeve will help with the election committee and I want you, Rory, to help Dessie with postering the area. We need to hit every lamp post in Redrock.'

'Mother, that's not fair,' Rory whined. 'I have my own plans.'

Mother shrugged, 'Sacrifice is part of politics. It will make you a stronger person. After the elections, you can do whatever you want.'

Rory didn't wait at the bus-stop with us.

'I need time to think,' he said vaguely and set off in the direction of the railway station at the harbour, head down, kicking at stones.

We watched him go. Rory gave the impression that he thought Mother was going up for election to the Dail just to annoy him.

I was excited trying to imagine what it would be like to have a mother who was a TD. Mother dominated everything that we did. All our friends adored her. Dessie O'Hanlon and a bunch of other men were in love with her. Almost everyone in the town and on the Hill liked her, except for the Calhouns and a couple of Fine Gaelers. Even the fact that Dad was missing had turned into a plus. People admired her for refusing to collapse under the pressure of three kids and a job. I felt that she was certain to get elected. It seemed somehow pre-ordained. This latest move of Mother's had taken us by surprise, but now that I thought about it, it wasn't really surprising at all; going up for election was simply a new stage in Mother's development. Sometimes, it seemed that we were mere spectators at the drama of her life. We spent most of our waking lives either dealing with the consequences of Mother's actions or speculating about what she was going to do next.

I wondered what Dad would have thought. I decided that Dad would have been proud of her. Then I corrected myself. Dad *is* proud of her. After all, I reminded myself, Dad *is* out there somewhere. It was important to keep that in mind. I glanced about me at the familiar row of houses, Butch Cassidy the butcher, across the road The Tall Ships pub, Mahony's mini-market on Main Street, the grey-faced church opposite with a few leering gargoyles still visible from our side of the street. If Mother got elected, we would no longer be the Buckleys from Church Street whose father was missing. Instead, we would become the children of the local TD. Overnight, we would become an exotic species. People would hit on us for favours. We would be famous. Mother would be powerful, wealthy, respected, perhaps even feared, though maybe that was a bit strong because I couldn't recall anyone in the area ever being afraid of the last local Fianna Fail TD, a little man with thick glasses who seemed to know everyone's name and always appeared surprised when people remembered his. I wondered if Mother's cumann had already spread the word about the election. I was sure Mrs Donovan would have spent half the night on the phone to everyone she knew.

'Think she'll get in?' I asked.

'No problem,' Maeve replied. 'In fact, I wouldn't be surprised if she was Taoiseach within a couple of years.'

'It looks like it, doesn't it?'

'With Mother, anything's possible.'

Maeve thought for a while, 'I'm going to write her speeches.'

'Are you going to tell people?'

'No, what they don't already know, they'll find out soon enough. Anyway, I bet most people already know.'

The bus came and we got on. Maeve scrutinised the driver's face to see if he knew about Mother, but the driver just took her money and handed her a ticket.

'Move up the bus and stop clogging up the doorway,' he

told her. We examined the faces of the other passengers on the bus to see if they knew, but they all appeared unaware of the fact that they were sharing a bus journey with the youngest son and only daughter of the area's next TD. An old woman turned to Maeve. I was sure she was going to congratulate her on having such a great Mother.

'If you don't quit staring at me, I'll get the driver to stop the bus and put you off.'

For once, I did not spend the journey thinking about Leonie Powers or Sabina Blazer or any of the other Hill girls or about playing guitar in a rock group or being a famous soccer star or any of the usual things. Instead, I fantasised about my part in Mother's election campaign. Beside me, Maeve got out her notebook and biro and worked on a speech for Mother.

'How do you spell destiny?' Maeve asked.

We became so preoccupied that we almost missed our stop.

At school, I waited for someone – a teacher, Father Caraher, Conker Connolly – to come up and say something about Mother's bid for election. Nobody did. I was so caught up in wondering about Mother that I could not pay attention to anything else. During French class, when everyone in the class was taking it in turns to read out paragraphs of a Maupassant story, I went into a dream. Ms Lewis, the pretty red-haired French teacher who Conker Connolly fancied even more than he fancied Mother, called out my name. It was only when she lost her temper and her voice turned as shrill and insistent as a madly steaming kettle that I snapped out of it. She put me outside the door.

'It's for your own good,' she piped. 'You'll thank me one day.'

Being outside the door didn't bother me. Now that I was free of distractions, I could think without being disturbed. I stared at the smudged, cream-coloured wall until it dissolved into an image of a teeming O'Connell Street. There was no traffic, just people, more than I had ever seen before, more even than during the Christmas rush or after international soccer matches. I saw Mother on a platform addressing a massive crowd, like De Valera in an old black and white photograph. At the front, photographers snapped and reporters hustled while hysterical party enthusiasts waved flags and chanted Mother's name, 'Kath–leen Buck–ley, Kath–leen Buck–ley'. Fathers carried their children on their shoulders in an effort to give them a glimpse of Mother as security men whisked her through the crowds to a waiting limousine. Some people screamed, others waved frantically from high windows and from the tops of lamp posts. Next, I saw a motorcade like the one that had carried President Kennedy through Dublin's streets. Mother stood tall and dignified in the back of an open-top limousine, a hand raised, turning left and right, with a stately smile, to acknowledge the crowds. From somewhere above the car, as if I was watching from the rooftop of a tall building, I saw myself sitting beside Mother as she received the adulation of the crowd. I had on a suit and tie, my hair was brushed slickly back like Robin the Boy Wonder in his guise as Bruce Wayne's ward. I looked smart and confident. Maeve and Rory were in front, beside the driver. Maeve looked radiant in a flowery summer dress. Rory wore a black monkey suit and dicky-bow. He looked uncomfortable and surly as ever but there was a new sparkle in his eyes. A security man stood on the running board. Another in sunglasses perched on the back, scanning the crowd for assassins.

As we moved through the streets, the surging mass reached out to touch our car. It was intoxicating. Everywhere you looked there were swaying, fluttering flags and banners. Scattered voices rose and fell like the sound of waves crashing against the pier. I was reassured by the steady mumble of the limousine underneath. We were now a royal family, I realised; I was the youngest son of the first woman Taoiseach in history. It was important to behave in the correct regal fashion. It was only proper that I too should respond to the acclamation of the masses. I raised my right hand, put a stately smile on my face and turned left and right giving slow, almost lethargic waves, the way I had seen Mother do. I nodded at the vast blur of people, picking out a face here and a face there for a smile, winking at babies and small children when I could spot them, occasionally raising both hands over my head in triumph like an Olympic gold medallist. How wonderful it would be to live like this all the time, I thought. I caught Mother's eye. I could feel that she was proud of me, too. I felt the rays of her smile, felt warm joy suffusing me. I felt like a rock star. I knew that if I threw myself into the crowd now, thousands of hands would catch me and pass me back to the car over a sea of faces. I anticipated an earthquake of applause. Heart thumping wildly with joy, face fixed in a terrifying grin which I imagined was a generous beaming smile, I spun slowly around with both hands clasped over my head in a victory salute. A cheer rumbled deep in my throat to echo the roar which was rising all around me.

I loved everyone. Including the madwoman who was standing on the bonnet of our limosine staring at me and waving her hands around.

It took several slow seconds to realise that the madwoman on the bonnet of the limousine was, in fact, Ms Lewis. I wondered what she was doing standing on Mother's limousine. Then I realised that there was no limousine. Mrs Lewis was standing transfixed in the yawning doorway with her mouth tight. Suddenly the crowd vanished, along with flags, noise and security men. Behind Ms Lewis, I saw that my classmates were strangling themselves with giggles. Mortified and confused, I dropped my hands and lowered my head.

'*Mon cherie*,' Ms Lewis said gently, 'I think you had better come back down to earth before you do yourself damage.'

Rory was in charge of postering around the harbour area, Maeve was appointed personal assistant and chief speech-writer and I was given the task of organising cups of tea and coffee for the election committee meetings which were to be held in our house every morning.

'Why do I have to do *all* the posters?' Rory asked. 'Why can't your people from the cumann do that. Isn't that what they're for?'

'Oh, excuse me,' Mother said. 'My eldest son is refusing to help out even though he knows we're stuck, is this what I'm hearing?'

'I'm just saying—'

'I see. The most important event in my life and in the life of this family and I'm getting cheek from my firstborn. It isn't worth it, all this pain, for what? So that my own flesh and blood can drive daggers into my back. Would you rather that I did nothing except wash your socks for the rest of my days?'

Rory looked ashamed. Embarrassed, he picked up the bag of posters.

'I never said I wouldn't do it,' he mumbled and went out.

Mother turned to me, pointing her finger at her head and making twirling motions, 'Your brother's a bit thick, you have to spell it out for him sometimes.'

She put her arms around me and crushed me into her chest, 'Not like you, the bravest of them.'

I smelled her sweet, stinging perfume, the soft tang of sweat and the ancient musky scent of her black dress.

'It will be nice to have you around the place, now that I am entering the most difficult phase of my life.'

'Helping your Mother get *what*?'

Father Caraher stared at me for a moment. With difficulty, I repeated my request to be let off school for three weeks to help my mother get elected to the Dail. Then his big ugly face broke into a big ugly grin.

'Elected to the Dail, is it? Oh, that's a good one, the best I've ever heard. Go back to your class before I laugh myself to death.'

At home, Mother was in the middle of a strategic planning meeting with Dessie O'Hanlon when I told her what the priest had said.

'What's the eejit's name?' she demanded and picked up the phone.

'Father Caraher,' I said.

I waited in the doorway while Mother got on to Father Caraher.

'Daniel is now engaged on a project that is far more educational than anything he could possibly learn in school,' I heard her say.

I winced every time Mother said my name. It was humiliating to have my future discussed while I was in the room. I thought that Mother could have sent me to the shops to buy groceries or something.

'I don't see what you've possibly got to object about, Father Caraher. It's only for a few weeks and I can't do without Daniel. I hope you realise that this is for his own good as well as the good of the nation. Yes, I realise that he's only twelve and half but he's a most mature and responsible child. Besides, it will be good for his stutter.'

Mother's voice turned breathy and seductive.

'One of the areas I'm particularly keen to re-organise is the whole business of State funding for schools. I have always believed that the best and most forward-thinking schools should get first preference. You run such a progressive yet disciplined school, Father Caraher, and Daniel's always raving about your own qualities as a leader. I just know that my election will be a very good thing for Daniel and for a school as co-operative and excellently led as yours. I'd be delighted to meet you to discuss the matter – after I am elected, of course. Do we understand each other, Father Caraher?'

There was a long pause, punctuated by Mother saying 'yes', 'of course' and 'I see'. After a short while, she smiled and thanked Father Caraher for all his trouble. She told him she'd be in touch and put down the phone. She passed me in the doorway, lighting a cigarette.

'He's having your homework sent around,' she said. 'There's never any problem when you're dealing with a man of straw.'

Mrs Donovan said that they were behind schedule with the area canvass.

'We need to average fifteen hundred people a day. So far, we're only doing half that.'

Everyone in the front room looked at her.

Dessie O'Hanlon leaned back on his chair with a smug face, 'The reason we're not doing that is very simple, Jenny. Today is our first day of campaigning, so how can we be behind if we haven't commenced yet?'

Mrs Donovan blinked, 'I know that. I was just trying to make sure everyone else knew the situation.'

Mother put out her cigarette in the ashtray. Maisie Dorney and Mrs Vincent sat on either side of Mother at the end of the table while Dessie O'Hanlon, Alberta Biggins and Shay McCloud, sat at the other end.

Maisie Dorney leaned forward, 'I think something should be done about Butch Cassidy.'

A hush fell on the room. Maisie glanced at Mother and for a moment I thought that Butch must have been threatening kids with his cleaver again.

'I know he's your next door neighbour, Kathleen, but I got six gigot chops off him last week and they'd gone off and when I complained he refused to take them back or refund my money.'

Maisie looked around the table for support but all she got was blank looks.

'And this isn't the first time it's happened,' she added darkly.

Jenny Donovan straightened up, 'Mind you, Maisie has a point. I got a chicken off him last week which tasted like old Wellingtons.'

A resolution was passed that once the election was over, someone would be detailed to deal with Butch Cassidy. In the meanwhile, Mother proposed that Maisie Dorney should keep a file.

'I'll be delighted,' Maisie Dorney said. 'What that man is doing is a sin against meat.'

Mother nodded to me to bring more tea and coffee. I gathered the tray full of used cups and empty pots and slid through the open door into the hall. So far, the election committee had gone through eighteen cups of coffee and two pots of tea. Nobody seemed to be in any hurry. In the kitchen, Rory sat slumped over a book. I bent down to see the title, *Narciss and Goldmund* by Herman Hesse. Rory suddenly looked up with bloodshot eyes, making me jump back.

'Are they finished yet?'

'Not really, they're still doing strategic planning.'

'Yeah, right,' Rory said and slumped down on his book again.

At Rory's feet was a bag of posters. He had been out all night postering and now he was waiting for the meeting to finish so that he and Dessie O'Hanlon could go in Dessie O'Hanlon's car to poster the crossroads and the seafront areas. I felt sorry for him having to work with Dessie O'Hanlon. There didn't seem to be any point talking to him so I made fresh pots of coffee and tea, arranged clean cups and saucers on the tray and went back inside. I arrived as Shay McCloud, the committee's burly, bald, election strategist, was rising.

'Kathleen, we need to maximise audio-visual campaigning techniques to give us the large-scale penetration we require.'

'Oooh, yes,' Mrs Vincent said.

'I agree,' Maisie Dorney said.

'Ah, speak English, will you,' Mrs Donovan said. 'You've been "maximising" and "minimising" all morning and I can't make head or tail of it.'

Shay McCloud smiled at Mrs Donovan to show her that he was not offended, 'Jenny, you're right to say what you believe. I just want you to know that I welcome and even encourage your objections. It's not easy to embrace something new.'

'Hmmph,' Mrs Donovan said.

McCloud waited until Mrs Donovan settled, then raised his fist in the air and passionately declared, 'We are going to bring the Fianna Fail party into the twentieth century. We will use the very latest developments in communications to win this seat and to catapult Kathleen Buckley to her rightful place in the Dail.' McCloud glanced around him to see how his speech was going down. Reassured by the blank looks and puzzled expressions, he produced a notebook, 'I'll just factor a few ingredients into the scenario.'

The cumann was in awe except for Mrs Donovan.

'Why don't you just factor off with yourself,' Mrs Donovan said.

A flurry of voices rose in the air like seagulls swooping on a fishing boat that was sneaking into harbour with a full catch.

'Oh Jenny, that's not fair,' Mrs Vincent said.

'Give 'im a chance, dearie,' Alberta Biggins said.

Dessie O'Hanlon had to thump the table to get people to shut up, 'Oh, now, Jenny, Shay has his own poetic way of explaining himself.'

'Explain? That's a good one. You'd need a degree in nuclear physics to know what he's going on about.'

Shay McCloud ignored her. He prowled the table like an evangelist, punching the notebook when he wanted to emphasise a point.

'First we hire a bus with speakers on the outside. We call it the "Kathleenmobile". Everywhere we go we blast out the message and we show the people that we mean business. Then we get special glossy photographs taken of Kathleen, not by a hack but by a top-class professional. We'll make Kathleen look like a Hollywood movie star – which, of course, she does anyway.'

Mother graciously bowed her head to acknowledge the compliment.

McCloud continued, 'Next we'll stage-manage the rallies so that every speech resembles All-Ireland Day at Croke Park. We'll get our friends in the music business, sports, the arts and the Church to be photographed with Kathleen. I'll make sure the newspapers are there.'

The cumann gave a 'coo' of approval. I felt so excited I nearly joined in.

McCloud arrived back at his place at the table and leaned forward, face grave, 'For the pièce de résistance, ladies and gentlemen, we hire a camera crew and make a film of one of Kathleen's speeches.' McCloud held up his hands to stem the flood of questions. 'We show the film in every parish hall, every cinema and every community centre in the whole of Redrock. By the time we hit election day, the whole area will be penetrated and saturated with Kathleen Buckley's image and message. Ladies and gentlemen, the people of Redrock won't be able to resist voting for her. It'll be like electing their best friend.'

There was a silence. Even Mrs Donovan seemed too stunned to speak.

Delighted with the reaction, McCloud sat down and closed his notebook.

Dessie cleared his throat, 'Now, what do you think, Kathleen? You're the one going up for election.'

Mother held out her hands for peace, 'I'm a simple woman. I see things in a simple way. I don't know anything about modern communications or any of that stuff, but I do know unless the people of Redrock know what I stand for then there's no point going up for election.'

'Exactly,' Mrs Donovan said.

Mother raised her hand with her fingers splayed. With her free hand she ticked off the points.

'I stand for unity, harmony, integrity, honesty, patriotism, the Irish language and free dental treatment. I also want to kick the Brits out of our country.'

'Hear, hear.'

'I hope you don't mean me?' Alberta Biggins said.

Everyone looked shocked and immediately turned to reassure her that they didn't mean her.

'Of course not,' Mother said, 'you're different.'

'You know you're one of the best, don't you?' Dessie O'Hanlon said as he squeezed her knee. 'We wouldn't kick you out, you know that.'

When Alberta Biggins was sufficiently reassured, Mother raised her hand for silence.

'If Shay says we need to make a film to get my message across then that's fine with me.'

Shay McCloud rose to his feet, 'We're going to change the face of Irish politics.'

Mother smiled, 'And by the way, I have a new campaign strategy.'

They all hushed to hear Mother's new strategy.

'As you all know, we do not speak English in this country.'

Everyone looked bewildered.

'We don't?' Alberta Biggins said. 'What language do we speak?'

'We speak Hiberno-English, our own language, our own creation, based on the ancient Gaelic tongue and Celtic tradition.'

There was a gasp. Mrs Donovan applauded, pitter-pats that sounded like a mouse running up a wall.

Mother held up a hand, 'I think there's a huge difference between our English and the language of that dumpy-looking bitch of a Queen of England who's German anyway. No offence, Alberta.'

'None taken, I'm sure.'

Everyone was elated with Mother's explanation.

'Oh, that's brilliant,' Mrs Vincent said. 'Where's Maeve? We must get that put into one of the speeches.'

'Hear, hear,' Dessie O'Hanlon said. 'What do you think, Shay?'

Shay McCloud drew in his stomach, 'Yes, I think that Hiberno-English could impact us on the electorate with maximum efficiency'.

'Someone take him out and shoot him,' Mrs Donovan sighed.

The woman was small, dark and gravely belligerent, cheeks as pink as a smacked bottom. She stood in the doorway of the Grandview supermarket and refused to let Mother pass. 'I'll have no more children for this country. It's not worth it. Six of them, all on the dole and what are you going to do about it?'

Mother drew herself up, 'I shall personally undertake to do my best to get all your children jobs.'

The woman shrugged and walked off. 'Ye're all the same,' she shouted back.

'Never mind,' Mother sniffed. 'You always get a few sourpusses.'

At the entrance to the Pier End pub, Mother was stopped by a large woman wearing a brown coat which billowed around her ankles like curtains in a gale.

'The country's banjaxed,' the woman said. 'We're a

banana republic without the bananas. In another couple of years we won't have a country to vote for. The rest of the world's laughing at us and I don't blame them. I'd laugh meself, only I've no sense of humour anymore.'

Mother appeared a little shaken, 'Once Fianna Fail are in power, we'll get the country back on its feet. It's a question of willpower. Once the will is there, the rest will follow.'

The woman shrugged and broke into a smile. 'You've a great face, do ye know that? Ye look like Liz Taylor. You'll get my vote anyhow – at least we'll have a bit of glamour in the Dail.'

At Mahony's mini-market, Mother was broadsided by a tall woman who windmilled her arms at her.

'Hell is waiting for us all,' she said and pushed past.

'Vote Fianna Fail,' Mother shouted after her.

At Wallace's fishmongers, a man stopped Mother to ask for the price of a brandy.

'It's doctor's orders, I haven't long,' and he coughed melodramatically into his fist.

Mother gave him a pound and he thanked her and told her he would definitely vote for her before he went.

'Is it always like this?' Maeve asked.

'Politics is never easy,' Mother said. 'Your country demands a lot.'

Maeve turned to me, 'I don't like the way some of these people are talking to Mother. I think we should do something to the next person who starts with her. Maybe I could kick them in the ankles. That would make them stop.'

'Let's wait and see,' I said. 'It takes all kinds.'

A middle-aged housewife with a red nose stood in the doorway of her house and told Mother she'd sell her votes to the highest bidder.

'There are eight votes in this house and ye can have them all if ye get two sons of mine jobs.'

'I'll do my best, I promise you that on my word of honour,' Mother said.

'I'll wait and see,' the woman said. 'If anyone had told me ten years ago that I'd be bringing kids into this world to have them sit on their backsides, I'd have laughed.'

In The Harbour pub, Mother was mistaken for a Fine Gaeler. On Main Street, she was swarmed by a group of old-age pensioners who thought she was wonderful. At the pier, she spoke to the fishermen and the fishmongers and received a rapturous reception.

'I saw your last film,' a man shouted. 'You were brilliant but I think you should go back to Richard.'

Outside Jimmy Lassiter's pub on top of Redrock Hill, a well-dressed middle-aged woman walked up to Mother.

'I wouldn't vote for you in a million years because you're the bitch whose husband ran off with a floosie.'

For an instant, Mother's face collapsed into the anguish of a small child when something they love is snatched from them.

'Thank you,' Mother said politely and walked on with dignity.

'Never in a million years,' the woman shouted.

Mother went around with a stiff, expressionless face on her for an hour after that.

'Are you all right, Mother?' Maeve asked. 'Do you want me to get you a drink of water or something?'

'No thanks, Maeve,' Mother said as she tossed her hair back. 'Sometimes, you have to put up with an awful lot in politics.'

Maeve and I walked up and down the pier for hours wearing sandwich boards in the freezing cold. In front the boards read, 'Vote for my Mother, Kathleen Buckley.' On the back, they said, 'Kathleen Buckley, Fianna Fail, No 1.'

Lots of people said they were going to vote for Mother. Then they took another look at us and went away laughing.

'This is the most embarrassing day of my life,' Maeve said.

'I'd rather be in school,' I said.

I was waiting at the bus-stop outside our house with a bag of posters when a green Volkswagen pulled up. Maisie Dorney leaned out.

'Hop in, we'll give you a lift.'

I sat in the back between Maisie's sons Seth and James and a sandy-haired lady with a permanent grin who turned out to be Maisie's sister, Rita. Within seconds of driving off, the car was humming with a strange chanting sound. At first I thought there was something wrong with the engine, but slowly I realised that everyone around me was saying a Hail Mary. When the prayer ended, Maisie Dorney looked in the overhead mirror.

'Seth please,' she said

'Hail Mary, full of grace . . .' Seth began.

We were halfway to Grandview when Maisie called my name. I was bewildered. I couldn't think, couldn't speak, couldn't do anything except sit there and feel them all looking at me. Maisie called my name again. I felt embarrassed in the eyes of God. I couldn't remember any of the words, even though I had been listening to them in church and in school all my life.

'Daniel, are you all right?' Maisie said.

I tried to say something but nothing came out except a rasp. What was the matter with these people? Didn't they know I had a stutter? I hadn't been to 'stutter lessons' for two weeks because of the election. I felt nervous and confused. Maisie cleared her throat, a boom like the harbour cannon alerting the lifeboat.

'Daniel?' she said.

'Y-yes.'

'Hail Mary,' she said.

'H-hail Mary.'

'Full of Grace.'

'Fa-fa-full of Grace.'

Beside me, James pretended to look out of the window. It was the longest car journey I have ever taken. Finally, after what seemed like a day, I was dropped off in Grandview. That night, I lay awake for hours because the words to the Hail Mary wouldn't stop running through my head.

'Hold my hands, children, this is the big one.'

We waited with Mother in the corridor of Leary's seafront hotel. In a moment, Mother would walk into the packed throne room to make her final election speech. Mother wore a long blue dress and her hair flowed across her white shoulders. She wore a pearl necklace. She looked vital, lovely, stylish. She looked even better than she had when Dad was around.

Maeve took my arm, 'You know, she really does look like a film star.'

Shay McCloud held the door open a crack so that we could hear Dessie O'Hanlon's introduction. Tomorrow morning, the voting would begin.

'You'll do it, Mother.'

'You'll be brilliant.'

'You're going to be Taoiseach one day, everyone says so.'

Mother turned to us, eyes wide, 'God, how do I look? Is my mascara running? Maeve, is it?'

'Your eyes are fine, Mother,' Maeve reassured her. 'Relax, it's your night. It'll be great.'

'You look ba-beautiful, Mother,' I said.

'Yeah,' Rory said. 'You look great.

'How would you know?' Mother snapped. 'If I lose this election, it'll be all your fault.'

Mother was angry at Rory for leaving a thousand glossy posters on the Redrock bus last week. The posters had been intended for the 'final push'. In the end, the 'final push' had to make do with a few hundred old posters, thousands of hand-outs and a couple of trips around Redrock in the 'Kathleenmobile', a second-hand Ford Transit with speakers attached to the roof that made every speech sound as though it were being spoken underwater. At the time, Mother said it had been an 'insignificant hiccup', but the closer it got to polling day, the more Rory's lapse had seemed to upset her. For the last couple of hours, it was all she talked about. Now it was a disaster on a scale with the British invasion of Ireland. We heard Dessie O'Hanlon's voice rising to a screech.

'Ladies and gentlemen, I give you, the next Fianna Fail TD for Redrock and our future Taoiseach, Kath-leen Buck-ley.'

'You're on, Mother,' Maeve said.

'Oh God,' Mother whispered. Her face went pale, 'Oh my God.'

Maeve tried to push her into the room but Mother refused to budge, 'Come on Mother, this is the last leg. You've been brilliant all week, don't stop now.'

'Just give me a second.'

Inside, the crowd roared.

'Give me a second please,' Mother shouted.

Everyone drew back and gave Mother space. She touched her cheeks. After a few moments, she took a deep breath, then stood with her hands by her side. 'Right, here we go,' she said. 'Wish me luck.'

'Good luck, Mother,' we said.

As soon as Mother walked in, the crowd rose to their feet and gave her a rousing reception. They waved Fianna Fail banners, some of which had Mother's photo on them. The applause increased as she took the stand and graciously accepted a kiss on the cheek from Dessie O'Hanlon. She raised a hand and the crowd hushed. Her voice was strong, resonant, intoxicating. We made our way to the back and stood on one of the tables.

'Ladies and gentlemen, my fellow Fianna Failers, my friends and family, it is an honour to be chosen to win the seat for Fianna Fail.'

There were cheers followed immediately by tumultuous applause and foot-stamping.

'I am proud to lead the crusade against the forces of ignorance. Redrock has had the misfortune in the past to be neglected by sleeveens and chancers. Our own late lamented colleague and TD, Dinny Blackstone fought hard and well for the people of this community and I intend to continue his great work.'

Mother paused for the applause to die down.

'But I don't have to tell you about the local politician who thinks more of going to the bookie's than he does of the welfare of his own people. I don't have to mention any names. With politicans such as these around, is it any wonder the country is in difficulties? I will make the people of Redrock one promise: I WILL NEVER ABANDON YOU.'

Beside us, Mr Mahony, the mini-market owner, appeared to be overcome with emotion, 'God, she's the spit of Elizabeth Taylor.'

Up at the podium, Mother smiled knowingly, 'Well, I know just what to do about the gombeens.'

She leaned forward dramatically on the platform. She thumped the stand in front of her. The room jumped.

'It's time the people took their REVENGE.'

At the mention of revenge, there was an unexpected, intense silence in the room. People were not sure how to react. It was as though Mother had cursed while reading the lesson at Mass.

Mother sensed the mood and smiled. She held her hands out.

'There's nothing wrong with revenge. It's been getting a bad press for hundreds of years, and do you know why? Because the other parties are afraid to rock the boat. I'm not ashamed to say that I want revenge for the wrongs that have been done to our nation, to its people, to its culture and architecture, to the very fibre of our society. Well, I'm not afraid to take revenge. I'm sick of the FOOLS, the CHARLATANS, yes, the GOMBEENS. With your help, my noble friends, I'm going to sweep these fools off the political map of the country like sweeping crumbs off a table. I feel humble and proud to be chosen as the one to reclaim my part of this great nation for the REAL people of Ireland, the people of Parnell, the people of Emmet and Grattan and Wolfe Tone, the people of Padraig Pearse, the people of REDROCK. So, my friends and neighbours, I'm here tonight to tell you that we will take this seat and we will have our REVENGE, make no mistake about that.'

She paused, leaned forward again, smiled. I could see the light in her brown eyes, see the skin of her face glowing. I felt a surge of love shoot through my veins. I looked at Maeve. She grabbed my hand to show she felt the same way. We wanted this speech, this atmosphere to last for ever.

'It's one small step for the people of Redrock, but a giant leap for the entire country.'

This time, the approval was deafening. It was followed by cheering and stamping and a great banging of cups and plates off tables. Mrs Donovan had to be assisted down from the top of a table where she had suddenly appeared, hand on heart, wailing the national anthem. Vincent Reddin, Paulie's father, was shouting something from a table at the other side of the room. Everyone ignored him.

Maeve turned to me with a radiant smile, 'Brilliant, isn't she?'

Half of the people in the room seemed to be on the tables, some of the men with swirling pints in their hands. I saw Vincent Reddin's mouth open before he was swallowed up in the chaos. Mother's voice rose above the cacophony.

'I know what the people want – they're crying out for leadership, vision, common sense and free dental treatment. I'm going to take this seat for the honour of the country. This is more than a political campaign. This, my friends, is DESTINY.'

The room broke up in hysteria. From our table at the back, we saw Mother standing with head back and her hands in the air for a few seconds before a mob of ranting, air-punching, cheering soldiers of destiny engulfed her and carried her off. Shay McCloud and the bishop jumped onto the podium, held each other's hands and danced a jig.

'I've a feeling they liked her,' Rory said drily.

'What did you think?' Maeve asked. 'She used some of my words.'

'It sounded good,' I said. 'Which bit did you write?'

'The bit about one small step for Redrock . . .'

'Hah, I might have guessed,' Rory said. 'You couldn't even write something original.'

Maeve hung her head. Rory smiled a wry smile and sipped his Guinness. He took out a packet of Gauloises, lit one, and blew a stream of white smoke from between his lips as he leaned back against the wall. Suddenly, people swarmed around us, clapping us on the back and shaking our hands and telling us what an extraordinary woman we had for a mother.

'I'm so excited,' Mrs Vincent said. 'That was a masterful bit about the one small step for Redrock.'

'Well, she's got to win this election first,' Maeve said.

'She'll walk it,' Mrs Vincent said. 'Like she says, it's destiny.'

Rory stuck it for about an hour, then he slipped away through the side door.

'What's the matter with your brother?' Mrs Donovan asked. 'He's a face on him like a cow licking piss off a nettle.'

'He's all right,' Maeve said. 'He's just gone home to get the party stuff ready for tonight.'

'Oh, that's good,' Mrs Donovan said and turned to us with a big grin. 'Now who wants a nice bubbly glass of lemonade?'

We watched as Mother was carried past by a large group of supporters who were chanting her name. It was like Cleopatra's entrance into Rome, except for Dessie O'Hanlon who was running alongside, holding onto Mother's hand and kissing it. With her free hand, Mother blew us a kiss.

'See you at the party,' she shouted.

The returning officer tapped the microphone for quiet.

'Therefore I declare Kathleen Buck –'

A roar as big as the sea erupted in the hall.

'– ley of Fianna Fail to be elected.'

Our new life began in an explosion of banners, flags, streamers and hats. Maeve pointed to a pair of men's underpants that was dangling from one of the chandeliers.

'Well, I betcha that's something that never happened to The Beatles,' Rory said.

A line of people surged through the room, dancing, singing, cat-calling, chanting. Maeve kept jumping up and down.

'My mother's a TD, my mother's a TD.'

Even Rory was agog. 'I always knew she was going to win.'

For a week after Mother was elected, neither Maeve nor I went to school or even phoned in an excuse. Our Mother was a TD and that was all that mattered in the world. The exhilaration of being swept up in Mother's new life meant that we couldn't sleep, couldn't eat properly, couldn't think about anything except Mother. People came up to us to shake our hands and tell us what an amazing woman we had for a mother.

'Mother, are we middle class now?' Maeve asked.

Mother put down her cup of tea and gazed at us, 'We don't need to put a label on ourselves. You just limit yourself that way. I work for a living. I pay my way. It doesn't bother me if they call me working class or middle class.' Mother laughed, 'Just as long as they don't call me a Fine Gaeler.'

Mr Wolkenski brought all his pupils together in the same class. There were fifteen of us, all ages. I noticed one man who must have been in his seventies sitting between a fat middle-aged housewife and a child of six. We each had to prepare a two-minute speech to deliver on the following Saturday, which would be the final afternoon of lessons. The speeches would be made in a room at the back of Wynn's Hotel in Dublin. All of our relatives and friends would be invited. The speech could be about anything we wished. It would be the final nail in the coffin of our speech impediments.

'Spech is ver important, only yor own verds,' Mr Wolkenski said. 'Yor own verds, own verds,' he said to each person in turn in case there was anyone who hadn't copped on.

When I couldn't think of a topic for my speech, I consulted Maeve.

'Write about being the son of a politician,' she suggested. 'I bet nobody else could deliver a speech on that.'

'That's a brilliant idea.'

Mother promised to come along on Saturday. We decided to keep the subject of the speech a secret from her. I wanted it to be a surprise as she sat in the audience. I wanted her to be proud of me.

'I'm looking forward to your speech, Daniel. What's it called?'

'Eh, it's ca-called, "Yes, there is life after a stutter".'

'Very good. I'm rearing a family of politicians.'

I worked on my speech on the bus to school, at lunchtime, in my bedroom at night before going to sleep. At home, I rehearsed in the mirror. Sometimes I practised on strangers on the bus.

'Hello, it's a fa-fine day, isn't it? I see United won again la-last night.'

Most of the people I talked to simply stared out the window. I didn't mind. It was enough that I was instigating conversations for the first time in my life. I became fired up with excitement and enthusiasm. I got my only suit cleaned and pressed. I picked all the blackheads out of my face. I began to feel like a real person instead of the family dummy.

On the day of my speech, I came downstairs in my suit, my hair slicked back with a handful of Rory's Brylcreem. Maeve said I looked like James Dean's younger brother. Mother was on the phone talking to Dessie O'Hanlon.

'What's the matter with your hair?' Rory asked.

When the phone call was over, Mother took me aside.

'Daniel, I am *very* sorry. Something has come up. I wish it could be cancelled, put off or dodged but it can't, not even for something as important as your first stutter-free public speech. I know you'll be brilliant. Maeve and Rory will have to tell me all about it when I get home tonight. Maybe you could deliver it again, just for me.'

The excitement went out of me like air from a punctured tyre. I watched Mother wave goodbye and leave the house. Mrs Donovan was going to drive everyone in and bring us all back again. I heard Mother's car start up and rumble off. Into my line of vision came Mrs Donovan's face. She smiled at me. For a moment, I thought she was going to ask Maeve how I was feeling.

Wynn's Hotel was full of farmers because there was an agricultural show on in the RDS. Everywhere we went, men were propped in corners discussing tractors and silage. It took us twenty minutes to find the room. In the end, I made the speech with a few stammers and a mammoth pile-up every time I came to the word 'politician'. Rory and Maeve and Mrs Donovan and a hundred or so people I had never seen before gave me a big round of applause as they did to every other one of the day's speechmakers. Later, I found out that the audience had been composed of relatives of the present class as well as people who had been cured by Mr Wolkenski. At the end, I didn't feel happy or proud. I felt numb, as though I had achieved nothing. Even when Mr Wolkenski came up to me afterwards to shake my hand, I had a hollow feeling inside. It didn't make any difference that for the first time since I had begun his classes, Mr Wolkenski smiled. He was so happy that I could see clearly the different shades of pink that separated his gums from his false teeth.

'Gut, ver gut. You gut buoy,' he said. 'I vill zee you again nex term.'

When Mother got home, I refused to talk to her. At first she tried to cuddle me and make me recite my speech for her, but when I wouldn't respond she grew serious.

'Daniel, I've explained what happened. If that's not good enough for you then I'm just very sorry.'

Mother took the others into the kitchen to show them her new publicity photographs. I sat in the front room watching television but I could still hear their voices.

'They took a long time to do but I think it was worth it,' Mother said.

Maeve was ecstatic, 'They're wonderful.'

'You look like . . . you look like,' Rory began.

'I know,' Mother said. 'I look like *her*, but sure there it is, I can't help the way I look, can I?'

'You're much better looking than Liz Taylor, Mother,' Maeve gushed. 'The photos are still wonderful.'

When Mother and the others came into the front room to watch television, I wandered out to the kitchen. The photographs lay on the table, glossy, black and white portraits that showed Mother posed on a chair, dark eyes gazing at a spot above and to the right of the camera.

Without thinking, I put the photographs under my

jumper and sneaked out of the house, leaving the front door on the latch. I ran down to the harbour and out onto the east pier. It was a tantalising, wicked feeling to have Mother nestling between my jumper and my skin. It was as though I had her in my power to do with as I liked.

In the glow of the shore lights, I removed the photographs from under my jumper, tore them in half and flung them into the dark waters. I experienced a delicious mixture of guilt and euphoria. My only regret was that it was too dark to watch the torn halves of Mother float away.

FIVE

Desperate Dan

THE DOG IS on the edge of the runway. It is lying on the grassy verge with its tongue out watching the planes landing and taking off. Five ship inspectors and ten baggage handlers plus a couple of airport security men are in the process of surrounding it. The dog appears perfectly happy. It doesn't seem to be in a hurry to go anywhere.

I am closest. Another step and I will be within jumping range. The dog still isn't interested in me. My heart is pounding. As soon as the dog is looking in the opposite direction, I will jump on it. The trick will be to hold onto it until the others arrive. What if it bites me? Which part of me will it go for? I cover my crotch with my hand. Behind me, I hear a scuffle of feet.

'Go easy now, Big Balls,' says a voice at my ear. 'Grey-hounds can be fierce.'

Chasing a vagrant dog around a runway is not standard ship inspector practice. In fact, in my time at the airport, I have only heard of it happening once before. On that occasion, six years ago, a terrier escaped from a damaged dog-box and spent two hours on a hangar roof before it was caught. It took a breast of chicken to coax it down. In the light of this incident, Frank Nails wrote a memo to Chief Magaw recommending that breasts of chicken should become standard issue for ship inspectors. You could never tell when one might be necessary, he wrote. All that was required was an office fridge. Magaw wrote back that a fridge in an office of ship inspectors was unthinkable. Breasts of chicken could be fetched from the canteen, should the need ever again arise. However, he commended Nails for his initiative.

Before the crisis, there was just one flight on the ground, a British Midlands from Manchester. Nothing else was due for half an hour. Old Brendan Toombs doddled out to check the baggage hold on the British Midlands. The rest of us except for Frank Nails, gathered around *Pure Lust*, a pornographic magazine that Dominic Root had seized in the Departure lounge toilets. Today, Chief Magaw was not due in until teatime. The Minister of Agriculture was coming in on a flight from Brussels at seven. Magaw wanted to be on hand to front the honour guard of ship inspectors that would line up in the Arrivals hall to greet him. The Minister was new. All we knew about him was that he was ugly and wore thick round glasses. Magaw had issued instructions that those on duty should make sure that their uniforms were clean and neatly pressed. Dominic Root had been put on the morning shift which meant he would finish work at four.

'Do you think I'll lose any sleep just because that bitch doesn't want me to meet the Minister?' Dominic Root said. 'You must be coddin' me. Granny can fuckin' well have the Minister all to herself. I'll be in the Ivy House slurpin' on big creamy pints when youse are all lined up like fuckin' traffic bollards.'

I am still a junior ship inspector and therefore not entitled to a uniform. This is only my fourth year as a full-timer. A ship inspector has to be on permanent staff for at least seven years before he gets a black uniform and a white-tipped peaked cap. As a junior ship inspector, I wear a Department of Agriculture armband. Magaw had left me a reminder to get my armband cleaned.

This morning, first thing, I took my armband into the passengers' toilets opposite the office and scrubbed it with a bar of green airport soap. When Carla's face floated into my mind, I scrubbed harder. Last night, Carla came home with a kitten that Donald Logan gave to her as a present. The kitten's name is Mr Poopy and the first thing it did was to attack my bare feet. Carla thinks Mr Poopy is cute, but I've told her that I want it out of the place by the time I get home tonight. There we were yelling at each other as Mr Poopy watched us with big eyes. Then Carla rang Donald and told him she was sorry but she was going to have to return the kitten. I slept on the sofa and Carla slept in the bed with Mr Poopy. I think we were both surprised to find ourselves fighting over a kitten, but a row had been brewing ever since Carla got back from London. I still haven't forgiven her for being three days late. She says I'm being too possessive and I need to be more flexible.

I am not going to phone her. I am sick of my life revolving around phone calls to Carla. I am going to be strong.

I scrubbed the armband like a maniac until her face went out of my mind. The moment I came out of the toilets, Dominic Root came up to me, wearing an inscrutable, officious expression.

'Excuse me sir, have you visited a farm on this trip?' Then he feigned surprise, 'Oh, it's you, Daniel. Well, goodness fuckin' me, I didn't recognise you in your new uniform.'

'Someone get me a pair of sunglasses,' Frank Nails said. 'Your man's uniform is blinding me.'

'Christ, boy, I'd say that's the most impressive armband we've ever had here,' said Desperate Dan. 'Sure you could almost send it out to inspect a plane by itself.'

'Eh, very nice, you know, whatever,' Harry Dunne said, pointing vaguely in the direction of my arm but smiling at Dominic Root.

My gleaming armband provided the morning's main source of amusement until the discovery of *Pure Lust*.

Dominic Root turned the pages of the magazine, pointing at pictures of naked women and going 'ak-ak-ak'. We roared. Frank Nails sat in the armchair under the flight monitor screen and looked disgusted. He folded his *Independent*. 'You sound like a barnyard. You should be ashamed of yourselves.'

Everyone ignored him.

'I took a look at one of those yokes once,' Nails continued stuffily. 'I may not be an expert on anatomy but I know God did not put man on earth so that he could place his private parts into a woman's mouth.'

Dominic Root looked at him, 'I agree with you.'

Frank Nails was mystified, 'You agree with me?'

'Of course, I think every man should keep his private parts where they belong – in his right hand.'

Everyone roared. Root's 'ak-ak' went off and we were roaring again.

'There's nothing funny about pornography,' Nails shouted over the din. 'It's a good job I haven't a hurley handy.'

That was when Old Brendan Toombs burst through the wails of laughter to say that there was a dog loose on the runway. We rushed out of the office, skidded on the polished white tiling of the empty Arrivals hall and scrambled for the sliding doors to the tarmac. Frank Nails made for the canteen.

'I'll get the breast of chicken,' he shouted.

On the tarmac, we ran smack into a wall of noise from the jet engines. For a moment, we milled around like ancient bachelors at a marriage fair. Old Brendan Toombs had to roar to be heard over the noise.

'The box fell off the belt and it got out. I think it bit one of the handlers.'

Desperate Dan put his nose to Old Brendan Toombs' glasses, 'Christ, boy, I don't care how it got out, I just want to know where it is now.'

A few hundred yards ahead, the dog ambled gracefully across the tarmac in front of a taxiing Boeing 797. We could make out the pilot waving at it to get out of the way. As we watched, the dog trotted to the side of the runway and flopped down on the runway's grassy verge. It lay there, tongue lolling, watching the plane go past. Desperate Dan spat on his hands, strode forward like a sergeant in the Marines.

'Right boys, let's do it,' he shouted.

Fifteen minutes later, we had the dog surrounded. There was still no sign of Nails with the breast of chicken.

'He must have had to catch the fuckin' chicken first,' Dominic Root said.

Before this, the most exciting thing to have happened in the history of ship inspecting was the great foot and mouth epidemic of 1969. The disease broke out in England and thousands of cattle had to be destroyed. Ship inspectors at the airport, Dublin Docks and at every other port in the country had gone into overdrive to prevent the disease reaching Ireland. Planes and boats were checked and double-checked, private yachts were boarded and inspected, meat and animal smugglers were caught and punished and the animals either put down or sent back to the country of origin. The sole of virtually every shoe to touch Irish soil had to be doused in disinfectant, irrespective of whether or not it had been on a farm. Ship inspectors worked long hours, disinfected millions of shoes, interviewed thousands of people, apprehended, quarantined, sent back or destroyed many more thousands of animals. In the end, the threat to Irish beef was averted. Foot and mouth stayed in England. The ship inspectors not only saved Ireland from a plague that would have cost millions and been the ruin of many a farmer, they also managed to detect half a dozen drug smugglers, a couple of runaway teenagers and a stowaway who had been living on frozen caviare for months in the hold of a Russian freighter. The older ship inspectors such as Desperate Dan, Old Brendan Toombs and Chief Magaw, still talked of the crisis as if it had happened just the other day. The pride in their voices gave it historical importance. They made it sound so glamorous. They saw themselves as battle-scarred veterans who had saved Ireland from a disaster worse than the Great Famine.

'You'd never know when we might be needed again,' Desperate Dan warned.

The greyhound is licking its paws.

I take a step closer. The dog looks up at me. There is

love in its eyes, as if it thinks I am its master come to claim it. It expression reminds me of Mrs Lally, my old neighbour, who came in on a flight from London last week. I saw her coming down the escalator but, before I could turn away, she waved. She was delighted to see me after all this time. We made small-talk for a few minutes. Mother, Maeve and Rory were all fine I told her, along with all the usual nonsense. Before she left, she gave my hand a squeeze.

'It's great to see how much you've improved,' she said.

Harry Dunne approaches on the dog's blind side with a muzzle and leash. In a couple of seconds, Harry Dunne is behind the dog. Poised with his tongue out and his brow corrugated, he attempts to measure the distance between the muzzle in his hands and the dog's head. It is a shock to see him so animated. He looks as though he is either about to pounce on the greyhound or suffer a heart attack.

The dog seems unaware that it is about to be captured. As everyone begins to close in, taking small tentative steps, careful not to make any sudden moves, I realise that this is my chance. If I capture the dog, I will cement my place in ship inspector history. I will no longer be Daniel Buckley, junior ship inspector, I'll be Daniel Buckley, captor of the greyhound who escaped on runway seven. I may not be able to compete with the great foot and mouth crisis of '69, but at least I will cease to be Daniel Buckley with the bit of a stutter, the missing dad, and the mother who used to be a TD.

I zero in on the dog's hind legs. Please God, don't let it bite me. I am just about to throw myself at the dog when someone brushes past to step onto the grassy verge.

'Stand aside, Big Balls,' Desperate Dan says.

The dog looks at Desperate Dan. Dan kneels and makes a clucking sound in his throat.

'Here, boy. That's a grand lad now.'

The dog gets up, trots the few yards over to him. Dan pets its head, ruffles it under the neck, chats to it as if it is his own dog. Everyone is astonished. The dog lies down at Dan's feet.

I have blown it. To get at the dog now, I will have to

leapfrog over Dan. If I try that, I will probably get tangled up with Dan and scare away the dog. If I'm lucky, the dog will bite Dan's leg off.

While Dan is distracting the dog, Harry Dunne steals up behind. With a deft movement, he slips the muzzle over the dog's head. The dog doesn't bark, doesn't try to run, doesn't do anything much except gaze lovingly at Desperate Dan.

'Now, there we are,' Harry Dunne says.

When Harry Dunne leads the dog away, it goes quietly. Dan puffs himself up, and is immediately seized by a sudden spasm of coughing. When he is finishing coughing into his fist, he grins at me.

'Now, bet you didn't know I used to be a champion greyhound breeder, did you?'

Just as the dog is being put into the back of an airport security van, Frank Nails comes lumbering up with a breast of chicken in a clear plastic bag. Dominic Root is waiting for him.

'You're too late,' he shouts. 'It decided to have the roast duck instead. Ak-ak-ak.'

At lunchtime, Dan insists on bringing me upstairs to the Sky High Lounge. He orders a club orange for himself and a pint and a sandwich for me. He likes to treat me from time to time. I think it gives him a sense of superiority. The capture of the greyhound appears to have jogged his mind back to the great foot and mouth crisis of '69.

'Christ, boy, it was the real thing. I didn't get a wink of sleep for two weeks. A soft Dublin lad like you wouldn't have lasted a day.'

Desperate Dan can be irritating and dogmatic. He occasionally, deliberately breaks wind and giggles like a schoolboy. But I find him a lot less objectionable than Chief Magaw or Frank Nails or even Dominic Root who is great company but whose constant 'ak-aking' can get on your nerves. I watch Dan sip his club orange. He doesn't drink any more, he says.

'It wasn't doing me any good so I gave it up before it gave me up.'

He seems to get as much pleasure from watching me drink a black, creamy pint of stout as I get from drinking it. After his great success capturing the runaway greyhound, Dan is all prattle about what makes a great ship inspector. His latest theory is that great ship inspectors are made, not born. I would hate to see Dan if he ever captured a runaway elephant.

'It's the kind of job that you have to work at. A ship inspector needs to learn three things – are ye listening to me, boy? He needs to be vigilant; he needs to pay attention to detail; and, most of all, he needs to have a good bullshit detection meter. Once he has these, he's halfway home.'

I am glad that Dan has forced me to go to lunch with him. If he hadn't, I probably would have gone off someplace on my own and ended up by phoning Carla. I have managed to block her out of my mind all day, but now I am feeling a little frayed. Why doesn't Carla phone me? It is up to her to apologise.

Dan is in the middle of telling me why a good ship inspector should always carry a supply of peppermints when he suddenly begins to cough. When he finishes coughing, he takes out his hanky, gives his lips and chin a rub and stares out the window at the planes taking off. Just as I am about to ask about the connection between ship inspecting and peppermints, Dan suddenly reaches in his top pocket and pulls out a ten pound note. He thrusts the note into my hand.

'Now, what do you think of that, Big Balls?'

'It's a tenner.'

'No, Big Balls, it's an alarm clock.'

'Why are you giving it to me?'

'I'm not giving it to you, I'm showing it to you. There's a big difference.'

'It still looks like a tenner to me.'

'Does it now?'

'What else would it be?'

'You tell me. Take a good look.'

I hold it up to the light to see if there is a watermark. There is. I crumple it in my hand to see if it will flake or fall apart. It doesn't.

'Just a tenner,' I say.

Dan's sullen, sunken-cheeked face suddenly cracks into a rare smile. Either he is delighted with me or he is confirmed in his original impression that I am an imbecile. It is difficult to tell. Even in his more accessible moods, Dan often bears a startling resemblance to Grumpy from *Snow White and the Seven Dwarfs*. In the Arrivals hall, I have often noticed young children pointing out Dan to their mothers. Once, a little girl even approached him for an autograph.

Dan likes to think that he is always one step ahead of most people, including younger ship inspectors and especially Dubliners. He has a simple philosophy: everything that comes from Kerry is wonderful, everything that comes from Dublin is rubbish. According to Dan, most good film and rock stars have their origins in Kerry.

'Jack Nicholson? His grandmother was a Sneem woman. Mick Jagger? Sure I knew his uncle well.'

Once he told me that David Bowie was from Kerry. When I said I didn't believe him, he looked at me in horror.

'Bowie's an ancient Kerry name. Go down and check the parish register if you don't believe me. His people are from Dingle.'

It has become an unwritten rule of ship inspecting that Dan can claim Kerry origins for whoever he wants without fear of contradiction.

I hand him back the tenner. He puts it in his pocket as he gazes out at a Jumbo taking off.

'My son makes them. He gives me sackfuls and I don't know how to spend them.'

'You mean he works in the mint or something?'

'No, Big Balls, I mean that he makes ten pound notes.'

'You mean he's a forger?'

Dan looks at me, 'My son is an artist.'

'Your son makes tenners.'

Dan sighs, 'You know why? Because they're easy to spend. Other fellas make fifties and hundreds and get caught. My boy is really clever. He's been doing it for years and nobody has ever copped on.'

I don't trust Dan. He is always trying to catch me out. But I am intrigued by the idea of his son as an expert counterfeiter. I decide to humour him. 'Well, it fa-fooled me. Do you think he'd give me a few? You know, just for myself.'

'He might.'

'How many would he give me?'

'He's a bit peculiar about who he gives these yokes to.'

'How m-m-much does he give you every week?'

'Christ, boy, that would be telling.'

'Well, how about giving me that one in your pocket.'

Dan smiles a rueful smile, 'Ah no. I've plans for that. Sure it has to get us the next round. Wait till Monday, Big Balls. I'll see what I can do.'

Dan calls the lounge boy and orders another pint of Guinness and a club orange.

'I don't want another pint, I have to go back to work.'

Dan insists, 'Shut up, boy, you're getting a pint. You don't even have to put your hand in your pocket. Sure, what are you worried about?'

I give up. A little later, my pint arrives. Dan stretches. He gets a great kick out of making loud cricking and stretching noises, pretending that his bones are unknotting themselves. Then he gazes into the distance sadly, as if all the fun has gone from things now that he has told me about the tenners. We drink in silence.

After lunch, I say goodbye to Dan and head back to work.

'See you later, Big Balls.'

Before I leave the bar, something makes me turn around. Dan is still sitting where I have left him, gazing out at the airport, his expression vacant, scrawny ankles showing above his pink socks. His face is at once dreamlike and alert as though he is watching television with the sound off. I realise that I have forgotten to ask about the peppermints.

Frank Nails is on his knees trying to convince the statistics girls, Donna and Polly, to sit down beside us on the red plastic seats. He is particularly anxious for Donna to join him. Donna and Polly are amused. They hold their statistics folders and look at each other. Donna looks at her watch.

'I don't know. We've got all these questionnaires to give out. There's a stack more in the office for tomorrow.'

'Don't mind him, Donna,' Dominic Root says. 'He's only on the scout for a missus.'

'Ladies, once again I'm extending you an invitation to pass the time of day with some lonely ship inspectors.'

'As long as that's all you're extending,' Dominic Root says. 'Ak-ak-ak.'

Polly giggles. Donna pretends to be shocked, 'Oh Dominic, that's awful. How could you?'

'You have to watch yourself with that fella, girls,' Dominic Root says. 'You should have seen what he was doing in the office this morning, shouldn't they, Harry?'

'Whatever,' Harry says vaguely.

Frank Nails gets to his feet and scowls at Dominic Root, 'I'd like to apologise for the company some of us are forced to keep.' He turns to Donna again, 'Come on, sit down just for a few minutes.'

'OK,' Donna shrugs. 'We can spare a few minutes.'

Donna sees me coming and waves, 'Hello, Daniel. How's it going?'

'Hi,' I say. 'It's going fine.'

Polly and Donna sit down beside Dominic and the others. Donna gives the seat beside her a wipe and motions for me to join her. I sit down beside her. All the seats are now taken. Frank Nails can't believe it. He stands in front of us with his hands on his hips.

'Well, I like that. That's just lovely, that is,' he says.

'It's all right, dear, you can sit on my knee,' Dominic says and the others laugh as Frank turns around to stride back to the office.

'Here, Frank, there's room beside me, if you like,' Polly says, making space on her seat.

Frank Nails' voice floats back, 'It's all right, I'll get a chair in the office.'

Donna is dressed in a red jumpsuit. She has an attractive,

133

friendly face with clear green eyes. Desperate Dan says that she's forty if she's a day. Today, though, she looks younger. I notice that her red hair is tied up with a coloured ribbon.

'Your ha-hair's nice.'

Donna touches her hair, smiles, 'Oh thank you, Daniel.' She turns to the others, 'You see, chivalry is not dead. It lives on in the younger generation.'

Donna turns to me, 'You had a bit of excitement this morning.'

'Oh yeah, the greyhound. Dan caught it.'

'I know, I was watching from my window upstairs. I don't think there's been that much drama around here for years.'

'Since the fa-fa-foot and mouth epidemic of 1969.'

'Probably. I wasn't here then.'

For a moment, I wonder if Donna is going to slag me about my failure to grab the dog while I had the chance. Then I realise that Donna is not like that. Ever since I have known her, she has been encouraging and friendly towards me. Donna is one of the few people I know who never says a bad word about anyone, not even about Dominic Root.

'How's Carla?'

'She's fa-fine.'

'That's good.'

I suddenly feel an urge to confide in Donna. Even though I am aware that it is early afternoon at the airport and that there are four other ship inspectors as well as Polly, the Stats girl, sitting on the red plastic seats outside the office plus at least four plane loads of passengers due to descend into the Arrivals lobby at any moment, I suddenly find myself looking into Donna's green eyes. I urgently need her to like me, to find me sincere, engaging, even desirable. I want her to make things better.

'Donna?'

'Yes, Daniel.'

'Actually, well I . . .' I clear my throat. 'Carla and I have been going through a bit of a rough pa-pa –'

'There we are,' Frank Nails plonks a wooden chair on the

floor, in front of us. He ignores me and gives Donna a huge grin.

'Now, Donna, what's the story. Did you buy yourself that second-hand car yet?'

'Not yet, Frank.'

'I don't know how anyone can live in this city without a motor. I'll help you check one out if you want.'

Dominic Root leans over, 'Watch yourself, Donna. He might show you his hurley stick.'

'Thanks, I'll watch myself,' Donna says calmly. 'By the way, Dominic, I'd like to offer my congratulations.'

Dominic is perturbed, 'For what?'

'Well, I believe today was the second time in fifteen years that you actually made it onto the tarmac.'

The explosion of raucous laughter that follows brings the Customs guys out into the lobby to see what is going on. When they see that it's only the ship inspectors they go back behind their corner. Dominic Root doesn't give one of his 'ak-ak-ak's. Instead he smiles sweetly.

'I'll get you back for that, Donna,' he says.

To be polite, I wait a few moments. Then I get up and wander inside to look at the flight monitor. There are five flights down. I check my armband and go out to the sliding doors.

'Daniel,' a voice calls.

I look back in time to see Donna's hand rise slowly over Frank Nails's head like a belly-dancer's snake to give me a wave.

As I wander between planes on the tarmac, I think about Carla. This time, I don't try to block her out.

Carla and I have a brilliant relationship except that we never have sex any more.

When we first began living together, we had sex at least once a night, sometimes twice. Carla loved to get on top and shout and often lost herself so completely that I sometimes felt like a spectator at our own lovemaking.

After a year though, sex between us fell away. We sort of got out of the habit. I think that we've had sex half a dozen times in the past two years.

Now we have cuddles instead. Carla says we're going through a 'bonding stage'. She says that our sex life will be reactivated when we buy a house.

'It's no harm. Most couples experience a period of calm. We just have to work our way through it.'

A couple of years ago, I read about 'Red Sex' in a magazine. 'Red Sex' happens when the sexual chemistry between two people is too strong for the bounds of ordinary behaviour. It is when people suddenly have to have each other there and then. Sex between them is wild, passionate, abandoned, dangerous, on the edge, glorious and wonderful. Men and women who have just met have been known to throw off their clothes in crowded restaurants in broad daylight and make love there and then on top of a table. Couples do it in lifts, in offices, at the movies, even in the toilet of an aeroplane.

I saw a couple fucking each other's brains out up against one of the speakers at The Clash concert in Trinity a few years ago. When they finished, the crowd gave them a bigger round of applause than the band.

The most exotic place that Carla and I have ever made love was on the floor in the apartment. Once I got excited because I thought Carla was tearing at my behind with her nails until I discovered that I was lying on one of her cactus plants.

I keep thinking there is something wrong with me because I have never experienced 'Red Sex'.

A large jumbo, engines screaming, crosses a runway ahead of me. After Carla and I make up, perhaps I will bring her out here to the airport one night. We will sneak aboard a jumbo and make love in the cockpit. Maybe I can borrow a couple of uniforms.

First, though, the kitten must go.

The Minister of Agriculture's flight is on the ground.

Frank Nails, Desperate Dan, Harry Dunne, Old Brendan Toombs and I are lined up at the bottom of the escalator watching for the first sign of the Ministerial entourage. Passengers stream down the escalator and stare at the six of

136

us standing there. Nobody comes in to get their shoes sprayed.

Chief Magaw is standing in front. He waddles across to the baggage belts and back again, never taking his eyes off the escalator or relaxing the smile on his face. He reminds me of the class swot who can't wait to get into the new teacher's good books. Frequently, he is forced to get out of the way of incoming passengers which makes his grin appear even more strained. I try not to catch his eye. He has sent me over to the incinerator twice in the last hour.

'Keep an ear out for the phone now,' he says. 'Shout if you hear it.'

We don't look like much of an honour guard. Desperate Dan is so hunched up that he gives the impression that his head has retracted into his body. Old Brendan Toombs, who Dominic Root swears is in his seventies, tilts alarmingly to the right now and again as if about to topple. I notice that his eyes are closed. Customs men, baggage handlers, airport security guards and passengers barge through our lines from the sliding doors behind us with distressing frequency. If nothing else, tonight's experience is an excellent demonstration of how difficult it is to keep an honour guard of ship inspectors in line when the airport is busy.

Magaw suddenly rushes in the direction of the toilets, 'I'll be back in a minute,' he says. 'If the Minister arrives tell him to hang on.'

Everyone relaxes. Desperate Dan hands me a packet of peppermints.

'Oh yeah,' I say, 'what are these for?'

Dan winks, beckons me closer. I lean over, thinking I am going to hear one of his dirty jokes.

'It's so you'll never have breath like this, boy. *Ha!*'

Dan blows a blast of rancid breath into my face. I recoil as if shot. Dan skips around behind the red plastic seats, grinning like an elf. The other ship inspectors, obviously in on the joke, shriek like baboons. I decide to ignore Dan for the rest of the evening.

'Any sign?' Magaw asks anxiously when he returns.

'Not a squeak,' Dan says, looking at me with a glint in

his eye. 'Christ, the air is very bad in here. We'll have to get a fan or something.'

A group of noisy passengers begin their decent.

'He's bound to be with this lot,' Frank Nails says.

There are flights from Leeds, Manchester, Tenerife and London. Within seconds, the Arrivals lobby is jammed. People mill around the baggage belts, searching for suitcases. They ram each other with trolleys. A small, lost girl wails for her mammy, who comes running. More passengers stream off the escalator and come through the sliding doors from the tarmac.

A large, ungainly woman with red, curly hair looks up at the Department of Agriculture sign. She breaks off from the crowd from the Leeds flight and approaches me.

'Have you been on a farm?' I say.

The woman nods. Without looking too closely at her, I escort her to the office. She stands on the mat and lifts a high heel as I fetch the sprayer. Usually I give the sprayer a few test runs against the floor mat but this time I forget. When I press the lever, a dense shower of liquid soaks the woman's dress and tights as well as her high heels. She lets out a loud, rough roar, like a footballer yelling at a referee. It is definitely not a voice that is usually associated with a high-heeled, well-groomed fortyish woman or indeed any woman.

'Look at my blooming tights,' a man's voice says. 'You've bloody well ruined them.'

'I'm very sorry.'

The woman whips off her red head of hair, and sighs. Then she sits down on a chair and stares at me in misery. Her face crumples into that of a middle-aged man wearing rouge and mascara. The man is wearing a flowered dress that clings to his large frame. He does not look as though he wants to be a woman any more.

'Oh bloody hell, I can't keep this up,' he says in a gnarled, Yorkshire voice. 'It's been one 'eck of a bloody dreadful day.'

I am about to ask if he is OK when he breaks down in front of me. I feel guilty for drenching him. I am also confused to find myself alone in the office with a crazy person.

'I've been doin' this for years and this is the first time it's all gone wrong. The wife would kill me if she found out. I wouldn't 'ave come in here at all except I'm a farmer and when I saw the bloody sign I just didn't bloody think, did I?'

He looks at me and I nod. I realise I am clutching the sprayer in my hands in case he makes any sudden moves. Before I can say anything, he is gabbling at me as if I'm his psychologist.

'I'm probably the first transvestite you've met.'

I nod.

'I thought so. I thought I'd the whole business all worked out. Every few months I take a trip, as a woman, to Dublin because over 'ere nobody knows me. I always change in the men's toilets in Heathrow. First my underwear started killing me. Then, I trip on the bloody stairs and wreck me knee – it's bloody crucifying me. Now this.'

Looking miserable, he squeezes some of the liquid out of the hem of his dress. He puts his head down and his shoulders shake as a succession of long, soft sobs escapes him.

'I knew I shouldn't 'ave come. I was pushin' my luck.'

'Would you like a gla-glass of water?'

He suddenly stops sobbing and stares at me wide-eyed.

'You won't tell anyone, will you? I swear I'll never wear one of these bloody things again. They've brought me nothing but bloody grief.'

'No, I won't. I don't even know your na-name anyway,' I add, hoping it will cheer him up.

He smiles, grabs my hand and starts shaking it, 'Thanks, mate, I won't bloody forget this.'

I am trying to diplomatically extract my hand from his grasp when a shadow falls across us from the doorway. I look up to see the faces of Chief Magaw, Desperate Dan and a man I take to be the Minister staring down at us. Harry Dunne is trying to squeeze in for a look. I pull my hand away and stand up.

'And this is the spraying room,' I hear Chief Magaw saying. 'That's Daniel Buckley there, eh, spraying a passen . . .' his voice trails off. 'Eh, spraying a passenger.'

The Minister takes off his glasses. The transvestite farmer, suddenly aware that there are people in the doorway, rises swiftly to his feet, plops the red-haired wig back on his head and suddenly becomes brisk.

'Thank you, young man, you've been a great help. Excuse me.'

The farmer makes his way past the Minister and the other ship inspectors in the doorway and out into the Arrivals hall. Desperate Dan is looking at me with an amused smile. He is still there when Magaw and the Minister leave to continue the Minister's tour.

'Christ, boy, that's the last time I ever let you look at those peculiar magazines,' he says.

Carla is curled up on the sofa. A tiny orange and white face peeps at me from under her arm.

'Hi, Groover,' she says. 'Mr Poopy, look who's here.'

She puts down the kitten that Donald Logan bought her. The creature looks at me for a moment, then it attacks one of Carla's plants.

'I thought you said you were going to get ra-rid of it.'

'I changed my mind,' Carla says. 'Daniel, I think you're over-reacting. It's only a kitten, for God's sake.'

I look at the kitten. Now it has its claws stuck in a Ray Bradbury paperback. I notice a small puddle of discoloured water on the kitchen floor.

'I thought Donald agreed to take it back.'

'Oh, Daniel, I can't, it was a present. Look at it. It's just a teenchy weenchy kitten. It can't possibly do any harm to anyone.'

Something in Carla's off-hand manner gives me an urge to be wicked, 'If it rips any more of my album covers I'm going to have it pa-put down.'

Carla's mouth falls open, 'Put down?' She stares at me as if I am a murderer. 'Put down? Daniel, what's the matter with you?'

'Nothing. I hate ca-ca-cats.'

Carla points a long finger at me, 'If you *touch* this kitten, I'll never speak to you again.'

'Fa-fine.'

I sit down in front of the television and switch it on. For an hour, Carla plays with Mr Poopy while I blank my mind with television. When I am angry or frustrated, I find that the most efficient method of calming myself is by watching crappy programmes. The crappier the programme, the more I unwind. If I am really angry, it can be hours before I realise what I am watching. It goes back to my days as a chronic stutterer when I found it a lot easier to watch television than to talk. After a little while, I realise that I am watching 'Gardener's World'. I am aware of the kitten launching a surprise attack on Carla's cactus, but I ignore it. It is Carla's plant, not mine. If it comes near me, I will stamp on its tail.

'Don't you want to want to know what I did today or are you going to stay mad at me all night?' Carla asks.

I don't answer.

Carla continues in a reasonable voice, 'Well, this morning I painted that huge skull and crossbones backdrop for The Undertakers From Hell. And just before you came home, I finished designing the rhinestone studded trousers and Hawaiian shirts for The Amazing Fantasticks. What do you think of that?'

On 'Gardener's World', they are demonstrating the best method for replanting fuchsias. I tear myself away.

'That's very good,' I say.

'Yes, I thought so. Where's my "Congratulations, Carla"?'

'Congratulations, Carla.'

'Thank you.'

I am aware of Carla coming over behind me and slowly putting her arms around me. I can smell her perfume. She snuggles her nose into my neck and giggles. I try to remain stiff and unyielding. I want to stay mad at her. In a few seconds, I am giggling too.

'Oh, I've missed you, Groover,' she says.

'I've missed you too,' I say.

'Let's never fight like this again, it's stupid. Promise?'

'OK, I promise.'

'We used to never fight.'

'I know.'

'I love you, Groover.'

'I love you too, Carla.'

She climbs over the back of the sofa, into my lap. She stretches herself languorously before putting her lovely face next to mine. I am surprised at how oriental and mysterious her eyes are up close. She looks like a different person. We kiss.

'Daniel?'

'Yes?'

'It's just a teenchy weeny kitten. Can't we keep it till it grows up?'

SIX

The Vigil

THE STORM sloped into the town like a thief. It rattled the bells on the masts of *The Ave Maria*, *The Timbucktoo*, *Erin the Brave*, *The Last Chancer*, *The Aisling*, *The Sea Breeze* and rocked all the other boats at the harbour. It sent spits of rain into town on a fast breeze that splattered on windows and howled across the rooftops like an old dog.

'It'll be over by teatime,' Mrs Donovan said, in her smug know-all voice. 'It's just a squall.'

Even when sharp cracks of thunder pealed down the black sky over Redrock Mountain and lightning sizzled white and petrifying over Church Street, making the houses look like the ghosts of houses, most people thought that it would soon blow over. I had just turned sixteen. I thought I was too mature to be afraid of a storm but every time the wind howled or lighting flashed it made me tremble.

After dark, the storm strutted up Main Street, tearing television aerials from roofs and rolling bins down the streets like tumbleweeds. It flung a bin through the window of The Tall Ships, sending drinkers scrambling under a hail of glass and rain. At the harbour, it plucked a rowing-boat out of the boiling water and impaled it on the light-house railings. People walked home in slow motion against the wind with papers, wrappers and other rubbish plastered across their legs and bodies. Raindrops tumbled in the yellow haze of the street lamps like a multitude of sprites haunting the town.

By midnight, Mrs Donovan had shut all her windows and sealed the tops and bottoms of her doors.

Ulysses was wailing in the hallway. I heard the cat dragging itself down the hall to my bedroom. Pushing the door open, it glared at me with a pink eye. The other eye hung by a bloodied thread from its socket. Its mewling grew into a low growl. It seemed to blame me for the state it was in. It was about to leap at my face when the wind blew something over in the yard with a crash.

I woke up. Ulysses was nowhere in sight. The wounded mewling was now our phone which had been ringing for ages. The room smelt of stale beer. I heard Rory's soft breathing in the bed across from me.

A light went on across the landing. I heard Mother came out of her bedroom and shuffle down the stairs to the phone stand in the hall.

In the light from the landing, I saw Rory stir in the bed opposite, then sit upright. His blond hair stuck up. The soft light played on the top of his head as though he was wearing a halo. When he saw me looking at him, he cleared his throat as though about to say something, but then he thought better of it and looked away. Instead he coughed, flopped back down in the bed and pulled the covers up to his throat.

At midnight, the scrape of Rory's key in the lock had been engulfed by a sudden deep gush of howling, followed by a thud as the front door hit the wall. The wind rushed down the hall and up the stairs to our bedroom like a demon trying to get to Rory's bed before he did. Eventually, there was a series of grunts, followed by a slam and the wind was outside again. Rory squelched his way up the stairs. In the bedroom, he stood panting. I heard his wet greatcoat clump onto the floor. His jumper stuck on his head. Eventually he yanked it off, then fell into bed with his shoes on.

'Crap night,' I whispered.

'Shut your stupid fucking gob.'

Rory was in his final year at university and he lived in a basement flat in Rathmines. He came home at weekends or when his money ran out. He worked as a waiter and a barman to get money to live on. Mother paid his fees and helped with the rent. His exams were coming up but he seemed to have more interest in rehearsing with his new band. He kept saying that university produced bourgeois shites and he did not want to be a bourgeois shite for the rest of his days.

'I might not bother doing finals,' he said. 'An arts degree will be fuck-all use to me if I'm playing in a band.'

'You're crazy,' Maeve told him. 'Don't throw away three years of your life.'

Rory shrugged, 'I'll be on the road soon and then you'll never have to see me again.'

Downstairs, Mother murmured, as if praying. There was a sharp ding as the phone went back on its cradle. I knew from Mother's fast footsteps coming back up the stairs that it was bad news. I hoped that she would go back into her bedroom and keep whatever it was from us until morning. For a second, I wondered if it could be news about Dad. The light in our room came on, poking sudden fingers into our eyes.

'Manus Rock's boat is missing,' Mother said softly. 'Get dressed – quick as you can, please.'

She stood in the doorway for a moment, then turned and went out, the tangled cord of her green dressing gown dragging behind her. I heard her go back down the stairs to Maeve's room.

I got out of bed and searched for my clothes. The air was freezing against my flesh. My new jeans felt as though they had frost down each leg. Sea Dogs, they were called.

Manus and I had gone into town the previous Saturday to get them. Manus watched while I tried them on. In the shop mirror, the blue jeans went really well with my red shirt and yellow and black striped waistcoat. The flare was so wide it covered my shoes.

'The sharpest, coolest flares in Europe,' the man in the shop boasted. 'Sure the whole of Germany's wearing them.'

Manus had looked at my new jeans with mild amusement.

'What do you think?' I asked.

'You look like someone out of Deep Purple,' he announced finally, in that off-hand tone he used whenever he had to comment on something that he considered was beyond human understanding.

Outside on the street, I checked my reflection in every shop window I passed.

'I think the flare is too wide,' I said.

'Stop fretting,' Manus said.

'Maybe they make me look like a weekend hippy.'

'You look OK.'

'Why didn't you get yourself a pair?'

'You must be joking. I wouldn't be seen dead in a pair of those things.'

Manus gave me a lopsided smile and now the memory faded.

I finished dressing. Rory lay in bed, waiting until I left the room before beginning his own resurrection.

In the kitchen, Ulysses was curled up in a ball in the corner. I felt removed from events, as if all this was happening in a daydream. On the shelf, the clock on the American radio said 3 am. I was surprised to find it still working. Last Monday, in the middle of dinner, the radio had exploded. Everyone ducked as it shot off the shelf to shatter on the floor.

Rory shook his head, 'I'm not fixing that thing again.'

'Please, Rory, I'll pay you,' Mother said.

'No way,' Rory said, then he thought about it. 'Eh, how much?'

'A pound.'

'Fiver.'

Rory eventually fixed it for two pounds, although this time it took him the best part of a day. The radio now gave a continual low buzzing sound, even when it was switched off.

'That thing's a fire hazard, Mother,' Maeve said. 'We should throw it out.'

'I like it there,' Mother said. 'It gives me a good feeling in the mornings.'

146

Maeve leaned over to me and whispered, 'She thinks if she throws that out we'll never find out what happened to Dad.'

Outside, the wind moaned against the window. Dark shapes danced and flew. I wondered whether to put on the kettle, then I felt guilty. How could I think about breakfast when my best friend and his crewmates were missing at sea in the middle of a storm? I decided that there must be something wrong with me.

Mother came in, 'Where's the other fellow?'

'Getting up,' I said.

'We'll just have to wait, I suppose.'

Mother wore her blue trouser suit and grey blouse, beige raincoat draped loosely on her shoulders like an actress during a break. She filled a teacup with water and poured it into a plant. She refilled the glass and went across to take care of another plant.

In the euphoria following her election victory, Mother had forgotten to water her plants for weeks. Most of the plants died. She sat with each drooping or withered plant for a while then slowly and lovingly wrapped it in paper and put it in the bin. Nowadays, she was very careful about tending her plants.

Maeve padded in and sat on her favourite wooden chair in the corner. She brought her knees up under her and squatted like a tiny Buddha. The chair creaked under her. She adjusted her thick-rimmed glasses and stared at the floor. I noticed that she was clutching her red notebook and biro. She held the pen so tightly that her knuckles were white.

'You're not going to take notes, are you?'

'I don't feel like talking,' Maeve said without looking at me.

'Are you OK?' I said.

'Yes.'

After Maeve left school, Mother appointed her as her private secretary and chief speech writer. Maeve spent so much time going around with Mother that she began to dress like her, look like her, at times even talk like her.

Maeve didn't bother to look for a job or apply to college, 'I already have a job. Why should I look for another? Anyway, I've decided I'm going to be a TD someday.'

'You'll have to go to university first,' Mother said.

'Why? You didn't.'

'Ah, yes,' Mother said. 'But I'm different.'

Rory appeared in the doorway. His face was pale and stricken and his hair stood out as though he had just pulled his fingers out of a light socket.

'Anyone see my denim jacket?'

'Has anyone seen my denim jacket, *please*,' Mother corrected.

'Yeah, right,' Rory said. 'Well, has anyone?'

Rory stood slumped against the kitchen door. His eyes were open but the rest of him seemed to be out cold. Even from where I stood I could smell the drink off him. Nobody had seen his denim jacket.

'There's a vigil on the east pier,' Mother said. 'I want all of us to be strong and positive. We have a duty to the Rock family. We will stay as long as it takes, and we will do whatever has to be done, do I make myself clear?'

We all nodded.

'Good.' She looked at Rory. 'Brush your hair, please. I'm not going down with you looking like a scarecrow.'

'I'm all right,' Rory said.

'Rory, just do as I say, please.'

For a moment, I thought he was going to ignore her. But then he yawned, and went down the hall to the bathroom for his hairbrush.

'Coats and scarves, everyone,' Mother said. 'I want you all well wrapped.'

We got ready. When Rory returned, he looked exactly the same. He still seemed a bit unsteady on his feet. He was dressed in his denim jacket, jeans and a scarf. He refused to wear his greatcoat because it was already wet.

'You can have my fur coat,' Mother said.

'No way,' Rory said.

'Why not? It'll keep you warm.'

'I'll be grand.'

'Fine, freeze if you want,' she said. 'Don't take any notice of me, I'm only the Mother.'

Maeve looked pensive and troubled, 'Why did Manus's boat go fishing in the middle of a storm?'

Mother wrapped an extra scarf around Maeve.

'Because nobody was expecting a storm. It was calm as a bathtub when the boats went out. You can ask him yourself when he comes back. Now let's go.'

Before we left the house, Mother took me aside, 'Get the fur coat and bring it with us anyway. Put it in a bag. Don't let the other fellow see you. I don't want him catching his death.'

The street glistened like new shoes. Above us, the church loomed dark and predatory. The cold stung my cheeks, forcing me to squint. It felt strange but oddly exciting to be leaving our little house as a family, at such an early hour and without breakfast. It felt like an important adventure, something that none of us wanted to miss even though we knew that it was a serious situation involving our neighbours and friends. As we walked through the town, we saw lights on in various houses. You could feel the news of the missing boat humming in the air. A light went on in Dorneys'. We were the only ones on the street.

Maeve snuffled into her sleeve. She stopped to wipe the rain off her glasses. I kept an eye on her on the way down to the harbour in case she walked into a lamp post or was blown off her feet by the wind. Rory looked fragile and vulnerable in his flimsy denims. I could have offered him the spare baseball cap that was in my coat pocket but I knew he would either ignore the offer or thump me. Rory believed that whatever pain he was suffering could only be relieved by passing it onto me as soon as possible. I had Mother's fur coat in a plastic bag. As soon as he really started to freeze, he would be glad of it.

I read once in a magazine that if you concentrated hard enough, you could send out good feelings to a person who was in difficulties. There was a chance that your thoughts could make the person feel better, possibly even grow stronger. I tried to send out the image of a hissing turf fire to Manus, but the cold made it difficult to sustain. My face was damp and stinging from the rain. There were chills running up my backbone. I couldn't imagine what it must be like on a small fishing boat in a storm like this. I said a prayer in my head: Dear God, please bring them home safely, especially Manus who has his whole life ahead of him. Amen.

Manus had never really wanted to be a fisherman anyway. He always boasted that he was only working on the boats to get money.

'One day, I'm going to do something, really do something,' he said. 'All I have to do is figure out what it is.'

Along the east pier, dark shapes were huddled into the doorways of the fish merchants and the various shacks that stretched half the length of the pier. The storm sent waves shuddering into the pier wall, scattering spray against the walls like buckshot. Every thirty seconds, a blaze of whiteness from the lighthouse at the end of the pier surged past. Some people shone flashlights out to sea.

Elias Powers, the harbour-master, Father Mulryan and a couple of the older fishermen crouched in the gateway of Donnie Kelleher's fish merchants trying to light a paraffin torch. Shadows flickered on the pockmarked walls behind them. The torch whooshed with flame. The men's faces turned scarlet and sinister. They followed our progress with pink, jittery eyes. Powers cupped his hand to his mouth.

'Keep your kids clear of the edges, Kathleen,' he shouted. 'I don't want any more accidents tonight.'

Mrs Donovan suddenly appeared, orange-coloured in the light from a torch. Her face was shiny with spray.

'They're lost,' she said. 'Nobody could survive in this for long.'

'Keep your voice down, for God's sake,' Mother snapped. 'Who else is on board?'

Mrs Donovan leaned over and put her hands on Mother's shoulder, 'Captain Zachary Durrant, Kenneth Hardy and young Francis Simmons from Donegal who's only sixteen.'

'Please God, they'll be all right.'

'It's a shocking tragedy. It's the worst thing to happen to Redrock in my lifetime.'

'It's not over yet. There's always hope.'

'Maybe so, Kathleen. Anyway, it's all we can do now to comfort the living. Lord have mercy on them.'

The families of the missing fishermen waited behind the harbour-master's hut at the head of the pier, as was the custom when a family's loved ones were missing at sea. Someone had fixed a torch onto the roof of the hut where it flared intermittently in the wind. Even when people were standing still, they looked as though they were moving to some internal private rhythm.

Mrs Rock saw us and nodded. Mr Rock and Manus's sister Patty and his brother Donal stared out to sea, their faces still and hard. Mother went over to them. I hung back, not knowing what to say.

May Hardy, Hatchet's wife, emerged from the darkness. She threw her head back and swigged out of a small bottle. As she drank, her hood blew down and her curly hair spilled out behind her. Father Mulryan went to her and put her arms around her. She patted him on the back.

'I'll be fine,' May Hardy said. 'Look after the other ones.'

She offered him the bottle and he took a swig.

A few weeks earlier, Paulie Reddin and I had been drinking in The Tall Ships. Paulie bought a five-quid deal and made the mistake of showing it to Hatchet Hardy. Hatchet came up to us at closing time. He put his arms around our shoulders. 'I wouldn't mind a few blasts back in my place,' he said.

When Hatchet Hardy said that you were coming back to his place to smoke your dope, it was not a good idea to argue. We pretended to be overjoyed.

May Hardy met us at the door. She made us tea and toast while we sat in the front room of Hatchet's cottage and rolled joints. After two joints, we were giggling like fools.

'Is that what that stuff does to ye?' May said. 'It just makes ye laugh like an eejit, is that it?'

'Will ye give it a rest,' Hatchet said. 'The lads and myself are enjoying ourselves.'

'If ye have to smoke that stupid stuff to get a laugh then ye must be very hard up.'

May stoked the fire in the grate, then stood up, 'I've seen enough of my man wrecking himself.'

After May left, nobody said a word for ages. The music clicked off. Hatchet was asleep in his chair. Paulie and I slipped out of the house like mice.

Mother's words rose above the screeching wind, 'Eileen, the sea has no right to such young lives. Manus will come home safe. I know it in my blood.'

'Please God,' said Mrs Rock.

In the light from the torches, people's shapes were unfamiliar. Maeve grabbed my sleeve and held it tight.

Behind us, a man's voice rose from the darkness, 'Why the fuck isn't every lifeboat and fishing boat in Ireland, fuckin' Wales and Scotland out searching. Where's the fuckin' Army helicopters? Eh?'

In the flickering light, I made out the squat figure of Vincent Reddin, Paulie's father. He was stamping up and down the pier, oblivious to the rain and the wind and the spray lashing his face.

'Launch every fuckin' boat, that's what I'd do, yis'd find them in no time, it'll be like Dunkirk.'

Finally, Father Mulryan came over and led him away.

'Now Vincent, you're a bit out of order tonight,' Father Mulryan said.

Just as the figures disappeared from sight, we heard the sound of a slap.

Rory kept his head down and his hands deep in his pockets. He stood behind a lifebelt stand, scarf flapping urgently in the wind like a distress signal. Mother came back to ask us how we were.

'Fine,' we lied.

Maeve pointed to Rory. 'He must be freezing. He's only got a denim jacket on.'

'Mmmm, that fellow. Not half as cold or miserable as the

poor lads who are out at sea somewhere.' As Mother walked away she whispered to me. 'Now's the time. Give it to him.'

I walked over to Rory with the plastic bag. He stared at me as I took out the coat and handed it to him. His lips were blue. He knew that if he wore it he would look stupid but the alternatives were to go home or to carry on freezing. After a few seconds, Rory took the fur coat and put it on. I left him before he became so embarrassed that he felt compelled to give me a thump.

From time to time, we sneaked looks at Rory in Mother's fur coat.

'He looks like a caveman,' Maeve said.

'At least he's warm,' I said.

Mother stood beside Mrs Rock until the flames on the torches died and first light peeped over the horizon like a baby's head.

When the helicopter went over, everyone cheered.

'I don't know why everyone's so happy,' Mrs Donovan said. 'It's only a helicopter.'

With the morning light, the wind eased. Mother sent us to fetch tea and sandwiches from the early pubs. Rory strode off in the fur coat like a rock star.

Mother was delighted, 'I knew he'd like it once he had it on. I'll probably never get it back now.'

By the time we got back to the pier, the sky was the colour of blood. Mother sent us to give each person a sandwich and a hot drink.

'This is like the loaves and the fishes,' Maeve said.

Mother dispatched Mrs Donovan to Harris's hardware to bring back blankets. Mother thought it would be a good idea for everyone on the pier to get a break from Mrs Donovan's insistent pessimism.

'Otherwise, somebody might push her into the harbour,' she said. 'I might do it myself.'

When everyone on the pier had been fed and given a hot drink, Mother beckoned us to her. Reluctantly, sulkily, as slowly as he could, Rory shuffled over to us like a great bear. Mother put her hands on his shoulders. There were tears in her eyes.

'Don't you ever go to sea,' she turned to look at Maeve, then me. 'All of you. You're making your mother very proud. That's all I wanted to say. Now, that didn't hurt, did it?'

She handed Rory a five pound note.

'Get something to eat in the Pier End or one of the early pubs,' she said.

Then she spun around and strode back up the pier with her hair rippling behind in the breeze. Rory fingered the five pound note.

'They do brilliant toasted sandwiches in The Tall Ships.'

The first body was brought in at noon. The flag on the lifeboat flew at half-mast so everyone knew they had found a corpse. As the boat pulled into harbour, people watched without a word. The only sounds were the lapping of the water against the pier walls and the occasional mew of a seagull. We watched as Elias Powers came to the edge of the pier, hunched down and was helped aboard the boat.

'It's young Simmons,' Mrs Donovan said.

Simmons was from Donegal. He had no relations waiting but you could still feel the anxiety increase.

'He was the nicest boy you could wish to meet,' Mrs Donovan said. 'He had a face like an angel off the Sistine chapel.'

Father Mulryan went on board, knelt and gave the corpse the last rites. Someone else went off to ring Simmons's people.

Suddenly, nobody was tired or wet or cold anymore. Everyone just wanted the sea to reveal the results of the storm.

The Cockleshell from Donabate brought in bits of wreckage, including a lifebelt from the missing ship. The lifebelt was lying on the deck as the boat passed into harbour. I could make out the name, *Celtic Mist*. It was like being kicked out of a dream. My best friend was out there somewhere. Perhaps the next time I saw him he would be stretched in a coffin in his best suit, face unnaturally white, more composed than it ever was in life.

A voice rose in the air, singing a hymn. Elias Powers stood on a pile of fish crates outside Donnie Kelleher's fish merchants, his gravelly voice soothing even those who had been on the pier since the start. When he finished, the mood was sorrowful but optimistic.

'God is good,' a voice said.

An hour later *The Sarah-Jane* from Redrock chugged into harbour. The moment we saw the white tarpaulin on deck, we knew there was a corpse under it. At that moment I wished that Manus could be missing forever like my Dad, rather than turn up cold and pale on the deck of a fishing boat. As *The Sarah-Jane* passed, we could make out a pair of white sneakers sticking out from underneath the tarpaulin. Mrs Durrant let out a sigh that was heard by everyone on the pier. Her shoulders went limp. Father Mulryan, May Hardy and some of the other women gathered around her. She didn't cry or tremble or fall down. She seemed too far gone to do anything except be led quietly away.

'Two drowned, two missing,' someone said behind us.

'They didn't drown,' Mrs Donovan said. 'It was the cold that got them.'

'Oh Jenny, will you shut up, please,' Mother hissed.

'Just an opinion, everyone's got a right to express an opinion,' Mrs Donovan shrugged to show that it was only a matter of time before everyone saw that she was right.

The sky turned blue and innocent, speckled with white, slow-moving clouds. Soon, it was hard to believe that there had ever been a storm. Someone spotted another boat heading in from the south-west. As the boat drew near, we saw that it was flying a full flag which meant that they had rescued someone. There was a rush to the edge of the pier.

'Go easy,' Elias Powers shouted. 'Keep back from the edge everyone, for God's sake, will you?'

People ignored him. They leaned forward to get a better view. It was like a bizarre, real-life quiz game. Who had been saved, one or both? Hatchet Hardy or Manus Rock? As the boat drew closer, we could see figures on the bridge. Manus was wrapped in a blanket. He stared straight ahead like a statue being delivered. He looked ghostlike, preoccupied, as though he were just passing through on his way to somewhere else. For a second I thought he was dead and rigor mortis had set in. Would they have propped him up in front like that so everyone could get a good look? Then Manus turned his head to look at the people on the pier and I felt a chill in my heart. Even at a distance, I could see that there was no expression on his face. His blue eyes were stern as crystals.

'It's a miracle,' a voice said.

'Thanks be to God.'

As the boat passed, I felt a sudden rush of joy. My friend was alive and standing a few hundred yards away from me on the bridge of a fishing boat. Before I knew what I was doing, I waved. I just caught myself before shouting out his name. Everyone around turned to look at me. I dropped my hand. I felt as though I had blasphemed.

'Sorry,' I said to their backs but they either didn't hear or else they ignored me.

'Kathleen's youngest, he's a bit slow,' someone said.

Mrs Rock walked past me, eyes as fixed and unblinking as a zombie's. The rest of the Rock family followed. Mr Rock, relieved but strained-looking; Patty, red-eyed from crying; and Donal, scratching under his arms as if he had fleas. Mother slapped me on the shoulder.

'Now,' she said.

Her face blazed in triumph as if Manus's rescue had all been her doing. I was trying to decide whether to go after the Rocks or wait until tomorrow to call on Manus when Mrs Donovan appeared in front of me, expression grim and knowing.

'Trust a proddie to come back from the dead,' she said.

May Hardy stood at the edge of the pier. I thought she was going to jump into the water. Then someone put their arms around her and gave her a hug.

When night fell, she was still there.

Mr Wolkenski gave me a glass of water and a bowl, then led me to a chair that was in the middle of the room. I sat down. He spread a towel at my feet and indicated that I should gargle. I took a sip and began, but he stopped me.

'Het back, het back pleez.'

He went behind me and pulled my head back so that I was looking at the ceiling. I gargled with difficulty. Water dribbled from my mouth. I heard splashes.

'Now, louder, do louder pleez.'

I did as he said. There were more splashes. I felt trickles going down my cheek to my neck and under my collar. A drop somehow reached my nipple and made me tingle. I thought that this was the stupidest exercise yet. How could gargling improve a stutter?

'Louder, pleez.'

I gargled as loudly as I could for as long as I was able before spitting out into a bowl. Mr Wolkenski studied my face.

'Ah gut. Now, pleez. Do more.'

After a half-dozen gargles, my throat felt like it was made of jelly. My collar was soaked. The floor under the chair was wet. I noticed that the towel appeared dry.

'Vait,' Mr Wolkenski said.

Mr Wolkenski walked over to a table in the corner. He opened a drawer, pulled out a chart and unfolded it. When he was finished consulting the chart, he produced a fountain pen, removed the top and wrote something in a small black notebook that he picked up from the desk. Then he put the top back on the fountain pen and put it back in his pocket. He tossed the notebook on the desk.

For a moment, I thought he was going to tell me I was never going to be cured.

'Ver gut,' Mr Wolkenski said. 'See you nex veek.'

'They hit a Brit submarine,' Mrs Donovan announced.

Mother nearly dropped her glass of Guinness, 'Do you really think so?'

'The Brits have been operating their manoeuvres in the Irish Sea for years. I mean, how many of our fishing boats have caught their nets on a British submarine and been dragged for miles. How many?'

'I think you're right, Jenny,' Mother said. 'I never thought of it.'

157

'Stacks of them. Absolutely stacks,' Mrs Donovan continued. 'It's a disgrace and something should be done.'

'I agree,' Mother said. 'It's about time someone raised the matter in the Dail.'

Elias Powers called to the house to thank Mother for her work on the pier. He said the search had been called off. He was sure they would never find Kenneth Hardy now.

'The sea keeps some bodies for itself. Others it gives back the moment it has finished with them. The lucky ones, like Manus, it gives back alive. Nobody can make sense of the ways of the sea.'

Elias Powers wanted to know if Mother could persuade May Hardy to come to the funeral service for Zachary Durrant.

'It would be good for her. She's been on the pier for two days and nights.'

Mother brought Maeve and myself with her to the Hardys' house. I hoped May would not remember me.

'Who is it?' May Hardy called from behind the door.

'It's Kathleen Buckley, May. I came to see if there was anything I could do.'

'No thanks, I don't need any TD coming down here to gain a bit of free publicity,' May Hardy called from behind the door.

'I'm really sorry, May,' Mother said. 'I thought I might be able to help. I too am the wife of a man who is missing. I was hoping you would come to the service for Zachary tomorrow morning.'

The door opened a crack. May Hardy's face was ashen.

'Did you ever have a funeral for your husband?' May asked.

'No,' Mother said.

'Why not?'

Mother looked confused, 'We never found any trace of him.'

'Well then,' May Hardy said. 'When the sea gives back my man, that's when I'll go to a funeral, not before.'

The door closed.

After the church service, a bagpiper, Zachary Durrant's

cousin, led the cortège through the town in a traditional sailor's send-off. The piper was a small, red-faced man, with a beer-belly that protruded over his kilt like a trapped balloon. The bagpipes were a lot bigger than him. When he started to play outside the church, it was like watching a man wrestling with the udders of a cow. For a moment it looked as though Zachary Durrant's funeral could turn into a farce. People looked away, started a conversation, examined their fingernails, anything rather than watch the bagpiper lose control of his pipes. Then the pipe lament sang out in the clear sky and the piper led the way down the street from the church, with five hundred people treading slowly behind.

The whole town seemed to be standing on the pavements to pay their respects. We watched from the corner of Finlay's flower shop on Main Street. I looked for Manus but couldn't find him in the procession of familiar faces.

At the service earlier, Manus had come up to me.

'See you after,' he whispered and walked up the aisle to join his parents in the pew.

I noticed how different his face seemed. His nose had been thin and sharp but had a bit of meat on it. Now, it looked as though someone had replaced it with a cheaper, narrower model. The eyes, too, had undergone a transformation. They were now watery blue instead of piercing. The sea had diluted Manus's face. I wondered what my face would look like after an ordeal. Would I have the nerve to go out again if I was the only survivor?

Rory and Mother stood in front of us. I glanced across at Maeve who was standing on tiptoes, trying to peer over the heads of the crowd. The coffin was carried by Zachary Durrant's four brothers and two of his uncles. They were followed by the parents, Jack and Polly Durrant, a couple in their eighties. Everyone had their heads up, looking straight ahead. Nobody was crying. People shuffled along the footpaths on either side all along the winding road to the harbour. At the graveyard, wreaths were piled into a large mound by the side of the open grave. Father Mulryan read a brief prayer. Then they lowered the coffin. Father

Mulryan helped Mrs Durrant to spoon the first earth onto the coffin. The dirt hit the wood with a noise that reminded me of currants being dropped into a weighing scale. I remembered when Mother used to make teacakes for us when Dad was coming home from someplace. It was always supposed to be a surprise but as soon as he came in he smelled them. It was impossible to keep a secret from Dad.

Mrs Durrant looked dignified and distant as though she had cried all her grief out and was left with just enough strength to get through today. People filed past in a silent line. We waited at the back while Mother spooned in some earth.

I was surprised that everyone appeared so relieved by the act of burial itself. I had expected weeping and a strained, nervous atmosphere. Instead, people seemed quite relaxed. The Durrant family thanked people for coming and invited them back to the house for a drink and a sandwich. After the burial, Mother went back to the Durrants' and we walked home. I looked out for Manus on the way but I couldn't spot him. I figured he had also gone to the Durrants'.

There was a piece of sail tied across the broken window of The Tall Ships, like a giant eyepatch. As soon as Manus and I walked into the lounge, faces peered at Manus from every corner. We made our way towards a table at the back. People at the bar nodded to Manus. Paulie Reddin came up to shake his hand.

'Glad to see you're all right,' Paulie said.

'Thanks,' Manus said.

We sat at a table at the back. A lounge boy came by and we ordered two pints. It was a while before Manus relaxed enough to take a sip of his pint.

'I thought people were going to shout at me,' Manus said.

'Why?'

He shrugged, 'I feel lucky but I feel guilty too. I can't explain it. I wish they'd found Hatchet Hardy.'

Neither Hatchet Hardy nor Captain Durrant could swim,

a common thing amongst fishermen. Manus had done a course in water survival.

'That was what saved me,' he said.

Manus was silent for a while. He fiddled with a beer mat. Then he tore it in pieces and put it in the ashtray.

'I thought we were going to make it in. We'd been out in loads of storms before without any problem.'

I glanced around to check if anyone was looking at us. Nobody was.

'Hardy and myself were on deck, securing the hold, when something made me look up. There was this wall of water standing over us. Next thing I remember I was in the water. After a long while – I don't know how long – one of the ship's lifeboats floated past, upside down. I swam under, climbed between the seats and hung on. For hours I bounced up and down like a bucking bronco. I must have conked out. Next thing I remember I was being taken up into the light and wrapped in blankets.'

Manus lifted his pint, 'Now I'm not Manus Rock anymore. I'm your man, the only survivor of *The Celtic Mist* disaster.'

We drank our pints. I called the lounge boy over and ordered two more. I realised that I had something in common with Manus. I wasn't Daniel Buckley anymore. Instead I was the youngest son of the TD, Kathleen Buckley – 'your man with the stutter' as I once heard someone say. If I'd had a choice, I would have preferred to be Daniel Buckley from Church Street who had a brother and sister, a mother and a dad.

I wanted to ask Manus if he was ever going to go to sea again, but I couldn't. Perhaps he didn't know himself yet. It was best just to savour the moment and be glad my friend was alive.

'Do you want to go into town this weekend?' I said. 'We could go to a m-movie to something?'

At first I thought Manus wasn't listening to me but then I saw that his attention was distracted by Mother who had come into the lounge and was shaking hands with people.

Manus shrugged, 'I don't think it's a good idea to make

any plans. Maybe I will go into town with you. I just don't know. Maybe I'll go away for a while. It's hard to say what I want to do.'

Manus's expression became agitated and he narrowed his eyes as if trying desperately to remember something, 'Don't take it personally.'

'It's OK,' I said. 'I'll g-give you a ring.'

'Yeah, give me a ring,' Manus relaxed.

'I think . . .' Manus began 'I'll just stay for one more.'

'No problem,' I said.

When the lounge boy came back with the drinks, he took my money but refused to take Manus's.

'On the house,' he said and cleared off before Manus could say thanks.

SEVEN

The Visit

I AM DRIVING a runaway Morris Minor. In a panic I have jammed my foot on the accelerator. Now I can't seem to lift it. The car is bucketing around Dollymount Strand like a tank. At any moment I expect a woman and child to appear in front of us like skittles to be mown down.

Beside me, Carla's cool voice tells me to calm down.

'Use the brake,' she says. 'You're doing really well for your first time – use the brake, the brake, *look out*.'

The car suddenly mounts a sand dune and leaps into grey sky. Carla grabs me. For a second we hang in space. I feel as though we are on a rollercoaster that has snapped its cable at the climb's highest point. Any second now we are going to plunge backwards.

The car splashes down on a sandbank. We bang our heads on the dash.

Everything is peaceful. There is nothing on the horizon except green sea, grey sky and rolling, beige-coloured sand. Overhead, seagulls are cawing. A playful breeze beats against the window. Carla reaches across me to turn off the engine.

There is nothing like smacking a car into a sandbank on a deserted beach to ram home a person's sense of inadequacy.

'I am not cut out for this driving thing,' I say.

Carla rubs the mark on her brow where her head hit the dash.

'Don't be so hard on yourself. You just need a bit more

163

practice. You'll be grand after a few runs up and down the beach.'

Even on Dollymount Strand, with nothing near us for miles, I find it difficult to reach the brakes or the gearstick with any fluency. The driving wheel itself seems to be set at an uncomfortable angle. There is something odd about the positioning of the pedals. I have to take my eyes off the road to change gears. I hate this car.

A speck of blood lands on my hand. I touch my forehead, feel a graze.

'Oh, you're cut,' Carla says. 'Poor thing. Here, let me.'

Carla takes out a white hanky and presses it to the spot on my forehead, 'You're lucky that you have me to look after you.'

A week ago, I fell off the back of Carla's Kawasaki 150. She drove over a length of hosepipe that was lying in the middle of the road and I just bounced off. I landed on my arse. Luckily, there was nothing coming. At first Carla worried that I had hurt myself, but when I wobbled to my feet and she saw that I was all right, she burst into laughter. For a moment I thought she had driven over the hosepipe deliberately, knowing that I would go flying.

'Oh Daniel, I'm sorry, you were lying there with your legs in the air. You looked like you were about to give birth.'

It took her ten minutes to convince me to get back on the bike. That night, I saw an ad in the paper for a 'second-hand Morris Minor, excellent condition, £400'. It was a sign. Carla was delighted. She promised to teach me to drive.

'Driving a car is like riding a bicycle or painting a wall. Nobody can be expected to do it brilliantly first time around. It's all a matter of confidence.'

This is my second emergency stop in twenty minutes. When I am behind the wheel, everything outside the car seems unreal. I keep expecting lights to flash and buzzers to sound. I'm beginning to think that I can't tell the difference between driving and a video game.

Carla gives my forehead a wipe, 'Now. The bleeding has stopped. Would you like me to drive?'

'No, it's OK,' I say. 'I think I ba-better do it myself.'

'As you wish.'

I start the engine and put the car into reverse. Carla looks out the window and guides me as I back the car out of the sandbank. I manage the feat without difficulty. I even remember to look in the mirror. I put the car into first. There is a gentle groaning of gears. Then we are clopping along the beach at a steady pace. I smoothly change into second gear. Then I go to third.

'Very good,' Carla says. 'See, you're a good driver.'

I am aware of the sea to our left but I daren't glance at it in case I hit a bump or something and lose control of the car again. We are on a smooth stretch. The car coasts along. The gentle rhythm of the engine is hypnotic. There is nothing to do but keep the wheel steady and watch the sand ahead of us. I begin to feel confident. I dismiss my earlier problems as beginner's nerves. I push the accelerator to forty, then fifty. The tranquillity of the ride is now intoxicating.

As soon as the driving lesson is over, Carla will drive us to Clontarf to visit Mother. It is Carla's idea.

'It's only a few miles away so we might as well,' she said. 'Besides, it must be three weeks since you visited your mother.'

'Actually, it is four weeks.'

'Oh Daniel, how could you? Your poor mother.'

'I don't want to stay too long.'

'We'll just stay for a while. Anyway, I've an important appointment this afternoon that I can't miss.'

Mother and I have had our differences lately. I see her at the doorway of the bungalow in Clontarf, pointing at me. I watch as she narrows her eyes to take careful aim. Her tongue protrudes between her lips, her arm goes back and she throws the teacup like a cricketer. Maeve arrives in the doorway, just too late to stop her. I see the teacup tumbling in the air towards me. Before it hits, I observe a floral pattern on its side.

'Well, you have to hand it to her,' Maeve said afterwards. 'Not many old dears can throw a teacup as well as our mother.'

I snap out of it to look at my watch. I have not run into anything for ten minutes. If I keep going as well as I am now for another ten, I may drive the Morris Minor to Mother's myself. It is only up the road. I feel that I am really getting the hang of this car now.

Carla begins to hum to herself. She is a good driving teacher. She is very encouraging and she never raises her voice unless she is screaming at me to hit the brakes. We get on brilliantly ever since she gave Mr Poopy back to Donald Logan. Now we don't fight anymore. We watch videos together and cuddle on the sofa. I buy her Walnut Whips. She buys me Aeros. Carla says that we are back to our old selves.

'Every couple goes through a bad patch,' she said last night. 'I think we handled things in a very civilised way. I'm rather proud of us.'

Tonight Carla and I are going to a gig in the Baggot. The Silent Screams are playing yet another special one-off concert. This time it's to celebrate the recording of their debut album. They are keeping seats for us in the front row. Carla is excited because the *Sunday Independent* is doing a fashion spread on her design work for the band.

'It could mean a lot of work for me. My fees will go up. It'll be terrific.'

Carla's involvement with The Silent Screams seems to have done her career a lot of good. Every day, there are phone calls from bands, singers, cabaret artistes, even one from a film producer. Carla is definitely going places. For her sake I pretend to be excited too.

Soon, I will turn around and drive back down the beach. Maybe I'll take it up to sixty. A flock of seagulls rises up before us, shrieking. The birds scatter into the sky. They are the only sign of life for miles except for a plane that is poised in the distant sky. It is one of ours. I can just make out an Aer Lingus shamrock. Donna's face comes into my mind. She has promised to buy me a pint sometime. The thing I like about Donna is that a person can talk to her openly without getting laughed at or slagged. She and I have always got on well. I think of her as a good friend. Donna what? I realise that I can't remember her surname.

'Daniel?' Carla says.

I wonder if Donna is going to go out with Frank Nails. He is really keen on her. He is always trying to chat her up. Dominic Root is convinced he wants to marry her. As a friend, I should warn her about his weird eating habits and his obsession with hurling . . .

'Daniel, I think you should –'

Kingston. That's it. Donna Kingston. Or is it Kindon? I hope she doesn't go out with Frank Nails. I think I would lose respect for any woman who found him attractive.

'Daniel . . . Daniel . . . for heaven's sake, *Daniel, watch out!*'

Carla grabs the wheel as a stream of water whooshes across the windscreen. For an instant, I think I must have hit the button for the windscreen wiper spray. My foot finds the brake and the car sloshes to a stop. I have driven into the sea.

Carla puts her hands to her mouth. Water is spreading at our feet. The engine is gargling.

'I don't think I have ever met anyone like you,' Carla says. 'Now get out and push.'

'Oh my God, you're wounded,' Mother says and reaches for my forehead.

'I'm fine, Mother, it's nothing.'

'What do you mean it's *nothing*? I'm your mother, I'm the best judge of whether something is *nothing* or not. Let me see.'

Mother tries to pull my head down. I allow her to do it. I don't wish to cause a scene, especially since we have just arrived. I hope she won't notice that my jeans and shoes are wet from pushing the car out of the sea.

'Hello, Kathleen,' Carla stands on the step with her hand out, but Mother ignores her. My forehead is all-engrossing. Maeve's worried face pops up beside Mother's shoulder.

'Oh, Daniel, you came. What's going on?'

'We had a slight mishap, Maeve,' Carla says and gives Maeve a peck on the cheek. 'Daniel banged his head.'

'Oh.'

Mother fingers my graze. I feel a stab of pain.

'God, it's septic.'

'Mother, it's not septic. It's just a graze.'

Maeve takes Mother's arm, 'Mother, leave Daniel alone. He's a big boy now. Let's bring our guests into the front room.'

'All right, I was just trying to help,' Mother says. 'I didn't know you had a car.'

Carla rushes her answer, as she always does when speaking to Mother, 'We bought it last week, it's a Morris Minor, Daniel was always saying we couldn't really be adults until we drove a car.'

Mother shakes free of Maeve, steps back. Her eyes open wide in horror.

'You hurt your head in a car crash? When? Where?' She glares at Carla, 'Who was driving?'

Carla looks as though she has swallowed a bee.

'It was just a sandbank, Mother. We were driving on the beach.'

'What were you doing driving a car on a beach? Is a road not good enough for you?'

Maeve takes Mother's arm again and leads her down the hall, 'That's enough, Mother. We can't stand here all day. We've made a special surprise for Daniel and Carla, haven't we?'

'Yes,' Mother says hesitantly. 'It took us all morning. I'm just a bit worried about Daniel's head.'

'I'm fine.'

The hall is dark and smells of old newspapers and cardboard boxes. The rooms are tiny and the thin, white walls look as though you could easily punch through them. Even after ten years, the hall of Mother's new home still reminds me of a corridor in an office block. We pass Mother's room. The door is open. On the wall over Mother's double-bed, I can make out framed newspaper clippings of her first election victory, a photograph of herself with Charles Haughey, a couple of campaign posters and a romantic portrait done by a second-rate artist. A wedding photo of Mother and Dad is on the bedside dresser. In the front room, we sit on two small sofas either side of a coffee table. Mother and Maeve take one sofa, Carla and I the other. Maeve has tried to give the place a bit of character. She has put up all the prints of famous paintings from our old home – Renoir's 'Garden Party', Manet's one of the couple in the boat, Salvador Dali's 'Hanging Christ'. Maeve has even stuck up a couple of family snaps to give the flavour of home. I wonder if Maeve misses the old place. I wonder if she still has the Aisling copybooks.

Mother produces a tray with cups, saucers and a teapot while Maeve carries a dish of teacakes. The teacakes are obviously our 'surprise'. Mother begins to pour the tea.

'OK, everyone, here it is,' Mother says.

We each take a cup of tea from Mother. My cup has the same floral design as the one Mother threw at me on my last visit. I am amazed that there are any left. Mother fusses over Carla. She insists on spooning sugar into Carla's tea even though she knows that Carla doesn't take sugar. Mother is on what can be termed her best behaviour. We have been here nearly five minutes and she has mentioned neither Dad nor the British Secret Service. Maybe Maeve is right. Maybe she is getting better.

Maeve passes the dish of teacakes, 'You haven't had one of these for years, have you, Daniel?'

I hold one of the smug round cakes and pluck off one of the burnt currants studded on top.

'I hope they're better than your hamburgers,' I say.

Maeve feigns outrage, 'Daniel that's not fair. I'm a good cook. Does he slag you too, Carla?'

'All the time. He's desperate.'

'Daniel was always the joker in the family,' Mother says.

I bite into the teacake. There is a faint tang of soap, as if a few flakes of laundry powder had somehow slipped into the mix. Definitely Maeve's work. Maeve looks to me for approval.

'Gorgeous,' I say.

I remember our excitement as young kids whenever Mother got out the Bird's Teacake Mix. It meant that Dad was due home. The teacakes were his 'surprise'. We watched as she poured the packet into a bowl, put in egg yokes, milk, sugar and currants then whipped the mix with a wooden spoon until it was creamy. We held the tray steady as Mother filled each paper cup in turn then placed it on the tray. When the tray was in the oven, she let us take turns licking the wooden spoon. Wolfing the teacakes down hot from the tray was the most fun. It didn't matter that they burned our throats. The taste was tender, honeyed, delicious. The heat tickled our noses. Dad often came home to find only a few of his 'surprises' left.

'Aren't the teacakes great?' Mother says. 'It's been years since we had them.'

'Really good,' Carla says with her mouth full.

'Oh, Carla,' Mother says charmingly, 'after you've finished your tea, you must go out to the back garden and see Maeve's rockery. It's just fantastic.'

Maeve is embarrassed, 'Oh, Mother. It's just a rockery.'

'It's a work of art, Maeve. You should be proud of it.'

I notice that there is a small trail of sand leading into the room. The trail stops at my feet. My feet make soft squelching noises when I move. It is a miracle that we are here at all. The Morris Minor clanks and gurgles as though it has seaweed in the engine. My arms ache from the exertion of pushing the car out of the sea and then half a mile along the beach until Carla got it started again. How could I drive into the sea? What's wrong with me?

'You're a good driver,' Carla said. 'Except that you have the concentration span of a fly.'

Today, Mother wears a blue trouser suit and red shoes. Maeve wears a black polo-neck, dark knee-length skirt, black tights and a pearl necklace. She wears red shoes just like Mother's. Apart from the lines around the eyes and a slight puckering at the mouth, Mother could be Maeve's big sister.

Mother stares at me as if she can't believe I am really here.

170

'I'm glad you've come,' Maeve says. 'Mother and I have been looking forward to it all day, haven't we, Mother?'

'Yes,' Mother says. 'I'm very glad you're home.'

The kitchen wall is a shrine.

Rory's name is spelled out in thick black marker across the length of the top R.O.R.Y. B.U.C.K.L.E.Y. Underneath are photographs, press clippings, various full-length posters of Rory's band, The Fabulous Roadrunners, a *Hot Press* cover of Rory and the band and a framed newspaper article with the headline, 'The New Wild Men of Irish Rock and Roll'. Rory's old jeans are hanging there, along with his leather jacket and a framed photograph of Mother's fur coat which Rory wore on stage in the band's early days.

Mother beams at me, 'Well, how about that? I ask you, is that a wall or not?'

'It certainly is a wall.'

'I knew you'd like it. Maeve and I were up all night doing it. I think it does him justice, don't you?'

'It's amazing.'

It amazes me that Rory should have a wall dedicated to him in a house he has rarely visited. By going away, Rory has become a hero, just like Dad. Whereas I, who stayed in the country, have teacups thrown at me.

With a glance to check that Maeve is still outside, Mother whispers, 'What did you think of the teacakes?'

'Eh, they were la-lovely.'

'Good. I was worried that Maeve would make a mess of them. She's a great girl but in a kitchen she can be absolutely lethal.'

Through the kitchen window I can see Maeve and Carla walking in the small garden. Maeve is pointing to something on the ground. They duck out of sight. I wonder what Carla thinks of the Rory shrine. She is sure to have noticed it earlier on her way out to the garden with Maeve. Mother is looking at me as if she is expecting an answer.

'Pardon?'

Mother says, 'I said, I kept an eye on her, you know – just in case.'

171

Mother takes me by the arm and brings me to the sink by the window. Carla pops up and waves. I wave back. Carla points to something on the ground and indicates that I should rush out to see it.

Mother blocks my way, 'Daniel, I want you to do something very important for me.'

Every time I visit, Mother always tries to get me to do something weird or impossible or both. Last time she had cornered me in the hall when I was leaving. Her eyes had burned at me with messianic zeal.

'I've had Charlie Haughey himself on the phone to me for weeks pleading with me to take back that seat for the party,' she had hissed. 'I need you to run my campaign.'

As politely as I could, I had declined. Mother had chased me out of the house, screaming that I was a traitor who had betrayed his own mother. That was when she flung the teacup at me.

Now I am ready for anything. Here it comes.

'Daniel, I want you to go to Manchester and bring Rory home.'

The shrine should have tipped me off to expect something like this. The last time Mother and Rory met was Christmas six years ago. She told Rory that Haughey had asked her to become Foreign Minister in the next Fianna Fail government and Rory laughed so hard that she went at him with a bread knife. Rory found it hard to forgive her for that. When I tried to intervene and get everyone to make up, he pushed me away.

'I'm sick of you trying to make everything hunky-dory all the time.'

Rory left for Manchester a few days later and has been there ever since. I have no idea what he is doing over there. He may still be in a band. Maeve went over to see him a few years ago but he wouldn't come back with her, not even for a visit. She said he was living in a squat on Moss Side and that his hair was really long. I doubt if Rory would be glad to see me turn up on his doorstep. There is no telling how he would react. He could either buy me a pint or hit me. I will have to discuss it with Maeve. I wonder what

Rory would say if he knew that Mother had erected a shrine to him. He would not be surprised that Mother still finds it easier to worship those who are absent than the ones who are still around.

I turn towards the window. Maybe Carla and Maeve will come back and Mother will have to drop the subject. Mother touches my arm and turns me around to face her.

'This is his country. He should be here with his own family. I've been thinking about it for a long time and I really want you to go. Are you listening to me, Daniel?'

'He wouldn't come back for Maeve. Why would he listen to me?'

'You're his brother. He'll come back for you.'

'Mother, Rory is thirty-three. He has his own life to lead.'

Mother shrugs, 'I'm still his mother.'

'Rory hasn't been in touch for years.'

Mother holds a hand to her face, 'I'll pay for the ticket. I'd hire a jet if I thought it could bring Rory back.'

'I've a la-lot on my plate at the moment. Can we talk about it next week?'

I notice the wrinkled skin on Mother's hand, the tips of the elegant fingers withered and sunken. One of the finger-nails appears bruised and discoloured. The image of Mother that I carry in my mind is vibrant, youthful with translucent skin and a clear gaze, the way she looked the night of her great speech in Leary's Seafront Hotel. I cultivate this image of Mother. I keep it in my mind as protection against the Mother who screams and throws cups; the Mother who accuses Carla of being a Fine Gael spy; the Mother who sends petitions to Argentina requesting a military invasion of the North to throw out the British. Mother takes her hand down from her face. I notice the hollows under her eyes, the flaking skin at her temples, the grey streaks in her hair. I feel that this is the first time I have really looked at Mother for a long time. I feel guilty for not visiting her more often. Now that I am here I can't wait to leave.

'I am sorry that I ever sent you to that eejit Wolkenski. I think he ended up doing you more harm than good.'

173

'Mr Wolkenski was fa-fine. He did me a lot of good.'

'I should have sent you out of the country while I had the chance. There was a doctor in Holland who was a world expert in curing your little problem.'

'Mother, don't fuss.'

She moves towards the shelf, 'If you hold on, I might be able to get his name. Maybe we could give him a ring now.'

'It's OK, Mother. I'm fa-fine, really.'

'No, you're not. Sometimes, I think you're getting worse. You should be over it by now.'

'It's not a big problem anymore.'

'It was my own fault for not taking you seriously enough when you were small. It was just that there was so much to deal with back then – the cumann, the schools, money, the mortgage. I can't be expected to look after everything.'

'I don't need any help.'

Mother takes an address book from the top of a shelf and rummages through it. I look up at the shelf, expecting to see the American clock radio.

I try to keep calm because I know that if I get rattled my stutter will come back and Mother will win the argument. I am just composing a brief stutter-free speech in my head to prove my point when the kitchen door opens and Maeve comes in, followed by Carla.

'It's a lovely garden, Daniel,' Carla says. 'You really should go out and see what they've done. The new rockery is gorgeous.'

'I'll look later.'

Maeve comes up, nods at the wall, 'Well, what do you think?'

I smile, 'A masterpiece. But why?'

Maeve goes red, 'They were great days.'

Mother stops rummaging in her address book, 'Maeve, I've got great news. Daniel is going to Manchester to bring Rory back.'

'Oh,' Carla says and quickly pretends to look out of the window.

Maeve clasps her hands, 'That's brilliant. When?'

I shrug, 'I dunno. Ask Mother.'

174

'Listen, Daniel,' Maeve says, taking me by the arm and leading me to the window just as she used to do when we were kids and she had a wonderful secret for my ears only. 'The ESB bill came. I need to get your half.'

'I'll send you a cheque on Monday.'

'Thanks.'

'What about the phone bill?'

Maeve grimaces, 'Jesus, it hasn't arrived yet. I'm dreading it. I think she rang Argentina again.'

When I turn around, I notice that Mother is staring at me. At first, I think she is staring into space, then I realise that she is gazing at the top of my head. She gives a sharp intake of breath. Everyone looks to Mother, then to me.

'Mother, are you all right?' Maeve says.

'Daniel, your wound,' Mother says, staring at the top of my head.

Everyone looks at my head wound.

'What about it?' I say.

'It's swelling,' Mother says.

The house is a red brick, two-storey in a quiet terrace. A large 'For Sale' sign leans from an explosion of weeds in the small, overgrown front garden. The white paint on the window-sills is peeling. I realise that what we are looking at is Carla's 'important appointment'.

'This is it. What do you think?'

'I don't know. It looks OK.'

'Wait till you see inside. The agent said . . . here he is now.'

A bald man in a grey suit blusters across the road. Why do they all have grey suits? There must be a secret rule for those fellows. The agent sees us, produces a set of keys and jangles them at us.

Carla gets out of the car. I follow. This is the first house we've looked at for a month. It is a sure sign that our relationship is back to normal.

'Sorry I'm late,' the man says. He fumbles with his keys, opens the door. 'I've had such a busy day, you wouldn't believe. The house market is jumping at the minute.'

The hallway is bare and dusty. The man switches on the light. I trip on something. A lump of stringy carpet is standing up, attached to a rotted slab of wooden floorboard. A nail sticks out of the floorboard, making it look like a medieval mace.

'Congratulations,' says the bald agent. 'You've discovered the only part of the floor in the whole house that needs a bit of fixing. The rest is almost perfect.'

He puts the floorboard back and pats the carpet into place over it. Then he shows us around the empty rooms. The rooms are small but compact. There is neither dry rot nor damp but all the walls need stripping and there are holes in the plaster work.

'All the lights work,' the agent assures us. 'They just need fittings. The plumbing is fine. Just expect to find a few leaks here and there. It's an old house.'

In the kitchen, Carla is charmed by the old-fashioned iron stove. She pats it like a dog. The wooden steps leading to the back garden have woodworm and the long back garden itself looks like a lost world.

The agent stands in the kitchen doorway and scratches his stomach with his keys, 'As you can see, this is a house with a lot of character.'

What he means is: 'This place needs months of back-breaking work.'

'I'd just like a word with my boyfriend,' Carla says.

'Of course, take your time,' the man says and leaves us.

Carla turns to me. She is excited, 'Daniel, do you like it?'

'Yeah, it's a good house.'

Carla appears apprehensive, 'Do you think you could ever live here?'

'Sure.'

Carla is relieved, 'Good, because I made a bid yesterday.'

'You did *what*?'

'I had to do something fast otherwise it would have been snapped up. It's going at a good price. It's a nice area.'

'You mean we're ba-ba-buying it?'

'We could do great things with the rooms. You can help me paint the place. It's a good place to bring up children.'

176

I jump, 'Children? You mean? Are you . . . ?'

Carla laughs, 'No, no, of course not. But you have to consider everything when you buy a house, you know. It's a huge investment.'

'You could have asked me.'

Carla gazes at the stove, runs her finger across the ironwork.

'You were working,' she says in a small voice. 'I was busy. There wasn't time.'

She turns to me, gives me a squeeze and smiles, 'I'm so glad you like it. I have a good eye, haven't I? Think about how great it'll be once we've done it up.'

'I still think . . .'

'I know I should have talked to you but we've looked at so many houses that you didn't like, I didn't want to waste your time. I had a feeling you'd like this one. I wanted to surprise you.'

'You surprised me all right.'

I feel a cold storm rising in me. I hate to have things sneak up on me. Who needs the hassle? Life is difficult and unpredictable enough. I go over to the kitchen window and look out at the jungle I will have to tame if Carla has her way. Today is not a good day. First I nearly drown us; then Mother tries to send me to Manchester to track down Rory; now I'm being blackmailed into buying a house. I try not to think about The Silent Screams gig tonight.

'Daniel, what's wrong?'

'It's OK, forget it.'

'Are you angry?'

'I said OK.'

'Forgive me? I was only doing my best.'

'Right.'

Carla walks over to join me at the window. I go numb inside.

'Don't go sulky on me like this, Daniel.'

'Who's sulky?'

'You've cut off from me again, as if I'm not here.'

'I know you're here.'

'Sometimes, I don't think you see me as a real person.'

'What are you talking about?'

'You treat me as if I'm a character from one of your television programmes or videos. I might as well be Minnie Mouse.'

'I don't watch Ma-Minnie Mouse.'

Carla comes in close to look me in the eye. I get uncomfortable when she does that. I take a step away.

'Daniel, I feel like I'm the only one who's making a commitment here. If you don't want to buy a house with me just say so and we'll tell the agent that we're not interested. I'm perfectly happy to do whatever you want. The only thing is, it's very hard sometimes to know what *it is* you want. Think about it. I'll be at the car.'

Carla goes out. I listen as her footsteps reach the front door. I hear her trip over the loose carpet, then the yawn of the door opening. As soon as the door closes, my numb feeling dissolves.

I feel utterly stupid. I realise that Carla is doing what's best for us. I can't imagine why I got angry in the first place. She is right. This is a wonderful house. It feels like a potentially great home. Sometimes I can be so insensitive. Why does she put up with me? If I don't act fast, Carla's 'surprise' will be spoiled. There is definitely something wrong with me. Tonight, I'll take Carla out to dinner at The Penguin. We'll have swordfish steak and Death by Chocolate. Suddenly I remember that we are going to the Baggot to see The Silent Screams. I decide to buy her a Walnut Whip instead.

I leave the kitchen and walk out to the front door. The loose carpet is sticking up again. I force it back down with my foot and stamp on it a couple of times.

Outside, Carla is leaning on the Morris Minor. The bald agent sees me coming and stands to one side. Carla looks up.

'When do we move in?' I say.

I feel like a rock star.

The jacket is dark red with hundreds of tiny white stars sprinkled all over and a black collar that gives it a distinguished feel. It is an Edwardian drape like the ones Teddy Boys wear except that Carla has altered it. Now it looks like the smoking jacket of an earl. In the mirror, I look taller, more handsome, glamorous.

Carla is delighted, 'It's you, definitely. I think you should wear it tonight. Knock their eyes out at the Baggot.'

I feel good. We are the owners of a second-hand car, we are about to become owners of our first house and now I have a new image. It is all thanks to Carla.

I am just about to tell her that she can reclaim Mr Poopy from Donald Logan, and bring it back into the apartment, when the phone rings.

I twirl across the room in my new jacket to pick it up, 'Hello?'

'Big Balls.'

'Dan, is that you?'

'Christ, boy, who else would it be? The bloody Pope?'

'How are you?'

'Grand. I've been trying to get you all day. There's a foot and mouth alert at the airport. The Chief wants all hands on deck.'

'You ma-mean now?'

'No, I mean last summer. I mean immediately. Get a taxi. There's a voucher here for you. See you soon.'

'Dan, I've got plans for this evening, I –'

'And, Big Balls?'

'Yes?'

'Don't make a bags of it. See ye.'

I put down the phone. Carla stares at me. I shrug.

'You're not going to believe this,' I say. 'I've got to go to work.'

Carla folds her arms and frowns, 'I suppose I'll have to drive you.'

I can smell the disinfectant at Customs.

The ship inspectors are outside the office, filling watering-cans from two large six-gallon drums. The odour is so powerful that some of the passengers cover their noses as they stream past.

The moment I arrive, the other ship inspectors stop dead with their watering-cans in mid-air and gape at my new red jacket. I am still wearing the jacket in the hope of meeting Carla later at the Baggot. Now I realise that this may have been an error of judgement. I am also getting queer looks from some of the passengers streaming past.

'Well, Daniel,' Desperate Dan says 'did your granny let you borrow her night gown again?'

'How are you going to get an armband on that yoke?' Dominic Root says. 'We'll have to disinfect it first.'

Dominic is just starting an 'ak-ak' when Magaw steps forward.

'Daniel, get your armband on and take tarmac duty with Dan. You'll find the stuff in the back room. Tonight, you're going to earn your wages.'

I slip on my armband. In the back room, Dan lifts an armful of mats and hands them to me. Then he grabs a watering-can and leads me through the sliding doors to the tarmac.

'We've got twenty-six flights in two hours,' Dan smirks. 'Do ye think ye're up to it, Big Balls?'

Outside, the air is cool and the night is lit by light from the control tower and the glow from the landing lights on the runways. We walk across the tarmac towards a British Airways jet that has just landed. I feel more at home on a noisy tarmac than I did in Mother's house in Clontarf.

It is humiliating being taken for granted all the time. First Carla decides we should visit Mother. Then Mother decides I should visit Rory. Finally, Carla decides we should buy a house. It is as though my life is happening *despite* my participation.

The image of the shrine to Rory haunts me. It occurs to me that the only way to get appreciated in my family is to disappear. Maybe it is about time that I went away to London or to Texas.

I have not seen Rory in years. He is living a new life in Manchester so why should I bother him? The last thing he needs is his goody two-shoes little brother arriving on his doorstep to nag him to come to visit his shrine. I don't want to go all the way to Manchester just so Rory can call me a 'lickarse'. Maeve can go in my place. If she's gone any longer than a week, I'm sure Mother will erect a shrine to *her*.

We arrive at the British Airways plane just as the landing stairs pulls up alongside. The mats are heavy and it is a great relief to put them down. In a few moments we will make a vast square of disinfected mats on the ground that no passenger will be able to avoid.

Suddenly I become aware of liquid running down my trousers. Then I notice that my hands are wet and bloody in the lights from the aeroplane. My jacket and jeans are soaked. Could I have somehow cut an artery on the way across the tarmac? I feel panic rising in my stomach.

Dan stares at me, 'Christ, boy, what have ye done to yerself?'

I frantically examine myself for wounds before discovering that the dye from my new red jacket is running. I realise that the mats that I have been clutching to my chest are already dripping with disinfectant. The combination of red dye and orange disinfectant has had a toxic effect.

As I watch, the top pocket of my new red jacket peels off and wafts across the tarmac in the wind from the jet engines.

EIGHT

The Band

THE FABULOUS Roadrun-
ners faced the audience and posed in semi-darkness with
their heads down as rotor blade noises from the soundtrack
of 'Apocalypse Now' blared out across the huge banks of
speakers at either side of the stage. It sounded as though
helicopters were passing through the hall. The soundtrack
was Rory's idea.

'Most bands just go on stage and play. We're going to
take people into a new dimension. They won't know what
hit them.'

Frankenstein stood in front of the stage and tilted his
square head back to gulp from a flagon of cider. Batman
stood beside him waiting for his turn. A girl dressed as a
banana swept past on the shoulders of Count Dracula.

Robert Duval's voice crackled across the hall, 'I love the
smell of Napalm in the morning. It smells like victory,' and
the soundtrack faded.

The silence that fell was unexpected and prolonged. In
the murk, nobody moved. I stood beside Joey Boland at the
side of the stage. Joey waited with his hands on the faders
of the lighting control, ready to immerse the stage in red
and orange light. I craned forward to try to see what was
going on. Maybe someone had broken a string. I was
eighteen and excited at being a roadie for my brother's
band. I felt confident and needed. Whatever the problem
was on stage, I was sure I could sort it out.

'Play your fucking music,' The Wolfman yelled.

'Hey, what happened to the helicopters?' a cowboy shouted.

Paddy Cool took a cautious step forward with his guitar. He lowered a pair of thick industrial goggles to squint across at Rory.

'Now?' he said.

'Yes, now, for fuck's sake,' Rory hissed.

Paddy Cool struck a vicious ear-splitting chord, the stage blazed into light and the band went into the first number. In the flashing lights the hall became a jumbled, twirling mass of waving hands and frantic, exuberant faces, some wore make-up, others wore masks, most were pale and youthful. In front, Snow White pogoed into one of the light stands. A few punks spat at the band. Rory strutted all over the stage, in Mother's fur coat, bellowing into the microphone:

> Ah met ma bayba in a telephone booth,
> My bayba told me she was in da mood,
> I wore my fav-or-ite birth-day suit,
> To meet mah bayba in a telephone booth.

Rory flung himself into the audience. The audience threw him back. Paddy Cool tried to leap on top of an amp, mistimed his jump and crashed into Mao's drums. Mao kicked away his drum stool and hit whatever drums were left standing. Gordon, the skinny bass player, posed at the back in his long, black leather coat and sunglasses looking cool with a cigarette dangling from his mouth, concentrating on his bass. A mini-skirted nun looked up at him adoringly from the side of the stage.

Rory seemed to lose all self-control when he performed. Every time he threw himself into the audience I expected them to suddenly open up like the waters parting for Moses to let him break his neck on the floor. When he climbed to the top of one of the speaker stacks and balanced precariously with his arms out to receive the roars of the crowd, I wanted to look away but couldn't. The spectacle of my brother endangering himself both thrilled and terrified me. He looked so frail and ludicrous in the fur coat, glaring out at the audience with mad eyes. I rushed through the crowd to a position directly underneath Rory, ready to catch him should he topple. In the end, he climbed slowly down to the stage, punched the air, then sauntered over to the microphone stand. I doubt if he even noticed that I was there. The sustained burst of discordant guitar noises and cymbal crashing that finished the song sounded like a car-crash. The applause was even louder.

'Thanks, it's great to be here,' Rory shouted, just before an empty beer can bounced off his head.

When the gig was over, I watched the roadies take down the drums, put them in their cases, and gather up all the leads and bits of equipment. They unplugged the amplifiers and pushed them over to the back door of the hall to wait for the van. This was the third time I had seen Rory's band and I still got a thrill out of the bustle and noise. Even clearing up after a gig seemed a lot more exciting than sitting in a lecture room listening to lectures on 'The Ambiguity of Philosophy' or 'Samuel Beckett's Melancholic Muse'.

In the dressing-room, Rory was ecstatic, 'They loved "Telephone Booth". That has to be the first single. You could tell that they really accepted us.'

Joey Boland agreed, 'Yep, getting hit on the skull with a beer can is a sure sign that you've been accepted.'

Mao passed a fat joint to Paddy Cool who was opening a bottle of red wine by pushing the cork down with his finger. In the corner, Gordon was wrapped around the mini-skirted nun, his bass guitar strapped across his back like a rifle. Captain Blackbeard, the Student Entertainments Officer, came up to shake Rory's hand and give Joey Boland an envelope filled with money.

'That was the best fancy dress ball we've ever had. Yis will be back next year,' Captain Blackbeard said.

Rory saw me and came over, 'What did you think?'

'Brilliant,' I said.

'What about the helicopters?'

'Superb. I thought they were real.'

'Yeah,' Rory smiled. 'It wasn't bad for a third gig. I think we're nearly ready for the Baggot. Want a lift?'

On the way home in the van, Mao rolled a joint on the top of an amplifier while Paddy held a flashlight on him. Gordon sat on an amplifier at the back with the mini-skirted nun on his knee. I sat on the floor in the corner.

'There's only one thing that bothers me,' Mao said, 'how can we be a New Wave band with a name like The Fabulous Roadrunners?'

'What's wrong with the name?' Rory said.

'It's a bit too rock and roll, isn't it? It hasn't got the street credibility of names like The Stranglers, Magazine, The Damned, The Clash, The Ramones. Why can't we change it to something really alternative like The Scumbags From Hell or The Open Sores? Then people will really notice us.'

'I've a great idea,' Rory said. '*We'll* be The Fabulous Roadrunners and *you* can be The Scumbag From Hell.'

'Let me off here,' said the nun. 'I've got school in the morning.'

Joey Boland stopped the van to drop off the nun. Mao passed the joint to Rory.

Rory stretched, 'When we play the Baggot, the record companies will be strangling each other to give us a deal.'

'I'm glad it's that simple,' Paddy Cool said.

'It is, if you're as good as us,' Rory said. 'This time next year, I want to be touring the States.'

Rory put a Graham Parker tape into the tapedeck and put his feet up on the dashboard. 'Hold Back the Night' came on.

Later, we piled through the door of Rory's basement flat in Rathmines and flopped down on chairs and on Rory's bed in the corner. Rory went to the record player and stuck on 'Eddie and the Hot Rods Live at the Marquee.'

'This is one of my favourites,' Rory said to me. 'We're going to be as good as this someday.'

Eddie and the Hot Rods sang '96 Tears' and Rory began to dance around the room. Mao lit a fat joint that sparked as he inhaled. Paddy Cool opened another bottle of wine. Rory made everyone get up to dance. At first they moved sluggishly but when Eddie and the Hot Rods went into

'Gloria', even Mao began to jump around. When people fell or crashed into tables, I helped them back on their feet. When the dancing was over, Rory snapped the cap off a bottle of Heineken and handed it to me. It was the first time I remembered that my brother gave me something other than a thump. He made me feel like a member of the band.

'If you're doing nothing next week, the band is going on tour down the country. We could use another roadie,' he said, pretending not to care if I came along.

'That would be ba-brilliant,' I said.

This was obviously the start of a new mature relationship for Rory and me. Now that we no longer had to share a room at home, we got on extremely well. From now on, we could look out for each other as brothers should.

Rory invited me to stay the night, 'You can sleep in the bath. There's a blanket under the table.'

In college next day, I felt queasy and exhausted. I couldn't concentrate on what the professor was saying. My head was full of electric guitars and helicopter noises and my underwear was still damp from the tapwater that had dripped on me all night while I slept.

When I got home, Mother was waiting for me.

'You could have phoned. You knew I'd be worried.'

'I told you that I ma-might stay with Rory.'

'You must have whispered it.'

Mother sat down at the table and lit a cigarette. Usually, if I stayed out late or didn't come home, I got harangued for at least twenty minutes. Today, Mother appeared distracted. Ever since she became a TD, she always seemed to be in a hurry. It was as though she had suddenly entered Camelot. In the mornings, she was magically whisked away to the Dail. We saw more of her on television than we did at home.

'It's like being a royal family,' Maeve said. 'Except that we don't have a palace.'

I was about to ask her if anything was wrong when Maeve came in.

'What was it like?'

'Great. The band are getting tight now. Rory has invited me to be a roadie on their tour next week . . .'

'A roadie? Gosh, how exotic. Are you going to do it?' Maeve asked.

'Yeah', I grinned.

Mother took a drag on her cigarette, 'You'll do no such thing. You've got college.'

'It's only for a couple of weeks. I'll be fa-fine.'

'I never knew that Rory could sing,' Mother said vaguely. 'When he was a child, I don't even remember him humming a tune.'

Maeve smiled, 'It's all right, he's in a New Wave band. Not being able to sing is an advantage.'

'Oh, I see,' Mother said. 'Well, as long as he's happy.'

Mother got up to go to a meeting.

'Behave yourselves, I have to sort out the country's problems,' she joked.

Maeve sat down and took Mother's place at the table. She lit a cigarette and drained it in several long drags, the same way Mother smoked hers when she was tense.

'I think she's going to marry Dessie.'

'Dessie? She would never do that. Would she?'

Maeve stared at a point on the floor. Her eyes narrowed.

'I hate his little moustache and the way he plasters his stringy bits of hair across his scalp with Brylcreem. He felt my leg once. Did I ever tell you that?' She smiled, 'I stabbed his hand with a fork.'

I tried to make light of the situation, 'She won't marry Dessie. She wouldn't do that to us.'

'Why shouldn't she? Rory's left home, you're in college. I'm nearly twenty. If she marries him, I'll join Fine Gael,' Maeve said.

I had always presumed that Mother would stay married until Dad came home or his body was discovered. I couldn't imagine Mother ever marrying Dessie. Dessie and I had never spoken. In fact, we hardly ever made eye contact. I suspected that Dessie regarded me as backward. Whenever he was around, my stutter always seemed to get worse. At least I didn't have to talk to him or hear any of his jokes. I was glad I was going on the road with Rory's band. For a while I wouldn't have to think about Mother and Dessie or even Fianna Fail. I smiled to myself as I thought about my brother rushing across the stage at the previous night's gig with the microphone stand out in front of him like a lance. Now Rory wore the fur coat off-stage as well as on.

'It's my image now,' Rory told me one night. 'Any fool can be *in* a band. The Fabulous Roadrunners *are* a band. That's the difference. That's why we're going to be the next Boomtown Rats.'

For a week I sleepwalked through college lectures. I day-dreamed about being on the road. I tried to work out how to save enough money for a leather jacket. I went into town and got my hair spiked. Now that Rory wore the fur coat all the time, maybe he would lend me his leather jacket.

On Saturday morning, I arrived at Rory's flat in Rath-mines just as they were loading the van. Rory allowed me to carry all the guitar amplifiers and the drums by myself and even let me help with the huge p.a. speakers. On the way to the gig, I sat in the back in the middle of the equipment, wedged between two bass bins. Occasionally, someone passed me the stub of a joint.

By the time we got to Mayo, my neck was stiff and my legs had pins and needles. Dangles was a long wooden hangar with a stage that was six feet high. A silver globe glittered from the ceiling and the walls were hung with ropes, displaying ribbons of blue and green. Posters for Margo, who was due to appear the following week, were everywhere. Rory and the band went to the bar next door while Joey Boland and I set up the gear.

We got to the bar halfway through the nine o'clock news on television. Mother suddenly appeared being interviewed by a reporter.

'The Fine Gael government is like a leaking boat. I see it as my duty to push them out to sea. I owe it to the people of Ireland,' Mother said.

When the interview was over, people at the bar turned around to nod at Rory.

'That's the eldest boy,' a man beside me whispered to a companion. 'I hear he's a bit wild.'

A man came up to Rory and shook his hand, 'Congratulations on having such a wonderful woman for a mother.'

'Eh, thanks,' Rory said.

The promoter was a short man with a long grey beard. He stood in the dressing-room door and assured the band that he was anxious that they should enjoy their first visit to Dangles.

''Cos if you enjoy it, the punters will enjoy it. If there's a good vibration about yis on the floor I'll have yis back. Don't forget to play the anthem, sure ye won't, lads, eh?'

'Sorry,' Rory said. 'We're a New Wave band, we don't play national anthems.'

'Ha ha, lads, that's a good one,' the promoter laughed as he went out. 'See yis after.'

'What's all this crap about an anthem?' Rory asked Joey Boland.

'Don't ask me,' Joey said. 'I'm only the manager.'

'It's unprofessional not to know how to play the national anthem,' Paddy Cool muttered.

The audience of teenagers sat on the wooden benches at the sides of the hall and refused to dance. There wasn't even a smattering of applause when the band finished the first song. Many didn't even look towards the stage at all. The only display of interest had come earlier, during the helicopter noises, when some of the younger ones became frightened and ran out.

'Hey,' Rory shouted from the front of the stage. 'This is a New Wave concert.'

No reaction.

'We're gonna destroy the whole town tonight, OK?'

Nothing.

Rory went down on his knees with the microphone, 'I said Ooooooh. Kayyyyy?'

They didn't even glance at him.

Rory turned to us, 'What's the matter with them? Was it something I said?'

The band stampeded through 'Something Better Change'. Nobody moved. Then they tried 'Gloria'. Still nobody got up to dance. In desperation, they played their encore, a speeded up assault on 'Climb Every Mountain'. Rory screeched the lyrics like a demonic preacher. Rory was on his knees screaming into the microphone when a priest walked on stage carrying a large box. The promoter followed, holding his hands up to indicate that the band should stop playing. Rory stopped singing and stood up. The music died away. The audience rose to their feet and scampered to the stage with eager excited faces.

Gordon came over to the lighting control at the side of the stage where Joey Boland and I sat transfixed. He lit a cigarette.

'Does anybody know what country we're in?' Gordon said.

The priest took the microphone from Rory's hand, 'Hellu, hellu, can you hear me? Well, I'm delighted to say that it's time for the youth club raffle for the Spanish holiday. Oh, and of course, Harding's pub has donated a gallon of Jack Daniels as a runner's-up prize. So, as you can see, it's all happening. Now if everyone will just gather around the stage here for a moment, I'll call out the numbers.'

'I think we're in the wrong business,' Joey Boland said.

It took us an hour to take down the gear after the show. I carried all the band's amplifiers and packed away the drums. Rory said that the band was 'breaking me in'.

'When you get really good, we'll let you carry the p.a. on your own.'

We ran out of petrol outside Naas. There were no street lights. We had to use a flashlight to talk to each other.

'I can't believe anyone could be so fucking thick,' Rory said. 'Did you not think of checking the petrol gauge now and again?'

'I forgot,' Joey Boland whined.

'You forgot,' Mao said. 'You're not a manager, you're a great steaming lump of cowshit.'

After everyone told Joey what an idiot he was, we tried to figure out what to do. In the end, it was so late and we were so tired that we slept in the van. I curled up between the bass bins with my jacket across my knees and an old scarf as a pillow.

In the morning, I awoke just as Joey was returning from Naas with a milk bottle of petrol.

'Enough to get us as far as the garage,' he explained. 'I met a girl down there who thought we were brilliant last night.'

'She must have been completely out of her head,' Mao said.

We got a full tank in Naas and drove on to Rathmines where Joey dropped Rory and myself.

'I'll pick you up at two,' Joey said.

'I don't want to go back to the flat,' Rory grinned. 'I want to stay on the road. Let's eat.'

Rory and I ate lunch in a small dark café. We were tired and sore but we had a tingling sensation in our bones.

'Congratulations, it's called road fever,' Rory explained through a mouthful of beans. 'Now you'll never be able to go back to a normal life.'

'That's fa-fine with me.'

'When we get our deal, we'll have our own Mercedes van with plush seats and even beds in the back. Just wait until after we play the Baggot and blow them all away.'

I gave Rory half of my green beans. I was relieved to see him eat them. He needed a lot of nourishment to fuel his energy for the stage.

Joey picked us up at two and a few hours later we were driving through Cavan's rolling green hills, passing strange expressionless men who stood in fields beside equally expressionless cows. Nobody waved. Everyone we passed seemed to know we were coming.

'I'm not smoking any more of this stuff,' Mao said, tossing his half-smoked joint out of the van. 'I'm beginning to get paranoid.'

'You're not paranoid,' Rory said. 'They *are* watching us.'

'I wonder if they like New Wave music?' Paddy mused.

In the centre of the empty Twinkles ballroom, an old man leaned on a mop and coughed twice into his hand.

'How yis?' he winked.

'We're grand,' Joey Boland said. 'Will there be a big crowd tonight, do you think?'

'Oh aye,' the man said in a Northern accent. 'Bag crowd, rite enough. A vurry bag crowd.'

'Oh good,' Joey Boland replied, looking confused.

'Go on, ask him,' Mao urged.

Behind Mao, the rest of us watched with interest.

Joey cleared his throat, 'Do you think they'll like New Wave music, you know, punk rock?'

The old man grinned a toothless grin, 'Oh aye, they'll like it rite enough, I'd say. As long as yis can dye-dill.'

Joey looked at us, then back at the old man, 'Dye-dill? What's that?'

'Yis don't know what a dye-dill is, do yis not?'

'No.'

'Here then hold me mop, I'll show yis.'

Joey held the mop as the old man stretched himself, then commenced an Irish jig. His steps rang out against the wooden floor.

'Ah diddle-ee-dye-dill, diddle-ee-dye-dill, diddle-ee-dye-dill eye-dill-dye,' he sang.

At midnight, the hall was full of young people. When The Fabulous Roadrunners took the stage, it was so hot and smoky that we could scarcely breathe. With the opening bars of 'Telephone Booth', a man plummeted from the balcony and was caught by the crowd. Young girls stood at the front of the stage and screamed at the band until tears ran out of their eyes. A girl was thrown up in the air, skirt billowing like a parachute. Girls balanced on their boyfriends' shoulders and waved their hands at the band. A fight broke out at the side. A man with his arm in a cast cleared a space by wielding the broken limb in front of him like a club. A pair of panties flew in an arc across the stage, followed by a wellington boot. Rory stood on stage and sang, fascinated by the wildness of the crowd. He didn't try to throw himself from the stage or hang from the ceiling. He just couldn't compete with the audience. For once, I could forget about him and enjoy the gig. As an encore, the band played an extended version of 'Telephone Booth'. The crowd made a human chain and jived around the edge of the stage.

After the house lights came on, the band fought their way to the dressing-room through a tangle of reaching hands and yelling faces. Joey Boland and I had to keep people from tearing the band's clothes off. In the dressing-room, the band collapsed, sweat running down their faces. When they got their breath back, they looked at each other with satisfacton.

'Now you know what it's like to play a Wild West Saloon,' Mao said. 'The only thing missing was the shoot-out.'

'It just doesn't come any better than that,' Rory said. 'We're ready for the Baggot.'

Paddy Cool slumped over, 'Tell us, are we a New Wave band or a punk band?'

'It's all the same,' Rory said. 'Just as long as we don't sound like Steely Dan.'

'But we're not a punk band, are we?'

'Well, not really I suppose,' Rory said. 'We're more New Wave.'

'Good, then I don't need these fucking things anymore,' Paddy Cool said and threw his industrial goggles across the room. 'I can't see a bloody thing on stage with them on.'

From outside came the sound of banging and thumping. Something went over with a crash.

'I wish all audiences were like this,' Paddy said.

The door burst open and Joey Boland appeared, haggard and choking, 'You better watch yoursleves, lads. They want to know why you won't play the anthem.'

'Fuck them,' Rory said. 'Tell them New Wave bands don't play national anthems.'

There was a thud on the dressing-room door.

'You can tell them yourself,' Joey Boland said. 'I think they're gonna break it down.'

From the stage came the sound of crashing.

'That sounded like your cymbals, Mao,' Paddy said.

Mao stood up, 'Aw, mother of God. They're not even fucking paid for.'

A swell of voices rose outside the dressing-room door. 'Kick it in, kick it in,' someone yelled. There was a loud bang.

'I told you we should have learned to play the anthem,' Paddy Cool said as he raised his guitar and held it like a baseball bat. 'It's so bloody unprofessional.'

Gordon sat on a chair smoking a cigarette as he flicked through a newspaper, 'They're just children. They'll calm down if you don't provoke them.'

Rory picked up a Coke bottle and stood back, ready to take on whoever came through the door. Joey Boland and Mao stood behind Rory. I went over to join them. Beside me, Mao took up a karate position.

'I didn't know you knew karate,' Paddy said.

'I don't,' Mao answered, 'but the crowd outside the door don't fucking know that, do they?'

The dressing-room door abruptly burst back on its hinges, revealing a doorway jammed full of faces and fists. It was hard to tell the difference between the girls and the boys. Everyone snarled and spat. In the centre was a tiny skinhead with full red lips.

'Playthefuckinganthem,' the skinhead said.

Rory smiled and stepped forward with his hands out, 'We don't know the anthem. We've never played the anthem. We're a New Wave band.'

'*Playthefuckinganthem*,' the skinhead screamed.

Everyone took a step back.

'We don't know it,' Rory repeated.

'Ye play all the English stuff, don't ye? Why won't yis play the Irish anthem?'

'Well, we –'

'*Ye're a fucking disgrace to Ireland.*'

'Look,' Rory said angrily. 'If The Clash played here or Thin Lizzy or The Boomtown Rats, you wouldn't expect them to play the anthem, would you?'

The skinhead stepped into the room. He held up his fist, 'Everyone who plays here plays the fucking anthem.'

'You mean The Clash play –'

'*Ye're not Irishmen.*'

Gordon got up, folded his newspaper and raised his guitar to defend himself. 'This is all so juvenile,' he sighed.

Rory appeared to reach a decision. He took a deep breath,

drew himself up to his full height. He towered over the skinhead. Now, he seemed to be taking delight in the situation. He gave a suicidal grin that chilled my heart and sent a tremor of fear through everyone in the band.

'Sorry, we don't know it. But you know, even if we did, we wouldn't fucking play it for *you*.'

The skinhead's teeth gleamed, 'Then yis'll not leave here alive.'

The skinhead pulled at the broken door hanging from the wall and attempted to wrench it free. The crowd helped him and soon the door was ripped off its hinges and stamped and kicked to splinters.

Paddy Cool shook his head, 'Fucking unprofessional.'

The crowd, led by the tiny skinhead, started forward.

My brother was going to get mangled, just because he was in a rock band and was standing up for his principles. I had to do something to save him. Mother expected it of me. Dad expected it of me. A mysterious impulse suddenly propelled me forward. I found myself walking briskly towards the crowd in the doorway.

'Excuse me,' I said politely as if I was just popping out for a can of Coke.

As I made my way through them, I expected a punch or a kick, but they let me pass. There were about thirty people with the skinhead. Most of them looked as though they wanted to bite someone. I was surprised at how calm I felt. It was as though I was outside myself, watching it all happening to someone else.

Behind me, I heard Rory say menacingly, 'Come on. Let's see you really start something.'

I climbed up onto the stage. The microphones were still standing. Joey hadn't bothered to turn off the p.a.. I said a quick prayer to God to not let me forget the words, stood at the microphone and sang.

'Sinne Fianna Fail ata faoi gheal ag Eir-air-eann.'

My voice echoed in the empty hall. It sounded sweet as a choirboy's and stutter free. Within seconds, I caught sight of a commotion to my right at the entrance to the dressing-room. I saw the the skinhead and his friends rush out. A moment later, the perplexed faces of Rory and Joey peered at me over the heads of the crowd. I stood with my hands behind my back like a schoolboy at a Feis so as not to give any offence. Suddenly, other voices joined in. Mao, Paddy, Joey and Gordon climbed onto the stage to sing into microphones. Rory stayed where he was. The voices became a chorus. When I forgot the words, I moved my lips. I heard a tremulous falsetto soaring above everything. When I looked down, I saw the tiny skinhead singing with eyes closed, face flushed crimson with emotion.

When it was over, the crowd stomped and cheered as if the band had just finished another gig. Rory looked disappointed. He went back to the dressing-room without saying a word to me.

'Brilliant, lads, best gig in years,' the tiny skinhead said, shaking our hands. 'Yis'll be back, no doubt about it.'

Later, while we were loading the van, Rory came up to me. 'Lickarse,' he said and walked away before I could say anything.

We were halfway to Dublin before Joey Boland realised we had left without getting our money.

'I'll tell you what I think,' Paddy Cool said.

'Please, don't,' Rory said.

'I think that tonight was the most unprofessional situation I've ever seen in my life.'

'You want us to become a showband and play the anthem every night, is that it?' Rory said.

'I mean, what's the difference?' Paddy Cool said. 'It's only an anthem, a few seconds of music.'

Rory glared at Paddy, 'I'll tell you the fucking difference. If we were in a showband, your name would be plain old Dermot Wiggington, not Paddy fucking Cool.'

Paddy was unperturbed, 'I just think that if we play the gigs and take the money we should play the anthem.'

Rory decided to be reasonable, 'Look, I'll explain it again.'

'Please, do,' Paddy said.

'The Fabulous Roadrunners are not a showband, never were a showband and never will be a showband. We're a

New Wave band. We play our own songs or songs we like by other New Wave bands. Is that clear?'

Paddy Cool snorted, 'Then why do we play "Climb Every Mountain"?'

'Yeah,' Mao said. 'That's from "The Sound of Music" for fuck's sake.'

'Hey, take it easy,' Gordon said. 'I like Julie Andrews.'

'Everyone's being too serious,' Mao said. 'At the next gig let's take off all our clothes and run around shouting, "Hallelujah". That should get a reaction.'

'Shut up, Mao,' Rory said.

'I was only trying to help,' Mao said.

Gordon leaned in from the back, bass guitar protruding over his head like a rifle, 'If this band plays the national anthem, I'm leaving. It's a matter of principle.'

'I'm just saying that I wouldn't mind a few bob now and again,' Paddy said, backing down. 'I mean, when was the last time we got paid?'

Mao nodded, 'I owe me old dear a fucking fortune.'

Rory leaned back in the seat with a smug expression, wagged a finger at them all, 'Wait until the Baggot. After that, I guarantee you that this band is gonna take off.'

The next night at the Fox and Hounds pub in Killybegs, we arrived to find a hand-written sticker stuck across the band's poster:

'Tonight, Back room, The Fabulous Roadrunners featuring Rory Buckley, See Kathleen Buckley's eldest boy make a career in music. Admission, £1.'

Rory stood with a stormy face, 'Who the fuck did this? My music has got nothing to do with my mother,' he said.

'Our music has nothing to do with music,' Mao said.

'It's only a sticker,' Joey Boland said. 'It doesn't impugn our integrity as a band.'

'If that's not taken down, we don't go on.'

'That's a bit extreme, isn't it?' Joey Boland said.

'Put it this way, if it doesn't come down, then *you* can sing with the band tonight.'

'I think I'd better talk to someone,' Joey Boland said as he went off to find the promoter.

197

'That's telling him,' Mao said.

Mao and Paddy Cool watched Joey Boland leave with some disdain.

'Maybe we should get a new manager,' Mao said. 'I've got a bad feeling about this guy.'

'Let's drive off without him,' Paddy Cool said.

'Only one problem,' Rory said. 'It's his fucking van.'

'Good point.'

A man appeared at Rory's elbow, 'Excuse me, are yis the Buckley boys?'

The man was red-faced with a beer-belly and an ingratiating smile. At first, I thought he was looking for money.

'Yes,' I said. 'We're the B-Buckleys.'

The man smiled, 'Can I have a private word?'

Paddy Cool and Mao went up to the bar to join Gordon who was chatting up the pretty barmaid.

'I don't have any money on me,' Rory said.

The man's smile grew wider, 'I knew your mother and father years ago, when they were first married. I'm from Sneem, same as your father.' He nodded at Rory, 'I was at your christening.'

'Good for you,' Rory said. 'I still don't have any money.'

I saw the smile go from the man's face, 'No need to be rude.'

'It's OK,' I said. 'Rory's on stage in a few moments, he's got a bit of an artistic temperament.'

'Spit it out,' Rory said.

The man looked at his feet, 'I just wanted to tell yis that I saw your father last year. I worked with him on a site in Islington. I thought ye should know.'

We looked at him for a moment.

'What's that supposed to mean?' Rory said.

'You saw Dad?' I asked. 'L-last year?'

'I did,' the man said, glancing at Rory nervously.

'What the fuck are you talking about?' Rory said.

'There's no need to get aggressive with me. I'm only telling you what I saw with me own eyes.'

Rory bent down until his face was inches from the man's, 'And for a few bob you'll tell us where he is, is that it?'

The man shrugged his shoulders, 'I don't want your money. I wouldn't have mentioned it at all except . . .' he trailed off.

'Except what?'

'Well, when I went up to say hello, he just walked away from me and pretended he didn't know me. I said, "Hold on, John, it's me, Mick Clohessy," but he just kept walking.'

'I don't blame him,' Rory said.

Mick Clohessy put on a sincere face, 'I'm sure your mother would want to know. I heard he was coming back. That's the only reason I mention it.'

'He's coming back?'

Clohessy threw up his hands, 'It was only a rumour. He left the site before I did but one of the lads said he heard him talking about going back to Ireland.'

'I've heard enough crap for one night,' Rory said.

Rory strode off to the bar and ordered a pint. Clohessy stood and watched him, then turned to gaze blandly at me. I felt as though I was on a lift that had suddenly plunged, causing my insides to fall asunder and turning my feet to jelly. Clohessy's words hung in the room like the edginess before a fight. I wanted to run from him as I would from a wild animal. I needed to be a child once again, back on Redrock pier with Mother shielding me from the rain. Then I had known my place in the world. When there was a problem I had Mother to help me. I had always dreamed about finding Dad alive. But in my dreams it was always Dad himself who turned up, not a little man with a beer-belly who brought a rumour that sucked all the air out of the room and made it hard to breathe, to think, to turn away. For an instant, I wanted to shake this odd, little man who was standing in front of me. I wanted to force him to take me to Dad. Then even if he told me to go away, I would know for sure that he was alive. Suddenly, I wished that I had never met Mick Clohessy. He stood waiting for me to say something. There was an explosion of raucous laughter from the bar.

'Maybe you could let me have your address and phone

number,' I said after a while. 'My m-mother may want to talk to you.'

Clohessy handed me a piece of paper with his name and address already written out, 'You can get me there any Saturday or Sunday.'

'Thanks,' I said.

I was about to leave and join Rory at the bar when Clohessy touched my arm, 'By the way, you wouldn't have enough for a pint, would you?'

I gave him a pound and said I would contact him later.

'First, I want to think about things,' I said.

I joined Rory at the bar. He didn't look at me. Instead he drained his pint and turned to leave.

'I'm going for a walk,' he said.

The rest of us stayed at the bar and drank pints of Guinness. Mao and Paddy went back to the van to snort lines of coke. After a while, Gordon followed them back. When it was time to go on stage, there was still no sign of Rory.

Ten minutes after the band was due on stage, the promoter appeared in the doorway, 'Is it going to be a disco all night or what? It's gone nine-thirty.'

'Just give us a minute,' Joey said. 'Eh, we're just tuning the guitars.'

The promoter's face said that he didn't believe a word, but he wasn't going to argue about it now.

'On stage in five minutes or you can pack up and go home.'

I went out to look for Rory. I walked down Main Street but the only people I saw were kids on the way to the gig in the hotel. After ten minutes, I gave up. I was on my way back when I saw Rory a couple of hundred yards up the street looking in the windows of a pub. I stopped in a doorway and watched him as he stood on tiptoe for a few minutes, scanning the pub. He seemed to be looking for someone. Then he turned away, put his hands in his pockets and crossed the road in the direction of the gig. If he noticed me following, he gave no sign.

On stage, The Fabulous Roadrunners were on their

second instrumental version of 'Telephone Booth', when Rory leaped onto the stage. Rory flung himself against the speakers, into the front rows, headlong off the stage to roll on the floor. His eyes were wild, his mouth twisted in a snarl, yet he appeared lost as though he had been taken over by forces beyond his control. In the middle of 'Love Me To Shreds', he ripped a patch off the fur coat and presented it to a girl in the front row who giggled. At the end of 'Telephone Booth', he poured a pint of beer over his head. I had to dash on-stage to snatch the microphone from him in case he electrocuted himself. During 'White Riot', he hurled himself from the stage onto the chandelier in the centre of the ceiling where he hung, swinging from side to side, long legs almost touching the floor. The bouncer told him to get down. During the encore, Rory stared into the audience, raking faces with the intensity of a spotlight. For a moment, I thought he was scanning their faces looking for Dad. When it was over, Rory roared 'goodnight' and led the band off the stage to scattered applause.

'Motorhead are better than youse,' someone shouted. 'And they're crap.'

By the time I packed away the equipment and got to the dressing-room, Rory had a straw up his nostril, inhaling a line of coke off a mirror. The others stood behind with studious expressions, as though about to award marks for Rory's snorting technique.

'The party starts here,' Rory shouted. 'You've heard of road fever, now meet white line fever.'

'You bolix,' Mao said. 'Leave some for us, will ye?'

Back in the hotel, we persuaded the night porter to bring us drinks. Gordon arrived with a group of girls who seemed delighted to see us. Rory and Joey pulled in their chairs either side of a pretty redheaded girl. Paddy Cool and Mao bought a bottle of tequila and a bottle of orange juice and started mixing their own tequila sunrises.

I couldn't relax so I decided to go to bed. Before I went up to the room, I told Rory I would leave the door open for him. His glazed eyes dismissed me as if I were a bellhop. For a moment I thought he was going to tip me.

As I started up the stairs, I saw Mao, stripped to his underwear, galloping across the floor towards the night porter.

'Excuse me, I require music,' Mao said in an unconvincing imitation of an English lord. 'Does this establishment possess a grand piano?'

In bed, I thought about what Mick Clohessy had said earlier. I tried to figure out a plan, a way of dealing with the situation, but I was too exhausted. A feeling that I had sinned crept over me. I longed to go to someone for forgiveness. The image of the tall grey church opposite our home appeared before me, as cold and dark as it had been on the night of the vigil on the pier. The image faded and I thought about Mrs Durrant's face as she ladled dirt onto her husband's coffin. Her expression was sad, but there was a kind of peace in her eyes, an acceptance of loss. I realised that I had never cried for Dad. There had been no body, no funeral, no ritual of grieving. I wondered how I would feel if Dad arrived at one of the gigs or if he showed up suddenly at home. I would talk to Rory tomorrow and together we would sort it all out.

I woke up to see a naked woman standing over me in the murk. At first, I thought I was dreaming. Then I heard her speak.

'He'll wake up.'

'No, he won't,' Rory said. 'He sleeps like a log.'

A hand reached out, pulled the woman's arm and she vanished. There was a faint rustling before everything went quiet. I fell back into drowsiness. I was on the point of dropping off when I heard the bedsprings jangling in the distance. Gradually the jangling got faster and louder. A woman's voice began to moan softly. Then she started to call out.

'Oh, my God,' she said. 'Ooh, my God.'

'Yes, yes, grrnnnn,' Rory answered.

I turned over slowly. I saw my brother's bare behind poised in mid-air, a pair of shapely legs wrapped around his waist. His behind began to thrust back and forth in time to the moans. A pale hand materialised to stroke my brother's back, then dig its nails in hard as the tempo increased. Suddenly Rory and the woman began to moan together. They seemed to be attempting to bite each other's faces. The woman uttered a series of high-pitched 'woa-oh-ohs'. The 'woa-ohing' and jangling got faster and Rory's grunts grew louder and the whole noisy business went on for what seemed like hours before eventually, with a gigantic spasm of springs, the whole room seemed to shudder. When they finally finished, the couple dropped off quickly in a tangle of limbs, hair and bedclothes, leaving me bug-eyed in my bed and as stiff as a plank.

In the morning, the woman was gone. I rose, dressed and went downstairs for breakfast. Rory came down later and got stuck into a bowl of Rice Krispies. He didn't mention the woman.

By the time we were in the van and on the way to the next gig, I was ready to dismiss the incident as a weird dream. Then Rory bent forward to put on a tape and I caught a glimpse of three angry red lovebites of varying sizes arranged on his neck as neat as a trio of flying duck decorations on a living-room wall.

At three, the van pulled up outside a huge flat-roofed building. There was a long banner over the front door, THE MIDLAND'S BIGGEST INDOORS ROCK FESTIVAL. Underneath was a list of bands: 'Fumbling Maggots, Theatre of Pain, The Four Marilyns and, from Dublin, The Fabulous Roadsweepers'.

'Roadsweepers?' Rory said. 'Who's responsible for this?'

Joey got out of the van, 'I'll just go and see someone about it.'

The band went off for a drink. The gig was at six o'clock. There was a p.a. in the hall for the festival, so we had only to put up the drums and guitar amplifiers. When it was done, I left Joey to mind the gear and walked down the street to be on my own for while. Outside a music shop, I stopped to look at the guitars and pianos and other instruments in the window, then I went in. It took the assistant twenty minutes to find a recording of the national anthem.

'You're in luck,' she said, giving the disc a wipe with a cloth. 'It's the last one.'

I paid her and took the record. I noticed that the duration of the anthem was five minutes thirty-three seconds, at least four and half minutes longer than the quick snatch that most showbands played.

Back in the hall, Rory held up the record of the anthem and announced that he had solved the problem.

'Next time, we can play this and keep them standing around like complete fucking eejits with their noses in the air for five minutes. After that, maybe they won't be so quick to ask for it again.'

'Great. Now there's just one thing,' said Paddy Cool, 'when are we going to get rid of those fucking helicopter noises? They're driving me ga-ga.'

Rory didn't tell them that I had given him the record of the anthem or that it was my idea. He hardly acknowledged me at all.

That night, the band played to a few hundred teenagers and a couple of middle aged ladies whose sons were in The Four Marilyns. The promoter gave us our money and told us he would have us back.

'Yis are a bit loud and your man can't sing but yis are good crack,' he said.

As we were leaving, The Four Marilyns came on. The band was four guys who were dressed as Marilyn Monroe – blonde wigs, rouged lips, tight dresses. They sounded like someone going at a flock of geese with a chainsaw.

'That's exactly what we need,' Paddy said knowingly, indicating the blonde wigs. 'A good strong image.'

We were on the road for an hour when a familiar sound came on the radio. The song was so familiar that it took a few seconds before everyone recognised 'Telephone Booth'. Five pairs of hands reached for the volume dial forcing Joey to swerve into the middle of the road, where we narrowly avoided a petrol tanker.

'Watch it, lads, you nearly made me crash,' he shrilled.

'It's the demo tapes. Fanning's playing them,' Mao shouted.

'Shut up and listen, will you?' Rory roared.

We sat in the dark van and listened as The Fabulous

Roadrunners' first demo recording came over the airwaves. My spine tingled when Rory began to sing. His singing sounded completely out-of-key, but the guitar chugged along excitingly and the whole thing sounded energetic and appealing. Rory's voice got better all the time. During last night's gig, Joey swore that Rory had been in the right key at least half the time. Everything outside the world of the band now seemed irrelevant.

'I don't like the drum sound,' Mao said.

'Fuck off.'

'Shut your face.'

'Just listen.'

Mao held up his hands, 'OK, OK, no need to eat me.'

When it was over, Rory leaned forward, 'That's a potential number one. It's gonna be the first US single.'

I saw Mao and Paddy smirk at each other.

'Yep,' Mao said. 'Better than coming up the Liffey on a bicycle anyway.'

For the next week I tried to get Rory alone to talk to him about Mick Clohessy's sighting of Dad but Rory kept avoiding me. It amazed me that even though there were only six of us on the road, Rory was never alone. He spent most of his time with Mao. Before gigs, they usually disappeared into one of the cubicles for half an hour. On stage, Rory tied himself up with microphone cable, shouted out the lyrics as if he didn't care about anything and jumped into the audience to roll around on the floor until Joey or myself helped him back on stage. When Paddy played a guitar solo or when there was a break between songs, I saw Rory studying the audience as if he were thinking of waving at someone.

The Captains' Arms in Letterkenny had a tiny stage and a huge dancefloor. Over two hundred people were swinging gently from side to side when Rory began 'Climb Every Mountain':

> 'Climb every fucking mountain,
> Ford every fucking stream . . .'

After the first verse, the bald, bull-necked owner came out with a shotgun.

'Stop making a mock of that song, you heathen bastard, or I'll blow you to smithereens, so help me God,' the owner cried.

Rory smiled, bowed, then threw himself around the stage instead, which the owner didn't seem to mind.

Lefty's Bar in Cork had no stage at all. Rory walked among the tables as he sang. He dropped to one knee to scream a serenade at a girl in the audience during 'Climb Every Mountain' and got punched in the face by the girl's boyfriend, a burly biker. When his nose started to bleed, Rory smeared the blood across his face and kept singing.

> 'Climb every bleedin' mountain
> Ford every bleedin' stream . . .'

Lilly Casey's Backroom in Athlone was packed with young people in Mohicans and spiky haircuts. Rory encouraged them to dance. When they wouldn't, he ordered them to throw drink over him. He stood in his fur coat and got showered.

'Come on, what's the matter? Where's the Guinness?'

Guinness cascaded on him from all sides. Rory kept singing and falling about the stage. Afterwards, the coat stank but he refused to take it off.

'It was a brilliant gig,' he said. 'They'll never forget it.'

In the morning, the smell was so foul that even Mao refused to sit beside him in the van.

'I have some pride, you know,' he said.

Rory didn't sit beside me at breakfast or in the van. Once, I squeezed in beside him and tried to talk but he simply turned up the volume on the tape recorder and sang along to the song until I shut up. I followed him down the street in Moate but he spotted me and sprinted away. At meals, he behaved as though I was invisible. It was like being back in the bedroom at home when we were growing up. Even the others began to notice.

'All singers are mad,' Mao said. 'He'll be fine once he gets famous.'

'I dunno. I've never seen a man fall in love with a fur coat before,' Paddy said. 'I think we should separate them for their own good.'

Every night, at whatever hotel we happened to be staying in, Rory stayed up late drinking or smoking joints with Mao and sometimes Joey. After a boring and sparsely attended gig in The Parish Hall in Tuam, Rory and Mao took all their clothes off and went out onto the hotel roof to catch pigeons for breakfast. When it started to rain, they began to wrestle. The two naked men rolled in puddles with their arms around each other.

Paddy approached Rory's fur coat, 'Maybe we should dump this in the bath and wash it.'

'You'll probably have to kill it first,' Gordon said.

'On second thoughts, somebody else can do it,' Paddy said and left the coat there.

When I awoke, there was a spaceship ahead. It was coming right at us with all its lights smudged in the rain. As it drew nearer, rows of flaring green and red parted like huge jaws. I tried to shield my eyes from the brightness but my hands wouldn't obey me. The light turned crimson, then brilliant white. A foghorn groan hurt my ears.

The spaceship crunched into us head-on. I screamed.

I sat up suddenly with my hands at my face. There was a whoosh of air as the truck swished past trailing pennants of purple and red. It gave a blarp on its horn as it went: a lonely juggernaut looking for a mate.

'You OK?' Rory said.

On the dashboard, the coloured meters and dials flickered. Through the windscreen was a gala parade of roadlights. The road was launching white lines at the window just as it had been before I conked out.

'I'm grand,' I said. 'How about you?'

'Go back to sleep,' Rory said distantly. 'We'll be home soon.'

He gave me a loan of his fur coat.

Just before going on stage in Dundalk, the promoter came backstage to beg us not to play the anthem.

'They're a mixed crowd here, Catholics as well as Protestants. Whichever anthem you play first will start a riot. Could you just play a rock song at the end instead?'

'We'll think about it,' Rory said.

The meeting with Mick Clohessy still bothered me. Even when the band was at its loudest, I could hear Clohessy's words in my mind. I decided that it would do me no good to stay confused.

Next morning when the van stopped for petrol, I climbed out, went into the nearest pub and found a phone. It took me twenty minutes to get through to Bernard, Dad's brother, who still lived in Sneem. I worried that the band would go without me. Eventually, Bernard came on the line. He was surprised that I was ringing him. He was even more surprised when I told him what it was about.

'I'm sorry,' he said. 'I've never heard of Mick Clohessy. He's not from around here.'

I took a deep breath, 'Have you heard from Dad lately?'

'No!' Bernard exclaimed after a shocked silence. 'Should I have?'

When I explained about Mick Clohessy, Bernard sounded as sincerely apologetic as ever. He promised to contact me the minute he heard any news. I put the phone down feeling like an eejit. At least I had tried. I took out the piece of paper with Mick Clohessy's name and address on it. For a moment, I felt an urge to throw it away. Then I folded it into a tiny square and put it in the back pocket of my jeans where I wouldn't lose it.

'We want you to wash the coat or throw it away,' Paddy Cool said. 'We've taken a vote and we're not travelling with it anymore.'

Rory sat on a rock in the field by the roadside, drew on his cigarette and nodded to himself. He huddled deeper in his smelly coat. Paddy and Mao and Joey shuffled their feet on the dewy grass while they waited for his answer. Gordon and I watched from the door of the van.

'All right, I'll buy a new one,' Rory said and watched them smile. 'After the Baggot.'

The last gig of the tour was in Trudy's Nite Spot in Ballina. Rory was sitting on the side of the stage with his eyes closed when I cornered him. He rocked back and forth with his eyes closed, humming softly. The odour from the coat was like rotting fish. I took a step back. A piece of fluffy fur wafted down to the floor. Rory was disintegrating in front of my eyes.

'Rory?' I said gently.

'Four days to the Baggot,' he said without opening his eyes, as though he had been expecting me.

'Rory, do you think we should t-tell Mother about Mick Clohessy?'

'Sure,' he said. 'Give her a good laugh.'

'Maybe she won't think it's funny.'

'He's just a chancer. Forget him.'

I was about to try to get him to tell me what he really thought when he opened his eyes and smiled.

'Tell her whatever you like,' he said, his voice unnaturally soft. 'Keep me out of it though, I don't want to get involved in anything anymore.'

'Do you think . . . ?' I began.

'I don't know and I don't care,' Rory said. 'In a while I'll be in England or America with the band, and it won't matter.'

'OK,' I said and went to leave.

'Daniel?' Rory said and I stopped.

Rory's eyes were swimming in his head, 'If Dad shows up, ask him what the fuck happened to my treehouse.'

As I walked away, I heard Rory laughing softly to himself.

That night, Rory stalked the stage like a maniac. He took off the fur coat during 'Gloria' and continued to shed his clothing for the rest of the set. After seven songs he was down to his shoes, socks, underpants and vest. He sang energetically, passionately but, unfortunately, out-of-tune. Everyone was riveted to see if he was going to go all the way. Finally, during 'Climb Every Mountain', he kicked off his shoes, peeled off his socks and threw them into the audience. He wriggled out his vest and his hands were heading for his crotch when the promoter turned off the lights. In the darkness and pandemonium we managed to get Rory into the dressing-room before the police arrived.

'You know,' Joey said, 'if your brother ever learns to sing, this will be one hell of a band.'

On the way home in the van, Rory lay in the back wrapped in as many of his clothes as we had managed to salvage. His fur coat lay across his knees. For some reason, the fur coat no longer smelled bad.

'He must have bought it some deodorant,' Gordon said.

I fell asleep. When I awoke we were in Dublin, and up ahead on the quay walls, rows of seagulls perched, haughty as lords.

Rory leaned over from the back. He gazed at the birds with great interest, 'Anyone fancy a seagull on toast?'

'Yeah,' Mao said. 'I'm sick of scrambled eggs.'

'I'll cook the thing,' Paddy Cool called from behind, 'as long as somebody else plucks it.'

'You cannot be serious,' Gordon said.

'Where's the roadie?' Rory shouted.

'I'm here,' I said.

'Hold on tight.'

'I'm holding on.'

Rory leaned out of the window of the van with his arms out like a messiah. I held on tight to his legs as the van bumped onto the footpath and screamed along the quays.

'Get in closer,' Rory shouted.

'If I get any closer we'll be in the fucking Liffey,' Joey Boland said.

The engine thundered. Everyone except Gordon whooped like a Comanche. Mao leaned over my shoulder and roared 'Ger-on-i-mo' at the top of his voice. Any seagull left on the wall by the time Rory made his lunge must have been deaf, I thought. I held on firmly to Rory's legs. For a moment, I thought he was going to take us both out of the window. There was a sudden thump and Rory went limp. I was sure he had hit a telegraph pole. I hauled my brother back inside as birds scattered into the early morning blue sky. A cluster of small white stars splattered onto the windscreen.

'My brand new windscreen. The little bolixes,' Joey Boland said.

Rory turned around to show us a single, white, perfect feather sticking out from his beaming grin. On the wall opposite, in flutters of white, like heavenly newspapers descending onto the quays, the seagulls reclaimed their positions.

'Let's go back and get the rest of it,' Rory said.

An hour later, Joey dropped me at the bus-stop for Redrock.

'See you at the Baggot on Friday,' Rory shouted as the van pulled away.

I arrived home tired and dirty, feeling that I had been to another world weirder and far more punishing than the one I knew. Perhaps life in a band was not really what I wanted to do after all. At least with ship inspecting, you didn't have to hump amplifiers up and down flights of stairs until your arms and legs screamed for mercy. I didn't want to be a roadie anymore. I would do the Baggot and that would be the end. I was sure Rory would be relieved to be rid of me.

Mother was in the kitchen with Dessie and Maeve. They were drinking coffee and smoking cigarettes.

'Hi,' I said.

Mother held up a letter, her lip curled, 'This fellow Mick . . .' she began. 'He says he was talking to you and Rory.'

'Yeah,' I said. 'We met him in Killybegs. He just wants money.'

'See, I told you, Mother,' Maeve said, turning to me. 'He wants Mother to send him a cheque so he can go to England to track down Dad.'

'That sa-sounds like him all right,' I said.

I noticed that Maeve's neck was dirty. She hadn't washed her face either. That was unusual for her. She looked at me with big sad eyes. She could have been twelve again. Then I realised that after two weeks on the road with Rory, I wasn't much to look at myself. Every part of me seemed to itch.

Maeve said, 'Mother wants to put out a nationwide appeal.'

'What's wrong with that?' Mother said. 'I should have done this long ago.'

Dessie cleared his throat, 'Kathleen, I know that this is a sensitive subject, but something like that will hurt your chances if there's an election. I'm only thinking of your future.'

'The man's a chancer,' Maeve declared.

'Rory thinks he's a chancer too,' I said.

Mother looked up. At the mention of Rory's name, something beautiful and unspeakably sad happened to her face. She looked up at me with a strange hunger in her eyes as if she were longing for forgiveness from some unnamed act in her past. Perhaps she wanted me to absolve her of this letter and the intrusive man who was trying to introduce a ghost into our lives.

'He's just looking for a few easy pa-pounds,' I said. 'I think Rory's right. We should ignore him.' I smiled at her, 'Rory wants everyone to come to the Baggot to see his band.'

Dessie leaned back and patted his belly, 'There are other ways of checking something out, Kathleen. We could hire a private detective for instance. I know a very good, reliable fellow in Stonybatter.'

Later, when Dessie had left and Mother had agreed to phone the private detective, we made breakfast. I told them about Rory's band. I exaggerated all his qualities and didn't tell them anything about the bizarre behaviour or the fur coat.

A while later, I saw Mother go to the bin with the letter in her hand. She made as if to throw it away then paused, folded the letter in half and placed it under a box on the shelf. Then she picked up the phone and called a friend at party headquarters.

'Rory's playing in a marvellous new Irish musical group this Friday and I want you to support his first concert. Bring as many people as you possibly can. It'll be a great night.'

She was on the phone all morning. When she finished making phone calls, she turned to us with a satisfied smile.

'Now at least, my son is guaranteed a good turnout.'

Four days later, at least half the audience in the Baggot were middle aged and wore Fianna Fail rosettes. Mother sat in their midst. As Rory and I peeped around the corner from the dressing-room, Dessie O'Hanlon passed, carrying a tray of golden pints.

'Fair play to yis, lads,' he shouted. 'Rock and roll, ha?'

'I don't believe it,' Rory said. 'The record companies will think it's a Fianna Fail convention.'

'I've an idea,' Paddy Cool said.' Why don't we play the anthem tape and just mime. I bet it'll go down a storm with that crowd.'

Joey Boland came in with a worried face, 'Your mother has just left a list of another thirty names at the door. There are already sixty or seventy in for free as it stands. What do you want me to do?'

Rory sighed, sat down on a chair in the corner.

'We'll just go on and play, I suppose.'

Halfway through 'Telephone Booth', Mother approached the stage with her fingers in her ears. She beckoned Rory. The music slowly twanged away to nothing.

'Rory, it's too loud. I'm deafened. Turn it down, will you please?'

Some of the younger people in the audience laughed. Rory turned as if in a daze.

'Eh, turn it down, will you.'

That night, The Fabulous Roadrunners played the quietest gig of their career. Many young people walked out. Some stayed to gawp at the spectacle of Dessie O'Hanlon dancing with Mother in front of the stage. The Fianna Failers clapped their hands together in time to the music. They cheered every time Dessie gave Mother a twirl. Maeve was horrified. She sat at her table all night and scowled at everyone.

By the end of the night, the front of the stage was full of Fianna Failers dancing. Rory stayed in one spot and sang like a zombie. I didn't know whether to feel sorry for him or laugh.

Joey came up to me, 'It'll be a while before this band makes it to America.'

Afterwards, Mother came to the dressing-room with a bottle of champagne.

'That was just fantastic,' she said. 'I think you're as good as The Beatles.'

'Thanks, Mother,' Rory said.

'Tell us, Kathleen,' Dessie said, indicating Rory who sat glumly on a guitar case. 'Do you think he'll take a seat for the party someday, ha?'

Mao came up to me to whisper in my ear, 'You know what? I think your Mother is an amazing woman.'

I helped pack the drums and carry all the amplifers to the van. When the van was packed, I went looking for Rory but nobody had seen him.

'I think he went home,' Gordon said.

I didn't blame him for going home. It had been a pretty dismal night as far as he was concerned. No record companies had showed up. Only his family and half of the Fianna Fail Party.

In the dressing-room, I found Rory's fur coat piled on a chair in the corner. I decided to take it home and bring it over to the flat in Rathmines tomorrow.

When I picked up the coat, it fell to pieces. Hundreds of brown bits scattered everywhere. The dressing-room floor looked like a graveyard for small furry animals. Someone had slashed the coat to bits with a knife.

It took me half an hour to gather all the separate pieces and put them in a plastic bag.

NINE

Baby Elephants

CHIEF MAGAW adjusts his glasses and sifts through another batch of incinerator reports. He removes one that has my name on it. His brow wrinkles like an old lady's. It surprises me to notice that the chief has virtually no eyebrows. Why have I not noticed this before in all the years I have worked with him? It just goes to show that sometimes even the most obvious things can escape a person's attention.

Magaw studies the report, frowns, then holds it up in front of him. He squints through his glasses as he begins to read in a slow, formal voice:

'*To Whom It May Concern. This to state that I visited the incinerator at 11:26 am. I discovered the incinerator operatives experiencing severe difficulties attempting to subdue a crazed chicken. The chicken had apparently become unstable after ingesting a large quantity of disinfectant. I was able to assist in the beast's capture. We gave the chicken a fair trial, found it guilty of disinfectant abuse and fried it in a thick mushroom sauce. When I left, the incinerator was functioning normally and the operatives were picking each other's teeth with the chicken bones. Yours sincerely, Daniel Buckley, Ship Inspector.*'

He finishes and places the report carefully on the top of the pile.

'Can you explain yourself?'

'Well,' I say, 'I did write that the incinerator was w-working normally.'

Magaw sighs, 'That's not the point and you know it. I'm surprised at you, Daniel. You don't appear to be taking your job seriously.'

'Sorry.'

'Hmm,' Magaw takes back the report and places it on top of the pile. 'I had hopes that you might one day occupy the chair where I am now sitting.' He indicates the incinerator report, 'This kind of thing can only hurt you. Now, is there anything else you should tell me about the quality of your work over the past while?'

For a moment, I am tempted to show Chief Magaw the book of passengers' names for yesterday. Among those listed as having had their shoes sprayed are Princess Margaret, Captain James T. Kirk of the USS *Enterprise* and Buffalo Bill Cody. I could confess that I also made up the report about Burt Reynolds's toupee giving itself up after a brief but violent struggle in the spraying room. It would be like helping police with their enquiries in return for a reduced sentence.

'No,' I say.

'Good,' Magaw says. 'At least that's something. Tell me, Daniel, how long have you been with us now?'

'Fa-four years full time. Before that, I worked summers and Christmases when I was a student and afterwards.'

'Are you happy here?'

'Yes.'

'Is there anything that bothers you about the job? Is anything interfering with your work?'

'Eh, no.'

Magaw's face registers disappointment. He gives me one of those 'I've done everything I can for you' looks.

'I am very surprised that you would treat a serious position with such levity and irresponsibility. In fact, if you had not performed so well the other night when we had the foot and mouth scare, I would have no hesitation in recommending your immediate transfer from this office.'

He is about to say something else when the phone rings. He picks up the receiver and listens carefully. He becomes extremely interested.

'Baby Elephant? Of course, I understand.'

Another thing I suddenly notice about Chief Magaw is that he has more hair in his nostrils than on his head. The hair appears to be spreading round the corners of his nostrils onto his nose. There is also a large quantity of fluffy hair on his thick round neck. The chief is definitely an odd-looking fellow.

'Leave it to us,' he says and puts the phone down.

Magaw looks at me with sudden enthusiasm as if he has forgotten why I'm here. Then he notices the pile of incinerator reports in front of him and I watch his face sag.

'Right. There's just one thing I have to ask you, Daniel. It may not seem very important to you but it concerns your future as a ship inspector. I want you to consider your answer carefully.' He points a finger at me, 'Don't say anything you don't mean.'

I sit up straight.

Magaw leans forward, his eyes narrow, 'What I want to know is, are you sorry?'

'Eh, yes.'

Magaw slams his hand on the desk. I give an involuntary jump.

'It's not good enough just to be sorry, Daniel,' he looks around him in apparent frustration. 'What I mean is, are you very, very sorry?'

'Yes, I'm very, very sorry.'

He looks into my eyes for an intense moment, then abruptly relaxes. Either he is content with my answer or he has decided that there is no more he can do for me.

'Very well. Let's hear no more about it. Now go back to work and tell the others that the baby elephant for Dublin Zoo is coming in on a London flight tonight.'

Outside, I nearly bump into Desperate Dan and Dominic Root who are on the edges of the red plastic-covered chairs trying to hear what the chief has been saying to me.

'Come on, Big Balls,' Dan says and takes me by the arm and leads me to the bottom of the escalator to watch the passengers coming down. Dominic Root follows, keeping an eye on the door of Magaw's office.

'What did the ould wagon say?' Dominic hisses. 'Go on, tell your Uncle Dominic, ak-ak –'

Dan hushes him, 'Keep it down or you'll have Magaw out.'

Dominic ignores Dan, 'Did he find the one about the outbreak of cannibalism in Customs?'

'Not yet.'

'Pity. I'd love to hear his reaction to that.'

I wonder if Magaw will have me transferred. He is not a person you can trust. He says one thing to your face and does the opposite behind your back. Unless I do something truly spectacular very soon, such as capture an escaped lion while armed only with a watering can, my career at the airport is over. I will go down in ship inspector history not as a captor of escaped dogs or as a hero of foot and mouth scares but as the author of years of misleading incinerator reports. It is not exactly what I had in mind for myself when I began this job. I am aware that I am drifting through not just this job, but my entire life. I need to have a long think about things. If Carla comes home tonight, I will talk to her about it. Carla is good at calming my fears. She says that it is important for a person to focus on the 'inner self', to find out what their true consciousness is really feeling. Whenever Carla has a problem, she goes away somewhere, sits in the lotus position on the floor and focuses on her 'inner self' until the solution to the problem reveals itself. Usually the answers are obvious to everyone except the person themselves, she says. When Carla is not around though, I can't seem to focus on anything for long. I think Carla is better at focusing on my 'inner self' than I am.

Dan gives me an amused smile, 'Did he find the one about the rabid seagulls?'

I shake my head.

Dominic Root cuts in, 'How about the one about Lassie's teeth?'

'I don't think so.'

A throng of squat, sun-tanned men in Hawaiian shirts and multi-coloured shorts come down the escalator. They guffaw and slap each other's backs. Most have legs as thick as beer barrels and faces so red that they look as though they are about to burst.

'That reminds me,' I say. 'The baby elephant is coming in tonight.'

Dominic snorts, 'Aw sure, that fuckin' baby elephant has been coming in every night for the past month.'

'You can say that again,' Dan says.

'Who was it brought in the fifty piranha fish from the Amazon? Remember that? They forgot to arrange to feed the feckin' yokes, so halfway across the piranhas started eating one another. By the time they got here, there were only three left.'

'I think that was some nightclub in town,' Dan says.

'Fuckin' nightclubs. Those places are a law unto themselves. The wine is watered and the champagne is only cat's piss with a label on it.' Dominic examines his fingernails, 'You know, it wouldn't surprise me if they put the baby elephant in with a bunch of fuckin' piranhas.'

Frank Nails comes around the corner at Customs and walks jauntily toward us. At that moment, Dominic Root's smile is the closest thing to a piranha's I can imagine.

'Here he comes,' Dominic Root says. 'The ship inspectors' answer to Casanova.'

'How are ye men?' Frank says as he passes us on the way to the office.

'Hello there, Frank,' Dominic Root gives him a disarming smile, waits for Frank to pass, then sings, 'She's once, twice, tha-ree times a lady . . .'

Frank Nails stops in his tracks.

'What's that supposed to mean?' he demands.

Dominic Root stops singing, feigns a look of innocence, 'What's what supposed to mean? Have you got something against singing or something?'

'No, but I've something against being made a show of. What do you mean "three times a lady", hah? Is this some kind of a big laugh with the lads now just because a man takes a woman out? Is that it, hah?'

'Kindly keep a civil tongue in your head when you're

addressing me,' Dominic Root says loftily. 'I don't know what you're talking about.' He begins to sing again, 'She's once, twi –'

'Right, we'll see who'll be laughing in a minute.' Frank Nails starts for Dominic who immediately giggles like a schoolboy and runs behind Dan.

'All right now, that's enough,' Dan says in a firm voice. 'Act your ages now. There are passengers around.'

Frank Nails turns for the office, 'If I'd a hurley stick on me, some people wouldn't be so quick to laugh.'

Dominic Root puts on an innocent face, 'What? What? It's a free country. I can sing if I want to.'

Dominic waits until Frank Nails is almost at the office door before singing in an exaggerated falsetto, 'Oh, Donn-a, Oh, Don-on-a . . .'

By the time Frank Nails reacts, Dominic Root is almost at Customs.

'Funny joke, ha ha,' Frank Nails says to Dominic Root's vanishing back and marches into the office.

I feel crushed that Donna would let herself down by going out with Frank Nails. I wonder if she let him kiss her.

When the hall is almost empty, Dan and I take a walk out to the baggage dock. There is nobody around. A plane crosses the open area at the end of the building. The noise of the engines makes it difficult to hear. In a short while, I will be off duty. I can't wait to leave.

I hope Carla will come home tonight. I haven't seen her since the night of The Silent Screams gig in the Baggot. When I got home after twenty-four gruelling hours of taking precautions to protect the country against a possible epidemic of foot and mouth, there was a note taped to the fridge door.

'Groover. I've gone down the country for a few days. See you soon. Love Carla. P.S. I know you'll save Ireland, yet again.'

I don't blame Carla. I have been most neglectful of our relationship lately. It's not good enough to buy someone you love a Walnut Whip every now and again and presume that everything is fine between you. There is a lot more to a relationship between two people than Walnut Whips. I don't mind if Carla has gone off with someone else for a while. I don't mind if she has gone off with The Silent Screams. She deserves a break. She's a wise person and I trust her not to do anything stupid. We both know that what we have between us is very special. When she gets home, I will ask her to come away with me for a fortnight. We will go to Greece or to the Canaries. I've never been off the island and Carla and I have never been on holiday together.

Dan gives me a playful punch on the shoulder that is meant to cheer me up.

'Don't mind Granny Magaw. They won't transfer you.'

Dan throws out his arms in a majestic sweep of the baggage loading area with its baggage carts, empty fuel drums and dismantled trolleys, 'Just think, Big Balls, someday all this could be yours – if ye play your cards right.'

'I'm thrilled.'

When he sees that I am not going along with his line, he grows sombre, 'Listen, what age are ye?'

'Twenty-seven.'

'I don't think you should be a ship inspector at all.'

'You don't?'

'No. A young fellow like you should be out in the world doing something interesting with your life. Tell us, are ye getting married to that girl of yours?'

'No, I well, that is I –'

'See, there ye are. There's nothing to keep ye here except yourself, is there? If I were you, I'd get on a plane somewhere and find out what it is that I want to do. Do a little soul-searching, you know?'

Dan's intrusion into my private feelings annoys me, 'Excuse me. Carla and I are in love. We don't need any p-piece of pa-paper from Church or State to p-prove it. OK?'

'All right, keep your hair on. Christ, boy, I was only making a point. I don't want you to make the same mistakes I did.' Dan reflects for a moment, 'Tell me, apart from your girlfriend, what would you want to stay here for at all?'

'It's my home.'

'Home? Ah, sure you can make a home anywhere. My home used to be in Kerry. Then in the fifties and sixties I lived in Ladbroke Grove. I've had three houses in Dublin in the past twenty years. Which one was my *home*? My wife, God rest her, passed away in a hostel in Ranelagh five years ago. That was *her* home for the last year of her life and it was mine too. Big Balls, there's no such place as *home*. It's just an illusion, put up by banks and building societies.'

I remember my own addresses: 'Number 3, Church Street, Redrock Town, Redrock, South County Dublin' where I grew up; a bunch of poky flats in Ranelagh and Rathmines where I lived when I went to college and before I met Carla; and my present address, 'Top floor flat, 95a Fitzwilliam Street West, Dublin'. Soon, Carla and I will have a house of our own. I wish I could remember the address.

'Why did you come back here then?'

Dan shrugs his shoulders, his neck disappears. He swivels to look at me. He scratches under his jaw.

'I was young and stupid like you. I thought I wanted to come home. Only when I got here, I found that my new home was like all the others – a temporary place to rest my head and dig a garden now and again. Now look at me. Stuck out here with a Big Balls like you.'

I want to ask about Dan's son's ten pound notes. Then I think to myself that I am already in enough trouble. To be arrested with forged ten pound notes on my person, at the same time that I am being reprimanded by my own department for filing misleading incinerator reports, is a situation I can do without. Beside me, Dan is having a coughing fit. He bends double for a series of racking coughs then straightens up slowly. He wipes some spittle from his lip.

'Are you OK?'

'I'm fine, Big Balls. I'm fine. Time to go back.'

By the time we get back to the office, Old Brendan Toombs has arrived to relieve me. Frank Nails is sitting on the red plastic-covered seats beside Donna and Polly. I get a little pang in my heart at the sight of Donna. Dominic Root is nowhere in sight.

Donna gives me a wave, 'Hi, Daniel.'

'Hi,' I say.

I remove my armband and stuff it in my pocket. I am careful not to smile at Donna. I don't want her to get the impression that I approve of her going out with that dung-beetle, Frank Nails. There is no way I am going for a pint with her now. She had her chance and she blew it.

'Good luck,' I say and wave goodbye to everyone.

I decide not to bother going in to say goodbye to Chief Magaw in case he has discovered the entry about Burt Reynolds's toupee.

'Bye, Daniel,' Donna calls.

'Bye,' I say quickly, without turning around.

I am at Customs when Dan catches up with me.

'Christ, boy, slow down will ye. Did ye not hear me calling?'

'Sorry, I was daydreaming.'

'I'll give ye a lift boy. I'm going into town myself.'

There are days when I hate Dan. Sometimes, I can't bear to stand next to him at the bottom of the escalator nor can I go for lunch with him nor even sit beside him on the red plastic-covered chairs. Rarely does a particular incident turn me against him. It is more a combination of his bad habits, the way he suddenly breaks wind in the office and his delight in releasing sudden loud belches behind you that make you spill your coffee. Most of all, I hate his habit of calling me 'Big Balls' in front of Donna and the rest of the Stats girls. My hatred never lasts long. If I get transferred, I will miss old Dan. He can be a pain and his personal habits are not the most admirable but he genuinely has a good heart. What is more important, he seems to like me.

On the way to Dan's car, I notice a thin stream of smoke rising from the incinerator at the back of the car-park. Dan sees it too and gives me a smile.

'Shut up,' I say.

'I'm saying nothing,' Dan says. 'I'm just relieved that it's still working.'

Dan's car is full of old issues of the *Kerryman* and discarded sweet wrappers. The passenger seat moves under me as I sit. I feel it swaying slightly as the car pulls off. Dan drives with his chin up and lips pursed as if about to blow a kiss to the car in front.

'The seat's perfectly safe,' Dan says, 'just as long as you don't make any sudden moves.'

On the way into town, I worry that there is something in my relationship with Carla that I am overlooking or taking too much for granted. Marriage is not the answer. Both of us agree that marriage is a silly, out-dated idea whose principal effect is to make people feel imprisoned. Buying a house together is all the commitment we need. I wish I could make Dan understand how things are between Carla and me, but I know it will take too long to explain. Dan was married for twenty or thirty years and he may get insulted if I sound too superior about the benefits of living together. I wonder if Dan is a committed Catholic. Perhaps he disapproves of living in sin. It is best not to bring up the subject. It will only make Dan jealous that he didn't do it when he was young. If Carla is at home by the time I get there, I will take her out to The Penguin, buy her flowers, romance her as I used to do when we were first going together. Then I will tell her about Greece. Just thinking about it makes me feel good.

When we arrive outside my apartment, I see that the Morris Minor is parked on the kerb. My heart gives a thump. I struggle to get the door open but it jams. Dan leans over to twist the handle in a certain way and the car door shudders open. Dan smells of cigarette smoke.

'I won't see ye for a little while, Big Balls,' he says. 'I have to go away.'

'Are you taking a holiday?'

'You could say that,' Dan laughs. 'I'm going in for a few tests. I should be out next week.'

I get out and close the door. Dan leans over, beckons me. He seems to want to say something else but I wish the boring old eejit would leave and let me get back to my life. I can't wait to get inside our apartment.

Dan winds down the window, 'Don't worry about Magaw. None of that stuff matters.'

'OK, I won't, thanks.'

Dan nods, dismisses whatever it was he was trying to say and begins to wind up the window, 'Goodbye, Big Balls.'

'See you.'

I bound up the steps, open the front door and go in. I hear Dan's car pull away from the kerb. I dash up the stairs to the third floor, slowing down as I pass Mrs Macken's door in case she hears me and comes out to talk. I scramble up the last few steps, stick my key in the lock and open the door. Inside, the first thing I see is Carla's coat draped elegantly on a chair.

'Hi,' I call.

Carla is sitting by the table overlooking the window. She looks worried. Her blonde hair, usually so firm and stylish, sticks up at the back. She looks defiant, like a child waiting to be scolded for a deed that the parent has yet to discover.

'Hi,' she says softly.

'You're home,' I say, overcome by joy at finding Carla home. I decide not to wait until tonight to tell her about Greece. 'Listen, I've been thinking that we should go on holiday someplace. We ha-ha-have never had a ha-holiday together. We could go someplace hot, like Greece or the Canaries. It'll be brilliant. What do you think?'

I notice that Carla is giving me a glassy stare.

'Are you OK?' I ask.

'I want us to break up,' Carla blurts out.

I sit down at the table, opposite her. I feel a shock spreading through me. I try to suppress it. In one way I don't understand what is happening but in another way it is as if I have been expecting Carla to say those words for a long time.

'I've been thinking about it and we have to break up,' she says. 'We're not going anywhere.'

'Where do you want to go?'

'Daniel, it's over between us. I'm very sorry. I've met someone else.' She expresses each statement firmly, with a glance at me for emphasis.

'Do I know the "someone else"?'

She won't meet my eyes.

'Donald?' I say.

She nods.

'*Fucking Donald.*' It slips out before I know what I am saying.

'It wasn't our fault,' Carla says calmly, as though she has rehearsed it. 'We both tried to stop it happening but it took us over. I don't expect you to understand but that's the way it happened anyway.'

I remember the first time I saw Carla at Sarah-Jane Cleary's twenty-first birthday party in the upstairs suite at The Old Sheiling. Carla had been standing by the record player with her friends, holding a bottle of Beck's. She wore a single earring that dangled below her collar. I thought she was so sophisticated. I was sure she would only look at guys who drove Porsches or Lamborghinis. We danced to 'Hold Back the Night'. Later, I got off with her in a broom closet behind the coat rack. For a while after we started going together, I thought of Carla as my beautiful ornament, a kind of female Porsche that only I could drive. During the seven years we have been together, she never wore the earring again. I don't remember even seeing the earring around. I wonder what happened to it.

'You don't have to worry about the house,' Carla says. 'I'll take care of it.'

'Are you going ahead with it?' I say.

Carla looks at me, 'Yes.'

'Are you going to buy the house by yourself?'

Carla turns jittery and defensive.

'I'm buying it with . . . someone else.'

'With Donald?'

'Yes,' she looks at me to gauge my reaction.

I remain seated and calm, even though I feel rage rising in me. The new house – the house that was to be *our home* – appears before me, then like a sandcastle, swiftly disintegrates. The image of that grey-suited eejit of an estate agent showing Carla and Donald around the house springs into my mind. He must think that Carla is auditioning prospective husbands. I think about Donald kneeling by the front door, nailing down the loose floorboard. When I think about Donald doing battle with the overgrown back garden, I fantasise that some lost carnivore that has been hiding there for decades will rear up out of the jungle to eat him. Now I feel better. The thought is ludicrous, but it eases my rage and it makes me smile. I look up to see that Carla is smiling too. She must think I'm taking it well.

'OK, well, if that's the w-w –. If that's the wa-wa –,' I have to give it up.

Carla leans forward, 'Daniel I hope you understand. I tried everything to make it work. I tried not seeing Donald for a while. I thought that once you and I bought the house together, everything would be fine again, but I was just lying to myself. I got the feeling that things were never going to work out between us. I know that this is the right thing to do. I'm sorry if I hurt you . . .' she trails off.

I notice how very slender and fragile Carla's cheekbones are. Her fine, slightly curved eyebrows that, when raised, can give her face an amused, sexy look, the long, slender nose, and full lips and bright, vivacious eyes. She really has a lovely face. I want to get things over with as soon as possible so that I can resume my life. It is important to get the practical end sorted out first.

'Well,' I say, 'what do you want to do about this flat?'

Carla seems relieved, 'You can take it over if you wish, the lease is due for renewal next month. I'm going away for a while until the house is ready.'

I cannot afford to keep the apartment by myself. I will have to find a new home. That's OK. I can handle that. Besides, it will keep me occupied for a while. I think about Donald Logan's goofy grin and about the pink and orange Doc Martens I cut with my penknife. Fucking Donald Logan.

'When are you moving out?'

'Today. I'll keep coming back for my things,' she says, obviously relieved that I am not causing a scene. 'I'll look in to see how you're doing too.'

'No,' I say firmly. 'When something's over, it's over. I

don't need to be looked in on. I'm not one of your p-plants.'

It gives me a pang of pleasure to see that my rejection has thrown her.

'I'm sorry,' she says. 'I didn't mean it like that.'

'Yeah, well . . .' I begin.

I look out the window. A group of boys is hanging around beside the parked cars across the street. I see a girl with blonde hair go by on a bicycle. Two of the bigger boys kneel down at the window of a parked car while the smaller ones keep a look out. I wonder how long Carla has been waiting for me. She must have seen Dan's car pull up and drop me off. She must have heard the door slam and listened to my footsteps bounding up the stairs. As my key turned in the lock, perhaps she was composing the words she wanted to say to me. Then when I arrived, I guess she just lost her composure and blurted them out. It must be hard for her. I glance across. She is looking down at her feet, her face vacant.

'At least this way, you get to hang onto that stupid kitten,' I say.

She looks up at me, smiles, then almost immediately her face collapses in the sorrow of an infant weeping for a lost doll. I have never seen anything as charming or as heart-breaking. I will do anything to make her stop. I stand up and go to her. She puts out her arms to receive me and we hug. She buries her face in my chest and I feel her sobs go through me. Seven years of cuddles, kisses, rows, occasional sex, intimate meals, misunderstandings and all the rest of it crystallise in my mind in an instant and I lose myself in tears too.

'You're my father, you looked after me. You kept me safe,' Carla cries.

We hold each other and rock from side to side while we cry things out. It is a good feeling, as well as a sad one. In a way, it is the highlight in our relationship. It shows how brilliant we were together that we can break up like this. As long as we hold each other, I know that the phone will not ring, Mrs Macken will not call to the door looking for something and nobody will drop in unannounced. After a long time, we finish crying. Carla looks up at me with a smeared face.

'I'll never stop loving you just because we're no longer together,' she says. 'You know that, don't you?'

'Yes. I know.'

I wonder what she meant when she said I was her father.

At the window, I watch Carla getting into the Morris Minor. She glances up, sees me and gives me a wave. I wave back. She could be popping out to collect a pizza. The Morris Minor gives a familiar gargling noise and pulls away from the kerb. I watch the car until it turns the corner and disappears.

I turn on the television and sit on the sofa where Carla and I cuddled a few nights ago. I watch the children's programmes, the News and 'Star Trek'. The break-up is just one of those things. It has happened and I feel relieved. Already, I can feel myself getting over it. We were comfortable friends rather than lovers. That's why it was so easy to break up. No arguments, no recriminations, no screaming matches. I am proud of us, as Carla would say. I hope she will be happy. The break-up will mean a new beginning for both of us. Next month I will move out of the flat. I will have no address, no television, no girlfriend. I will be free. In a while, there will be no trace of us as a couple, except for a few photographs that Carla has somewhere.

Before she left, Carla told me that she is going off to France for a few months with fucking Donald Logan. The Silent Screams are recording their debut album in some château in the south of the country. The thought suddenly strikes me that I may be on duty the day fucking Donald and Carla return from France. It is possible that I could be standing at the bottom of the escalator with my armband on as they descend. Of course, I will immediately ask fucking Donald if he has been on a farm. Even if he says no, I will invite him to follow me. While Carla waits outside, Dan will spray every item in fucking Donald's luggage, place them carefully in leaky plastic bags, before putting them back in the suitcase. My trained eye will suddenly spot fucking Donald's severe case of foot and mouth. My fellow ship inspectors will hold him down and force his mouth open while I fetch the watering can of disinfectant and a funnel. I will then insert a funnel into fucking Donald's open mouth and pour a hundred gallons of orange-coloured disinfectant into his stomach until he swells up. Then I will jump on his stomach to make sure that the disinfectant circulates effectively. After fucking Donald explodes I will pronounce him cured, place what remains of his body into plastic bags and put the bags in his suitcase. It will give me great pleasure to enter his name in the book of passengers, 'Donald Fucking Logan'. After that I will hand the whole lot to Carla.

'Have a great life,' I'll say.

There is a gardening programme on. A middle-aged woman is asking the experts what she should do about the leaf-cutting bee that is attacking her bonsais.

'Whatever you do, don't hurt the bee,' the expert says. 'The leaf-cutting bee is extremely rare. You've very lucky that it has made its home in your garden.'

'What about my bonsais?' the woman wails, just as the phone rings.

I turn down the television and reach for the receiver.

'It was a conspiracy all along,' Mother says.

I think she is talking about the break-up, until I realise that she is rattling on about her election defeat. It is another of her themes.

'I have proof that Dessie O'Hanlon and Jenny Donovan were in league with Fine Gael against me. They wanted to get the yacht club built so they betrayed me – after all I did for them. I could just laugh at my own stupidity. How could I have let them do it to me? Where was my family when I needed them?'

'That's too bad, Mother. How's Maeve?'

'Don't mention that bitch to me. Your sister tried to lock me in my room today. Can you imagine? I gave everything I have and I'm treated like a prisoner.'

'I'm sorry to hear that.'

Mother goes into one of her political speeches. This is definitely one of her bad days. Even though it is eight years since she lost her seat, she still likes to practise her rhetoric on members of the family or anyone who will listen. I can hear her pausing during her rant, anticipating the applause of cumann members or the party faithful. I could tell her that my house is burning down around me and she will ignore me and keep on with the speech. I have learned that it does no good to argue with Mother when she is like this. The best method I have found to deal with her is to hold the receiver a few inches from my ear so that her voice sounds distant, less authoritative, less like Mother. I hold the receiver away from me until she is finished and then agree with whatever she has been going on about. It saves a lot of unnecessary hassle. I know that by tomorrow morning she will have forgotten the call.

'Charles J. Haughey told me privately that he feels that it's a crime that I am no longer in the Dail. He says that there's a post in his government for me if I can win back my old seat. Are you listening to me, Daniel? Are you?'

A feeling of panic suddenly grips me. I cannot take anymore of Mother haranguing me.

'Gotta go, Mother, I'm sorry.'

'I beg your pardon. Daniel?'

'The house is burning down,' I put the phone down.

I stand up, pace around the television set. My skin is itchy. I cannot stay in the apartment a minute longer. I know that in a few moments the phone will ring again. When I pick it up, Mother will say, 'How dare you', and carry on where she left off.

I get up, grab my jacket and start for the door. On the television the experts are examining someone's hydrangeas. The phone begins to ring. I open the door and go out. All the way down the stairs I can hear the phone ringing.

I take a taxi to the airport. The taxi man is one of those guys who responds to whatever mood the passenger is in. When he sees that I am a bit sullen looking, he leaves me alone and turns up the radio. I feel a numbness creeping all over me. It is the same feeling that I cultivated in school when The Barrel or Father Caraher humiliated me or made me feel self-conscious and guilty about my stutter. Now I allow the feeling to overtake me. In the back of my mind I know what I am going to do but I refuse to allow myself to think about it. It is enough to feel myself in motion. It is dusk by the time I get to the airport. A plane is climbing above the Departures building. I look out the back window but the sky is too murky to tell whether or not there is smoke rising from the incinerator. I give the driver a two pound tip for leaving me alone on the ride out.

It is an odd feeling to be back at the airport again. I walk through the side door to Customs, go through the Customs area and turn the corner to the Arrivals lobby. There is a London flight down. About a hundred passengers are waiting for their bags to appear on the baggage belt. Harry Dunne, the night man, is sitting on the red plastic seats. Harry is not surprised to see me but then, Harry is the type of fellow who is not surprised by anything in life.

'Evening,' he says. 'Couldn't stay away, hah?'

'No,' I laugh and sit down beside him. We watch the passengers collect their bags off the trolley.

I stretch and yawn.

'Harry,' I say, 'would it be all right with you if I stayed here tonight?'

Harry raises his hands, sticks out his lower lip, 'So be it. I've no objection. As long as you make the tea.'

'Thanks.'

We watch the last of the passengers, a large woman with a beehive hairstyle, struggle to place her suitcase onto a trolley. The suitcase falls off, her beehive goes lopsided. As one, Harry and I rise and go to the woman's assistance. We pick up the suitcase and put it back on the trolley.

'Oh listen, thanks, you're gentlemen,' she says and turns at the Customs corner to give us a wave, beehive wobbling.

I make small talk with Harry for a while. Then I get up, stretch my legs and wander into the office. I take down a blank incinerator report from the shelf beside the flight monitor and with a delicious feeling of guilt, I begin to write:

'To Whom It May Concern. This is to state that I did not visit the incinerator at midnight because of a severe emotional disturbance. Isn't it about time that the department provided overnight facilities for ship inspectors who encounter emotional turbulence during the course of their private lives? Perhaps the incinerator could be converted into a small hostel for ship inspectors. This simple, expedient manoeuvre should increase efficiency among all grades of ship inspectors and provide a harmonious and secure working environment for all. P.S. I did not visit the incinerator itself but I took a look out of the windows of the Departures terminal. There was no smoke rising. I feel it is valid to speculate that the incinerator was cold and dark and that no rubbish whatever was being destroyed. Yours sincerely, Daniel Buckley, Ship Inspector.'

I place the report in the drawer on top of the pile of incinerator reports in Magaw's desk. When Magaw opens the drawer in the morning, it is the first thing he will see.

Outside, Harry Dunne is talking to a couple of baggage handlers. The baggage handlers look totally fed up.

Harry chuckles, 'Guess what? The baby elephant has just touched down.'

'I don't believe it,' I say.

'It just goes to show that you can never know when something is going to happen, doesn't it?'

'Yes, it does.'

'I'll have to go with it so you can take care of the fort. It's a good job you're here, isn't it? Cheerio.'

Harry Dunne goes off to take care of the baby elephant and leaves me in charge of the office. After a while, there is nobody around, no sound at all except for the hum of the ventilation fans and the fluorescent lights.

I put my head down against the crackly red plastic of the seat and try to sleep.

TEN

Maeve's Party

THE TOOTHACHE started midway through a lecture on 'The Duality of Beckett's Monologues'. The lecturer, a bespectacled, curly-haired cherub who windmilled his arms constantly, was trying to make the point that, when you got right down to it, everything in Beckett had a dual meaning.

'It's important to remember that when Beckett says I, he means 'non-I', he said, gazing at a spot near the ceiling. 'Once you grasp that it is the sheer insurmountable otherness of selfhood that is at the very core of Beckettian alienation, then you'll be ahead of the posse.'

I was nineteen and sick of listening to long-winded lecturers whose principal calling appeared to be to make things more difficult than they really were. Usually, boring lectures put me to sleep but something in the cherub's whinging delivery seemed to make my toothache worse. At the end of the lecture, my tooth was screaming. By the time I got home to my bedsit in Ranelagh, it felt as though the right side of my mouth was on fire.

Next morning, I had just decided to skip college and to find a dentist when Maeve rang to tell me that the Gardai had found a Triumph Herald off Redrock pier.

'I think you should come home now,' she said. 'Mother says they're going to have it out of the water by noon.'

In the ten years since Dad disappeared, I had never forgotten him, but there were times when I simply did not think about him. Ever since the previous year, when I left home to go to college, Dad's presence in my mind had gradually diminished, like a kite drifting away on a high wind. Now that he was back in my life, I told myself that there was nothing to feel guilty or apprehensive about. If they discovered Dad's body and Mother became upset, I was sure that Maeve and I would hold things together between us, the way we used to do.

By the time I got home, my toothache had eased to a dull throbbing. Mother was in the hallway, talking on the phone, cigarette in her mouth. It was strange to see Mother at home during the day. Ordinarily she was a working politician and usually in the Dail or attending a function. Maeve stood behind her in the kitchen doorway. She rolled her eyes, as if to say, 'all the trouble I've had to put up with'. Mother frantically beckoned me to her, cupped her hand over the receiver.

'They've sent a crane', she said out of the corner of her mouth and went back to her call, 'Now, are you saying to me that the Irish Navy has no frogmen or that there are frogmen available but you have no intention of sending them to me?'

As I left the room, Mother was saying, 'Excuse me, do you know that you're speaking to the TD for this area?'

In the kitchen, Maeve was distracted. When I came in she feigned a cheerful nonchalance.

'That's her fourth Government department in the last half an hour. She's putting off going up there. I don't think she really wants to see the car.'

The kitchen was untidy. On the counter, plates were piled up. There were papers strewn about as though someone had been searching for a particular news story. A mop lay across the sink, dripping onto the floor.

'What about Rory?'

Maeve saw me looking at the mop, walked across to the sink and picked it up. 'He won't come. He says he's not going to fall for a spoof. I think he just doesn't want to come.'

Maeve placed the mop in a bucket inside the back door. She wore a black polo-neck and black jeans. With her dark hair cut in a pageboy style and her large brown eyes, she reminded me of a beatnik. There was a ding as the phone went down.

'Whoops,' Maeve said. 'Brace yourself.'

Mother appeared in the kitchen doorway, 'They've already sent two frogmen. There should be another frogman there by the time we arrive.'

The only thing I could think of when I saw Mother standing in the doorway with that familiar expression of triumph on her face was that I was glad that I didn't live at home anymore. I didn't miss the endless phone calls, the political strategy meetings, the important visitors to the house. I had a comfortable bedsit in Ranelagh, I was enjoying my first year of college and I worked as a ship inspector in the summer and at Christmas. For the first time in my life, I felt as though I was living my own life, and not Mother's, or Rory's or even Maeve's.

Mother's expression became morose, 'What about your brother?'

'He can't come,' Maeve said.

'He won't come, you mean. That's just like him.' Mother lit another cigarette. 'I've a good mind to go over there and get him but I wouldn't give him the satisfaction.'

'He said he was going out,' Maeve said.

Mother ignored her, 'Two teenagers found it when they were scuba-diving off the pier. They weren't even supposed to be there at all because it's such a dangerous spot. Imagine that.' She drew on her cigarette, blew the smoke out quietly. 'Do you think it's *him*?'

Maeve looked at me. 'I suppose we have to prepare ourselves, just in case,' she said.

Mother's lip curled, 'Prepare ourselves. How do we prepare ourselves for a body half-eaten by fishes? Do we run twenty laps around the Hill, Maeve? Do we do press-ups on Redrock beach?'

'Mother, I didn't mean –'

Mother cut her off, 'Don't talk to me about it now. Your brother should be here. Phone the police and get them to send a car to track him down.'

'I don't think –'

'Oh, you're all the same. I'll do it myself. I have to do everything on my own around here.'

Mother stayed where she was, taking long, slow drags on her cigarette. We said nothing for a while. Maeve looked at me to take the lead.

'I think we should go, Mother,' I said. 'We don't want to keep the f-frogman waiting.'

Mother giggled suddenly, into her hands. I felt a tickle rising in my throat. Maeve tried to suppress a laugh.

'What's funny?' Mother said sternly.

Maeve composed herself, 'Nothing. We'd better go and meet the –' she hesitated.

Mother's face seemed to leap and then settle.

'Meet the frogman,' Maeve said and burst out laughing.

This time, we all lost it completely and roared almost simultaneously. The word 'frogman' suddenly became the most hilarious word we had ever heard. The giggles were so overwhelming that I collapsed onto the floor. I caught a glimpse of Maeve who was holding onto a chair, her face twisted in apparent agony as she surrendered to the laughter that was sweeping her entire body. Mother held onto the doorway and tried to control herself.

'Stop,' she said without conviction. 'Oh, stop it now.'

Within a few seconds, Mother too was helpless. It was hard to know if what we were laughing at was funny or if we were releasing tension. Perhaps it was both. Whatever it was, we were complete fools for about ten minutes. The tide of giggles subsided only after all three of us were sitting on the floor.

Mother gave us a playful slap on the head each, 'You're dreadful, the pair of you, but I'm glad you're here.'

When I finally managed to get to my feet, I was so feeble it was like learning to walk again.

Maeve gesticulated at me breathlessly, 'Please don't mention that word.'

'What word?' I said innocently. 'You mean f—'

'*No!*' Maeve's eyes went tight and off she went again, silently this time.

'All right, that's enough,' Mother shouted. 'Let's go and see about this car.'

When we finally left the house, we were too exhausted to talk. We got into Mother's car and as she drove off she smacked into Mrs Donovan's bin. If we had had any energy left, we would have laughed again.

'Oh for heaven's sake, I don't believe this,' Mother said. 'Daniel, get out and move that bin, would you?'

I did as I was told and got back in the car. We drove to the harbour, parked at the east pier and got out. A crane stood at the end of the pier. We walked past fish merchants, fishermen and customers from the town, many of whom nodded to Mother with kind expressions as though they knew why she was there. When we reached the crane, there was a crowd of about a hundred people around it. When people saw Mother, they cleared a path. I caught sight of the boy Thing. He nodded but didn't come over. I couldn't see Mrs Donovan anywhere. Nobody said a word as we followed Mother to the end of the pier. Elias Powers was standing with a Garda sergeant beside the crane. Powers saw Mother and came over.

'They're nearly ready to lift it out now, Kathleen. I'm glad you're here. We were afraid that you weren't going to make it.'

The day was damp and cloudy with a mild intermittent breeze that was just strong enough to send a few white caps kissing against the harbour walls. The sea looked blue and welcoming. A windsurfer, stalled in the water a few hundred yards out, cupped his hands over his eyes to see what was happening on the pier. Behind the windsurfer, I could see white sails sprinkled across the bay. A frogman broke the surface just below us to give the Garda sergeant a thumbs up. The Garda sergeant turned to Elias Powers who nodded.

'OK,' he called to the crane operator. 'Give it a lash.'

We stood back as the crane's cable began to wind. There was a loud 'dang-dang-danging' noise as the cable became taut. It reminded me of the sound made by a Ferris wheel as it began to revolve. I expected to hear fairground music and delighted screams of people above us. Beside me Mother's white fingers dug into Maeve's arm but Maeve didn't seem to notice. She stared at the spot where the cable disappeared in the swirling water. A shadow became apparent just under the surface. The shadow stayed the same shape and size for a long time. Then suddenly the rear bumper and boot appeared covered in moss. Within seconds, the back of the car lifted clear of the water with a sucking sound. Soon the whole of the Triumph Herald dangled in the crane's chains. The front of the car pointed towards the sea as water gushed out in streams as from a giant watering can shot full of holes. The car's windows were black, and a carpet of glistening green moss covered the roof and bonnet. A lump of seaweed dropped from a door handle to splash in the water. It was strange how something taken from the sea could appear filthy yet washed at the same time. I couldn't tell if it was Dad's car or not. It looked like a toy swinging in the air, half covered in some-body's front garden. Mother stared at the car in reluctant awe, her face scrunched up as though she had just put her fingers in something slimy. Her eyes though were steely. She reminded me of a photograph I saw once in a magazine of people recoiling or holding onto the person next to them as they watched a horror film. In the centre of the photo-graph, a proud woman stared sourly up at the screen, chin up, determined not to give in to mere fright.

I thought of the last time I had been on the pier, at the vigil for the *Celtic Mist* when the sea had given back Manus Rock alive. The Triumph Herald had been lying under the water, only a few feet from us, like the last piece in a giant jigsaw puzzle. I could have gone to the end of the pier, looked down and seen it there. Perhaps someone on one of the fishing boats could have spotted it when they were bringing in the bodies and the wreckage. I felt shivery thinking about it. Manus came into my mind. A couple of months after the *Celtic Mist* tragedy, he had gone to Glasgow to work on his uncle Jamie's boat. I got a postcard from him a few weeks after he arrived. 'Having a brilliant time. I'll be home soon. All the best.' He was still there. I wrote to him a couple of times but got no reply. Someone told me he had got married over there. It wouldn't have killed him to drop me a line now and again.

The crane swung the car in a lazy arc, water dripping in a series of eruptions across the sea. Elias Powers pushed us all back. What would happen once the crane put the car down? Would everyone rush over and open the door to see if there was a body inside? That was why everyone was here. They wanted to gawp at the tragedy of another person's life. They needed reassurance that the person inside wasn't *their* loved one. Perhaps they were curious to see what a person looked like after ten years in the sea. For a wicked moment, I wished that the car would touch land, that the door would spring open and that Dad would step out looking exactly as he had on the day he disappeared. What would happen then? Would people run away? Would Mother run to welcome him home or recoil as if from a monster? There must be something wrong with me, I thought. How could anyone think such inappropriate thoughts on an occasion like this?

The car landed with a clang, and a moment later the Garda sergeant and Elias Powers hastened over to unfasten the chains. Water flowed over the stone ground, darkening it, foaming in the cracks. I expected the sergeant to turn to us first to ask permission before he opened the door. Instead he wrenched the handle, gave it a couple of powerful tugs and the door popped open. The Triumph Herald stood there as if ready for a test spin. I prayed that the car was not Dad's. I knew that if there was a body inside, then the crabs and prawns would have taken most of it. I did not want to find Dad's bones, held together by his clothes, like some scarecrow from the deep.

'Come on, stay with me now,' Mother said and we walked forward with her.

There was no body inside the car, just moss-covered seats, blackened windows and seaweed everywhere, even hanging from the steering wheel. For some reason, I glanced down at the floor by the passenger seat anticipating to see a pair of shoes. I saw only a puddle of water. I felt nothing. It was like being a spectator at someone else's life.

'Nobody home,' the sergeant said cheerfully, then caught himself as he realised that Mother was beside him. 'I beg your pardon, Ma'am. I wasn't thinking.'

'That's all right,' Mother said, as she looked into the dark interior. 'I'm not your Ma'am, I am Kathleen Buckley, the TD for this area. I think this might be my husband's car.'

The sergeant took a step back, 'Of course, Mrs Buckley. I knew you were coming. I apologise for not recognising you.'

The sergeant was a tall, sallow-faced man with a long prominent nose. He kept his notebook in front of him like a talisman to ward off any further lapses in judgement. Mother led him to the back of the car and they bent down to examine the licence plates. The sergeant wiped some green stuff away as Mother took a piece of paper out of her bag. Mother looked at the licence plate, then consulted the piece of paper. She nodded to the sergeant and he wrote down something in his notebook. Mother glanced across at us in an odd, almost indifferent way as though we were someone else's children and that was how we knew that it was Dad's car. Mother and the sergeant stood up, walked around to the front of the car.

'Is he –?' Mother indicated the frogman. 'Is he going to keep looking around down there?'

'Yes, Ma'am, eh, Mrs Buckley,' the sergeant replied. 'We've two of them down there. If there's anything to find, they'll find it.'

A finger touched my shoulder. I didn't have to look to know who it was.

'It must have been an accident, don't you think so?'

'Yeah,' I said, 'it must have been.'

'God,' Maeve said, just as I was thinking the same thought. 'Do you think . . . ? I hope it wasn't that.'

'No. I'd say he came down here to think or something.'

'Maybe he fell asleep with the handbrake off and it just rolled in.'

'Something like that.'

'I wish there was someone you could ask,' Maeve said.

An image had been building in my mind of one of the last times I had been in the Triumph Herald. Now something in Maeve's voice triggered the memory. I was in the back seat, six or maybe seven years old. We were coming home from a spin around the Hill. Maeve and Rory were squeezed in the front beside Dad. There had been an argument between them about who should get the front and Dad had resolved it by letting them both sit there. I had the whole back seat to myself and I crawled along it as we drove. We were turning a corner when a large man on a bicycle suddenly appeared in front of us like a vision. I don't remember the sound of the impact, just the vision's sudden disappearance and the pain as my shoulder hit the back of the seat. We watched in silence as a red, stunned face emerged over the bonnet of the car to glare at us as if we were maniacs. Dad got out and he and the man yelled at each other, the man towering over Dad. It was the first time I had ever seen anybody who was taller than Dad. Maeve turned around, her young face stark with worry.

'I think Dad's going to give him the clatters,' she said.

In the end, Dad got back in the car and drove away. We all turned around to see the large man in the middle of the road, holding his bicycle, fuming at us with his face as red as a flame.

'He wanted me to say I was sorry, but it was his fault,' Dad said. 'There's no talking to some people.'

Now that water no longer pumped from the car and there were no hideous surprises contained within its dank interior, people drew closer for a look. Some touched the roof, the open door. It occurred to me that someone might try to prise off a souvenir. I felt a violent rush of anger shake me. I had to grab onto myself as if struck by a freezing chill. I was about to say something when Elias Powers sensed the mood and moved forward with his arms out.

'OK, that's enough. If everyone could keep their distance here, please.'

'Is anyone inside?' a voice asked.

Elias Powers closed the car door, 'There's nothing to see now. Nothing to see.'

Mother came over to stand beside us. 'You know, when I was married to your father, I became a child. I didn't really exist except as his wife. It was only after he disappeared that I grew up. People respect me now. They don't look through me or dismiss me as some man's property. Today was the first day in a long time that I didn't think about John when I woke up – and now, here he is. I feel like a child again.'

We waited for fifteen minutes by the end of the pier. The sergeant found nothing of interest inside the car. Mother went over to sign a form before the sergeant could get the car taken away.

By the time the frogmen emerged, my toothache had returned. First it pulsed along the right side of my face. Then a series of sharp pains made me squint.

'What's the matter?' Maeve said. 'Are you crying, Daniel?'

'Toothache,' I said.

'Oh no,' she said. 'Oh my God.'

Maeve went over to Mother and whispered something in her ear. Mother glared across at me as though she had been slapped. She came over to me with a horrified face.

'Why didn't you tell me? How long have you had this?' Mother demanded.

I wanted to tell Mother that the toothache was nothing and that I would go to a dentist first thing tomorrow morning. Instead I heard my voice grow whiny as a spoiled child's.

'A week. It's really bad today for some reason.'

'Show me,' Mother grabbed my jaws. 'Come on, open up.'

'Mother, don't.'

'Open your mouth please, Daniel.'

I was aware of the crowd's attention shifting from the Triumph Herald to what was going on between Mother and me. A thought crossed my mind that I should break away immediately and run up the pier as fast as I could. Instead I opened my mouth. Mother peered in intently, shifted my head to catch better light, poked my teeth with her finger.

'Where is it?'

'On the right, at the side,' I mumbled.

'Oh, my God. Maeve look at this.'

A sharp pain pierced me and I groaned.

'We'll have to get that taken care of right away,' Mother said.

The top of a peaked cap appeared at the corner of my vision.

'Eh, excuse me Ma'am, eh, I mean, Mrs Buckley?'

'Yes, what is it?'

'We'll be taking the car away shortly. We'll keep you informed if we find anything else.'

'Thank you, sergeant.'

Mother let go of my jaws, 'Right, come on.'

Mother took me by the arm and marched me down the pier. Maeve followed for a while before dashing across to take my other arm. Along the length of the pier, people paused in shop doorways or at the quayside to watch us. I could feel them whispering as I passed. I felt like an innocent man on my way to jail.

'Where are we going, Mother?'

'I know just the man for you. I should never have let you take that bedsit. You're too young. You just can't take care of yourself.'

In the car, Mother dug down under her feet and came up with a blanket, 'Here, put this across your lap.'

'Mother I –'

'Just do it, please. You're run down. I won't have you catching pneumonia as well.'

We drove through Redrock Town and up the hill to the summit. At the summit we turned right with a screech of tyres. At the next screech I looked at the speedometer and saw that Mother was doing sixty miles an hour. I was afraid to open my mouth in case Mother drove into a ditch. Maeve leaned across from the back with a big grin on her face, staring straight ahead like an apprentice rally driver.

'Isn't this brilliant?' she said.

Mother jerked the car to a halt outside the gates of a flat-roofed house.

A plate on the gate said, DESMOND O'HANLON, DENTAL SURGEON.' My toothache disappeared immediately.

'Oh, shite. I should have guessed,' Maeve said.

'Now,' Mother said, with a scornful glance to Maeve, 'let's sort out things out once and for all.'

There were three squat, middle-aged women in the waiting room when we arrived. Mother swept me through the room to the door of the surgery. The women began to stand but then one of them recognised Mother and whispered to the others. They abruptly sat down again. When Dessie opened the door in a white coat and with a small glass mirror strapped to his forehead, he jumped back as if someone had poked him with a stick.

'My golly, Kathleen. How are you? And you've brought the family too. Well, most of them, hahaha.'

Mother let go of my arm, 'Didn't you get my message this morning? I rang five times?'

Dessie smiled, 'Oh Gosh, yes, well, I was very busy, as you can see,' he swung his hand in a broad gesture at the women in the waiting room, who were watching in fascination.

'They took John's car out of the harbour this morning,' Mother said as her face fell apart. 'I'm very upset.'

'Oh dear, oh dear,' Dessie said. 'If I'd only known.'

'I rang and I rang,' Mother gushed. 'I left a message and everything.'

'Now, now,' Dessie said as Mother collapsed into his arms. 'We'll see what we can do to fix things, shall we? Now you just let me take care of everything.'

'Why didn't you come? I was all alone down there,' Mother said as Dessie guided her into the surgery and closed the door.

Maeve and I stood at the surgery door and looked at each other.

'What does she mean all alone?' Maeve hissed. 'What about us?'

Behind us, in the waiting room, two of the three people were on their feet, staring at us. They appeared to have forgotten all about their toothaches. The lady who was sitting down smiled at me.

'What now?'

'We sit and wait, I suppose,' Maeve said.

245

Maeve and I read magazines for half an hour and tried to avoid the prying gazes of the women. Maeve flicked the pages of the magazines, glancing at the photographs and taking nothing in. She was rigid with anger. There was no point trying to speak to her. When Dessie finally called me into the surgery, I could scarcely walk upright because of the pain. Mother was nowhere to be seen. Dessie put me in the dentist's chair, got me to open my mouth and poked my teeth with a slim steel rod until my toothache flared up again.

'Ahmmm,' Dessie said. 'Ah, yes, it all becomes clear now.'

He pulled my chair up and looked at me, 'You have an abscess, my boy. I want you to go home immediately and gargle a glass of hot water mixed with a tablespoon of salt every hour on the hour.'

'Salt?'

'When the swelling goes down come back to me and I'll be able to have a go at it. I'm afraid you're going to lose it.'

In the waiting room, Mother was smoking a cigarette and Maeve was sitting on the other side of the room reading a magazine, deliberately ignoring her. I could feel the tension in the air between them. The three women were huddled together in the middle as if protecting themselves. Mother looked up and gave me a wide, delighted smile.

'Oh, isn't he the greatest dentist in the world? I knew he was the right one for you.'

On the way home in the car, Maeve and Mother sat rigidly.

'Tell your sister she's blocking my rear-view mirror,' Mother said to me.

'Tell my mother I heard her,' Maeve said.

Maeve shifted herself without looking at Mother. Dessie's fiddling about in my mouth had set the tooth off again. The moment I got home I gargled with a glass of hot water. That only seemed to make the toothache worse. A half-hour later I gargled again. The pain finally eased.

Mrs Donovan called around, 'Oh Kathleen, I can't believe it. It's incredible news, incredible. Just think the one day I go into town to buy a decent pair of shoes, this happens.'

'I'm really sorry about your bin,' Mother said. 'I just wasn't thinking.'

'Oh, never mind that now. You can buy me another one. It must have been terrible for you down on the pier like that without me. Tell me,' Mrs Donovan leaned forward and took Mother's arm, eyes alight. 'Have they found the body yet?'

Disgusted, Maeve and I went out to the back garden.

'She wants to invite Dessie to my twenty-first dinner.'

'Why, for God's sake?'

'She says that Dessie's almost a member of this family now and that he's entitled to come.'

'You could always stab him with another fork.'

'I told her I'd rather not have a twenty-first birthday dinner at all than have that slithery bastard there.'

'That was fairly definite. What did she say to that?'

'She hit me with her bag.'

'Well, maybe you could just have him over for dessert?'

'That's not funny, Daniel.'

'Sorry,' I said.

Maeve's hands twisted and fiddled with the belt buckle of her black jeans. I knew that she was waiting for me to save the situation.

'Look,' I said after thinking it over for a while, 'why not let her do what she wants. Sit through it as though it was a party meeting. You and I can go off and have your *real* twenty-first in town somewhere the next night.'

Maeve brightened, then turned away to stop me noticing, 'No, that won't work.'

'Yes it will, is there anyone else you'd like to invite?'

'No, I think the whole idea of a twenty-first in town is a bit . . . eh . . . it's a bit . . .' she hesitated, turned to face me, then quickly swung away again. 'Well, I wouldn't mind inviting Malachi Spain. He's nice. What do you think of him?'

'He seems nice enough. Is he your latest?'

'Kind of. Sort of. Yeah, I suppose he is.'

'We could order a special cake and everything. It'd be great.'

She smiled, 'OK then, where'll we go?'

'We can decide tomorrow.'

Maeve gave me a smile, 'Yeah,' she said 'I think I'd like that.'

That night I slept in my old bed. The toothache had gone. Mother had insisted that I stay home until I got the abscess cleared. It felt good to be sick and to have responsibility for myself taken away from me. Now that I was home again, it felt like the right place to be. I kept expecting to hear Rory's footsteps on the stairs, the sudden whump as he threw himself onto the bed and the struggle and strangled curses as he removed his clothes before clambering under the sheets.

I dreamed that I was at a twenty-first birthday party for Maeve on the pier. Maeve, Rory and I sat at one end of a long table while Mother sat at the head, pouring endless cups of tea out of a large black teapot. Hundreds of onlookers gathered around us to watch the party. We didn't mind. We were used to being looked at. Mother got up to make a speech. She smiled at everyone, held her hands out to the crowd.

'I am here all alone,' she said sadly.

We kept telling her that we were there with her but Mother shook her head.

'All alone.'

Dessie O'Hanlon appeared in his white coat, wheeling a giant birthday cake in the shape of a Triumph Herald. The cake had green icing all around the top and green candles in the middle.

'Here we are now,' Dessie's fingers twiddled the ends of his moustache, 'One big happy family.'

He sliced downwards with a knife and the cake erupted as seaweed, sea crabs and thousands of tiny slithery things scuttled across the table towards us.

Mother sat at a table in the back room of Leary's Seafront

248

Hotel. She had a pen in her hand and paper in front of her. Maeve sat just behind her with the files and a notebook. I sat opposite, at the side of the door facing Mother. Earlier, Mother had been adamant that I should accompany her to the weekly clinic with her constituents.

'I'm not having you moping around the house all day. You can come and help out. It'll do you good to see others who are not as fortunate as you.'

The first constituent to come in the door was a small man who limped. The man didn't see me.

'Hello, James, don't tell me you've turned down another house?'

The small man smiled, 'It was the wrong shaggin' place for me, you know. Sure you couldn't swing a cat in it.'

'How many houses have you turned down now?'

'Ah, sure I don't remember.'

Maeve handed Mother the notebook. 'Thirty-six.'

'Ah, no, not that many,' James says. 'I'm sure it's only thirty.'

Mother sighed. 'I'll see if I can get you a bigger place.'

Next in was a young woman who wore leggings with images of palm trees emblazoned down the side.

'He's fired me again, just because I'm pregnant and can't reach up to the top shelves. You'd think there was a law against getting pregnant in this country.'

Mother took down the details and promised the young woman that she would do what she could to get her her job back.

'You'd better. Otherwise I'm going to murder me husband for getting me pregnant again.'

The next constituent was a tall weedy woman with short, spiked hair. Her mother-in-law had thrown her out because she had broken up with her husband and now she had lost her job as well. She needed somewhere to live fast.

'It's only you can do it for me, Kathleen. Ye got me grandmother a place before she died, God rest her, and now I need a place too.'

'I'll see what I can do,' Mother said. 'Ring me on Thursday.'

249

As Maeve went to the door to let the next constituent in, Mother suddenly put her hands to her mouth as she started to giggle. Maeve looked at me and I rose to go to Mother. Mother held up her hands.

'Sit down. I'm fine, really I am,' she said and put her head down as she was overcome by giggles.

I felt a dreadful chill run through my stomach. We went to her and tried to get her to stop. Maeve held her head up. I took her hand. It felt warm and moist. I slapped it a couple of times. I didn't know why. I had seen it done on television and I thought it might help.

'Ow,' Mother said and took her hand away. 'That hurt. Now leave me be, I'm fine. Just a bit of giggling. No harm to anyone.'

Mother composed herself and adjusted the sheets of paper in front of her. As I went back to my seat I heard her muttering to herself. The constituents went by in a blur. A fat man who had had a fistfight with his foreman and been fired wanted his job back or 'that fucking foreman's head on a plate'. A small, stooped woman needed a free bus pass and a medical card. A skinhead wanted a job in either the Army or, if he couldn't have that, he wanted Mother to get him into the Foreign Legion. An old woman wanted to move away from her flat because of the junkies who lived next door.

After a while, the stream of people became like a procession of scavengers tearing invisible pieces from Mother. It was Mother's job to know answers, solve problems, intervene on people's behalf. She conducted her business in a patient, friendly way, yet each person who came to her took something from her face when they left. In between constituents, she sometimes stared ahead of her like a woman searching for something in an empty room. I wondered if Maeve still had the photograph of Mother and Dad as a young couple out in the town. Mother's face had been bright, inspiring with a wide smile that glowed in her eyes. Now Mother's face was bitter. She reminded me of Rory in one of his foul moods. It shocked me when I looked at Maeve's face and saw exactly the same bitter expression.

They looked like a pair of theatrical sisters who had just failed their last audition.

At home, Mother was restless. She smoked cigarettes, fiddled with the pots and pans in the kitchen and drove Maeve mad with queries.

'What about the replies to the council? Did you phone the social welfare people? How long will it take to get your man out of that house into the new one?'

'I've got it all under control, Mother,' Maeve said. 'Leave me alone, please.'

'Where's Rory?' Mother said suddenly. 'He should be here to help us out.'

Next morning, Mother drove me to Dessie O'Hanlon's. On the way, she was preoccupied. She appeared to have forgotten I was in the car with her. When she dropped me off, she handed me an envelope addressed to Dessie.

'Tell him to ring me later,' she said.

Dessie's eyes narrowed when I handed him the envelope, 'Yes, thank you.'

He showed me to the chair and went out of the room with the envelope. When he came back, his face was watchful, hesitant. I got the impression that he had made a pact with himself to take revenge on me for bringing him the letter. Dessie poked around in my mouth with a variety of long steel instruments. Then he gave me a sharp prod and told me to be brave for a minute.

'Now I'm just punching a teeny-weeny hole in the gum so the poison will drain out. It'll only be sore for a little while. But it'll make the pain go away. Then in a few days we can yank it out and the pain will be gone forever, won't that be great?'

I prayed that Dessie would get an abscess someday. I hoped that whoever he went to for treatment would talk down to him as though he were a complete moron, the moment he was helpless with his mouth open. It saddened me to think that Dessie's teeth were probably in excellent condition. All dentists had good teeth. Nobody in their right mind would go near a gummy dentist. Perhaps the only way that Dessie would ever feel the agony of toothache would be if someone smacked him in the mouth with a wheel clamp. To take my mind away from Dessie, I thought about Desperate Dan. One day, soon after I began work at the airport, Dan had come up to me where I sat on the red plastic-covered seats, shot his false teeth out of his mouth and caught them when they were inches from my nose. His face looked as though his entire mouth had fallen out which, in a way, it had. When he had finished laughing at my shocked reaction, he popped them back in his mouth.

'Got them all out when I was forty,' Dan said. 'Best thing I ever did. No more toothaches.'

Now as I sat in Dessie O'Hanlon's dentist's chair, I felt fluid running down my gum. Dessie gave me a beaker of lukewarm water to rinse out my mouth. I spat into a sink by the chair.

'I'm sorry I wasn't on the pier to help you all out,' Dessie said with his back to me. 'Tell your mother I'll try and make it to Maeve's twenty-first.'

Dessie didn't bother showing me to the door.

When I reached home, Mother was tending a plant in the hallway. 'Well, what did he say?'

I told her what Dessie had said and she ripped a leaf off the plant.

'Is that it?'

'Yes.'

'It's just not good enough, after all this time,' she put down the plant and wandered vacantly into the front room to look for her cigarettes. 'It's not good enough.'

In the morning, a Garda called to the house to tell Mother that they had found nothing at all in the car.

'If there was anything the little sea crabs took it away,' the Garda said. 'They are the fellas who do all the damage. You wouldn't think it to look at them but I've seen a —'

'Yes, thank you, Garda,' Maeve said. 'I think we get the message.'

When the Garda left, Mother went to the phone and called in sick to her office in the Dail.

'This is weird,' Maeve said. 'She never gets sick. She's got all these big meetings this week and now she's cancelled the lot. I'm worried about her.'

Mother refused to take any phone calls unless they were

from Dessie O'Hanlon, 'I'm expecting him to call or drop down to the house. Until then I'll be in my room.'

Late in the afternoon, when Dessie still hadn't phoned, Mother rang Dessie's surgery. Dessie's secretary said that he had gone on holiday for a week and that his practice was being taken over by Dr Caldwell until his return.

'What about my son's abscess?' Mother said. 'Do you expect him to go to a stranger with it?'

Mother took the phone into the front room and made calls. Whenever Maeve or I went in, she cupped the receiver and told us to get out until she was finished. She spent most of the evening on the phone. When she came out she went straight to bed without mentioning my tooth.

'What's up?' I asked.

'I dunno. I hope she's better by tomorrow.'

'Was it the car that did it?'

'I hope so.'

'You hope so?'

Maeve's face was grave, 'As long as it's not about Dessie. Anything is better than Dessie O'Hanlon.'

By the morning of Maeve's twenty-first, my toothache was just a faint presence in my mouth. Mother appeared to have cheered up. She and Maeve went out for a long walk. When they returned, both of them went around the house humming to themselves as if they knew that something wonderful was going to happen. It was a while before I could corner Maeve to ask what was going on.

Maeve did a pirouette, 'She's giving up politics.'

'Our Mother?' I said. 'I don't believe that.'

'She wants to start a shop on Main Street, with me as her partner. We're looking at a place tomorrow. She says to think of it as a belated birthday present.'

'That's great, eh, I think.'

'It's brilliant,' Maeve said and did another pirouette.

'I thought you wanted to be a TD someday.'

'Nah', Maeve said. 'I've changed my mind. I want to run a shop with Mother. I'm really looking forward to tonight. It'll be just family. I'm so excited.'

I rang Rory and told him to come out for dinner.

'Why should I? I didn't get a dinner for my twenty-first.'

'Let me speak to him,' Mother said.

I handed Mother the receiver.

'Rory, this is an important family occasion. I want all my family around me. Besides, I've got a big surprise for you that you've got to be here to see. No, I can't tell you now. You'll see what it is tonight.'

We bought food in the town. People occasionally told Mother that they were sorry about the car and Mother thanked them. It surprised and delighted me to see how well Mother was coping with things. Even when Mr Mahony told her how glad he was that the car had been found and that he said a prayer every morning that the body would turn up soon, Mother just shrugged, said 'thanks', then asked for a look at the head of broccoli that was on the counter.

'I think she's almost over it now,' Maeve said. 'She's serious about the shop. She's even called off the cumann meeting tomorrow so we can look at sites.'

After Mother sent Maeve off to the pier to buy fish, she and I sneaked into Hannon's bakers on Main Street and collected the birthday cake she had ordered earlier by phone. She wouldn't let me look at it.

'Just guard it with your life and go home now and hide it in the closet under the stairs.'

When everything had been brought back to the house Mother sent Maeve and me down to The Tall Ships while she cooked. When Maeve offered to help, Mother laughed.

'It's very good of you' Maeve, on your own birthday but I really want to cook this meal without watching my house burn down around my ears, thank you very much.'

In The Tall Ships, Maeve had a glass of white wine and I had a pint of Guinness while we kept an eye out for Rory. The Fabulous Roadrunners still hadn't managed to get a record deal, Joey Boland had resigned and Paddy Cool had quit to join a showband. Rory still believed that they were going to be the next Boomtown Rats.

254

'I'm glad we found the car,' Maeve said. 'I think it's been therapeutic, don't you?'

'I think it has helped,' I said.

'I think she's had enough.'

'I can't imagine her out of politics.'

'I know,' Maeve said, and we both sipped our drinks.

After a while, Maeve turned and smiled at me, 'Well, Daniel what's it to be – a newsagents or a mini-market?'

Rory came in, looking like a Hell's Angel in his leather jacket and jeans. He slouched over to us and pulled up a chair.

'Hello, Rory,' Maeve said.

'Hi,' I said.

Rory nodded, and looked about him as if pressed for time, 'Where's the old dear?'

'She's in the house,' Maeve said. 'We're not to go in until eight. Thanks for my present, Rory.'

'Present?' For a moment Rory was confused, then he remembered it was Maeve's birthday. 'Sorry. I left it in the flat.'

'Yeah, sure,' Maeve teased. 'I'll come over tomorrow and collect it, OK?'

'Eh, OK,' Rory said and went up to the bar for a pint.

'He thinks I can't see through him,' Maeve said proudly, 'but I can see through everyone, can't I?'

'You certainly can,' I said.

'Thank God Dessie isn't coming,' Maeve said. 'This time I really would have gone for him with a fork.'

We both laughed.

At eight, we arrived at the door of our house. There was a candle burning in the window and balloons tied to the door.

'It's like New Year's,' Maeve said.

'Yippee,' Rory said sarcastically. 'Let's make a chain and dance around the street.'

'Oh come on, Rory, loosen up. It's my birthday.'

Mother opened the door and beamed at us. She wore her lowcut black dress with the set of pearls from her election night victory. She kissed each of us on the cheek and welcomed us home.

255

'It's great to have my whole family in their own home,' she said. 'I was beginning to think I might never see us all together again.'

Mother seated us at the table. There was an extra chair at the table with a napkin in place in front of it but no knife and fork. We presumed it was in case Mrs Donovan dropped in, which often happened during family occasions. For a first course we had smoked salmon on brown bread. Mother wouldn't let anyone help.

'This is a birthday party so you just enjoy yourselves,' she said and left the room to get something else.

'She's on good form,' Rory said. 'There must be something wrong.'

'Don't be so cynical, Rory,' Maeve said.

'Sorry, just making a joke.'

Later, when the first course was over, Rory asked for seconds. Mother told him if he still wanted more after the main course and the dessert she would be delighted to oblige.

'For the moment, just eat what you're given, please.'

We were halfway through the main course of steak, sliced potatoes and broccoli in cream sauce when Mother announced that she had a very special surprise that she would unveil during dessert.

'It's something we've all been looking forward to for a long time.'

'Dessie O'Hanlon's head on a plate?' Rory asked cheerfully but Mother just tittered.

'Mrs Donovan's mouth on a p-plate?' I suggested.

'No, this is something that's going to change our lives,' she said as she left the room.

'Oh, is that all?' Rory said, his mouth full of steak. 'God, I thought it was going to be something really important.'

'Will we tell him?' Maeve asked me.

'Why not?' I said.

'Tell me what?'

'I'll tell you a secret,' Maeve said. 'She's going to give up politics.'

'Yeah, sure,' Rory sneered. 'And I'm going to join Fianna Fail.'

Maeve appeared hurt, 'All right, don't believe me. Just wait and see.'

'Yeah. I'll wait and see.'

The dessert was a chocolate ice cream with chocolate flake topping. It was nice but it was nothing special. We had had it before on lots of occasions.

'Come on, Mother,' Maeve said, 'where's the surprise?'

'Coming,' she said.

Mother disappeared into the kitchen and came back with the cake, candles blazing.

'Now, before you blow these candles out,' Mother said, 'I want you all to close your eyes. We have a very special guest who has come a long way to be with us tonight.'

I saw the smile freeze on Maeve's face. Rory looked around as if someone was playing a big joke. Mother put the cake on the table. She smiled and rubbed her hands together. Her eyes looked at us but went right through us. She may as well have been staring at waxwork dummies. We watched her take her hands down and slowly move towards the door which was open a crack.

'Children, today I received a very special phone call from a very special man. Someone you haven't seen in a long time has come a long way to be with you tonight.' She began to open the door. 'Say hello to your father.'

There was a slow creaking as Mother pulled the door open. Her smile grew wider. A tear ran down Maeve's face and stopped at the edge of her chin, poised to drop.

Mother giggled, 'Welcome, welcome. Come in John and say hello to your family and, of course, wish your daughter a happy birthday.'

The dark hallway leered at us. The only sound was the squeak of Mother's hand on the door handle. Mother's eyes watched someone come into the room. She smiled back at someone who was slightly taller than her. She reached out a hand and took thin air and guided it to the extra seat at the table. Then she sat down beside the chair and smiled at us. She looked as fresh and youthful as she had in the photograph Maeve had found in the bookcase years ago. She placed her hand on the table napkin in front of the extra chair as if covering the hand of another.

I felt suddenly helpless and disconnected from what was happening, as though I were looking at a scene on television. I summoned up the same numb feeling I had taught myself in school whenever anyone made fun of my stutter. When I went numb inside the words did not hurt me. Only this time I felt ice in my guts as well, an abrupt realisation that the situation was beyond control and that all I could do was wait for it to take whatever course it would.

'Now Rory, say hello to your father. Rory's got his own band. They're really good. He had his photograph on the cover of *Hot Press*, didn't you, Rory?'

Rory sat slumped in his chair, a resigned look on his face as though he knew this was going to happen, He didn't say anything.

'And the birthday girl, Maeve. Have you got a kiss for your father, Maeve? Of course you have. John, she's been a terrific help while you were away, you've just no idea.'

There were tears streaking Maeve's face, but she kept looking at Mother as if she hoped that Mother would pull out of it and run to her for a hug.

'Finally, the baby, he was only . . . what age were you when John went away, Daniel? Oh, very young, seven I think or maybe nine,' Mother giggled again. 'Anyway, here he is, a student at UCD and he's a ship inspector at the airport. I gave him strict instructions to keep an eye out for you. You can be proud of him.'

Mother pretended to listen to something that her visitor said, then threw her head back and laughed.

'Oh, my gosh, did you hear that children?' she said. 'John, you're dreadful. I told you before I won't have jokes at the dinner table.'

When Rory got up suddenly and left the room Mother didn't notice. We heard the front door open and slam.

'Mother?' Maeve said. 'Mother, I think it's time to go to bed.'

She stood up and walked over to Mother and put her hand on her.

'What?' Mother said. 'What was that?'

'Bed,' Maeve looked at me for help.

I went over and the two of us helped Mother to her feet and led her down the hall.

'I'll be back in a moment, John,' she called, then turned to us. 'For heaven's sake, don't let him go out the door tonight, will you? God knows when we'll see him again.'

We took Mother up the stairs to her bedroom and Maeve undressed her while I drew the blinds and locked the window so she couldn't climb out. Mother talked all the while, a rambling stream of memories of when we were young, stories about Dad, sayings from her own childhood. There was nothing about politics, Fianna Fail or Dessie O'Hanlon.

When she was in bed and growing drowsy, Maeve and I went outside.

'I'll take first watch,' Maeve said. 'You go downstairs and tidy up.'

'Maeve?' I said.

'What is it?'

'I'm sorry.'

Maeve shrugged, 'What can you do?'

I went downstairs. The front door was open so I presumed Rory had gone back to his flat. I left the door on the latch in case he had just gone to The Tall Ships and intended to come back later. Then I went into the front room and blew out the candles on the cake. After that I cleared away all the dishes. The clearing up kept me from thinking too deeply about anything. When it was done I took the birthday cake, two plates, two forks and a knife upstairs to Maeve.

'This is ridiculous,' Maeve said, 'but it's a good idea.'

'How is she?'

'Asleep,' Maeve said. 'We'll decide what to do tomorrow. I can't think about anything tonight.'

'We should have seen it coming,' I said. 'Why didn't we?'

'I think you're doing pretty well if you can see what's coming for yourself. Nobody can predict how anybody else is going to react.'

259

'I thought she was doing so well.'

'She was,' Maeve said. 'She'll be fine.'

'She will?'

Maeve finished her piece of cake and put down the plate, 'Of course she will. We're going to open a shop, Mother and me. Wait and see.'

We sat on the stairs outside Mother's room and ate cake until we were too full to eat another bite. Then we got pillows and blankets from my bedroom and fell asleep on the floor outside Mother's door.

In the morning, we woke to Rory's snores, coming from his own bed in his old bedroom down the hall.

ELEVEN

Homecoming

DAN'S BED IS on the unhealthy side of the ward. To his left is an empty bed and to his right is a patient who lies covered in plaster, arms stretched out to drip stands on either side like a crucified mummy. The mummy is such an arresting sight that I bump into Dan's bed and nearly fall on top of him. Dan remains asleep, his cheeks sunken, mouth lopsided as though his face has fallen in. At first I think he is in a bad way, but then I notice that his teeth are grinning at me from a glass on the bedside table. Across the aisle, on the healthy side, two patients in the other row of beds are boisterously entertaining visitors and a third is reading a book.

None of the ship inspectors know what is wrong with Dan exactly. Harry Dunne says it's a hernia while Dominic Root is convinced that Dan's throat has collapsed due to the effects of constant loud belching. The only thing that everyone knows for certain is that Dan has had an operation. I believe I am the only ship inspector so far to visit Dan.

I love the smell of a hospital. The rooms are clean and warm and the nurses so friendly and sexy in their spotless white uniforms. In hospital, all a person has to do is to get well. Someone else changes the sheets, does the washing up, puts out the bins and scrubs the floors. I think how great it would be to fall ill for a few months with an illness that isn't life-endangering but which requires constant attention and monitoring. I sit by the side of the bed, a box of chocolates named 'Happy Flavours' in my hand. I bought the chocolates in the hospital shop, attracted by the box's bright colours and the breezy letters of the title, even though I had never heard of the brand. On my way up the stairs to the second floor, I could feel everything shifting about inside. Now the box looks cheap and shoddy. I should have paid the extra fifty pence for the Milk Tray selection.

When Dan shows no sign of waking, I cough loudly. I have a lot to do today and I can't afford to waste time sitting around. Dan stirs, his right eye opens. At first he doesn't recognise me.

'Hello, Dan,' I say and give him a smile. 'It's me, Daniel.'

His eyes open fully. He lifts a hand to his face and seems relieved to find it still intact.

'Big Balsh,' he mumbles wearily as he sits up.

He rubs his face, then gestures at the glass holding his teeth. I hand him the glass. Dan removes his teeth from the glass and pops them into his mouth. After a couple of test grimaces he looks like himself again.

'The biggest Big Balls of all,' he says indifferently.

Dan tries to lift himself higher in the bed, then realises that his right arm is attached to a tube from a clear plastic container on a drip stand. He looks surprised to find it there. For a moment, he appears to consider tugging his arm free.

'Feckin' thing,' Dan says. 'I can't even go to the jacks without pulling this yoke around with me.'

'Can I g-give you a hand?'

Dan's face suddenly contorts and his face twists to the right. 'Hold your horses now,' he says breathlessly.

As the seizure continues, Dan puts his hands underneath him and attempts to rise from the bed. At any second I expect his teeth to shoot out of his mouth and land on my lap. I have never seen anyone in such abject agony. I decide that it must be a heart attack. I am about to call the nurse when Dan lets off a long, flapping fart. Dan gives me a look of such imbecilic bliss that I smile too. I glance over at the healthy side of the room. Nobody is looking at us. It is ironic that Dan is now in one of the few places in the world where he can break wind all he likes without offending anyone.

I move my chair back. 'I'm glad to see that you're feeling better.'

'Ah, it builds up in ye after a while. Sure ye have to let it go.'

I notice that there are no flowers on Dan's bedside table, no fruit, not even a card, even though he has been here a week. I hand him the box of 'Happy Flavours'.

'I got you something.'

'Thank you, Big Balls.'

Dan examines the chocolates. He turns the box over and finds the price tag which I have forgotten to remove.

'One pound and ninety-nine pence,' Dan reads. 'Is that all you think I'm worth?' he says without a hint of a smile.

'Sorry, I thought you'd like them.'

'Have you ever eaten one?'

'No.'

'Then how do you know I'd like them?'

Dan holds the 'Happy Flavours' in his hand as if he cannot decide whether to toss them in the bin or fling them back at me. I decide that this is going to be a short visit. Dan tries to lift himself in the bed again. This time he almost upsets the drip stand, but when I try to help he waves me away angrily.

'Christ, boy, what do you think I am, an invalid?'

'When are they letting you out?'

'Oh, in a while. Don't look for me till ye see me coming.'

I notice that Dan is squinting at me in a peculiar way.

'You were never really a Dan, were ye, Big Balls?' he says.

'Pardon?'

'No, I didn't think so. Ye've always been a Daniel, haven't ye?'

'Well, Daniel's my name.'

'I don't suppose anyone has ever called you Danny?' Dan says, scratching at his arm in irritation at the place where the drip goes into it.

'No.'

'Ye wouldn't ever think of changing it to Danny yourself?'

'Why should I?' I feel myself growing irritated.

Dan laughs, 'Some people are born Dan, some get called Danny and others, I suppose, stay Daniel all their lives. I've always been Dan. You'd know it, wouldn't you? I thought about calling my son Daniel but I decided that I couldn't do that to him. It would be too much of a burden.'

Dan's face is devoid of its usual smirk. He actually appears serious. If I didn't know better I could almost swear that he is trying to pick a fight.

'Tell me,' Dan says, 'are ye going to stay a waster all yer life?'

'Eh, no, I mean, yes. W-what are you on about?'

'What year were ye in when ye dropped out of university?'

'Second.'

'Ye should drop what ye're doing now and go back to it,' Dan says in the same condescending way that some of the members of Mother's cumann used to do.

'That was years ago,' I say. 'I'm working now.'

Dan ignores me, 'If I'd had *your* chances, I'd have done a lot more with my life. I wouldn't have pissed it up against the wall the way you're doing.'

I feel an overwhelming urge to push Dan's drip stand out of the way and punch him on the nose. He's the one who is in hospital, yet here he is talking to me as though I'm the one who needs help. I am tired of his sneers and his cynicism, the farting and belching. He has called me Big Balls for the last time. I think of all the lies he has told me over the years. I remember the spoof about his son being a master forger of ten-pound notes and that makes me angry too. I came here wishing that Dan would get well soon but now I would like to see him covered from head to toe in plaster like the mummy in the bed across from him.

'Dan,' I say, determined to tell him what I think of him before walking out, 'I don't want you to ca –'

'Hish,' Dan says as he watches someone enter the ward.

I look up as Donna bears down on us, carrying flowers and a basket of fruit. Donna wears a red jump-suit and red shoes and has her hair scraped back into a pony tail.

'Oh, Dan, you're looking great.'

'Donna,' Dan says, as softly as a lover's greeting, 'come here to me, my little darling.'

Donna kisses Dan on the cheek and presents him with the flowers and the fruit. She smiles at me.

'And look who's here too. How are you, Daniel?'

'Fine.'

'What do you think, Daniel? Isn't our poor sick colleague looking well all the same?'

'Eh, I suppose so.'

Dan snorts, 'Sure, what are ye asking him for? He wouldn't know.'

She turns to Dan, 'I can't stay long. My sister's giving a yoga class and I'm already late. I just wanted to look in on you and give you these.'

'You're very good,' Dan says. 'Me and Big Balls here were discussing the lad's future.'

'He was winding me up,' I say, suddenly embarrassed in front of Donna.

Dan holds up the box of 'Happy Flavours'. 'Do ye see this cheap box of chocolates he brought me?'

'I shouldn't have b-bothered,' I say, getting to my feet.

'I'd offer ye one but I don't want to poison ye,' Dan says.

'Now, boys, that's enough,' Donna claps her hands. 'Dan, you're awful, really you are. I think that Daniel is very good to bring you anything at all.'

'Hmmmmph,' Dan says, playing up his disgruntlement for Donna's benefit.

I offer Donna my chair but she prefers to sit on the edge of Dan's bed. For a few minutes they talk about the airport and Donna's car and other things that they have obviously discussed before while I sit there like a waxwork. The box of 'Happy Flavours' lies on the bedside table where Dan has left it. When neither is looking I switch it to the table beside the crucified Mummy. The mummy's table is laden with Get Well cards and baskets of fruit. I may as well give the chocolates to a popular fellow like the mummy than a grumpy old bastard like Dan. After a few more minutes of small talk, Donna leans over and kisses Dan on the cheek again.

'I must run. I'll look in tomorrow.'

'Why don't ye take yer man with ye?' Dan says, cocking a thumb in my direction.

'Would you like a lift, Daniel?' Donna says.

'Er – yes, please.'

'Goodbye, Dan, see you soon,' Donna waves and I follow, without bothering to say goodbye to Dan.

I hear a chuckle, 'Goodbye, Big Balls.'

The lift is between floors so we take the stairs. On the way down, Donna asks me how things are. I think about telling her about the break-up with Carla but I decide against it. In return I may have to listen to the current state of play between Frank Nails and herself and I couldn't bear that. I tell her that everything is going fine. Outside, we walk across the car-park to Donna's car, a yellow Nissan Sunny.

Before we drive off, Donna suddenly turns to me, 'I don't know if you've heard, but they pulled a tumour out of his stomach, you know.'

'I didn't know.'

'You might not be seeing Dan for a long while. If they move him to a hospice, he may not come back at all.'

As we drive out of the car-park, I feel dreadful. I want to rush back into the hospital, up the stairs and apologise to Dan but something prevents me from asking Donna to stop the car. I feel like such a heel for not being more compassionate and understanding but I also feel a sense of relief from being out of there, away from Dan's bad form and his illness.

'I just didn't know,' I say, as though I should apologise to someone.

'It's sad,' Donna says. 'Dan is such a vibrant man too, and he's only sixty-one.'

'What about his family?' I say. 'Have they been in to see him?'

'Dan's a widower. I think he has a brother in Kerry somewhere but they haven't spoken for years.'

'What about his son?'

Donna smiles, 'Dan has no son.'

'No son?'

'I'm afraid not.'

Today started off really well. I was going to do a lot of things to get my life in order. The first was a simple visit to my colleague in hospital. Now I feel as though I've committed a crime.

'I'll be going in regularly,' Donna says. 'Do you want me to keep in touch with you?'

'Yes. That w-would be great.'

Donna hands me a card, 'In case you need me.'

The card lists Donna's home number and address. It also gives her surname, Kennedy. We don't say much on the way into town, but I feel a closeness between us. Dan's illness suddenly makes the question of Frank Nails irrelevant. I have been selfish and small-minded, I realise. I will have to start improving my understanding of others.

By the time Donna drops me in Mountjoy Square, I have made up my mind to become a more caring person. I thank Donna for the lift, she gives me a peck on the cheek and I get out. Before she drives off, she winds down the window.

'You know,' she says seriously, 'perhaps you should have bought Dan a more expensive box of chocolates.'

I watch Donna's car drive away then I cross the road to Mr Wolkenski's building. The outside of the building is still pockmarked and abandoned looking. Inside, Mr Wolkenski sits on a wooden chair in the middle of the room, bony hands clasped in his lap. He looks a bit pockmarked and abandoned too. Today, we are on the ground floor because Mr Wolkenski is too frail to climb the stairs anymore. My first 'stutter lesson' in four years is also my last with Mr Wolkenski who is retiring next week. When I phoned yesterday to ask for this final lesson, he said he was surprised to hear from me again.

'I tot your lil problem vas unter control,' he said.

At first he resisted the idea, but when I told him that I had something very important to do today and that I needed his help for the last time, he consented.

Now Mr Wolkenski looks at me with light blue eyes set in a sallow face. His face hasn't changed much, the rest of him now just appears skinnier and more delicate.

'Chair. Sit, pleez,' Mr Wolkenski says, indicating a bank of chairs against the wall.

I select a chair and sit opposite him.

'Vatch, pleez.' He opens his mouth slowly, takes a deep breath and screams into my face, 'Aaaaaaaagh.'

I sit back on the chair.

'Do loud, pleez.'

I open my mouth and give a pathetic 'aah'. Mr Wolkenski shakes his head. Once again he screams as loudly as he can in his weak voice. I try again. It is difficult to find the motivation to scream into the face of an elderly man sitting directly opposite. If I had a poster of an alien or something to look at, then I could let my imagination run. My scream sounds little better than my previous attempt. After a few more tries I conclude that I achieve the best results by closing my eyes. That way, at least, the screams sound good to me. After a while, screaming in the dark becomes a pleasant, uplifting experience. After a particularly satisfying blood-curdling yell, I open my eyes to find Mr Wolkenski staring at me as if my nose has fallen off. Have I somehow traumatised Mr Wolkenski? Is my screaming technique too effective?

'Sorry,' I say.

It takes me a few seconds to realise that Mr Wolkenski's stare by-passes me to focus on a spot behind. When I turn, I see a tiny mouse on top of a chair. The mouse gazes at us without concern.

Mr Wolkenski takes off his shoe and immediately presses it into my hand, 'Do, pleez. Now.'

Displaying a surprising degree of strength for such a delicate-looking man, he pushes me off the chair in the direction of the mouse.

'Do, now,' Mr Wolkenski shouts with such force that I almost run to the far wall.

Mr Wolkenski's shoe is a black brogue with a curlicue pattern on the toe. In my hand, it feels heavy and awkward.

It surprises me that a frail man should wear such a weighty, cumbersome shoe. Perhaps it explains why it always used to take him so long to get up the stairs. Holding the shoe by the toe, I approach the mouse. The mouse watches me lift the shoe then, almost casually, avoids my first half-hearted swipe. It jumps off the chair and scuttles along the floor. I chase the tiny creature along the walls with Mr Wolkenski's shoe upraised. Every time I get near, the mouse ducks in between the piles of plaster that are all along the wall. I hurl the shoe and succeed in giving the mouse a glancing blow. I am certain that I hear a squeal. To my relief, it vanishes down a hole in the corner. I pick up the shoe and dust it off. When I turn around Mr Wolkenski is poised on the chair as if ready to make a leap for the door.

'It's all right, Mr Wolkenski,' I say 'The mouse is gone.'

Mr Wolkenski unfurls from the chair, reaches out a hand to me with an agonized expression.

'Shoe,' he says.

I give him his shoe which he puts back on. For the rest of the lesson, Mr Wolkenski stares at the hole in the corner with an expression both alert and petrified. He pays more attention to the hole than he does to my screaming. Finally, when I am unable to scream any more, Mr Wolkenski shakes my hand and tells me that the lesson is 'finish'.

'I ken do no more fer you,' he says.

We walk to the door where I hand him a twenty-pound note. He pushes my hand away.

'Last time is free,' he says without a smile.

'Thanks. Well, goodbye then.'

'Yez, yez, gut bye,' he says and guides me out as though he is relieved to finally be rid of me.

Outside, my throat feels raw and parched. I go into the newsagent's on the corner to buy a Coke. The drink feels cool and fizzy going down but afterwards I still feel as though the inside of my throat has acne. I usually felt more self-confident after a 'stutter lesson'. Recently, I have been feeling down. I needed a boost after the break-up with Carla, the trouble with the incinerator reports, Mother's phone calls and everything else that has swamped me over

the past while. Now, though, instead of feeling more confident, I just feel drained and a bit silly. Going back to Mr
Wolkenski was probably a waste of time. At least I did not
have to pay for a lesson in screaming and mouse-chasing.

On the corner of Mountjoy Square, I hail a taxi and
climb in.

'Redrock, please,' I say and am gratified to hear that my
voice sounds fine.

'Oh, Jaysus,' the taxi man says. 'What do you want to go
to Redrock for?'

'Eh, I . . . well –'

'I'll never get a fucking fare back from out there.'

'I have something to do there . . .' I begin.

'I'm supposed to be on me lunch break soon. Then it's
me sister's birthday and I'm supposed to pick up a present
for her. Just my bleedin' luck to get a fare to Redrock.'

The taxi man scratches his stubble and looks at me in the
mirror. I experience a strange sensation of guilt, as though
I have ruined this man's day. Why is it that everyone I
meet today makes me feel guilty about something?

'If you like,' I say, 'you can drop me at a taxi rank.'

The taxi man lets out a long sigh, 'Oh, I'll bleedin' take
ye. Don't worry your head about it. You're in the hands of
a professional now.'

After a muttered and largely unintelligible soliloquy, the
taxi man lapses into sullen silence.

I had thought that I was over Carla. Then, one day last
week, I came home from work to find that all the plants
were missing from the apartment. Next day, the wardrobe
had vanished. After the wardrobe, it was the chest of
drawers and the chairs. The following night, the sewing
machine and all the paintings had disappeared. It was as
though the place was being ransacked by a team of invisible
elves. I could feel their eyes on me every morning as I
walked out the front door. At this stage, Carla has taken
everything of hers except the television and the sofa. Tonight, I expect the invisible elves to finish the job. I wonder
if they will leave the bed.

I blame Donald Logan. I hate his tattoo, his goofy laugh,

his deep-set eyes and that helmet of thick blond hair that makes him look like a demented Viking. Rock stars are the only people in the world who wear sunglasses indoors. The other night, I dreamt that Donald Logan and I were sharing a platform high in the air, preparing for a bungee-jump. At the last moment I refused to jump and Donald laughed at me. He produced a photograph of Carla kneeling on a bed, naked. Then he stuck the photograph between his teeth and hurled himself backwards into space. While Donald was still free-falling, I leaned over to un-clip his bungee cord from its harness. Unfortunately, I woke up before he hit the ground.

We pass a Fianna Fail election poster stuck to a telegraph pole. Apparently, there is a local government election going on. The writing on the poster says, 'Vote for Donnelly. You know it makes sense'. The face shows a beaming, puffy-cheeked man. It reminds me of all the times that I saw Mother's face staring back at me from election posters. I think about the election that followed immediately upon Maeve's twenty-first birthday party. Before the campaign, Dessie O'Hanlon ran off with his dental assistant, an act that came as a surprise to nobody except Mother. In the first week of campaigning, Mother crashed the car into the bus-stop outside our house, denounced Mrs Donovan as a Fine Gaeler at the campaign meeting and tried to stow away on board a fishing boat. When Mother refused to leave the house, saying that she was expecting a phone call from Dad, even her own canvassers gave up. By the halfway stage in the election campaign, Maeve had radically re-assessed Mother's chances of getting re-elected.

'Only if all the other candidates die suddenly before polling day,' Maeve said.

Mother lost the election and was quietly dropped by the cumann. The phone stopped ringing, people stopped calling around and suddenly nobody wanted favours done. Mother went to bed and stayed there for weeks. A year after the election defeat, Maeve convinced Mother to sell the house and move to Clontarf. We didn't even meet the people who bought our home. The sale was handled by an agent.

'She needs a new start,' Maeve said. 'We'll open a shop or something. Everything will work out for the best.'

After Maeve sold the house in Redrock and rented the place in Clontarf, I felt lost and homeless. I worried that when Dad returned he would not know where to find us. He would have to ask Mrs Donovan where we were. I failed my exams in English and History. Then I failed the repeats. I worked part-time as a ship inspector in the summers and at Christmas. I stayed in the new house in Clontarf as seldom as I could. I couldn't connect with the sheer dullness of the new place and I didn't like seeing Mother so lost and angry all the time. For the first time in my life, I couldn't smooth things over. All I could think about was that I had somehow failed the family. Even in the seven years I lived with Carla, whenever I thought of *home* it was the house in Church Street that came into my mind. I often imagined myself scaling the mountain in my old back garden or prowling around the house in the early hours in Dad's dressing-gown.

Now I am on my way to Redrock for the second time in weeks. It just goes to show how quickly things change. Life seems to plod along in the same casual way, then next moment it shifts utterly and for ever.

The taxi man chain-smokes cigarettes, even though there are No Smoking signs prominently displayed. We pass through Grandview and drive out along the coast road. In Redrock, the landmarks of my youth flow past – the steps leading up to the railway station, Molloy's multi-coloured newsagent's, the entrance to the east pier with all the fish merchants' shacks stretched into the distance, the sour-smelling harbour with its ugly yacht club, Leary's Seafront Hotel. Then we are in the town itself. As we pass Mahony's mini-market, I see that Arnold Schwarzenegger and Sigourney Weaver are still in the window, dominating the other vegetables. Then we are at the church.

'Just here,' I tell the taxi man.

The taxi pulls up on the corner beside Butch Cassidy the butcher's. I hand the taxi man the same twenty-pound note that Mr Wolkenski refused. The taxi man gives me change and I get out. Despite myself, I tip him a pound.

'Good luck,' the taxi man says grimly as he drives away.

I walk past Butch Cassidy's. Inside, Butch is dismembering a side of lamb. I see nobody I know in the street. I stand outside the door of my old home and knock. I feel tense but determined not to stutter or let myself down. I had thought about phoning the people to tell them I was coming. Then I decided that if I was going to get turned away, I wanted it to happen on my old doorstep rather than on the telephone.

The door is opened by the same stooped, blue-eyed man I met on my previous visit. He doesn't seem to remember me. I take a deep breath.

'Hello, I'm sorry to bother you. My name is Daniel Buckley. My family used to live here ten years ago. I was wondering if I could come in for a quick look at my old home? I won't stay long and I won't get in the way.'

'Oh,' the man says, 'I see.'

He is about to say something else when a voice calls him from behind.

'Who is it, Bill?'

A stout middle-aged woman appears by the man's side. I hear a child's voice singing from the kitchen.

'This young man used to live here,' Bill says in a quiet voice. 'He wants to know if he can come in to look around.'

My heart is thumping, I feel an urge to clarify things, 'I'll only take a couple of minutes. I promise I won't disturb anything.'

'Oh,' the woman says, 'well, I don't know.' She looks to her husband who shrugs meekly to show that it doesn't bother him. The woman turns back to me, 'What is it you want to do exactly?'

'I'd just like to see my old home once again.'

The woman hesitates, 'Oh, well, I've got the kids. We're just about to start lunch. I . . .' she looks to Bill for guidance.

'I don't think we've any objection, do we, Jean?' Bill says.

'No, I suppose not,' Jean says.

'I'm sure you'll find it very different than you remember. Come on in.'

I decide that Bill is a good guy. He is exactly the kind of person who should be living in our house. I'm not sure about Jean. She still looks extremely concerned. She looks like the sort who is suspicious of everyone.

'You know your way around,' Bill says. 'We'll be in the kitchen if you need anything.'

'Maybe you should go with him,' the woman whispers to Bill. 'You know, just in case.'

'It's OK,' Bill says. 'Let the lad have a look around.'

I watch them go back to the kitchen. A toddler's face peers at me from the kitchen doorway.

'Mammy, who's that man?' the toddler asks.

'Someone who used to live here, dear, now eat your scrambled eggs.'

The kitchen door closes as I walk up the stairs. The banisters are new, as is the yellow wallpaper. Upstairs, the landing is spotless. There is a new side-table and a flower display. The door to Mother's old bedroom is open so I glance in. Inside the room is bright and airy. There is no hint of the dark stuffiness that used to hang in the room like a curse. Everything about the room is different, even the position of the bed.

I back out of Mother's room and cross the landing to my old bedroom. The room is smaller than I remember. It is apparent that two girls occupy the room now. It is a surprise to find that the two beds are in the same positions. The bed that occupies my old space is covered in a brightly coloured duvet. The one that used to be Rory's has a neat blue bedspread. There are posters of male pop stars all over the walls.

After a while, I see myself as a three-year-old, sitting on the bed, calmly arranging teddy bears and other stuffed animals. Rory has refused once again to look after me, so I am playing on my own. In a while, Maeve will join me with her dolls and we will create our own little world to play in.

The image fades and I leave the room. I go downstairs to the front room. I hear the chatter of the family at their lunch.

The front room is unrecognisable except for the window

overlooking the street and the church opposite. There is a bright green sofa, a pine table and chairs, vases full of flowers everywhere. I go to the window and touch it. I remember one afternoon as a ten-year-old sitting down here with Maeve, blanking our minds on 'Blue Peter' as thumps and shouts came from Rory's bedroom above us.

'Dad's giving Rory the clatters again,' Maeve says.

I leave the front room and look in at Maeve's old room opposite. It is now a study of some kind. There is a desk and typewriter and paintings of brightly coloured flowers in vases on one wall. I walk to the kitchen door and pause. Inside, a woman's voice shouts, 'No, no, aw – now look what you've done.'

I am about to knock on the kitchen door when I hear a noise behind me. Outside, a car door slams and a man's voice says 'thanks'.

I hear the sound of something heavy being left on our doorstep before there is the scrape of a key in the lock. Maeve rushes out of the front room and comes over to stand beside me, face flushed with excitement. She has recognised the voice too. I feel my pulse pounding.

'Do you think we should call Mother?' Maeve says.

'Yes,' I say.

'Mother,' Maeve calls, then louder, 'Mother.'

A car pulls away outside and the scraping sounds continue. Behind us, the kitchen door opens but neither of us turns around.

Mother appears at my side 'What is it?'

'There's someone at the door,' Maeve says. 'Will I . . . ?' she moves towards the door to open it.

'No,' Mother says. 'Let's just see.'

We watch the door in silence for a few seconds until the key turns in the lock. The door opens and Dad stands there, a suitcase at his feet. He wears blue jeans, a denim shirt and a black jacket. His eyes are wide with surprise to see us waiting for him.

'Oh, there you are,' he says with a big smile as wide as a river. 'For a minute then, I thought you'd changed the lock.'

There are hurried footsteps on the stairs above me. Rory pauses, his hair standing up around his head, shirt sticking out. For a moment, his mouth makes a perfect circle.

'Dad,' he says.

We run to Dad and throw our arms around him. Dad drops the suitcase, sweeps Maeve up in one arm and holds the other out to receive Mother. I get to him at the same time as Rory and we both end up bouncing off the huddle in the doorway and hugging each other instead.

'John,' Mother says 'Oh, John.'

Maeve sobs, Rory giggles, Dad says 'now, now'.

I desperately try to think of something to say. All I can do is hold onto Dad's shoulder and grin at everyone. I *knew* that one day Dad would come home. I knew that he would not forget us. I don't care where he has been or what he has done over the past years. The only thing that matters is that we are a family again. I can feel tears welling up in my eyes as I hold onto him. I see that Dad's suitcase is bulging and behind the suitcase there is another bag filled with colourful, wrapped packages. Dad smells of America and sunshine and horses. I think about running upstairs to get the stetson from under my bed but I don't want to leave Dad. Maeve punches me on the shoulder.

'See,' she smiles 'His eyes are brown.'

'Hey,' I say, rubbing my arm where she punched me. 'All right, all right, his eyes are brown.'

I feel another thump on the shoulder from behind. Somehow, Maeve is behind me now. I turn around but instead of Maeve I see a group of people standing in the doorway, a fair-haired woman, two young blonde girls and a stooped man with blue eyes. The man looks at me with concern. I can feel tears streaming down my cheeks.

'Are you all right?' the man asks.

I turn back to my family but the image has vanished. There is no Dad, no Mother, no Maeve, no Rory, just the back of our old front door. It takes me a while to accept that I was looking at an illusion. Now I feel weak and dizzy. I want to leave the house immediately and get into the street where I can breathe. I start towards the door but I wobble and have to grab hold of the banisters. Bill takes my arm and leads me to the kitchen.

'You're all right. Just sit down for a moment.'

'What's the matter with the man, Mummy?' one of the girls asks.

'Maybe we should call a doctor,' Jean says.

'No, he'll be fine,' Bill says. 'Coming home was a bit of a shock, was it?'

I look up at him and nod.

'Would you like a cup of tea?' he says. 'Give him a cup of tea. The lad will be fine, won't you?'

'Yes,' I say, surprised at how loud my voice sounds in our old kitchen.

'There, you see. I knew he was OK,' Bill says. 'The changes were probably a bit much for you. I know how you feel.'

He sits down beside me at the table. 'I went back to my old street once and the whole place had been turned into office buildings. I felt like my family had been massacred or something. Everything changes eventually, even the place where you grew up. The only place it doesn't change is in your memory and sure that's the most unreliable place of all.'

A cup of tea arrives in front of me.

'Will I get the man a biscuit as well, Daddy?' one of the girls says.

'Of course. Get the packet of Jaffa Cakes down from the shelf there.'

'Oh, Bill, I was saving them,' Jean says.

'Give him a Jaffa Cake, for God's sake.'

I sit for a while and sip my tea as Bill chatters on. He doesn't seem to expect an answer. A Jaffa Cake on a plate appears beside my cup of tea. I pick up the Jaffa Cake and bite into it. The crunchy biscuit and orange taste immediately refreshes me. Behind me I can hear Jean whispering to the girls to leave me alone.

'He's had some kind of emotional shock.'

The skin on my hand still resonates from touching Dad's shoulder. I can still feel the rough texture of the black denim jacket and the firm, bony flesh beneath. It is difficult to believe that he was not real. Dad's brown eyes had exuberantly and vividly taken in each of us. He looked so delighted to be home again. He had made me feel part of a perfect circle for a few exhilarating moments, then disappeared again. The thought strikes me that perhaps Dad came home to say goodbye to me, to let me know that I had to let go of him, to get on with my own life.

I shut the image of Dad out of my mind. I have never felt so embarrassed. As soon as I can stand, I will thank Bill and his family for their kindness and leave. I know that I will never feel the need to come out here again.

Now Bill leans over to say something to me. He smiles and slaps me gently on the shoulder.

'I met your mother once, years ago,' Bill says. 'She was a great woman.'

As I carry Maeve's bag through the Departures hall, I keep an eye out for ship inspectors. For some reason, I expect Dan to appear at any moment to call me Big Balls and embarrass me in front of my sister.

'Here, let me carry that,' Maeve says. 'You still look a bit pale.'

'I'm fine,' I say.

Maeve wears all black again. She looks cool and composed, like a famous folk singer going on tour.

'Where is this incinerator yoke anyway?' Maeve says. 'I've always wanted to see it.'

'Not now,' I say. 'I'll show it to you when you return.'

'Pity,' Maeve says teasingly. 'I was looking forward to it.'

Maeve seems to be delighted to be leaving the country. I am relieved that she is the one to be visiting Rory in Manchester and not me. It will do her good to get away from looking after Mother for a while. Perhaps she will convince Rory to come home. I am not ready to go anywhere yet. I have to find a new place to live, get my life sorted out.

'Do you think Rory will come back with you?' I ask.

'Well, he sounded in great form on the phone. I'm going to have a nice visit with him. Then we'll see.'

'Did he hear any more about . . . ? Did he ever . . .' I can't bring myself to say it. The vision of Dad from earlier today is still too fresh in my mind.

Maeve shrugs 'Rory doesn't believe any of the sightings. He thinks that people say they see Dad so they'll have something interesting to talk to us about. It makes them feel important.'

At the ticket desk, I hand the bag to Maeve and she checks in. Maeve is leaving her return flight open. She might stay a week, maybe two, perhaps longer. It all depends, she says. Maybe someday I too will go to Manchester to visit Rory.

When Maeve finishes at the check-in desk, we walk slowly over to the Departure gates. There are ten minutes to spare before boarding begins so we go to the coffee counter. I order two coffees.

'It was nice of that fellow to give you a lift to the station,' Maeve says, eyeing a passing pilot.

'Yeah,' I say, 'they were a nice family.'

When I told Maeve about the visit to our old house in Redrock, I left out the bit about seeing Dad. Maeve thought I had done the right thing by going back to Redrock.

'Maybe you had to go back so you could leave home properly. We should take Mother back there someday too. There are a lot of people out there who still have fond memories of her.'

We drink our coffees in silence for a time. The airport is busy. I am not on duty again until tomorrow. I don't want to even think about the job until then. I watch a family of tourists struggling with their baggage. The father, a large, heavy-jowled man in lederhosen, is incensed at his children's inability to stack the suitcases on the trolley so that they won't tumble off.

Beside me, Maeve sighs, puts down her cup, 'Do you still keep an eye out for Dad, you know, when you're at work?'

'Sometimes.'

Maeve nods as if she knew the answer anyway, 'I think Dad's in America somewhere. I think he's got another family over there and a new life. I've no proof or anything but it just seems like the truth to me.'

'Do you think he'll ever come back?'

'Nah. Why should he? There's nothing to come back to really. It was all so long ago.'

'We were eejits to think he would, weren't we?'

'We weren't eejits. We were just doing our best. There's no right way or wrong way to handle things.'

Maeve seems to have grown younger and more confident since she decided to go to Manchester in my place. She reminds me of the way she was as a teenager, before she got obsessed with Mother's career. Maybe Maeve will find a new life in Manchester. The thought makes me sad but it fills me with happiness too. Maeve deserves a break. We all deserve a break.

I walk Maeve as far as the Departure gates. She makes a frantic search for her ticket before eventually finding it in her shoulder bag. She kisses me goodbye.

'You'll look after things, won't you?' she says and waves.

'I'll look after things,' I say and wave back.

Outside it is raining. The sky is growing dark and angry. I climb in and tell the driver to take me to Clontarf. It surprises me that he doesn't argue or say that he'll never get a fare back from there, but I suppose that airport taxi men are used to long drives.

I am glad I saw the old home today. I look upon it as the first step in getting my new life together. It has helped me to realise that I have no ambition. Apart from my work as a ship inspector and my family, I have almost no other interest. I will have to do something about that. As soon as I get the chance I will sit down and draw up a plan for myself. Perhaps I will phone Donna and ask her to go for that pint. Maybe I'll look for another job. Perhaps I'll go abroad for a while. There are lots of possibilities.

By the time I get to Clontarf the rain has stopped. I notice that the light is on in the front room. This time, Mother's face does not appear at the window. I put my key in the lock and open the front door carefully. Moving through the dark hallway, I bump against the coat rack but catch it before it falls. Cautiously, I open the door to the front room. Inside, sprawled across the easy chair lies Mother, telephone receiver tangled in its own cord at her feet. Mother's head is back, hair spread across her open mouth. She appears not sleeping but unconscious. I take off my jacket, go out to the rack and hang it, then return to the front room.

I gather Mother in my arms and lift. She sighs once and flops into my chest like a child's dolly, arms dangling. A cigarette butt with a long, delicate pillar of grey ash drops from her hand to shatter on the carpet. Her long, grey-streaked black hair swings jauntily as I carry her out into the hallway and down the corridor to her bedroom. I nudge open the bedroom door with my foot and tread slowly across to the large double-bed, the room black and yawning, the boards creaking. With one hand, I fold back the sheets before laying her down with a brief crackling of springs. I lift her head, pull a pillow under it, take off her shoes, then pull the bedclothes across her. I place the shoes under the bed.

Mother's bare breast is showing over the covers. In the pale light from the window the breast appears shrunken and wrinkled. The nipple that nurtured me when I was a baby looks like a lost button. Without really knowing why, I bend down slowly to kiss the nipple. It feels rough against my lips. Mother sighs again. I pull the covers back up to Mother's chin.

I remember being a child on the pier with Mother when the hailstones came. I remember how good it felt to be carried under her coat as she ran with me along the pier and through the town to our house. That night she let me into the bed with her and I stretched out in the long never-ending sheets. I always slept better in Mother's bed. I never had nightmares nor did I waken not knowing where I was. When I think back on it, I feel it was the only time in my life I felt truly secure. Mother created me, raised me, loved me. I think she did a great job, considering what she had to put up with. I forgive her for throwing the cup at me.

I take off my shirt and trousers and slip in beside Mother.

The sheets are cool against my skin. I lie there listening to Mother's troubled breathing. I know that it will take an eternity to get to sleep and that once I drop off it will suddenly be dawn. Something is gnawing at me, something I have overlooked.

Suddenly, I remember what it is. I rise quickly and shuffle down the corridor to the front room where the light is still blazing. I bend down by the easy chair to pick up the telephone receiver. It gives a tiny 'b-b-bring' when I put it back on its cradle. I turn off the light and pad back down the corridor to the bedroom, feeling a lot better.

I crawl back into Mother's bed. I make a vow to visit Dan tomorrow. This time I will bring him a box of Dairy Milk. If he complains about that as well, I will eat them myself. After that, I will send something to the family in Redrock. I still don't know their surname. I will address the flowers or whatever I choose to send to 'Bill and Jean and family, 3 Church Street, Redrock'.

Before I drop off, I think of Dad. I see him riding a horse in a desert, somewhere near Tucson, Arizona. Dad looks smaller now, his hair white, face lined. Even his moustache has lost its shine. His black stetson has a tear in the brim that flaps as he rides. Under the stetson, his brown eyes are weary and resigned. He looks haunted and ready to quit. There are no pearl-handled six-guns strapped to his waist and his horse is a dull grey colour instead of the blazing white of the stories that I told to Maeve. I watch as Dad turns the horse down a trail and is gradually obscured by dust.